Infernal Father of Mine

Book Seven of the Overworld Chronicles

John Corwin

ISBN- 978-0-9850181-7-7

Printed in the U.S.A.

EVERYBODY HAS DADDY ISSUES

Justin's reunion with his father starts with a punch to the face and their capture by Exorcists, a cult branch of the Templars supposedly disbanded centuries ago. The Exorcists banish Justin and his father, David, to the Gloom.

Fighting to escape exile, Justin discovers everything he knows about his father is a lie. Even worse, the man is a complete jackass who won't give a straight answer to the simplest of questions. But when they stumble upon a secret army being grown by one of Daelissa's minions, they realize much more than a healthy father-son relationship is at stake.

Justin and his father will have to escape the Gloom, bring back reinforcements, and crush the enemy before Daelissa marches her forces into the real world. Unfortunately, the army stands between them and freedom.

Daddy issues will have to wait. The war starts now.

Connect with John Corwin online:
Facebook: http://www.facebook.com/johnhcorwinauthor
Blog: http://blog.johncorwinauthor.com/
Twitter: http://twitter.com/#!/John_Corwin

Books by John Corwin:

Overworld Chronicles:
Sweet Blood of Mine
Dark Light of Mine
Fallen Angel of Mine
Dread Nemesis of Mine
Twisted Sister of Mine
Dearest Mother of Mine
Infernal Father of Mine

Stand Alone Novels:

No Darker Fate
The Next Thing I Knew
Outsourced
Seventh

To my wonderful support group:
Alana Rock
Karen Stansbury
Pat Owens

My amazing editors:
Annetta Ribken
Jennifer Wingard

My awesome cover artist:
Regina Wamba

Thanks so much for all your help and input!

Chapter 1

On a bright sunny day in the middle of a small cemetery, I punched my dad in the face.

David Slade staggered back a foot before recovering his balance. He rubbed his jaw. Grinned. "I suppose that wasn't the answer you wanted."

Breathing heavily, rage building inside, I stared at this man, unable to believe he was the same man who'd raised me. The same man who'd rented movies and bought pizza every Friday for family night. The same man who'd thrown baseballs and footballs with me despite my pre-supernatural clumsiness. The same man who'd once so gently kissed my mother.

I'd saved Mom from Daelissa. My long-lost little sister, Ivy, had left the Conroys and was now living with me and Mom. My family was so close to complete in a way it had never been before. And still this man insisted on abandoning us.

"Does this mean you won't come to the wedding?" my father asked.

Jackass. Somehow, I pushed back the anger. "Let me get this straight. I just told you Mom and Ivy are living with me in Queens Gate. Your family is waiting, and you're just ignoring us?"

David leaned against a tombstone. When I'd asked for a meeting, he'd chosen a tiny cemetery trapped between two new high-rise condominiums in Buckhead. The unfinished buildings loomed on either side, all gray concrete and rebar. "When you reached out to me about reconciling, I knew it was a bad idea. Does your mother know about this meeting?"

I shook my head. "No, but Ivy does. We were hoping to surprise Mom."

He crossed his arms. "You should have asked Alysea first. There are bigger things at stake here than just a happy family reunion."

"Bigger stakes?" I threw up my hands. "What have you been doing the past few months that could be more important than reuniting with your family?" The last time I'd seen him had been just after Vadaemos Slade escaped from Templar custody with the help of Daelissa and nearly killed me. It hadn't been more than a few months ago, but the man I faced now seemed completely different.

"Justin, do you think you can beat Daelissa's forces as things stand?" David's expression turned serious. "She practically owns the vampires, the Synod Templars, and probably a good portion of the Arcane Council."

I wanted to be an optimist, but couldn't. "Probably not. Right now it's just my friends and the Templars under Thomas Borathen's command." I narrowed my eyes. "What's your point?"

"What I'm doing isn't for me. It's for you too."

My blood pressure spiked. "What a load of bull. You're still betraying Mom to marry Kassallandra, that red-headed demonic ho-bag."

"I knew you weren't ready for this," David said. His amused grin returned. "I guess I'm expecting too much from an eighteen-year-old."

My teeth clenched. "I'm nineteen." *This man isn't my father. He's a stranger, and he doesn't give a crap.* I'd held such high hopes for this meeting. Buoyed by having Ivy and Mom back, it had seemed so simple to convince my father to come home. After Mom abandoned my father and me to live with the Conroys and Ivy, I'd thought David's entire reason for marrying Kassallandra was some kind of payback. Now I wasn't so sure about his motives at all.

My fists clenched as I fought back anger. "Mom says she can't tell me about you. About how you really met. I want to know the truth."

He pursed his lips. "Are you sure?"

"Don't you think I deserve it?"

A smile flickered across David's face.

"What's so funny?"

"I suppose it depends on whether you'd view the truth as punishment or reward, son."

"Don't call me that," I said. "You haven't even come close to earning the right to call me your son again."

He put up his hands in a surrender gesture. "I get it, son— Justin. I'd just hoped maybe what you'd been through had evolved your way of thinking."

"Not when it comes to family, *David*."

"Fair enough." He crossed his arms and watched me without offering more.

I crossed my arms. "The truth. Please."

"I am not, strictly speaking, a man." He paused, as if letting that sink in.

"Um, ok. You're Daemos, so of course you're not human."

David grinned. "Perhaps I should have phrased that a little better."

Something flickered in my peripheral vision. I looked up at the towering concrete structure to my right.

David followed my gaze. "What is it?"

"I thought—" A human silhouette appeared next to a support beam. Whoever it was seemed to know I knew he was there, because he didn't move from our line of sight.

"Did you bring along your Templar friends to watch your back?" David asked.

I shook my head. "Elyssa promised she wouldn't follow. Commander Borathen wouldn't send anyone without asking."

"Which means—"

"Yeah, we're about to have a situation."

The watcher's arm catapulted forward. Something flashed in the sun. We jumped back as a silver disc landed on the grass between us. The grass sizzled and hissed. Bright orange light flashed, smoke rising from charred vegetation, forming a perfect circle crisscrossed by blackened lines. The silver disc vanished.

"I think this is the situation you mentioned," David said. "Time to go."

The two of us raced toward the low stone wall at the back of the cemetery—or tried to. Before we'd gone two feet, we both bounced back from the edge of the circle.

"A sense of déjà vu just hit me," David said, touching the air at the edge of the circle, unable to push through.

My bounty hunter friend, Harry Shelton, had once tried to bring in my father. He'd trapped us in a simple magical circle designed to contain demon spawn. Because of my angel side, however, I'd been able to leave the circle.

I pressed my hands to the invisible barrier. "I can't get out either."

A group of hooded people filed from the small red brick church in front of the cemetery. Without a word, they made like a human train and encircled us while we watched, perplexed. They didn't look like Templars or act like Templars, and they sure as heck weren't dressed like any I'd seen before. If anything, they looked like monks.

"Who are you?" I asked.

A grim look passed over David's face. He touched my arm. Shook his head. "Exorcists."

"From the Catholic Church?"

"No. They used to be a division of the Templars, but some of them left to form their own cult."

"We are not a cult, demon," said a man, his face hidden beneath the black hood, though the robe strained to conceal his generous paunch. "We cleanse humanity of your ilk."

"You don't like demon spawn?" I asked. Stupid question, of course. Nobody seemed to like our kind. At least my friends had learned I was a kinder, gentler sort of demon spawn—all warm and fuzzy.

"Is that my old friend I hear?" David said, the relaxed look on his face belying what felt like a dangerous situation.

"I am no friend of yours, infernal creature," the man replied in an imperious British accent.

David tutted. "Really now, Montjoy, is that the way to treat someone you've known for so long?"

Who the hell is Montjoy? I clung to a brief hope David actually knew the guy and this was all some big misunderstanding.

"Subdue them," Montjoy said.

Hope faded, and smartassery took over. "Maybe someone should subdue your appetite," I said. "Or at least buy you a new robe." I thought I heard someone snicker, or maybe it was my imagination.

"You would do well to keep your mouth shut, Justin Slade." The man pointed a meaty finger at me. Rings adorned every finger, each one crowned with large jewels, though one with a fat gray stone stood out from the rest. "It will go better for you if you do."

"You mean I'll get candy and ice cream?" I said in a childlike voice. "Oh, gee, Mr. Montjoy, that would be swell!"

That time, someone definitely snickered.

"I'm curious. How did you know about this meeting?" David asked.

"I have agents constantly watching for you," the Exorcist said with an evil smile. "When you left your haven alone, I knew this was my chance."

David pursed his lips. "If you wanted a date, all you had to do was ask. Some flowers would be nice, too."

Someone in the group of Exorcists snorted.

Montjoy's face went bright red. "I said subdue them!"

Something stung me in the neck. I saw David's hand go to his at nearly the same time. A silver dart protruded from between his fingers.

"Why is it always in the neck?" I managed to say before feeling my legs fold and the impact of grass against my side. David

5

fell beside me, his eyes open and staring. I waited patiently for darkness to take hold, but consciousness remained. David blinked. I blinked back. I tried to open my mouth, to move a hand, a foot, a finger, but nothing responded. Even blinking took tremendous effort.

A female voice chanted in what sounded like Cyrinthian. The black line in the entrapment circle faded away. Hands gripped me beneath my armpits and legs. My view shifted to the brilliant blue sky as our captors hauled me from the ground and set me atop something firm. Though I couldn't move my fingers, I felt fabric against my bare skin. Using all my concentration, I closed my eyes as they began to water from staring into the brightness.

I felt myself move smoothly without the jarring bumps associated with a wheeled gurney. It was possible our captors had employed flying carpets or some other form of magical levitation.

"This is risky," I heard someone whisper near my head.

"Hush," said someone from the direction of my feet. "You know Montjoy hates it when we second-guess him."

"But this is bloody David Slade," the man said. "He didn't say we'd be going after bloody David Slade."

While both men had British accents, they didn't sound nearly as refined as Montjoy.

"We do what we're told, you ruddy git. Now, shut it."

The other man remained quiet. I heard car doors click open. Smelled the odor of stale cigarettes attack my olfactory senses. Heard doors slam shut. I opened my eyes and saw the ceiling of a vehicle. A moment later, an engine roared to life, and the vehicle lurched into motion. I tried in vain to move my head. A bump in the road sent it lolling to the side for a view of the back of David's head where he lay on a plain gray rug—presumably a flying carpet. We were in the back of a van, judging from the size of the cargo space.

What a happy family reunion.

It had already been spoiled by my wonderful father's refusal to give up his marriage plans. Was I being obtuse by demanding he come back to Mom? Was it really so important he marry Kassallandra to create an alliance between House Slade and House Assad? It seemed the threat of a Seraphim invasion would be enough to unite anyone with common sense.

Don't I have more important things to worry about now, like escape?

Not much chance of that in our condition.

Reaching inside for the infernal half of my soul lurking there, I tried to open its cage, hoping I could manifest into demon form. It was apparently as incapacitated as me. *Elyssa's gonna be pissed when she finds out I'm in trouble again.* Christmas was barely over and I'd already been captured by a cult. *I probably should have waited until the new year before embarking on another adventure.*

After what felt like hours, we finally stopped. I heard the passenger and driver doors open and slam shut. The rear doors opened. A breeze wafted in, tickling the hairs on the back of my neck.

My left pinky finger twitched.

Hope bloomed in my chest. *The drug is wearing off.* I'd need a bit more than my pinky to get us out of this situation, though. I closed my eyes in anticipation of the sun as I felt the flying carpet I rested on rise and move into the open. Birds chirped somewhere, accompanied by the honking of horns not far away. It sounded like we were still in the city.

Cracking open an eyelid, I saw a tall church of gray stone to the side. The carpet rotated and my head lolled to the left. A parking lot with several black SUVs came into view, bordered by a tall black iron fence embedded in a stone wall.

Creepy monks. Creepy church. Great.

We entered a door, glided through a hallway, and entered a large dim cathedral. Candles flickered from tall metal candelabras along the wall. We turned a corner and entered a sprawling semi-circular area in front of a choir loft. Metal cages to the left gleamed in the candlelight. A hand lunged for me from between the bars as the carpet drifted by, the filthy fingers so close, I felt the breeze of their passing. A man's face slammed against the bars hard enough to draw blood. He strained his grasping hand toward me, foam-flecked lips gibbering madly. Paralysis came in pretty handy right then because, otherwise, I would have crapped my britches.

7

My bearers rotated the carpet and the center of the chancel came into view. The podium and table where the priest usually stood were absent. A thick silver circle at least fifty feet wide was embedded in the stone floor. Something even more shocking than caged humans met my paralyzed gaze. Two arches stood side-by-side in the center of the circle separated by about ten feet of stone floor. I'd seen arches before—shiny black arches used for traveling the globe, and arches veined with white used to travel between the mortal realm and the angel dimension. But these arches were unlike any I'd seen before. One was drab and gray. The other shined like a sapphire.

What do they do?

My inner nerd completely forgot the dire situation for a moment as possibilities ran through my mind. In all my travels and adventures, I'd never heard of arches this color. Maybe the color didn't mean anything. Maybe the Exorcists had a really good interior decorator who'd grown tired of black and white arches. Unfortunately, I couldn't move my mouth to ask questions.

"You got him, Montjoy?" someone said, excitement in their voice. "I can't believe it."

"I told you he would eventually be mine," replied Montjoy. "It was only a matter of time before he left the haven of his household."

"We were preparing for one of the other subjects. Would you like to do Slade first?"

"I would be delighted," Montjoy replied. "I will lead the purging myself."

"Who's the kid?" someone else asked.

"His son," Montjoy said, spitting the last word with obvious distaste.

A man's face came into view, a thick gray beard bristling from his chin. "He's spawn. We can't purge him."

"No, I suppose not," Montjoy said. "He's an impetuous runt, though. I believe banishment would suit him fine."

The fingers on my left hand clenched. My right hand joined the party. *Come on, body. Don't fail me now.*

"What about House Slade?" someone else asked. "What if they find out we took him?"

8

"They are of no concern to me." Montjoy appeared in my view. "Place David Slade in the circle."

My carpet moved. Someone leaned down to my ear. "I'll let you watch," said one of the men from earlier. He sounded rather smug.

I welcomed the surge of anger. I felt a growl attempt to rise in my throat, though it was hardly audible. My carpet stopped near the side of the large silver circle inlaid in the stone floor. I watched as they pushed David's carpet into the center.

Why can they purge him but not me?

It didn't make sense. We were both Daemos, our souls bound in human form, one half in the mortal realm, the other in the demon plane.

One of the cloaked people turned David's head to face me—a final insult it seemed. He looked calm, or maybe it was just the paralysis. I was pissed at him. Angry with his disregard for our family. But this was too much. Somehow, I had to save him from the purge, whatever it was. A spasm moved my left arm. My right soon followed. I reached inside again, and found my demon half straining against the bonds of my own flesh-and-bone prison.

Move, damn it. Move!

Using every ounce of willpower I had, I wiggled my fingers. Felt my toes respond. Montjoy, obvious by his girth, climbed a tall pulpit, the wooden structure groaning with each step.

"Gonna eat them. Gonna kill them. Blood, blood, blood," gibbered a man from somewhere behind me. "Bathe in their juices. Drink pretty brains from pretty skulls." He laughed maniacally.

"Shut up, you filthy demon," someone said. I heard something impact flesh, and a grunt.

"You first, you first, you first!" screamed the crazy man. Something rattled against metal.

"Subdue him," Montjoy shouted from across the ring.

The mental patient launched into another tirade and abruptly cut off mid-scream. I imagined they must have shot him with one of their paralyzing darts.

9

The chunky figure on the pulpit raised his arms. Hooded Exorcists appeared from the shadows in the church, forming a ring around silver circle, hiding David from sight. Montjoy's voice rose in a chant. The figures in the ring raised their hands straight overhead, singing a response one might expect to hear from Gregorian monks. As they sang, their hands angled outward into V shapes, pressing against their neighbors' palms. The chant faded to echoes.

For a moment, silence reigned. Then Montjoy shouted a word. It might have been Latin, but I couldn't understand any of what they were saying. The circle of Exorcists responded with a shout of acclamation. Montjoy sang at a low pitch, words rising in volume. As he sang, I saw a form rising from the center of the circle. David floated, arms and legs outstretched, held rigid by unseen force, even as his head lolled forward.

My teeth clenched. A shudder ran through my body. I was awakening. Fingers responded to my commands. The leaden weight of my arms subsided. I could almost move my head. *Is anyone watching me?* I knew someone had been behind me a moment ago. Feigning paralysis until the last minute was vital.

My father's head suddenly jerked back. A long cry of pain tore from his throat. Blue vapor emerged from his nose, mouth, ears. The volume of the chant rose higher and higher, the cadence moving faster. Azure mist shrouded David's head, rising like a genie from a bottle. As it grew in volume, a face formed from the nebulous smoke.

"Oh, Montjoy," the face said playfully, even as David continued to shout hoarsely as if in great pain. "Your lifelong quest will end in disappointment, I'm afraid. For you see, I am not what you thought I was."

The Exorcist seemed to ignore him, though it was hard for me to tell from this angle. Montjoy raised a fist. He shouted a single word, and made a vertical slashing motion with his hand. The sapphire arch burst into brilliance, sparkling like a gem. The space between the columns slit open. Blue light, similar in color to the mist and the arch, lit the sanctuary, dancing like moonlight on the surface of a pool.

The blue mist swirled toward the opening. The smoky face cried out. "No, no! Please no! Don't send me back!"

All I could do was watch helplessly.

Chapter 2

Elyssa

Elyssa pushed herself up slowly, watching as a string of drool stretched from her face to the concrete. Someone had knocked her out. *The ninja.* She'd seen the shadow figure at the last minute but hadn't been quick enough to block the blow.

Justin!

She slid forward a few feet and peered over the edge of the twelfth floor of the unfinished condominium bordering the cemetery where Justin was meeting his father. Aside from a few black lines in the grass where the two men had been standing, there was no sign of anyone.

"Really?" she growled. "Can't he even wait until the new year to be abducted?" Elyssa leapt from the side of the building, grabbed a piece of steel rebar where it jutted from the concrete support beam below, and flipped from it to another bar of steel a floor below. She landed on the gravel soil moments later and raced to the cemetery next door.

Footprints littered patches of bare earth between clumps of dying grass. The ninja hadn't been alone—he'd had help. She counted at least ten separate pairs of footprints, not including David's and Justin's. They'd been standing at the center of the black ring. She snapped a picture with her arcphone, and called the one thing—person—she knew could help identify it.

"Hello, Elyssa," Cinder, the golem said in his calm, unassuming voice.

Elyssa had gotten somewhat used to the presence of Cinder despite its—his—origin as one of Mr. Gray's killing machines. He was also like a walking encyclopedia and seemed to relish research above all else. "I just sent you a picture."

"I have received it," he said. "It appears to be a symbol burned into grass."

"Can you identify what the symbol is, and how it was burnt into the grass?"

He paused for a moment. "I will do my best, Elyssa. Is there something wrong?"

"Justin has been taken."

"By his father?"

The question caught Elyssa off guard. She hadn't even thought of the possibility that David Slade might kidnap his son. After all, Justin was to play a very important role in the battle against Daelissa. What if his father had switched sides? Her stomach tightened. She couldn't rule out the possibility. "I don't know who took him. I saw them talking, and then someone snuck up behind me and knocked me out."

"If someone was able to sneak up on you, they must be quite skilled," Cinder said. "According to Justin, you are an amazing badass. I must admit, I do not quite understand how being analogous to a defective posterior makes someone amazing, but having seen you in combat, I must agree with Justin's biased assessment."

Elyssa wasn't sure what to say, so she changed back to the matter at hand. "Just find out where that symbol comes from. I'll be out in the field looking for leads."

"Very well," he replied.

She disconnected the call and stared for a long moment at the symbol, a circle with two lines crisscrossing each other. They didn't quite form an X since one line was a little higher than the other. It didn't look like any Cyrinthian or arcane symbol she'd seen before, but it did seem familiar. Elyssa didn't have any arcane abilities, so she couldn't fathom why a magical symbol would look even remotely

13

familiar to her unless she'd seen Justin use it. To the best of her recollection, she hadn't. He stuck to plain circles anytime he needed one to cast a spell.

Footprints surrounded the symbol. Elyssa tracked them into the small church up a slight rise from the cemetery. The quaint building was little more than a sanctuary with a few rows of pews. Dirt and soil marked the floor where the abductors had walked through the room. She continued on, emerging on a sidewalk covered by a cloth awning. It made sense why she hadn't spotted anyone entering the church. The covered sidewalk led to the street where cars would have to park along the curb or at a large parking deck across the road.

It was a good bet the kidnappers had parked here, ambushed Justin, and brought him out the same way. She spotted an ATM cash machine at a small bank across the road. Not daring to hope, she ran to the other side of the street and found the small piece of glass hiding the camera. It appeared to be angled just right to capture whatever happened across the street.

Elyssa wished she could contact Alysea, but Justin's mom and Nightliss had been called away on a Templar emergency in Colombia and were under a communications blackout. Plenty of options remained. She whipped out her phone and called Shelton. "I need you to meet me right away."

"Cinder told me about Justin," Shelton said. "Kid can't keep himself out of trouble for two minutes."

"I'm sending you a picture," Elyssa said. "Use the omniarch."

Shelton sighed. "It might help if I knew what you want me to do once I get there."

"Hack a camera."

"Got it. On my way." He disconnected.

Elyssa took a picture of an alley between the bank and the art supply shop next door. A short time after texting the image to Shelton, a portal shimmered open in the air. Harry Shelton appeared on the other side wearing his leather duster and a wide-brimmed hat. He stepped through, followed by Bella. The portal closed behind them.

14

"Elyssa, I'm so sorry," Bella said, her Spanish accent rolling the Rs ever so slightly. She brandished a wand. "I am ready to do whatever is necessary to help you get him back."

Shelton held up a hand. "Before you go blasting holes in buildings, let's do a little digging."

"Really, Harry, do you think I would go off on a rampage?" Bella quirked an eyebrow.

"I've seen you and Elyssa in action," he said. His gaze shifted to Elyssa. "Where's the camera?"

She showed him the ATM. "Can you hack the video feed from it?"

He looked it over. "Adam gave me a spell that might do the trick."

That came as no surprise to Elyssa. Adam Nosti had once been a conspiracy nut and was probably the best spell hacker she'd ever seen. "Well, why aren't you using it?" she said, impatient to begin. For all she knew, Justin wasn't even in Atlanta anymore.

Shelton's forehead wrinkled. "Don't rush me, woman." He took out his arcphone and fiddled with it. He grunted, tapped the screen, and nodded. "Hope this works." Standing to the side of the camera, presumably so it wouldn't record him, he pressed the arcphone over the glass.

Symbols flashed past on the screen followed by green static. Images of people and cars zipped past in reverse across the field of view of the camera, as did patrons visiting the ATM. A man in a huge fur coat reversed course from the camera to reveal two large black vans parked across the road. A procession of people in long, hooded robes walked backwards up the sidewalk and into the church.

"That's got to be the kidnappers!" Elyssa said.

"He was kidnapped by monks?" Bella said.

"Don't look like no monks I've ever seen," Shelton said.

The video rewound all the way back to the vans driving away from the parallel parking spaces in reverse. Shelton moved as if to pull his arcphone away.

"Wait," Elyssa said.

15

A few minutes later, David Slade exited the church from the front door, walking backwards and vanishing down the sidewalk. Justin had taken an omniarch portal to an adjoining construction site. Elyssa had given him a moment or two and used the portal herself to shadow him. She'd promised not to follow him, but had he really expected her not to?

"David was alone," Shelton said. "Dollars to dog nuts he had nothing to do with the abduction." He raised an eyebrow. "Can I stop recording now?"

Elyssa nodded.

Shelton took the phone off. Electricity sparked from the machine followed by a puff of smoke and the whirring of something spinning. Cash suddenly spewed from the front of the ATM and an alarm wailed.

"That's not supposed to happen," Shelton said, looking at the money wafting through the air.

"Call someone to open the portal," Elyssa said.

"Son of a—" Shelton gave her a disgusted look. "There ain't nobody there to open it."

"What about Ivy?" Elyssa asked.

Shelton shuddered. "That kid gives me the creeps."

Bella elbowed him. "Be polite, Harry." She looked at Elyssa. "She's there, but I don't have her number. Do you?"

Sirens wailed in the distance. Elyssa frantically waved everyone down the alley. "I have her number, but it's in a text Justin sent me. I'll have to look, but we don't have time right now."

A metal gate blocked the end of the alley. Bella took out her wand and, with a word, sliced the hinges with a thin beam of magic. The gate fell to the ground with a clang. Their path took a sharp right turn into another alley leading to a street. They hadn't gone more than a few feet when two police cars blockaded the exit. Elyssa spun and looked back the way they'd come. The police cars with flashing lights had cut it off as well.

"You'd think somebody just robbed a bank," Shelton said, jaw tight.

16

Elyssa looked up at the three-story buildings on all sides. There were no ladders, no fire escapes—no way up, and no way out.

Chapter 3

I saw a smile break out on Montjoy's face as the sapphire portal sucked at the billowing cloud of mist coming from David's mouth. Whatever the man was doing, it was probably about to kill my father.

"Please don't send me away!" the nebulous face in the cloud cried. Just as it neared the threshold between worlds, the smoky mass stopped swirling. The face bared wickedly sharp teeth. "Just kidding." Then it bellowed like a tyrannosaurus rex on steroids. The gale blew hoods from Exorcists and sent candelabras tumbling. Candles flickered out, leaving most of the sanctuary in pitch black. Someone screamed.

My night vision flickered on. I saw a smoky tendrils extending in all directions from the cloudy mass. They whipped around the circle like an octopus gone mad. One of the panicking Exorcists fell, crossing the silver line of the ring. A tendril lashed out, gripping the cloaked figure by the leg and lifting him high. It spun the Exorcist and flung him. The cry of terror cut off as the body smacked into a stone column.

A metal candelabra fell across the silver ring. I felt a rush of magic as the seal around the circle broke. Now free, the blue tendrils reached further, gripping another victim and throwing him across the sanctuary. Wood cracked as he smashed into a wooden pew. Shouts of terror echoed as Exorcists ran blindly. The smoky arms snatched each one with ease, sending them on short, brutal flights across the room.

18

Shrieks and cries erupted behind me, like those of overexcited chimpanzees. The cacophony rivaled the screams of the Exorcists as they battled the blue smoke creature in the middle of the sanctuary.

My body spasmed. I felt my limbs respond with agonizing slowness to my commands. It wasn't much, but it would do. Using all my effort, I pushed into a sitting position. Digging inside myself I found the demon half slowly waking from slumber.

"Subdue! Subdue!" Montjoy screamed.

I saw a familiar figure across the room—the same one that had thrown the silver disc at me and David. Unlike the others, this one was dressed in tight black Nightingale armor. It pulled a short rod from a holster at its side. The rod expanded into a thick black bow. The figure pulled back on the string and an arrow appeared from nowhere, nocked and ready to fly straight at David 's hovering body.

"No!" I shouted, jumping to my feet. My knees gave out as the attacker's head turned toward me. The arrow whistled for me. I ducked.

The sound of shrieking metal sounded behind me. I looked back and saw a large cage filled with people. Some looked unconscious. Others looked insane out of their minds. A man foaming at the mouth punched himself in the face over and over. Drool leaked from the hanging jaw of a woman, her fists full of her own hair as she tore it out by the roots without uttering a sound.

A short man with wisps of gray hair and wrinkly skin kicked at the cage door. The metal groaned as the man's bloody foot rammed it over and over again. I heard bones break. Saw the toes twist at odd angles. The man laughed hysterically and kept on kicking even as blood sprayed from the open wounds on his mangled foot.

I turned away from the wackos in the cage and crawled on hands and knees toward the crouching figure as it lined up another shot on David. "Stop!" I shouted.

This time, the attacker didn't turn to look. An arrow flashed forward. The blue smoke formed a wall, and deflected the projectile. The Exorcist ninja sprang forward, dodged a sweeping blow of a smoky tendril. A hand formed at the end of the nebulous tentacle and grasped for the attacker, but the ninja was too quick. The slim figure

19

dove and slid on its chest beneath the giant fingers, sprang to its feet, and kicked away the candelabra short-circuiting the ring. The ninja turned. Performed a leaping backward flip to avoid another swing of the smoky hand. Then it slid across the silver line, dropped to a knee, and touched a thumb against it.

I heard a faint hum as the circle snapped closed and saw the fingers on the giant hand sever and fade to sparkling mist where they'd crossed the silver line. David's body abruptly dropped to the floor. The blue vapor swirled back into him, vanishing.

Strength returned to my legs. I stood. Something crashed behind me. I turned to see the short old man, now free from the cage, leap at me, rotted teeth gleaming green by the light of a standing candelabra. Blood trailed from his foot as he sailed through the air. I held up my hands in defense. His mouth opened wide an instant before clamping onto my forearm. I shouted in pain.

"What the hell?" I tried to shake him off me. "Why are you biting me?" I gripped the few remaining strands of the man's hair and pulled. They came loose in my hand. His sweaty, oily head slipped from my grasp even as he opened his mouth and clamped down on my wrist, teeth gnawing at my flesh. I bellowed with fresh agony.

I punched his face but the blow didn't faze the crazy coot. I wasn't nearly at full strength, and despite the little old man's apparent ancient age and bad health, his grip felt supernaturally strong. Redirecting all power to my legs, I ran toward a stone column and slammed the insane man's head against it. Blood spattered at the point of impact. He burst into maniacal laughter, freeing my arm. I backpedaled.

A groggy Exorcist staggered from behind a pew. The old man saw a new victim and leapt on him, biting the robes and tearing at it with his teeth like a rabid dog. I ran, leaving the struggling pair behind, and headed toward David. A blur of black caught my peripheral vision. I ducked. Felt a foot clip my head, and stumbled to the side. My ribs glanced off a pew. My knees decided to give out again, and I fell in the aisle.

The shadow ninja vaulted a pew, elbow aimed for my chest as I lay on the ground. I rolled away. Heard the thud of impact. Gaining my feet, I watched the dark figure spring from the ground. Up close I noticed the curve of breasts and hips beneath the tight fabric.

A woman is about to kick my ass.

Not that Elyssa hadn't done so plenty of times before.

An entirely different crazed woman ran screaming from the dark, blood smeared all over her face. The ninja did a roundhouse, slamming the mental patient hard in the side of the head. The woman's body flipped sideways from the impact. Before her body hit the floor, the ninja raised a foot and slammed her in the ribs, pile-driving the body into the stone surface. The woman groaned but stayed put.

The unexpected pause before my imminent ass beating gave me much needed seconds to recover from the tranquilizer still clouding my control. Warmth flooded into my limbs. I felt strength roar through my blood. This chick was in for a surprise if she attacked again. I held out a hand and motioned her with my fingers. "Come get some."

Her foot flashed out. Instinct took over. I dodged back and felt air whoosh past my nose. Her fist blurred for my head. I juked right to avoid the thrust, but she blindsided me with her other fist and nailed me in the temple. I staggered backwards, regained my feet and took a swing at her. She jumped back from my clumsy retaliation. This time, the ninja held out a hand mimicked my "come get me" taunt.

I touched my aching head and glared at my assailant. Experience overrode my initial desire to charge in, fists blazing. I'd trained with Elyssa, but still wasn't anywhere close to her level of proficiency. This person obviously had similar training, not to mention supernatural speed and strength along with it. I needed to level up before contending with this threat. Unfortunately, I couldn't just run away. David might be an ass, but he was still my father and I had to save him.

The whistle of a projectile narrowly warned me in time to duck as a dart flew past my personal airspace. The ninja attacked. With a flurry of blows, each one seemingly quicker than the last, she drove me back down the aisle toward the front of the church. I felt static tickle the hairs on my skin as I crossed the silver circle. The

21

attacker paused. Backed off and regarded me, her mask concealing whatever smug expression lay behind it.

I decided to exploit her hesitation and blurred forward. I ducked beneath her swinging arm. Shot up from a crouch, and delivered a crushing uppercut to—thin air.

My gaze flicked around. The ninja was nowhere to be seen. *Where did she go?* I looked back at the circle. David lay prone in the center, unmoving. I felt a tap on my shoulder. Spun, and saw the ninja. A foot crushed into my chest. I flew backward, hit the ground skidding and rolling until I came to a rest against my unconscious father.

For a brief second, I felt the aether in the air dissipate as the ninja woman broke the circle. Just as quickly, she drew another circle and two slashes across it in the air with her finger before jamming a thumb to the silver. The air crackled and snapped as the new circle formed. She waved like a beauty pageant contestant, crossed her arms, and regarded me from behind her black mask. I grabbed David, and ran for the opposite edge of the circle. When I pressed a hand to the air, it confirmed my worst fears. She'd put up a physical barrier.

I reached for my pocket. My phone was gone along with my wallet. The Exorcists must have taken our belongings earlier. I felt David's pockets and came up empty. Setting him down for the moment, I walked to the edge of the circle near the woman.

"Why are you doing this?" I asked, straining to keep my voice calm.

She didn't answer, but remained standing and watching.

"Who are you?" I asked. "Show me your face."

Her head tilted slightly, as if considering my request. A chubby figure rose from behind the pulpit. Blood trailed from Montjoy's nose. He panted as if he'd just sprinted a mile—or more likely ten feet—considering how much energy it probably took to move his considerable bulk.

"Subdue the others," he told the fighter. "Quickly, now."

"You like that word," I said. "Maybe you should subdue with all the subduing."

22

Montjoy's lip curled into a sneer. "I will never rest until I cleanse your ilk from the mortal realm."

"You want to get rid of all Daemos?" I said, more surprised by his ambition than by the actual admission.

He wiped at the trickle of blood as it ran down his lips, and looked away, apparently choosing to ignore my question. Another Exorcist appeared from the shadows, walking with a slight limp.

"Set the candles back up," Montjoy snapped, obviously not a bit concerned with the injuries sustained by his comrade.

The Exorcist complied without comment.

The scattered screams and shouts of crazy people and their victims diminished to silence over the next several minutes. The mysterious fighter appeared from time to time, hauling incapacitated people to another cage and tossing them inside like sacks of garbage.

"What's wrong with those people?" I asked.

Montjoy spun to me, an amused expression partially hidden behind a tissue pressed to his nose. "Why, surely you know, young Slade."

"No, I don't, old Montjoy."

He walked right up to the edge of the circle, as if taunting me with the thin invisible barrier that kept me from backhanding him across the room. "They're possessed."

I raised an eyebrow. "Possessed?" I'd seen and fought summoned demons, but hadn't realized demon possession was actually a real thing and not something fabricated for entertainment. That said, I wasn't terribly surprised.

A smirk appeared on his face. "It seems your relatives haven't done a very good job informing you, boy." He looked at the tissue. Snapped his fingers, and an Exorcist produced another for him, taking the blood-soaked swab. "Demons crave our world. They love taking bodies on joy rides, much like teenage boys with fast cars or loose women. They wear out the bodies. Strain them and drive the physical shell insane."

"Like that old man?"

23

Montjoy pinched his nose shut in an attempt to stanch the blood flow. "That 'old man' is in his twenties." His voice sounded funny, but surprise overwhelmed my desire to laugh.

"Twenties?" I couldn't believe he was less than fifty.

"Some demons wear out bodies faster than others. It all boils down to what kind of demon inhabits the person."

"Purging them is an exorcism," I said, addled brain finally making a connection. "Does that kill the body?"

"No, not generally. It drives the demon back to their plane, and restores the human's soul back to full control." He sneered, displaying blood-stained teeth. "If only demon spawn were so simple to handle."

"We're not possessed," I said. "Why are you trying to purge my father?"

"Don't listen to his lies, Justin," my father said in a weak voice.

"Slade." Hatred added a rough edge to Montjoy's voice.

"You finally caught me after how many years?" David pushed himself off the floor, and made a show of counting his fingers. "Gee, I've lost count."

"You're mine now," Montjoy said. "Perhaps I underestimated what it would take—"

"You're a little old to be making rookie mistakes," David said. He rolled his shoulders and jerked his head side-to-side, cracking his neck. "I think you should let me go before someone gets hurt."

"Never!" Montjoy shouted.

"How do you two know each other?" I asked, eyeing them both.

"Poker night," David said, cracking his knuckles one at a time.

Montjoy pressed his hands to ears. "Stop cracking your knuckles, you infernal creature!"

"Or was it band camp?" my father said, holding up his pinky finger and twisting it to the side with a loud snap. Malice glimmered in his eyes.

24

"Your kind killed my family," Montjoy growled. "The Templars gave me a new mission in life, and I intend to fulfill it. You will be my crowning glory, Slade."

"Do the Templars still associate with you and your crazy cult?" David said. "I thought they kicked you out a long time ago."

"The Synod reached out to us after the Borathen infidels broke ranks," Montjoy said. "The Divinity herself has given us her blessing. She is the one who helped me find you, beast. She will show me how to destroy you."

"Just because demon spawn killed your family doesn't mean my father did it." I didn't think logic would work with this man, but at this point we had nothing to lose. "You're unfairly targeting him for the actions of others."

"You do not know him, boy." An unholy light shone in Montjoy's eyes. "You do not know his origin."

"Invite me over for tea sometime, Montjoy, and I'll tell you all about my childhood," David said, making a show of inspecting his fingernails.

I felt my eyebrows rise as I looked at David. I'd never heard him talk like this. He'd always been a lazy goof-off with few cares. His work as an artist rarely panned out to much, leaving Mom with the bulk of responsibility for keeping the household financially afloat. During my incubus puberty, I'd discovered his secret bank account with over a million dollars in it.

I looked at the stranger in my father's skin. "Who the hell are you?"

"That is a very good question," David said. "I planned on explaining myself to you, but my dear friend, Mr. Montjoy, rather rudely interrupted."

"I will return you to the eternal lake of fire, Slade." Foam flecked Montjoy's lips. "I relish the thought of you burning in perpetuity."

"Here's some advice," I said, poking a finger toward the angry fat man. "First of all, never get involved in a land war in Asia. Second, relishing the thought of anyone being tortured for all eternity is not gonna win you any friends."

25

"Especially when it's a nice guy like me," David said with a hurt look on his face. "Do you need a hug, Montjoy?"

"I don't need a hug!" the big man shouted, face beet red. The trickle of blood from his nose grew to a steady stream.

"Sir, your nose," the Exorcist with the tissue box said, and held out another tissue.

"Fix it!" Montjoy snapped.

The man dabbed at the blood for a moment to no effect and resorted to stuffing a wad in the Montjoy's nose.

David snickered.

The front doors to the church opened. Sunlight flooded in. Candles sputtered in the sudden breeze. A lone figure dressed in a silky white dress glided down the center aisle. She made a motion with her hand. A black tarp fell from where it had covered a circular stained window above the doors. Sunlight painted the hidden nooks of the Gothic church. It shimmered from the woman's Pantene-perfect golden hair. My breath caught in my throat. I backed away from the edge of the circle even as David's back straightened.

Exorcists fell prostrate, bowing in the presence of royalty. The man with the tissue box fainted. Montjoy narrowed his eyes, offering a curt bow to the one the Synod Templars called Divinity.

Fair skin and blonde hair aside, the woman looked identical to Nightliss. She was, in fact, her evil twin sister.

Daelissa.

Chapter 4

Elyssa

Police opened their car doors, aimed pistols over the sills, and shouted, "Raise your hands and get on the ground!"

"Give a guy a break!" Shelton shouted back at the police. "I just went out to get some milk and bread!"

"On the ground, now!" a cop screamed.

Shelton turned his head to Bella. "I am not getting arrested."

"I found Ivy's number," Elyssa said. She'd gone through her texts with Justin and finally found it. She dialed. The voice of a young girl answered after a few rings.

"Bigdaddy, calling from other numbers won't help," she said. "I told you I'm not coming back."

"It's Elyssa, not Jeremiah Conroy."

"Oh." She giggled. "I was just playing with Justin's hellhound puppy. He's so cute, even if his breath stinks."

"Ivy, we don't have much time. You know the omniarch in the cellar?"

"Yes."

Elyssa breathed a sigh of relief. "I need you to go down there right away. I'm going to send you a picture, and I want you to open a portal to the exact spot, okay?"

"You got it!"

Elyssa took a picture of the space behind a large green dumpster, and sent the image.

The sound of squealing tires heralded the arrival of a SWAT team. Police in bulletproof armor poured down the alley from the direction of the bank. Shelton looked at the police barring the other exit and growled. "You've got to be kidding me. I swear if they come at me, I'll use magic to stop them. Ain't no way in hell I'm letting noms take me in."

Bella gripped his arm. "No, Harry. We can't let noms see us using magic."

"She's right," Elyssa said. "Just give Ivy a minute."

"They'll see the portal open," Shelton said. "What's the difference?"

"The dumpster will screen them from seeing the portal," she replied.

"Down on the ground, or we'll open fire," said one of the men on the SWAT team. They aimed their assault rifles across the twenty yards separating them from Elyssa and the others.

"Hey, everyone!" said Ivy in a bright voice. She stepped from behind the dumpster, blonde hair bouncing and blue eyes alight with excitement. "What's all the excitement about?"

"Back through the portal," Elyssa said. "Hurry!"

"I said halt!" someone shouted and a gun exploded.

Ivy threw up a hand. A bullet flattened against a rippling shield inches from Shelton's chest. He staggered back, eyes wide with surprise. Ivy's lips peeled back into a snarl. "You tried to hurt my friends!" She threw her hands forward and a shimmering force threw the assault team back down the alley, guns clattering along the ground after them.

The police behind the cars at the end of the bank alley fired, but their bullets failed to penetrate the shield. Ivy squeezed her hand, and the police cars crumpled like tin foil. Someone shouted orders and the police went into a full retreat, voices filled with panic.

Bella looked horrified. Shelton barked a laugh. Ivy brushed her hands and smiled at Elyssa. "Are you guys ready to go?"

Elyssa nodded. "Yes."

They stepped back through the portal and into the cellar of the mansion. Elyssa deactivated the portal and gave Ivy a stern look. "You can't just go blasting noms with your powers. Didn't Jeremiah teach you any better?"

Ivy looked down and toed the floor. "Well, yeah. Bigdaddy— um, Jeremiah—he said I needed to be top secret with my abilities." She looked up. "But Daelissa told me I shouldn't worry so much, because taking over the world means you have to strike fear into the hearts of mere mortals."

Shelton and Bella exchanged looks of horror.

Elyssa decided it was time to have a much-needed talk with Justin's little sister. She looked at the other two. "Will you excuse us for a moment?"

"Take all the time you need," Shelton said. He took Bella's hand and fled up the stairs.

It had been a huge surprise when Ivy had shown up at the mansion the day after Justin's Christmas party. She'd apparently sneaked away from Jeremiah Conroy, as she'd done on several previous occasions, and come to live with Justin and Alysea, her mother. Justin had been overjoyed and immediately put plans in motion to meet with his father, arranging a meeting through his Aunt Vallaena. He'd hoped to surprise his mother with a family reunion when she returned from Colombia.

Despite the Ivy's tremendous abilities, she hadn't gotten out much. The Conroys had kept her close and mostly isolated. She'd attended Arcane University, but according to Justin, most other students shunned her. As if the Conroys weren't bad enough, the poor girl had grown up with Daelissa pretending to be her aunt. Kids were supposed to learn about world domination from television cartoons, not insane Seraphim posing as relatives.

This is not going to be easy.

Elyssa smiled. "Do you like Daelissa?"

Ivy wrinkled her forehead. "I used to love her a lot. Lately, she's gotten really creepy, and Justin says she's just plain crazy."

"Justin is right." Elyssa kept her tone sweet, trying to avoid an adversarial approach. "As Jeremiah has probably told you, normal

29

people—noms—don't react well to magic. In fact, it's against Overworld law to use magic where noms can see it."

"Why should we care? I mean, I could just incinerate the ones who don't like it."

Elyssa held back a grimace. "How many of you are there, Ivy?"

Ivy giggled. "Just one."

"That's right." Elyssa smiled. "There are billions of noms. If they all tried to kill you, do you think you could incinerate them all?"

Ivy pursed her lips and looked up, as if really calculating the odds. "I suppose I could blast a couple hundred before I got tired."

"In other words, they'd probably kill you long before you killed all of them."

The girl nodded. "Yeah, I guess you're right. They might be inferior, but there's so many of them that it's not a good idea to rile them up." She shrugged. "I mean, killing isn't that much fun anyway. When Bigdaddy—"

"He's not your grandfather, Ivy." Elyssa and Justin had to constantly remind the girl Jeremiah and Eliza had taken her when she was a baby, but they weren't related.

"Okay, fine. When Jeremiah wanted me to kill every vampire in Maximus's compound, I figured it was okay, because he told me they were all evil bloodsuckers." A frown crossed her pretty face. "But after meeting a few vampires, I realized that some of them are pretty nice. Felicia is really sweet."

Felicia Nosti hadn't started out as the sweetest vampire in the world, but Justin had somehow won her over to his side. Elyssa had to admit the former druggie had come a long way since the first time they'd met. "See? Just because someone is a vampire or a nom doesn't mean they're evil or inferior."

"Yeah, I guess you're right." She shrugged. "I mean, noms can become Templars, so even they have some potential."

"So, no more blasting noms?" Elyssa said.

Ivy nodded. "I promise not to, unless they're really evil." She tilted her head. "Why were you in that alley anyway?"

Elyssa wasn't sure she wanted to inform Ivy about the current crisis, but knew it would be a mistake to conceal it. "Justin was kidnapped."

The girl gasped. "Oh no. Who got him?"

"We're trying to figure that out right now." She motioned up the stairs. "Let's go meet the others and go over the clues."

"Elyssa?" Ivy said.

She looked at Justin's sister. "Yes?"

"Can I blast his kidnappers?"

Elyssa managed an uneasy smile. "Let's talk about that after we figure out who did it, okay?"

"Okay!" Ivy said in a bright voice.

They went upstairs to the planning room. Shelton and Bella were already inside talking with Cinder. The golem looked at Elyssa with a stiff smile.

"I believe I have narrowed down the possibilities for this symbol." He projected an image above the table of several similar symbols. "Templars used these symbols centuries ago to imprison various entities. In particular, they used them to combat those possessed by demons."

"You're saying the Synod Templars took Justin?" Shelton said.

Elyssa shook her head. "Those weren't Templars I saw in the video."

"A video?" Ivy asked. "Can I see it?"

Shelton looked back and forth from Elyssa to the young girl. "Uh, how'd the talk go?"

"I promised not to incinerate people unless they're evil," Ivy said with large innocent eyes.

Bella put a hand to her chest. "Madre de dios."

"A worthy goal," Cinder said in his calm voice. "I have found it is often better to think things through before resorting to deadly force."

"Well, that's what the adults seem to think." The girl shrugged.

"Anyway," Shelton said, displaying the video for all to see, "these are the perps who took Justin and his dad."

31

In the video, the hooded figures walked down the sidewalk with what looked like the unconscious forms of Justin and David on flying carpets.

"The Exorcists have him," Ivy said in a hushed tone.

All eyes turned to her.

"The Exorcists?" Elyssa said. "They don't exist anymore." She vaguely remembered a mention of them in her Templar history classes, but that was about it.

"I know all about the Exorcists," Ivy said in a matter-of-fact tone. "Daelissa bragged all the time about how she made the Templar and Exorcist organizations." She sighed. "I got really tired of hearing about it."

"What do you know?" Shelton asked.

"Daelissa told me she made the Exorcists into their own organization a long time ago." Ivy tapped a finger on her chin. "Sometimes when she came to visit Jeremiah, she brought along this fat guy named Montjoy. I think he's their leader. Daelissa talked about how she wanted to kill him because he was such a nincompoop."

Shelton's forehead wrinkled. "She called him a nincompoop?"

Ivy laughed. "No, but Bigmomma—Eliza—wouldn't let me say the words Daelissa said."

"Hold on a second," Shelton said. "You're saying there's an entire organization of people who exorcise demons from the possessed? Justin and his father are demon spawn. That ain't the same thing."

"I think Montjoy was looking for a way to get rid of demon spawn," Ivy said. "Before I got to know Justin it sounded like a really good idea."

"Because Jeremiah told you all demon spawn were evil," Bella said.

The girl shook her head. "No, Daelissa told me all that. Jeremiah told me vampires were evil."

Shelton grunted. "That doesn't make any sense. Vampires are on Daelissa's side, aren't they?"

"I believe I know why Daelissa wishes to purge all demon spawn," Cinder said. "The history I've uncovered from Ezzek Moore's personal journals indicates the Daemos fought against the Seraphim. Perhaps she sees them as a threat to her future."

"Yeah, and vampires are her allies." Shelton aimed a look at Ivy. "Did Conroy tell you why he wanted to kill the vamps?"

Ivy shook her head. "No, but he convinced me they needed to be killed."

"I hope to hell he doesn't know where you are." Shelton shuddered. "That old man scares me."

Elyssa paced back and forth, listening to the group talk as she tried to remember her history lessons about the Exorcists. Unfortunately, not much came back to her. "We need to find where these people are."

"There's one place Daelissa talked about a lot," Ivy said. "I can take you there."

A ray of hope warmed Elyssa. "Grab your gear, everyone." She headed out of the room. "We're going to pay the Exorcists a visit."

Chapter 5

"You have him," Daelissa said, not even glancing at the kneeling Exorcists all around her. She gave Montjoy a haughty look. "I am pleased with you."

The pompous ass bowed as much as his paunch allowed. "As promised, Milady."

"A promise kept is a promise kept, though it took the passage of centuries to see it through." The Seraphim made an exaggerated yawn. "Nevertheless, servant, you have done well."

Montjoy ground his teeth at the backhanded compliment. "The ritual failed to purge him."

Daelissa raised a blonde eyebrow. "Indeed?" She made a dismissive motion with her hand. "Leave me."

The other Exorcists evacuated, some of them carrying the unmoving forms of their fallen comrades. I wondered if David's blue mist attack had killed any of them, or if the demon-possessed people held sole responsibility.

Montjoy sputtered. "But—"

The Seraphim's eyes narrowed and lips curled down as she turned her baleful gaze onto the rotund Exorcist. "I said leave," she hissed. A pulsar of white light blazed to life in her hand, spitting sparks of darkness.

"What the—" I said. David bumped me, interrupting my thought, his eyes also regarding the strange spectacle. Daelissa was a Brightling, the upper crust of the angel social class. Her sister, Nightliss, was a Darkling. Despite the explanations I'd received, I still didn't understand why those of her particular persuasion were regarded as evil and second class, but I knew they used dark energy when channeling magic, whereas the Brightlings used, well, bright energy.

Montjoy continued to argue, despite the hazard to his health pulsing malevolently in her dainty hand. "I only wanted to—"

Daelissa raised her hand until the deadly energy almost tickled Montjoy's chin.

He waddled away faster than a duck on roller skates.

The bright sphere winked out, leaving a cloud of sparkling dust. The angel turned to David, a smile playing on her lips. "It has been too long," she said. "Have you missed me?"

"How could one not miss such beauty?" he said, all sign of irreverence gone. "You are as fair as the day I met you, Daelissa."

"And you are ever so handsome and charming," she said with a girlish sigh.

"You two know each other?" I said.

Daelissa's eyes flared, as if seeing me for the first time. "Who is this boy?" Her voice rose to fever pitch. "Who is this child? I did not order any boy servants attend me."

She doesn't recognize me?

"He's my servant," David said, voice smooth, even as he cuffed me on the back of my head. "I must apologize. The lackwit doesn't understand he cannot speak unless spoken to." My father snapped his fingers. "Keep your mouth shut, boy." His eyes flared with warning.

I backed away, bowing apologetically like I'd seen a dancing monkey do after someone put a quarter in its little red hat.

"Now, where were we?" David said. He reached out as if to touch Daelissa, but the circle prevented his hand from crossing.

"What is it?" she said, face blushing.

35

"Your servant put a barrier between me and your beauty," he said. "I long so much to feel the warmth of your fair cheek beneath my hand. To feel your supple lips press against mine."

"You do?" she said, sounding like a girl on a first date. "You have changed your mind?"

"My heart has never wavered, my sweet Daelissa. My mind, likewise, never thought differently. Necessity and fate tore choice from my grasp and made a poor life for me." He took in a deep shuddering breath. "Lovesick, I yearned for your fair sight, but lost hope as centuries passed I would ever see such beauty again."

"Oh, Davidius," she said, a tear sparkling in her eye. "I knew your heart chose me, and not Alysea. The others corrupted your mind. But now we can have what should have been ours millennia ago."

Millennia?

Holy French fries in a milkshake. How old was my dad?

"It is my dream, fairest of the fair," David said. "Everything is but dust and ashes without your beauty." He pressed a hand to his heart. "I feel naught but lovesick in your absence."

Daelissa heaved a longing sigh. "I knew you loved me then." She twirled like a princess. Her silky white dress flared wide. She stopped, looked at him. "Then and forevermore."

A longing growl escaped David's throat. "Were it not for this barrier, I would take you now, my love." He ran his hand down the invisible shield, sighing with such longing I thought he might burst into tears of pure testosterone.

"Make it so," she said, raising a hand.

"Help!" a man screamed. Two Exorcists dragged him into the sanctuary by a chain manacled around his neck. "Who are you crazy people? Help!"

"What is the meaning of this?" Daelissa cried, teeth bared like a lioness ready to pounce.

"We have found another of the pure ones, blessed Divinity," said one of the Exorcists. His face blanched when he saw the expression on her face. "Montjoy said you desired sustenance, holy one."

36

I noticed David's eyes flare with something akin to alarm. "Foolish servants," he said, slashing a hand through the air. "We will have our fill of each other first, my love. Then you can have your way with this food."

The angel's eyes turned back to him, widening as if suddenly remembering their conversation. "Leave the human chained here. I will feed after I have my love."

A smile touched David's lips. "Already do the flames of desire taunt me unto madness, most desirable of women. Loose me from these confines so I may taste your sweet skin."

"Oh, yes," Daelissa said, raising her hand.

"Almighty Divinity," Montjoy said, peeking around the corner of the partition to the right of the sanctuary. "I regret the intrusion, but this pure specimen will soon expire unless you use him now."

"Suffice it to wait!" she screamed, fists balled, face red like a girl throwing a tantrum.

He offered a forced smile. "I do not wish fear to pollute the specimen's purity."

Daelissa flung out a hand toward the chained man. His body jerked, hands flying straight out toward the angel. White tendrils flowed from each digit, streaming into Daelissa's. He made a horrible moaning wail, splitting the air with a cry wavering between pain and pleasure.

I grimaced and clamped hands over my ears so I wouldn't have to listen to the animalistic sounds tearing from the poor man's throat.

David clenched his teeth and glared at Montjoy. The Exorcist narrowed his eyes, lips widening in a greasy smile.

"What is it?" I whispered.

"She's borderline insane unless she feeds," he said. "Montjoy just brought her back from la-la land."

White light blazed in Daelissa's eyes. She made a soft moaning sound as the man's skin writhed with dark veins. Smoky shadows roiled from his body, and his eyes rolled up until only the whites remained visible. With a croaking scream, he collapsed to the

37

floor. The angel shivered, and gasped. She turned toward us, skin suffused with an alabaster glow. Her eyes narrowed.

"Davidius Slade," she hissed, voice crackling with fury. "You tried to fool me."

David sighed and shrugged as if pissing off the crazed angel was no big deal. I backed away slowly.

The movement caught her eyes. "Justin Slade." She spat the words. White fire filled Daelissa's palms. Without hesitation, she hurled the crackling infernos at me. They splashed against the magical barrier, dissipating with loud whooshes.

Montjoy appeared behind her. "I did not realize Slade was meeting his son, but I captured both for you."

"You did well," Daelissa said, glaring at me, another deadly inferno boiling in her hand. "You have made quite a name for yourself, boy. But you failed to fulfill Foreseeance Forty-Three Eleven. Your sister is the Cataclyst, and she is still loyal to me and my servant, Conroy."

Apparently, Jeremiah hadn't told the angel the truth about Ivy's current whereabouts. I didn't even know what to think about this Cataclyst business. Another Seraphim had referred to me as the Cataclyst—someone who would bring about great change. I decided it would be a bad idea to correct Daelissa.

"I may have failed," I said, trying to come up with something to get her off track, "but you still won't succeed."

Her fiery eyes narrowed. "You are still the blood of Alysea. Perhaps you can help me." She made a tutting noise. "Unfortunately, Ivy is too young, her voice not yet mature."

Dad and I exchanged confused looks.

Mature voice? Does she want me to make prank calls with her? "I won't help you with anything," I said.

The angel laughed. "Oh, but you will have no choice."

"Would you prefer to kill the boy?" Montjoy asked.

"Does it sound like I want to kill him?" Daelissa shrieked. "You idiotic toad! We will banish him. Send word to Serena and have someone waiting."

"See it is done," Montjoy said to one of the Exorcists. The hooded figure scurried away. "Your Eminence, perhaps we could send them to Kobol until Serena is ready to receive them."

"I will not give them another chance to escape." She flashed teeth at David. "Davidius is most slippery."

The Exorcist who'd left the room a moment ago returned. "It is done. She will be ready."

"Excellent," Daelissa said. "My mind will rest easy with this abomination no longer soiling Eden's fair lands."

"Why are you so intent on ruling again?" David said. "The cost was staggering last time, Daelissa. With your power, you could usher in a time of peace and serenity."

A low, growling laugh rose in Daelissa's throat. A cold, malicious smile spread across her lips. "What good is peace and serenity when there is no one to share it with, hm?" She paced outside the ring, eyes never leaving David. "You, of course, have someone. You chose her over me, I might remind you."

"I'm sorry—"

She cut him off with a slash of her hand. "Tell me, Davidius, and tell me true. What does Alysea have that I do not? Am I not more powerful? More beautiful?"

"You are the fairest of all," Montjoy exclaimed.

Daelissa backhanded him across the floor, and continued to speak as though she'd just swatted a fly. "I offered you the world. I offered you myself, and you *refused me*." Her last words emerged in an angry hiss.

"There was never a choice," David said.

Her blonde eyebrows rose. "What do you mean?"

"My choice never wavered from Alysea." He shrugged. "I thought I could stop your mad conquest with deceit and treachery. I failed."

"Lies!" Daelissa screamed. "You are lying to me. I know you loved me. Alysea poisoned your mind against me." A bright glow formed around her body. The air shimmered with heat. Any nearby Exorcists backed away, eyes wide.

39

"Maybe we could get you a subscription to an online dating site," I suggested, figuring the situation was far beyond reason at this point. "I'll bet there are plenty of guys looking for an angel who's into world domination."

"Enough!" Daelissa screeched. One of the wooden pews behind her smoldered. She spun to Montjoy who was only just now recovering his wits after the blow she'd dealt him. "Begin the ritual, you lazy swine. I want these two banished and in my service immediately."

"Y-yes," Montjoy said, staggering to his feet and promptly falling flat on his face. "Gather the others for the ritual," he shouted at the Exorcist he'd sent on the errand earlier as the other man helped his boss to his feet.

"Talk about melodramatic," I said with an offhanded wave of my hand. "Banishment doesn't sound so bad as long as I don't have to see either of you two again."

"I assure you it will not be pleasant, boy." Daelissa's eyes flicked to David. "Do you see what choosing Alysea has cost you, Davidius?"

"I'd say it spared me your constant bitching," he said.

"Fool!" Daelissa shouted. "We could have united our kingdoms and ruled together. You squandered it all for a silly girl whose fondness for these animals"—she indicated the still form of the drained human behind her—"cost us everything!"

"You," David said in a calm voice, "are a crazy, maniacal bitch."

"Quoted for truth," I said.

Daelissa's eyes flashed. "Your precious wife may be out of my reach for now, but I still have your daughter well in hand."

Thank god she doesn't know the truth.

David tensed, whether for show or because he didn't remember I'd told him about Ivy living with me, I didn't know.

"She will do anything for her Aunt Daelissa." The angel sneered.

David blew out a breath. "You think if I cared about her I wouldn't have taken her from you already?"

"She is your daughter," Daelissa said.

"She was a mistake," he said back in a flippant voice. "I gladly let the Conroys take her."

My stomach clenched at hearing his words. Did he really mean it, or was it a ruse?

"I knew you were cold when you spurned my love, Davidius." She arched a blonde eyebrow. "I see now you still care only for yourself with one exception." Her lips curled into a sinister smile. "Alysea, the dimwitted little fool, somehow touched your heart. You may not care for your daughter, but she does."

"What's your point?" David said.

"I can use Ivy to draw Alysea into the open." The angel tapped a finger to her lips. "While you waste away in exile, I will find and kill Alysea." Her lips peeled in an ugly smile. "I welcomed the pathetic creature back after the Conroys found her. She repaid me with yet another betrayal. I will enjoy tearing off her wings."

My father shrugged. "What makes you think I care? Do you really think I'd arrange to marry one of my own kind if I cared at all for Alysea?"

Daelissa bared her teeth. "You are obviously once again using your talents as you used them against me." She looked at Montjoy. "Proceed."

David clenched his fists, even though his face remained passive. Desperation filled me. Daelissa didn't appear to know Ivy was living with me, but if she managed to contact Ivy and lure her into a meeting, I wouldn't be able to do a thing about it. *Where are they sending us?*

Exorcists filed into the room, some of them limping from the previous battle with the possessed and that blue smoke from my father. Without a word, they formed a circle around the silver ring. Montjoy took his place atop the tall podium, the effort of climbing so many stairs causing him to huff and puff with each step. He reached the top and took a moment to catch his breath.

"Better stop with the fried foods," I said, trying to think of some way to delay this banishment. If we could only stop it for a day, it might give Elyssa time to realize something was wrong and find us.

41

Daelissa backed away a few paces. "I will enjoy this."

I had a distinct feeling I would not. "Can't we talk about it?" I tried to smile. "Daelissa, I know we haven't always gotten along, but deep down inside, I think you're probably a really cool person."

Her upper lip curled into a sneer. "Shut your mouth, pathetic worm."

"What the hell did I ever do to you?"

She bared her teeth. "You were born."

At that point, I decided there was no appealing to Daelissa's humanity—Seraphinity—or whatever it was called. I turned to David and whispered, "What are they planning to do?"

He shrugged. "Sounds like enslavement in an alternate realm if I had to guess."

The Exorcists in the circle began to chant, softly at first, voices rising into a sonorous song. Any other time I might have thought it sounded beautiful. Right then, it was just creepy. Spiders seemed to crawl up my spine as the magic inside the circle brushed against my skin. I closed my eyes and concentrated, trying to channel the aether, but felt it slide through my grasp like oily water. Their ritual was somehow preventing me from casting spells.

Damn it, do something!

Manifesting into demon form would accomplish nothing. David walked to the edge of the ring. He pressed a hand against the air, and muttered something under his breath. A glow spread from his hand, highlighting the curving outline of the invisible barrier. The ground trembled.

Daelissa levitated into the air behind the Exorcists. She smiled and waggled a finger. "Even you cannot escape this, betrayer."

David's voice rose to a shout. The ground buckled. Stone cracked beneath my feet, and a fissure raced toward the silver circle. It hit the ring and stopped. The volume of his voice grew louder until it rose above the chanting Exorcists. I heard the groan of metal. Felt the air grow hot against my skin. Saw the floor cracking and crumbling beneath our feet.

From the corner of my eye, I saw Montjoy slash his hand as he shouted a word. The air within the gray arch cracked like glass stressed to the breaking point. A spider web of fissures laced the air. With a roar, the fabric of reality shattered. A gale of wind tore at me and dragged me toward a ragged hole within the arch. Beyond it laid a gray void. I suddenly knew without question where they intended to banish us.

The Gloom.

I cried out as the wind dragged me toward certain doom. Unleashing the demon within, I grew long black claws and stabbed them into the stone floor. They screeched across the hard surface as I vainly sought purchase. Muscles snaked around my arms. A tail ruined the seat of my jeans, jabbing a hole through them as it sprouted like a prehensile weed. David's legs flew out beneath him, and his body sailed toward the portal. I wrapped my tail around David's arm before he flew past. The extra weight dragged us toward the hole. Sparks flew from my claws as they raked the floor.

I looked back. "Don't give up!" I shouted above the roaring wind.

My father gave me a calm, almost accepting look and shook his head.

I felt my shoulder muscles bunch and strain as I tried to stab one of my clawed hands into the stone. Rock chips sprayed as I jabbed them over and over against the unyielding surface. My claws couldn't take the pounding and snapped. Red-hot pain lanced up my fingers. My other hand lost its grip, and the wind seized us, hurling us into the jagged gray maw.

The last thing I saw before the gray swallowed the portal was the smile on Daelissa's face. I slammed into something hard, and everything went black.

Chapter 6

I sit on a bench in a park on a lovely spring day. Children nearby laugh and play. Dogs bark and chase Frisbees. A young girl licks ice cream as her smiling parents walk close behind, hand-in-hand. Something seems to move in my grasp. I look down and see a book with a pale leather binding. A title in gold letters, THE FINAL CHOICE, is the only thing on the cover. I open the book. Inside, it says, "Dedicated to Justin Slade." Unable to resist, I turn the page only to see a blank white space.

The earth trembles. The laughter of the children turns to cries of fear. I look up and see brilliant balls of white light streaking across the sky like stars falling to earth. In the distance, the city skyline crumbles to ash. People scream and run in all directions. One of the balls of light lands, leaving a blackened crater. Giant white wings unfurl and I look into the face of—of myself. Brightling Justin stretches out his hand. All the people nearby turn to face him, fingers reaching as if to touch his while milky white light drains from their bodies. Their bodies writhe with dark veins.

I try to scream, but cannot open my mouth. As if of their own accord, my fingers turn the page. Again, there are no words, only a dim ultraviolet glow.

I hear laughter and look up. The park scene has reset. Everyone frolics as if the entire world hadn't just been destroyed. I hear the sound of waves breaking and look for the source. There are no oceans near Atlanta. A great black tidal wave rises on the horizon, stretching from side to side as far as I can see. It swallows the city within second. The ground rumbles. Trees, houses, and bodies litter the wave like flotsam. Flying before the water on wings of dark light, I see Darkling Justin. As before, I can't scream or run, only watch as the dark wave washes over the park. When it is gone, all that remains is an empty world and a dark sky. As if watching a time-lapse video, I see vegetation growing, and animals emerging. The world seems to be starting over anew.

With a trembling hand, I turn the page and find gray.

The people walk with stiff gaits from one point to another. They are like machines, driven to their tasks. There is no laughter, no joy, only endless repetition. Nothing changes on the outside, but I smell the stagnation, the rot. I see an unmoving statue of myself standing in the center of the park. When I look at it too long, the eyes blink. The happy family from earlier passes me. They are no longer smiling, but straight-faced and serious. They stop before my bench and turn to face me. Half of their faces are nothing but skulls covered in rotting flesh.

"This is perfection," they say in unison. "Perfection, perfection, perfection—"

I jerked awake with a loud scream. David lay face down next to me. He groaned and pushed himself into a sitting position. Gray fog hung heavy as pea soup around us. Whether it was real fog or something else entirely, I couldn't tell. The ground felt stony beneath me. The air was neither humid nor dry, hot nor cold, just a Goldilocks medium.

What kind of crazy dream was that? It had seemed so real. And yet, something like a sense of purpose filled me despite the ache in my head. *I'm supposed to be here.* Then again, I might have just hit my head really hard. I looked frantically around me. "Daelissa is going after Mom and Ivy. We've got to get out of here."

"This certainly puts a pinch in things," David said, standing and brushing off his jeans.

I pushed myself up and faced him. "Amazing assessment. Did you hear what I said about Mom and Ivy? Do you even care?"

He folded his arms. "Of course I care, but panicking won't solve anything."

I wanted to grab him by the front of the shirt and shake him, but he was right. Escape from the Gloom was our priority, and I had absolutely no clue how to do that. As deep breaths calmed me somewhat, a stinging pain in my fingertips drew my attention. Blood caked my fingers where my demon claws had torn off. It looked like I'd ripped open a pregnant yak with my bare hands. I winced, and realized with a shock I was back in human form already. I usually had to beat back my demon side until it retreated inside its kennel. The raw, jagged remains of my fingernails stung. I sucked on my index finger to soothe it.

"My hand isn't healing," I said.

"I noticed." David knelt and inspected the floor. "I've never actually been in the Gloom. Not much to see."

"There must be a way out," I said, resisting the urge to run aimlessly through the thick haze around us. "Didn't Daelissa say someone would be here to enslave us? Do you see anyone?"

David held up a hand, and listened. "I don't hear a thing. Before we go running willy-nilly, I suggest we take stock of our surroundings."

Despite the moderate climate, the inability to see further than a few feet in any direction was absolutely suffocating. My feet scuffed against the hard floor. I knelt. The surface looked like stone. In fact, it looked a lot like the floor of the church. "Where did Montjoy get a gray and a sapphire arch?"

"Your guess is as good as mine. I don't remember seeing anything like them."

"Obviously the gray arch goes to the Gloom." I followed David as he moved through the fog. "He tried to exorcise you through the blue one. I assume it goes to the demon realm."

"Fair assumption." He put his hands out, as if feeling his way.

I kept following him through the thick fog. "Do demons need portals to possess people?"

He shook his head. "We have our own ways of crossing the veil between realms."

"Like demon-summoning runes?" My friends and I had been attacked by monstrous demons not so long ago thanks to a group of murderous battle mages called the Black Robe Brotherhood.

"Summoning runes simply bring a demon spirit into a temporary cage of flesh within the mortal realm. An actual demon portal means someone bound by flesh could step into our realm." He pursed his lips. "I'm curious what would happen."

"I'm not," I lied as the image of tossing a cat through the portal flashed through my mind. *Stacey would kick my ass.*

David knelt and tapped the ground with a knuckle. He looked around and grunted. "The Exorcists must have more than just the one demon portal. I can't imagine they ship all the possessed to Atlanta for purging." He motioned me to follow, and walked until he nearly stumbled over a wooden pew. "We're in the church."

My brow pinched with confusion as I ran my hand along the grained surface. "How is the church in the Gloom?"

"The Gloom is supposedly a shadow realm of the real world, or so I've heard."

"What's the difference between a shadow realm and the other realms?"

He shrugged. "Your mother might know." He shoved at a pew and failed to budge it. "This isn't good."

"What isn't?"

"Move the pew," he said.

I tried and barely managed to scoot the heavy oak bench. "I'm not supernaturally strong."

"Yeah, or the bench got a lot heavier."

Come to think of it, I felt punier than normal, and my hand still wasn't healing. Something was way off about this place. Before I could say anything, David started down the center aisle, feeling his way like a blind man while I followed close behind until we passed beyond the first row. He squatted and traced the ground with his fingers, making a thoughtful noise when they found the silver circle. We continued in a straight line until we reached the center of the circle.

Both arches were there, though they looked different. The demon arch glowed with a sullen red hue while the Gloom arch looked more or less as gray as ever.

I felt a flare of optimism. "Maybe I can use the arch to take us back through." I knelt, searching the floor until I found the silver ring around the Gloom arch.

"Don't you have to sing to it?" David said with an amused grin.

I shrugged. "No idea. I'm going to give this a shot first." Jamming a thumb to the circle, I willed it to close. At first, nothing happened. I closed my eyes and concentrated on the circle, commanding it to close over and over again until finally, I felt it snap shut.

"Doing okay?" David said. "You looked a little constipated for a second."

"I'm fine," I growled. "Let me concentrate." I willed the Gloom arch to open a portal back to the real world. Once again, it felt as if it resisted my will. As before, I kept pushing harder and harder until the center of the portal flickered.

A black barrier greeted us. David grabbed a chip of stone from the floor and tossed it at the darkness. It swallowed the stone without a sound.

"They must have blocked it with a spell," he said.

"Makes sense," I said. "Wouldn't be much of a banishment if the banishees could just hop back through." The foolish hope we might escape quickly died. My chest tightened as I thought of Daelissa hunting down my family.

"You're worrying about Ivy and your mother again," David said.

I felt my eyes flare. "Maybe you should try it sometime. It's called caring."

"Justin, Daelissa is only one Seraphim. Do you really think she'd try to take on your mother and Ivy?" His eyebrows rose in challenge.

"She might lure Ivy to her, brainwash her, and use her against Mom."

48

He crinkled his forehead. "No wonder you worry so much with an imagination like that."

My knuckles cracked as I fought back the panic and anger. "Just shut up and let me figure this out."

David sighed. "We could try the demon arch."

I looked at it for a long moment before finally deciding it might be worth a try even if the idea of entering the demon world scared the tinkle out of me. I closed the connection with the Gloom arch and worked on sealing the circle around the demon arch. As before, it took me several tries just to close the circle.

"Not working?" David said.

I grimaced. "Just barely. Something about this place makes it really hard to reach my magic." As if to confirm that theory, I spent the next several minutes fruitlessly trying to open the demon arch. Unlike the Gloom arch, I didn't sense any response from this one. I finally gave up. "This one must require an Exorcist singing ritual."

"I'm not much of a singer," David said, "so I can't help you there."

"Yeah, we're basically screwed," I said. I looked around despite my inability to see more than a foot in any direction. "We need to get out of here before Daelissa's people arrive."

"With fog this thick, it's no wonder they aren't here yet." My father blew out a sigh. "There's only one chance of getting out of here I can think of."

"And that would be?"

"The Obsidian Arch in the Grotto." He shrugged. "I don't know the odds of an accidental Gloom rift opening, but unless you have another suggestion, we should head there."

Nothing better sprang to mind. Cinder had once told me under usual circumstances, the odds of an accidental Gloom fracture around an Obsidian Arch were about fifteen percent. Standing here gave us a zero percent chance to escape. The math wasn't too hard to do, and I was willing to try anything to protect Mom and Ivy. Even without considering the odds, something felt right about going there. I couldn't explain the feeling, only that thinking about going to the

Grotto gave me a sense of purpose. It was a rather enigmatic feeling. Then again, I was standing right next to an enigma I used to call Dad.

David headed across the room, quickly vanishing from sight.

I shook my head and followed, determined to learn more about him. "I didn't know you could do magic. How did you crack the ground open just before they banished us?"

"I've learned a few things over the years."

I pshawed. "Years? How about centuries? Or better yet, millennia?" Dad looked like a well-preserved man in his early forties. "You once told me you were really only about forty. You lied to me."

He nodded. "Yep. I lied about a lot of things."

What the hell? "You don't even sound ashamed about it."

"Why should I be? I did what I had to do." He reached the large wooden doors to the church and pushed them open to reveal more fog.

"You lied to your own son, you ass." I almost punched him again. Seeing as how the last time I'd done that hadn't achieved the desired effect, I held back. "Why don't you just come out and tell me the truth?"

"I'm an old dude," he said, navigating the stairs in front of the church.

I waited in silence as he bent down and examined the sidewalk, hoping he would elaborate. Impatience overwhelmed me. "Are you going to tell me?"

"I just told you the truth," he said, forehead wrinkling. "Wasn't that what you wanted?"

"You didn't say *how* old you are."

"Really, really old."

I grabbed his arm and jerked him to his feet. "Keep it up and I'm going to beat the snot out of you, old man."

"I thought I raised you better."

Heat flared in my face. It took everything I had not to pounce on him and—what? Beat him into a bloody pulp? It wouldn't help a thing. My anger cooled. "You know what? You're not even worth my time." I stalked off in what I hoped was the general direction of the Grotto.

50

"Why couldn't they wait until night?" someone complained from somewhere in the fog.

I came to a stop and felt David bump into me. Putting a finger to my lips, I listened.

"You think they care if we can see or not?" another man replied to the first. "We're supposed to take them to the fortress."

"A little heads up would've been nice," growled the first man. "The worst part is I won't even get to see the look in their eyes when they realize they don't have their supernatural abilities." He chuckled. "I love that part."

"I think we should have a little fun," his partner said. "Let's kick some demon spawn ass." He spat. "I hate those inhuman things."

The voices were closing in on our position fast. I motioned David back the other way. He nodded and we carefully made our way down the street. I rammed my stomach into a parking meter and grunted.

"You hear that?" one of the men said.

They went silent. I listened hard, but without my supernatural hearing, nothing gave away the men's position. David waved me to follow. We followed the sidewalk, careful to avoid benches and other pitfalls that might trip us up.

"Come out, come out, wherever you are," one of the men called. He sounded farther away, but I couldn't be sure.

"Here, little chicky," his partner said in a mocking tone. "Come out and play, little demon spawn."

The men kept calling after us, but it was apparent they couldn't see through the fog any better than we could.

"Thank god they're idiots," David said as the men's voices faded into the distance.

"What do you think they meant by the fortress?" I asked. "Who the hell puts a fortress in the Gloom?"

He snorted. "Sounds like something Daelissa would do." He glanced over his shoulder. "Good news is, we just escaped whatever she had in store for us."

I blew out a breath. "But the bad news is being stuck in purgatory with a congenital liar and deadbeat dad is bad enough."

51

"Just because I don't conform to your notions of a perfect father, doesn't mean—"

I swatted the air with a hand. "If we ever get out of this mess, I'm done with you for good." I felt disgusted to think of this man as my father. He acted nothing like the father I remembered. Or was he simply someone I'd never truly known? "I guess everything I thought I knew about you was just an act, a show to make me think we were a normal family."

"I wouldn't go that far," he said. "I really enjoyed having a family experience."

"A family isn't an amusement park," I said. "It's not an experience; it's a life you build for yourself and those you love."

"Ah, the love thing," David said. "That was the first thing your mother taught me."

I stopped in my tracks and stared at him. "She *taught* you?"

"In a manner of speaking."

"What, you don't know how to love?"

"Not in the same way humans do."

I felt my eyebrows rocket upward. "What other way is there?"

His eyes looked skyward, as if he were thinking hard about it. "I remember the first time I saw her. I felt light as air. I wanted to touch her skin. I wanted to stroke her hair. I wanted to feel her naked body against mine."

"TMI, man!" I said, covering up my ears. I lowered my hands. "In other words, you lusted after her."

"At first. Eventually, she taught me what it was to really love someone." He gave a wistful smile. "Sometimes I regret it."

"You regret learning to love?"

"It's not a pleasant experience when you hit a downturn."

"You mean like getting into arguments, or arguing over the remote control?" I asked.

"As in the woman you love was just killed, and you're faced with an eternity of anguish and heartbreak."

I blinked a couple of times at his response. "She's not dead. Your argument is invalid."

52

"At the time, I thought she was." He rubbed his forehead as if warding off a headache, stopped, and turned to me. "I met your mother when humanity was in its infancy. We fought a war together. I thought she died. I then endured a very long period of time in which I propagated Daemos across the mortal realm, made up a bunch of meaningless rules to keep them in order, and tried to forget the agonizing ache in my heart. I then discovered Alysea was, in fact, not dead, but somehow a young girl being raised by—" He broke off, brow furrowed as he looked around our bland environs.

"What is it?" I asked.

"Just a strange feeling."

"In your case, I think we can safely say it's not puberty."

He laughed. "I'm glad you have my sense of humor, Justin."

"Keep going with the story," I said, not willing to be dragged off track.

"Ah, yes." He tapped a finger to his chin. "I don't know how I knew the girl was Alysea, but something inside me surged at the first sight of her. The following years of waiting for her to mature were more torturous than the centuries before because I had no idea if she would remember me."

"She did, obviously," I said.

"After a time." He pursed his lips. "I took her to the place I first told her I loved her." His eyes looked a little dreamy. "It was like flipping a switch in her mind."

He no longer seemed like the uncaring asshole from two minutes ago, but a lovesick boy. I had to wonder if maybe my dad had severe mental issues. "You make it sound like a fairy tale," I said.

"I suppose it was."

"Then what the hell happened? Why are you marrying Kassallandra?"

His gaze flicked to the side. "We aren't alone."

"Are those men back?"

He shook his head. "No. It's something else."

Ice seemed to glaze my stomach. "Something worse?" I almost didn't want to know if something monstrous lurked unseen in

53

the fog, like a giant spider, or snakes—or even worse—giant spider snakes.

"I'm not sure," he said, eyes sweeping the grayness. He motioned me to follow and set off at a steady pace.

I followed close behind. "How do you know someone is there?"

"Use your senses."

"Your incubus senses are working?" I hadn't thought to try them, especially since none of my other abilities seemed to function.

"Just barely. It's an effort to switch them on."

David was right. What was usually instantaneous instead took me several minutes of closing my eyes and concentrating intensely. Reaching inside to flick the switch was more like fumbling through a pool of black tar to tug on a heavy lever. When I opened my eyes, the fog glowed all around us, limiting my field of view even more. On the other hand, it made it a lot easier to detect where David was in relation to me. I jogged to keep up with him and simultaneously sent tendrils of my essence questing into the surroundings. Within seconds, I encountered something alive. It wasn't human, and it didn't feel like an animal. It radiated what I could only equate to a strange hunger mixed with an almost instinctual sense of duty. Despite the alien emotions, I felt a peculiar familiarity with whatever stalked us through the shroud of fog.

The last time I'd felt such a presence hadn't been so long ago. "It's a minder." I shuddered. The things looked like large flying jellyfish with ghostly tentacles.

"Exactly." He continued walking.

"You already knew?" The last time I'd encountered a minder was at La Casona. Battle mages with the Black Robe Brotherhood and a group of the creatures had chased me and my friends while we lured them away from their headquarters.

He cast a backward glance over his shoulder, dodging another parking meter without even looking. "I suspected. You confirmed."

Chills crawled up my back. "Those things live here. If one of them catches us it'll suck our brains dry."

"I don't think minders actually kill what they eat," David said. "Though, I have heard of possible brain damage."

"I need my brain as functional as possible, thanks." Extending my essence in all directions, I detected a few more blips on the radar. Whether they were minders or not, I couldn't tell. I'd seen one of them turn an entire group of kids into compliant little zombies. Granted, the minder had been protecting the boundary of La Casona and the secrecy of the Obsidian Arch within, but it was still creepy.

"I think we're heading in the right direction." David acted as if we weren't being stalked by one or more creatures of pure nightmare.

I opened my mouth for a retort when the ground rumbled beneath my feet. We stopped in our tracks as the fog cleared around us, revealing a cracked gray road running several hundred feet in either direction before vanishing into a wall of fog. We were in the ghetto for sure, though I didn't recognize this part of town. Dilapidated houses with worn, wooden siding lined the road in either direction. The church remained shrouded in fog somewhere behind us. Parallel-parked cars lined the sides of the road.

Before I could open my mouth to ask a stupid question, the ground buckled. Cars bounced like toys. David and I stumbled backward as a pickup truck teetered on two wheels before crashing on its side. The road cracked and crumbled with tremors. Cars bounced, alarms wailed, houses collapsed.

"Are they having an earthquake in the real world?" I asked, trying to keep my feet.

"Watch out!" David said, pulling me from the center of the street as a two-story house toppled over.

A complete set of railroad tracks plowed through the center of the street. Vines crept along the gravel bed, growing insanely fast. Within a minute, the railroad tracks ran the length of the fog-free zone. A railroad crossing sign sprouted between my feet. I leapt back with a yelp as it sprang up where my crotch would have been. A bell started dinging. The rumble of a locomotive sounded from somewhere in the wall of thick fog to my right. Its horn sounded a warning as a bright headlight suffused the mist.

A male scream jerked my attention to the left.

A red sedan sat in the middle of the railroad crossing. "Help me!" shouted a man inside the car. I saw his feet pound against the window over and over again, his screams never diminishing.

I didn't have a clue what was happening. Frankly, I didn't care. A man was about to meet a gruesome end if I didn't help him. I raced to the car. "Hold on, I'm gonna get you out of there." I jerked on the door handle, but it didn't budge. I punched the window. Despite feeling as if I'd just broken my fist, it didn't so much as crack the glass. The man cranked the ignition on the car. The starter whined. The engine thrummed to life. Just as hope entered the driver's eyes, the engine shuddered and stopped.

"No!" he shouted, pounding the steering wheel. He looked at me.

I pounded the bottoms of my fists against the window. "Unlock the doors!"

His eyes widened, and I suddenly realized he apparently wasn't looking at me, but at the rapidly approaching train. The earth trembled. Gravel rattled beneath my feet. I flicked my gaze behind me and saw the train streaking toward the car. Only one chance to save the man remained. Racing to the front of the vehicle, I pushed. My efforts failed to even rock it back and forth.

This thing is immovable!

"Justin, get out of there," David said, running over.

"I don't understand," I said, grunting and pushing to absolutely no effect. True, I wasn't feeling very strong, but even a normal human should be able to bounce a car on its shocks. The train barreled on, heedless of the car in its path. I felt my eyes widen with horror as I saw the engineer, a skeletal creature with sharp wicked teeth and long black hair trailing in the wind. It leaned out of the locomotive window and laughed maniacally in a feminine voice.

The laughter of the engineer and screams of the driver mingled into one ear-piercing cacophony of pain. I dove from the tracks as the train smashed the car with phenomenal force. It exploded, sending car parts flying. Something slammed into my back, knocking the breath from me. I sucked in a breath, wheezed a few

56

times, and pushed slowly to my feet. The man lay a short distance away, miraculously alive. The train had vanished from sight.

And then I saw the skeletal figure walking toward the man. Flesh hung from its naked form in wrinkled folds, the contours of bones clearly visible through translucent flesh. It cackled as the man tried to slide away from it. Despite the blood all over his body, the man abruptly stood and started running. Though his legs practically blurred with speed, he moved forward in slow motion. I could only watch as he screamed in terror at the creature reaching for him.

"You're mine forever," it said in a ragged feminine voice.

"No! I don't want to get married," the man shouted.

The anorexic woman leapt for him. The man cried out. They vanished in a cloud of gray mist. Before I could make sense of anything, the tracks vanished, leaving only the ruins of the houses and road. Fog billowed from all directions, rolling in on us like the tide. I managed to spot David before losing sight of him, and found him with an intrigued look on his face.

"That was interesting," he said.

"Interesting?" I said, groaning at the ache between my shoulders. "I think we just fell down the rabbit hole."

"Maybe we did." He shrugged. "In any case, I believe we just witnessed the beginning of a beautiful marriage."

"Now I know why I want to hit you all the time," I said.

He raised an eyebrow. "And that is?"

"Because you're an even bigger smartass than I am." I clenched my teeth.

He motioned me to move. "Let's talk while we walk."

What with the earthquake, houses falling over, and cars threatening to crush me, I'd forgotten about the minder trailing along behind us. I pushed my incubus senses outward and found several hovering only a few hundred feet away.

"If I'm not mistaken," my father said after a moment, "I believe we just witnessed someone's nightmare."

Chapter 7

Elyssa

The Church of the Divinity loomed across the street. The gray stone structure rose several stories high with a steeple stretching to the sky. The imposing building was shaped like a cross, with two huge wooden doors at the entrance. Elyssa, Ivy, Shelton, and Bella stood in an alley across the street, observing the area.

"Looks like a place for creepers," Ivy said.

Bella pointed at the stain glass windows. "Notice how filthy those are? It's like nobody is maintaining the place."

"The shrubbery looks wild too," Shelton added. "Then again, this neighborhood doesn't look all that wonderful either."

Closed businesses and run-down houses lined a street in dire need of pothole repairs. The few people wandering the sidewalks pushed shopping carts full of their belongings or drank alcohol from bottles in brown bags. In short, it was the perfect place to hide a rogue organization.

The front doors of the church swung open hard. A petite woman with blonde hair and fair skin emerged. She closed her eyes and faced the sun, as if enjoying the feel of it against her face. The doors slammed shut behind her.

"Holy fricasseed frog burgers," Shelton said. "She looks just like Nightliss."

Elyssa knew the face all too well. The blonde woman had once wiped her memories and tried to use her against Justin. Only

Nightliss had been able to restore what the blonde woman had taken. Fear chilled her heart while anger tightened her jaw. "Daelissa."

"She looks so cute," Bella said. "I hate to think someone hell-bent on world domination looks like that."

"She can be so sweet," Ivy said. "She isn't all bad."

"I, for one, ain't gonna find out," Shelton said with a shudder.

An old woman in ragged clothes staggering drunkenly down the sidewalk bumped into Daelissa. The angel's serene features contorted into disgust and rage. Brilliant light flashed. Elyssa blinked sunspots from her vision. The homeless woman was gone. In her place lay a heap of ashes on the sidewalk. Daelissa snapped her fingers, and a black stretched limousine pulled around the corner of the church and stopped. A young man hustled from the front passenger seat and opened the rear door for the Seraphim to climb inside.

"Should we follow her?" Shelton said. "Or check out the church?"

Elyssa looked at the limo as it pulled away. "Can you use a tracking spell?"

He shook his head. "It's a secure limo like the ones the Conroys use, protected against tracking spells."

"We don't have transportation," Bella said. "I could hotwire a car."

"Following Daelissa is dangerous," Shelton said. "Even if we do, it'll probably get us all killed like that poor bag lady."

"She is very tricky," Ivy said. "I tried to follow her a few times to see where she lived, and she caught me every time."

"You didn't have to worry about incineration," Shelton said, eyeing the swirling ashes on the sidewalk across the way.

"She would hurt me sometimes," Ivy said, a sad look on her face. "Daelissa told me pain was the only way to learn my lessons."

The limo turned a corner at the end of the street and vanished.

"I'm actually a little disappointed," Shelton said. "I'd expected her to fly away on a cloud of light or something more dramatic."

"She might be powerful as hell, but she doesn't have access to unlimited power," Elyssa said. "Even Seraphim have their limits."

59

"Tell you what," he said. "I'll wait until I'm sure she's all tuckered out before making a move against her."

"I'm going to check out the church," Elyssa said. "Everyone wait here."

She jogged across the road and up the stairs to the church. Something seemed off about the way the door shimmered in the sunlight. In fact, the sun seemed to reflect off of something just in front of the door. She found a twig on the ground and tossed it. It bounced off thin air just inches from the door. *A shield spell.* She didn't dare tamper with it. That left the windows. Jumping behind the brown-leafed hedge, she went to the closest stained glass window and tested it the same way. This time, the branch touched the window. Steadying herself, she drove her elbow into the glass. The material absorbed the blow and shot her elbow away from the window so hard, she stumbled into the bushes.

It's just like the enchanted glass on the mansion.

This had to be the right place to find the Exorcists. It was too well protected to be anything else. Elyssa wasn't ready to give up just yet. She ran down the side of the church and vaulted a tall iron fence guarding the parking lot. There was no sign of the vans used in the abduction, but that didn't mean anything. This place might have a secret garage, or this might not be the only place the Exorcists took their victims.

She tested the back door with a bit of gravel and found it too was shielded. Grunting in frustration, she turned to head back across the street when the hairs on the back of her neck spiked. She dove sideways and felt a whoosh of air brush past. Elyssa spun and saw the ninja who'd knocked her out before. It was obvious from the contours of the skintight armor the ninja wore she was female.

"Guess you can't win a fair fight, can you?" Elyssa said. She felt her lips peel back in a defiant smile. "Let's see how good you are when your opponent is ready for you."

The mysterious opponent assumed a defensive stance, but made no move to advance. Elyssa was tempted to move in but caution held her back. If the ninja knew she was here, that meant—she heard

60

a click and rolled away as a dart hit the pavement where she'd just been standing. The ninja took out a disc and hurled it toward Elyssa.

At first she thought it was a throwing star but quickly realized it was something else. She slid a sai sword from the sheath at her back and threw it. The disc shattered in mid-air. A fiery circle with a cross burned for a brief moment before vanishing in a pattern of smoke. Elyssa realized it must have been the device the Exorcists had used to trap Justin and his father.

"Where is Justin?" she yelled, looking around. She spotted small cross-shaped holes in the sides of the church. Metal tubes protruded through the holes. Several of them spat more darts her way. She dodged, but knew she couldn't avoid them all.

The darts bounced off an azure shield. "Get out of there," Shelton yelled, holding his staff out to maintain her protection.

With a running leap, Elyssa flipped over the fence. She and Shelton raced down the side of the church as more and more of the cross-shaped holes spewed darts. Shelton huffed and puffed, but maintained his shield. They crossed the road and ran into the alley.

Ivy and Bella gave them looks of alarm.

"We're getting out of here," Elyssa said, and went straight through the portal and back into the mansion. Shelton and the others followed her through, and deactivated it.

"I think they're onto us," Shelton said.

Elyssa smacked a fist into her palm. "That doesn't mean anything. We'll still get them." It had only been a few hours since Justin's abduction. She hoped and prayed they hadn't done anything to him. Somehow, she would figure out a way to break through the Exorcist defenses and save him.

Chapter 8

A nightmare? I didn't know what David was talking about. I opened my mouth to argue with him when I suddenly got a clue. The entire ordeal with the man, the train, and the corpse bride had been surreal and nonsensical. And yet, if I analyzed it as someone's bad dream, it made all the sense in the world. It still didn't explain the falling houses, the shifting terrain, or how the scene had appeared out of nowhere. It didn't explain how the man had survived a direct impact between a train and his car.

Unless. "The Gloom is dreamland," I said, not quite phrasing it as a question.

"I don't know if that's completely accurate," David said. He pursed his lips. "When the tire hit you in the back, it obviously injured you. That would suggest a physical representation of a dream."

"I couldn't move the car," I said. "I couldn't even budge it."

"Perhaps the representation of the dream was immutable."

"Maybe people's brainwaves recreate their dreams here," I said.

David tilted his head, as though listening for something. "A moment ago, we were surrounded by minders. Now they're gone."

"I noticed that too," I said, embellishing my situational awareness a bit since I hadn't even realized we were surrounded in the first place, thanks to my futile heroics. I snapped my fingers as a light bulb flickered on in my brain. "Minders feed off dreams. The dream attracted them here."

"Very likely," he said.

"Maybe that guy lives in one of these houses. Maybe his dream caused the minders to create his dream in the Gloom." It seemed too fantastical to be true. Then again, so did most things when it came to magic.

"It's possible," David said. "It also brings up a troubling idea."

I already had dozens of troubling ideas running through my noggin.

He furrowed his brow. "It was still daytime or early evening when they banished us here. Most people in Atlanta are still awake. I wonder what will happen when everyone goes to sleep."

"Oh crap," I said. "This place is going to be nightmare central."

"I don't know if the physical representations of the dreams can kill us and I don't want to find out." David's flippant attitude was gone, replaced with a far more concerned façade.

"Glad to see you're taking the situation seriously for once." I bit the inside of my lower lip.

He crossed his arms. "The minders showed up just before the nightmare."

"They're probably attracted to dreams like flies."

"If we sense them gathering, we'll need to be careful." David ran a hand through his hair. "It might mean another dream is forming."

"How are we—" I cursed and jumped back as a man on a skateboard whizzed out of the fog. The skateboard wheel hit a rock and threw him off. He yelped and vanished just before hitting the ground.

"I hate those kinds of dreams," David said, looking at the spot from which man and skateboard had disappeared.

My heart still raced. I didn't like surprises like that. "I'm going to drop dead of a heart attack if this keeps up."

David tilted his head again. "I detect one minder, but not as many as the last nightmare."

63

Using my own probes, I confirmed his assessment. "Quick dreams are probably appetizers," I said. "Nightmare brides and trains, on the other hand, seem like the main courses."

His lips pressed together. "I agree."

"We need to get to the Grotto, fast." I tried not to think about Mom and Ivy and the danger they might be in. "Have you sensed those men who were coming to get us at the church?"

He shook his head. "No. Unless they have a way to track us, I doubt they're anywhere nearby."

Something brushed against my senses, raising the hairs on my neck. Closing my eyes, I let my incubus probes wander the fog around me. More and more alien presences swept past, as if rushing toward a specific goal. I felt my face contort with each close call.

"Something is about to happen," David said.

"We should get a move on." I started walking. "I don't want to get sucked into another nightmare."

"Agreed."

A cluster of minders floated past us, their trailing tentacles entwining with others. The brain-like shape of their bodies glommed onto one another, almost as if they weren't entirely corporeal. Each passing sent vibrations into my incubus senses even though I had them turned on low. I was afraid to completely turn off my demonic awareness for fear I wouldn't be able to reactivate it.

"I think I'm gonna be sick," I said as uneasiness morphed into nausea.

"Close off your senses," David said. "Don't keep them bared like that."

I'd feel blind without them to guide me, but it was better than barfing. Hopefully, I'd be able to turn them back on later. With great reluctance, I flicked them off. The yuck-factor all but vanished from my guts. We walked forward a few more steps and entered clear air. I jerked to a halt. A shimmering starlit tapestry painted the night horizon. The Atlanta skyline sparkled in the distance. Hope surged in my chest but died within seconds as my eyes found a swarming mass of minders sweeping up and down the streets like ghastly flocks of birds. The creatures glided down the roads toward the center of town.

64

Even as they did, a wave of their comrades rushed past them in the opposite direction.

"They're coming right at us," I said in alarm. And they were—a wall of cloudy gray forms with wildly waving tentacles beneath. I stop, dropped, and rolled just as the minders swooped past. Numbing cold traced along my skin as their translucent tentacles brushed me.

Elyssa straddles me, fangs bared, and presses a cold blade against my throat. I feel warm liquid running down my neck. She leans close.

"You're a monster. You almost fooled me."

"Elyssa, I love you," I say in a wheezing voice.

She leans down and whispers in my ear. "I am your dark light. I will be with you at the end."

I am suddenly in a room with a table. Bookshelves surround me. A man sits in a chair across from me. He is muscular but otherwise looks quite ordinary.

"Good day, Mr. Slade." A slow smile spreads across his face. "You have passed the test. Your father is released from the death sentence."

"Underborn." Anger fills my voice. "You threatened to kill my father just to see if I could pass a stupid test?"

I hear a roar and spin around. Vadaemos Slade manifests into demon form and lunges for me. I dodge a clawed swipe that would have removed my head. Before I can manifest, he grips me by the neck and slams me to unforgiving asphalt. A battle rages around me. Monstrous moggies—Stacey's mutant cat friends—yowl as they trade blows with Vadaemos's hellhounds. Templars fight hellhound claws and teeth with swords.

It doesn't matter. I am about to die.

I squeeze my eyes and wait for the end.

The pressure on my throat vanishes. I feel cold metal along my bare back. When my eyes open, I see a plain concrete ceiling. I try to move, but my arms, legs, and even head are secured.

"Mine at last," Maximus says. He walks around me, inspecting me like a prized pig. "With your blood, I will turn the world into my own vampire nation. I will be the one in control, not Daelissa."

"Let me go," I say, trying to keep fear from my voice.

He leans close. Blood-scented breath reaches my nose. He whispers in my ear. "You are my little mouse now, boy. You are mine forever." He lunges for my neck.

I scream. I struggle. All to no avail. His fangs sink into my skin. Ecstasy and fear flood my entire being. Maximus rears back, blood—my blood—running down his face. He laughs, and I know I will never escape.

Ivy looks up at me with big blue eyes. "I love you, big brother."

I stand in a stone-lined hallway at Arcane University. Students flow around the two of us in the busy corridor. "I love you too, sis." I lean down to hug her, but she vanishes along with the world around me.

A voice speaks in the void. "The final choice must be made." Images of a burnt world, of a new world, and of a world rotting like an apple flash before my eyes.

I blink my eyes open and look into the blue eyes of my mother as she cradles me in her arms. I try to speak, but only baby noises emerge.

"Is he truly the one?" Mom asks.

Another face appears. "He will serve, and he will die." My father places a hand on Mom's shoulder. "Don't get too attached, Alysea."

My father leaves. A tear trickles down my mother's cheek. "I won't let you die, my son." She sings to me. I recognize the tune but can't remember where I last heard it. My eyes grow heavy. I cannot keep them open a second longer.

"Ah!" I shouted and looked wildly around. The minders had moved beyond us. I saw my father lying on the ground next to me. His face was absolutely white.

Before I could ask him what he'd seen, he shook his head. "What a ride."

"A ride?" Those visions had replayed some of the most emotionally traumatic parts of my life. But what David had said to my mom about me hurt the worst of all. Had it been a dream, or memory?

66

He looked back the way we'd come from. "Looks like the fog won't be an issue anymore."

I followed his gaze and watched as the line of minders erased the gray haze. "What the hell is going on?" I asked, feeling even more perplexed than before.

"I'd really like to know that myself." David pushed himself off the ground and stood. "On the other hand, without the fog we can find the Grotto a lot faster."

"Yeah, but those men can find us more easily too." I regarded him once more, unable to decide if I should ask what he'd seen. *My own father told Mom I would serve and die. He told her not to get attached!* The thought made me sick to my stomach, and I lost all desire to question him. Had it truly been a memory from my infancy, or just a minder-induced nightmare? I looked north and pointed. "It's that way."

"Let's go," he said, and took off at a jog.

I tried to run at a supernatural rate and only succeeded in tiring myself. "I hate this place. I hate feeling normal."

A bead of sweat trickled down David's forehead. "You and me both."

It felt awful to have no super powers. Considering how dangerous dreams made this place, we'd be hard pressed to avoid every surprise. "We're doomed."

He smirked. "Since we're already doomed, I might as well mention we don't have food or water."

That troubling thought hadn't occurred to me. "There aren't any people to feed from either," I said.

"Yep." His eyes turned back toward the section of town known as Buckhead where the Grotto sat buried deep underground beneath a fancy shopping mall. "To top things off, we have something else to worry about."

"Great, what else?"

"The fog will return." He motioned around us. "It seems when the mortal world sleeps and dreams, the fog clears."

"So we have until morning to reach the Grotto," I said, trying to judge the distance in my head. "It could take us hours to walk

67

there." My heart was already hammering from the jog even though I was in pretty good shape.

"That would be my guess," David said as we crested a hill. "Somehow, people dreaming or sleeping clears the fog."

"Don't Arcanes study the Gloom?" I said. "Wouldn't they know about this kind of stuff?" Before he could answer, another thought smacked me upside the head. "Harry Shelton's dad—"

"Jarrod Sager," David said.

I decided not to ask him how he knew the deceased Arcanus Primus was Shelton's dad. "Yeah, that guy. He was pushing—"

"The Gloom Initiative," my father interrupted again without even glancing my way as we trotted down a residential sidewalk.

I clenched my teeth to hold back a smart remark. "Surely they know all about this stuff if they were really studying the Gloom."

"Perhaps. The project was shrouded in secrecy. Apparently Daelissa thought she could find a way back to Seraphina through this place—"

"And bring through her army," I said, interrupting him for the hell of it, though I had nothing constructive to add. I wondered if she could the initiative was still active. *Was that why she sent us here?*

"Why are you so reluctant to tell me the truth about you?" I asked, using a tactic Elyssa had applied many a time when she wanted to catch me off guard with random question.

"I don't think you're ready for it yet," David replied.

"I put on my big-boy panties a long time ago, *David*." I glared at him to put extra emphasis on his name. "You're the one who's been acting like a child. After Mom left us, you got stinking drunk every night and left me to figure out why I could suddenly seduce any woman I wanted. Do you know how hard it was for me to resist abusing that ability? Do you know how close I came to dying because I didn't have a clue about the Overworld or Templars, or how most supers regard demon spawn as evil monsters?"

"I knew all along what you were going through," he said nonchalantly.

I almost tripped over my own feet. "You what?"

68

He shrugged. "I knew exactly when the change hit you, and most of what was going on in your life during your adjustment."

"Adjustment?" I shouted. "My girlfriend almost cut my throat because she thought I was abusing my sexual superpowers to take advantage of her!"

"Her love won out in the end though, didn't it?"

I opened my mouth to shout something back but only angry sputtering noises emerged. David grinned. The world flashed red. I dove into him. His back hit a brick mailbox. We bounced off it and landed on a grassy lawn. I wrestled him beneath me, straddled his chest, and reared back my fist. He looked up at me, one eyebrow raised.

"I can see you're upset, son—"

I punched him in the face. "You're damned right I'm upset, you lying bastard!" I lined up my fist for another punch when he pushed me off. I somersaulted backwards and flopped on my stomach. Anger burned behind my eyes. I rolled to my back and sprang to my feet.

"Let's stop with the hitting for a while," David said. He narrowed his eyes. "I don't want this to get ugly."

"You're not my father. You're dead to me." An angry growl rose in my throat. "Why did you make me go through hell when you could have told me everything?" I heard knuckles crack as my fists clenched tight.

"I'm dead to you?" He sighed. "That hurts." His easy smile returned along with a shrug. "I knew you weren't ready for the truth." He nodded down the road. "We should keep going."

"Not until you tell me why," I growled.

"Because I wanted to see what kind of man you were," he said.

"It was a test?" I heard my knuckles crack. "You son of a—"

He sighed. "I knew you weren't ready." With that, he resumed jogging in the direction of the Grotto.

I let out a frustrated shout and, seeing no choice, followed him, anger boiling as I thought about how cruel his little test had been.

69

As we passed through a residential neighborhood, I heard laughter echoing from nearby and detoured down a side street. A guy about my age stood in the midst of several pretty girls. He said something I couldn't quite hear, and the girls burst into laughter. One of the girls kissed him. The others broke into arguments about kissing him next. One took off her shirt and—the scene vanished.

"Another dream," I said.

A screaming girl raced around the corner of the house at the end of the street, arms waving frantically. Before I could wonder what she was running from, I heard a strange honking noise. My heart froze in terror as a clown appeared, ghoulish leer on his face as he raced after the girl, shoes honking with every step.

"Now that," David said, "is scary."

"I hate clowns," I said with a shudder.

The clown erupted with evil laughter and dove at the girl. She screamed one final time before they vanished. David looked at the skyline to get his bearings, and we resumed course. Dreams and nightmares sprang up all around us. One man stood screaming in his front yard as his house grew a mouth and ate him.

"Guess he can't afford the mortgage," David said.

I watched in horror as a young boy set a dog on fire, clapping and laughing with glee. I made a note of the address. *Serial killer in the making.*

As the number of dreams grew in density, more and more minders appeared, drifting down the streets, tentacles touching the people who I figured must be doing the actual dreaming. Far overhead, I made out people flying like superheroes. It seemed to be a popular dream. Further down the road, I watched as a young girl saved her family from a burning house, only to witness her parents and little sister crumble to ashes before her eyes while she cried in anguish. Before we'd gone far, the scene reset itself and the girl repeated the rescue.

"Talk about trapped in your own worst nightmare," I said with a shudder.

"We need food and water," David said some time later. He wiped sweat from his forehead. "I don't know about you, but I'm thirsty."

We'd made good progress, but I needed a break. "Me too."

David headed toward a nearby house. He tried the doorknob, but it was locked.

"We can't break in," I said. "Remember the car on the railroad tracks? I couldn't move it."

He lined his elbow up with the window and smashed it in one blow.

I felt my eyebrows rise. "How'd you do that?"

David shrugged. He reached through the window and unbolted the door. We went inside the seemingly empty house and into the kitchen. He stopped. "You hear that sound?"

"That low humming?"

He nodded. "The fridge is working." He opened it and looked inside. "It's cold." Grabbing a gallon of milk, he took a swig, set it down on the table and waited.

"I hope you didn't just kill yourself," I said, unsure how safe Gloom food was.

"I don't think we'll survive long without the necessities." A shrug. "Nothing to be lost by trying."

"Unless it gives you diarrhea."

He laughed.

After a fifteen minute wait, nothing happened, so I took a drink of milk myself. It didn't taste quite right—in fact it didn't have much taste at all. As if that was the cue to pig out, we devoured a basket of fruit in the middle of the table. None of it had much flavor, but at least it was filling.

"I couldn't smash the window of that car in the first nightmare, but you smashed the window to this house." I picked up a pencil from the table and broke it. "It doesn't make sense."

"It makes perfect sense," he said.

"Please explain." I had to hear this.

"The nightmare was a constructed dreamscape with a series of events determined by the mind of the dreamer." He took a swig of

71

water. "It was recreated here, maybe by the minders, and followed the exact sequence of the dream."

The logic made sense to me. "So a dream sequence is set in stone. We can't do anything to alter any part of it."

"Exactly." He waved his hand at the kitchen. "The environment here mirrors the real world when there's no dream sequence."

"We can affect the normal environment," I said. "If we break something here that's not broken in the real world, I wonder if it resets back to normal after a time."

"A good question," David said. He opened the pantry and dug around inside. "We just have to hope the food is nourishing."

"It certainly doesn't have much taste."

He removed a backpack from the pantry and started shoving food inside it. "Yeah. Everything here is like a pale shadow of the real world."

After filling the backpack, we resumed course for the Grotto, dodging dreamscapes as we went.

We trudged down residential roads for at least another hour, though it was impossible to know the exact length of time without a phone or watch, and finally connected with a main road leading into Buckhead. I managed to restrain the nearly overwhelming urge to ask my father about his past or why he'd lied to me all his life about who he was.

What if I'm really not ready for the truth?

I had no way of answering such a question. The secrets my family kept tended to be a lot more shocking than the average fare. Instead of, "Your uncle is an alcoholic," I might expect something along the lines of, "Your uncle destroyed a parallel dimension by accident." It was clear my father was no ordinary demon spawn. If he'd told the truth about being the first Daemos, how had he come into being?

I remembered the vision of my father telling Mom I would serve and die, and not to grow attached. The sick feeling returned in my stomach, like a knife in my gut. I wanted to throw up. I wanted to

72

shout at him and demand respect and love from my own damned father.

He never loved me.

A realization punched me in the gut. I knew what David meant about me not being ready for the truth. If knowing what he knew felt like this, I never wanted to hear it. I didn't want to know everything was a lie. I didn't want to know my wonderful, sheltered childhood was pure fantasy with my father and mother as the main supporting characters.

"You two, halt," said a commanding voice.

I raised my head from troubling thoughts to see a man riding a velociraptor guide the creature to a halt in the middle of the road. "Talk about a whacked out dream," I said, steering clear of the creature in case it started salsa dancing.

"I said halt!" the man roared.

"Justin," David said, eyes locked onto the man and his beast. "I think he's talking to us."

Chapter 9

I stopped dead in my tracks and stared at the man. He looked young, maybe in his thirties, though he wore a tailored suit and bowtie.

"You're real?" I asked. We'd seen so many dreamscapes, finding another person was almost surreal.

He displayed a wicked set of vampire fangs. "Oh, very much so."

"How did you know we're not dream people?"

"I've been following you for quite some time," he said. "Do you know how hard it is to find fresh blood in the Gloom?"

I backed away and saw David doing the same. "I'm sure you could find blood packs at a hospital," I said.

"I said 'fresh'." The vampire nudged the raptor toward us. Razor-sharp claws flashed.

"Cool dinosaur," I said, using peripheral vision to find a safe place to run. Businesses and high-rise condominiums lined the road. We might be able to get inside, but would the elevators work? "Did you find him at a pet shop?"

"When you've lived in the Gloom as long as I have, you discover a few useful tricks." He sniffed the air, as if discovering a wonderful aroma. "You're not human."

"Correctamundo." I bared my teeth. "So don't mess with us."

He laughed. "Don't even pretend you still have preternatural abilities. I know you don't."

"And neither do you," I said.

"Do you have a velociraptor?" He raised an eyebrow in challenge.

David and I exchanged looks. I shrugged. "You have a point."

"We're looking for a way out of the Gloom," my father said. "There's no reason for you to stay trapped here forever. Come with us."

"Escape? Escape?" the vampire said in a high-pitched whine. "There's no escaping from the Gloom." He leaned over his mount, eyes wide. "There are people here who kidnap others from the real world. I was abducted while taking an Obsidian arch nearly two decades ago. I've been trapped here ever since."

I thought back to the men who'd come for us earlier. "Those people tried to kidnap us too. Join us. Maybe we can all find a way out."

"I said there is no escape!" he shouted. He drew in a long deep breath, eyelids fluttering with what looked like ecstasy. "I have no more patience for this talk. I must feed. Follow me or Gloria Richardson will tear out your guts."

"Why did you name your raptor Gloria Richardson?" I said, preparing myself to make a break for a nearby gym I'd spotted nearby.

"She's the bitch who turned me into a vampire and broke up with me. I was on my way to see her, to beg for her to take me back when I was kidnapped." His eyes flashed. "Now, come!"

The vampire had obviously been trapped here far longer than recommended by the Surgeon General and was absolutely bonkers. Something about an insane vampire in control of a raptor terrified me beyond belief.

"Simmer down," David said, seemingly calm as ever. "Gloria obviously didn't know what kind of a man she was losing when she broke your heart. Lead on. We'll follow you."

The vampire regarded us a moment longer before spinning his raptor around and heading down the road. I nodded toward the gym.

75

David winked. We bolted toward the sidewalk and jumped a metal railing.

A screeching roar sounded behind us. I turned my head to see the raptor leap.

"Help me with this!" David said, pushing on the glass door to the gym. It didn't budge.

I rammed my shoulder against it and bounced off. Sharp talons sliced the metal railing behind us like butter. Metal clanged on the sidewalk.

"On the count of two," David said, aiming his foot at the door.

It took everything I had not to run screaming as I heard claws on the concrete behind us, waiting for an ebony talon to spear one of us in the back.

"One! Two!"

We kicked. The glass shattered. David shoved me through the opening. My head clanged on the metal push handle on the inside. I crawled through and rolled onto my back in time to see a claw slash at my father. He juked left. The talon sliced through the door's metal framing. I gripped his arm and jerked him all the way into a lobby leading to a hallway which seemed to end in offices. From what I could see, the only way out was a red metal staircase.

We descended into a room with punching bags hanging from metal railings, each one spaced about every square foot from its neighbor. A boxing ring sat near the back corner.

I heard a crash and an animalistic screech from upstairs accompanied by heavy feet clanging down the stairs. David and I ran through the forest of punching bags desperately looking for an exit.

"What if it dead ends?" I asked.

"I'm sure there's another way out," he said, shoving past another row of punching bags.

I heard ripping and thudding, and turned to see the raptor shredding the vinyl casings with its claws, hissing and smashing them so hard the exercise equipment flew off its chains and smacked into the walls. Timothy rode low, eyes shining with fury.

"There!" I said, pointing across an open area with artificial turf. Beyond it was another glass door. We raced across the padded surface. The thudding of bags and the hissing of the raptor grew closer.

"Nobody escapes Timothy Burkmeyer!" the vampire cried. "There will be blood!"

"Stop being melodramatic!" I shouted as I slammed my hands against the door handle. It swung open, depositing me in a courtyard surrounded on all sides by several stories of apartments. I spotted another metal door at the far end of the sidewalk and sprinted toward it. Glass shattered. Metal shrieked. I looked behind to see the raptor skidding on the concrete as it made a sharp turn to follow us.

David reached the door and opened it. A parking garage lay beyond.

"Oh, crap," I said. The raptor would be on us in two seconds in that place.

"Here," David said, jerking open another metal door to our right, revealing stairs.

We ran through. I slammed the door shut and raced up the stairs to the first landing, huffing and puffing. Sweat poured down my forehead, stinging my eyes. Something slammed into the door, leaving a three-toed dent. Just as many talons speared through the metal and sliced it to ribbons.

"Don't just stand there," David shouted. "Run!"

We climbed halfway up the four-story stairwell when the sound of metal slamming into concrete announced the raptor's entrance. I tested the door at each landing, but all were locked.

"Why didn't he just get off the stupid dinosaur and open the door himself?" I said, sucking in each breath.

We reached the top floor. There were two doors. David opened one. It led outside to the top of the parking deck. The doormat on the opposite one had folded inside the door jamb, preventing it from latching closed. I jerked it open and saw a hallway lined with doors.

"Which way?" I asked.

"We're dead if we go outside," he said, and ran down the hallway.

I pushed the doormat away and latched the door behind me.

David was already checking every door, but none opened. He stopped at a window halfway down the corridor, unlatched it, and poked his head out. I looked at a four-story drop and gulped.

"Safe to say the other doors are locked," he said, looking out the window. "But there's a balcony on either side. We might reach one."

I examined the balconies. "The one on the left is a little closer, but I can't grab the railing from here."

He nodded. "I can hold onto the waist of your pants. You can lean out and grab it."

My throat constricted. Even with supernatural abilities, the drop to the hard concrete in the small courtyard below would probably break my legs. In the real world, I'd heal. Here, I'd splat like a bug. I looked at him. "That would require me trusting you."

He pshawed. "Really now, do you think I'd let you die?"

"Maybe once I've served my purpose." I narrowed my eyes. "After all, I will serve, and I will die."

He flinched, eyes full of surprise. "Who told you that?"

"Nobody told me, David. I heard you saying it to Mom when I was an infant."

"How could you remember something from that age?"

I shrugged. "Does it matter? You said it, I heard it."

He released a grim sigh. "We have no choice. If you don't trust me, I'll go first."

Already the sounds of the raptor slamming claws against doors echoed down the hallway. I wasn't sure if it was the one leading into this hallway, or the one outside.

I shook my head. "I'll do it. After all, if I die, you'll be trapped in the hallway and Gloria Richardson will tear you apart."

"That's a rather cynical way to look at it."

"Here goes nothing." Taking a deep breath, I perched on the windowsill, holding the top half of the window for balance.

He gripped the waist of my jeans with one hand and the window frame with the other. "Good luck."

My butt cheeks clenched. "Don't drop me."

"Wouldn't dream of it." He smiled. "After all, you haven't served your purpose, Cataclyst."

Without further ado, I ducked under the top half of the window and stood on trembling legs. The balcony was just out of reach by a foot. A ledge with a gutter inches above my head prevented me from jumping. I had to trust my father. I leaned forward. For a brief instant, it felt as though I was falling. Panic sent my arms flailing. At the last instant, my jeans tightened at my waist, and I stopped, suspended above the deadly drop. David eased me forward a little more, and I grasped the railing in a white-knuckled grip.

"I'm letting go," he said.

"Okay," I wheezed through a tight throat. My legs swung off the windowsill. Wasting no time, I pulled myself up and over the railing.

David crawled out the window, holding on as I had. "Grab my arm."

The railing came up to my chest so I couldn't lean over too far. Our fingers were inches apart. "Can you reach any further?" I asked.

"I'll have to let go." His face looked pale. "You'll only have one chance to grab me."

I steeled myself. Nodded. "I won't let you down."

"Pun intended?" he said, offering a weak smile.

I showed him my teeth. "You haven't served your purpose yet either."

"Fair enough." He stood, leaned forward, and fell.

My hand gripped his forearm. All his weight jerked hard, and I thought my arm was about to come out of the socket. He slipped until only his wrist remained in my grasp. I groaned, clenching tight as I could. His other arm swung up, gripped my forearm. I released my hold on the railing, grabbed him, and pulled with all my might. His face turned red with exertion. My shoulder ached with the strain and it was an effort not to cry out. Doing so would alert the vampire. Using my feet as leverage, I leaned back, teeth clenched tight. His hand found the railing, and suddenly the weight eased from my body.

David pulled himself over and lay on the concrete, breathing heavily. "That was scary."

I was panting too hard to reply and simply nodded.

We were safe, but for how long?

Chapter 10

The sliding glass door on the balcony was unlocked so we let ourselves in. A television mounted on the wall hissed with white noise. Occasional images flickered onto the screen too quickly for me to discern what they were. I turned off the television. "This place creeps me out."

"I wonder if it picks up signals from Eden, or if those images are something else entirely."

"Eden?"

His lips parted. "That is our name for the human realm."

"Sure as hell doesn't live up to the reputation," I said, looking around the room. The apartment was obviously a bachelor pad. The couch looked like a relic from the eighties. Worn, shabby furniture crowded the small space. Gun magazines littered the coffee table. In fact, the only nice things in the room were the huge plasma television and the game consoles hooked up to it.

"This place could use a housemaid," David said, thumbing through one of the gun magazines.

I stepped inside the bedroom and found a metal locker against the far wall. I tested the handle. "Locked," I said with a groan. "Considering all the gun magazines lying around, I'll bet there are weapons inside this thing."

81

"Keys," David said, pointing to a hook on the wall near the door. The key ring was attached to a retractable chain like the kind someone wore at their waist. He tossed it to me.

I sorted through the keys, testing each one until I found the one that fit. I opened the gun cabinet and found an assortment of pistols and ammunition. "Jackpot!"

"You know how to shoot?" David asked.

"Just like a video game." I shrugged. "Point and click."

He chuckled. "Maybe you should go with the small revolver."

I picked up the six-shooter and examined the cylinder. "Any idea which ammunition it takes?"

David picked up a box of twenty-two caliber bullets. "It won't stop a velociraptor, but it might stop a vampire." He gripped a hefty silver pistol and slapped a clip into it. "Ah, now this is more like it."

I felt my eyebrows rise. "Do *you* know how to shoot?"

He pulled back the top part of the gun—whatever it's called—and flicked a lever on the side. "I've learned a few useful things in my years in Eden."

"You keep mentioning the mortal realm—Eden—like you weren't born and raised there."

"I've been a few places," he said, grabbing a spare bullet clip from a box.

I regarded my measly pea-shooter and nodded toward a long black rifle. "How about I take that too?"

He took it out of the cabinet, examined a slot on the side of the barrel. "You think you can handle a shotgun?"

"I've used them lots in video games."

"Just remember, you're not super-strong here." He grabbed a box of red shells and showed me how to load the gun.

"Looks easy enough," I said, and took the weapon. I loaded my revolver and grabbed a satchel from inside the gun cabinet so I could load it with ammo. Within a few minutes we looked ready to take on a small army. "I can't wait to blow Gloria Richardson's head off."

"I think we should avoid Timothy and pal altogether," my father said, peering out the bedroom window.

82

"How does he even have a dinosaur?" I scratched my head. "Unless they still exist in the Gloom, it just doesn't make any sense."

"If people in the real world can project dreams in this reality, it's possible Timothy dreamed up his raptor."

I considered the theory. "Sounds legit."

"It's the only thing I can think of," David said.

"Maybe we can make our own dinosaurs." I slung the shotgun strap over my shoulder. "It'd be better than walking."

"The Gloom has rules just like any other dimension." David belted a holster to his waist. "Timothy obviously knows them better than we do."

"He could make himself a tank and blow down the building," I said.

"But he hasn't." My father headed into the den. "Either he doesn't want to, or creating things takes more effort than simply thinking of them."

I decided to test our theory and thought of a sword appearing in my hand. Nothing happened, so I closed my eyes, and imagined it harder. When I opened them, my hand was still empty. "Yeah, I guess there's something more to it than just wishing something into existence."

We exited the apartment and were making our way down the stairs when an unpleasant thought occurred to me. "What if these dream guns don't work?"

David stopped, raised an eyebrow. "Everything else seems to work, so why wouldn't the guns?"

I shrugged. "Just paranoid thinking, I guess."

He smiled and patted my back. "Let's hope we don't have to use them."

I tugged on the shoulder strap holding the shotgun to my back, wondering if I'd be able to handle the firepower should the need arise. I imagined the kickback knocking me down, giving Gloria Richardson a free shot at liberating my guts. "I agree."

We made our way down to the first floor and went into the hallway. The place was eerily silent. I imagined people slumbering in their beds, invisible to us. What if another dream sequence started while we were in this building and the Gloom swallowed it up to create whatever landscape the dreamer created? The thought was unnerving to say the least. Would we be consumed along with the building or transported to another place? The urge to leave the possible deathtrap caused my stomach to clench.

David tested each door on the side of the hallway facing the street. They were all locked, and they looked too sturdy to kick down. "Looks like we'll have to exit blind."

I nodded, tension gripping my shoulders.

"Don't get nervous," he said. "It'll cause you to freeze up."

"Who's nervous?" I said. "I mean, if the Gloom decides to tear this place down because someone's dreaming about tossing a Frisbee to their dog in an open field, it only means we'll be squished to tiny bits."

He pursed his lips. "True. Maybe we should accelerate our escape."

"Good idea." I jammed the revolver into the pack and unslung the shotgun. "Let's do this."

We reached the exit at the end of the hallway. I eased open the door and peered into a hallway that connected the center courtyard with the sidewalk in the front of the building. I listened intently for a moment for the sound of raptor claws clacking or Timothy shouting curses.

Silence.

I pushed through the door and looked both ways. "Which way?" I whispered.

David pointed toward the courtyard. "We can sneak out through the parking garage. He might be patrolling the street we were on earlier."

I clenched the shotgun tighter and nodded. We jogged down the hallway and looked into the courtyard. No sign of dinosaur or vampire. We went right, down the sidewalk, and through the metal door to the parking garage. The place was deathly quiet. I took a few steps and felt a faint vibration in the ground.

"Did you feel that?" I asked.

David nodded.

84

I heard a faint rumble and felt a stronger vibration in the ground. Panic seized me, and it took everything I had not to run gibbering for the exit. It was a good thing too. I heard a hiss. David jerked me down behind a car just as Gloria Richardson walked around the corner and into the parking deck entrance. Another rumble shook the ground, and another.

"No, no, no!" Timothy shouted, whirling his mount back toward the exit. "I almost have them." The raptor stepped outside, and the vampire looked down the street.

Another thunderclap echoed. The ground trembled, and the car bounced on its shocks. David and I exchanged worried glances. The next boom set off car alarms all up and down the street. Dust and bits of concrete rained down. Timothy raised a fist and cursed at the top of his lungs, but even that was drowned out by the next shockwave. The cars parked on the street bounced like toys.

"If he doesn't move," I whispered, "I'm going to shoot him."

"Let's reverse course and go out the other way," David suggested, motioning toward the door to the courtyard.

"Make a run for it?" I asked, looking at the vampire. His attention seemed fixed on whatever horror was coming our way.

The car we hid behind jumped several inches off the ground as the next earthquake hit. The bumper hit me in the chest and knocked me onto my butt. I scrambled to my feet. "Go!" I hissed.

We ran for the door.

Something bellowed. It sounded like a lion with a locomotive horn caught in its throat. The entire parking deck shuddered. A chunk of concrete and rebar slammed atop a car. I looked left just as Timothy looked to his right. Our eyes locked. The vampire's gaze lit up like Christmas ornaments.

"Get them, Gloria!" The raptor wheeled around and loped toward us.

I jerked open the door. My father and I raced through, down the hallway and out into the street. A monstrous foot crashed down in the intersection to our left. Any cars that weren't crushed flipped and rolled away from the impact. Glass shattered on nearby buildings. I looked up at the behemoth lizard-like creature towering over the

85

buildings as it roared. Its head and arms looked tiny in relation to its massive body. The monster walked upright like a Tyrannosaurus Rex. Large spikes ran from the top of its head all the way down the tail.

And it was about to kill us all.

Chapter 11

Elyssa

Elyssa stalked back into the planning room at the mansion.

"This is crazy," Shelton said. His phone projected a live feed from a nom news station. People had taken videos of Ivy's brief encounter with the police.

"Authorities still can't explain how or why the robbers were able to crush the police cars," a female news anchor said as the video of the event played in the background. "Officers on the scene said something stopped their bullets before they ever reached the target. Bystanders have plenty of opinions on the matter."

The image switched to show a man. "Giant underground magnets, dude!"

It flicked to another interviewee. "Probably some precocious teenager with telekinesis," said an older woman. "These cell phones are mutating the rotten little parasites."

"Does this mean I'm famous?" Ivy asked.

"Shelton, don't encourage her," Elyssa said, shooting him a warning look.

He simpered and turned off the news. "Any news about reinforcements?"

Elyssa took a deep breath to ward off the knot of stress. It didn't help. "The Synod is sending troops into Atlanta. My father can't spare any men to assault the Exorcist church." Her heart ached with worry, frustration, and anger. Her shoulders and back felt taut as iron cables. All her options for saving Justin had evaporated, and she was out of ideas.

"How the hell are we gonna break in there without an army backing us up?" Shelton said. He slammed his fist on the table, sending marble-like ASEs bouncing. "Those people are doing only god knows what to Justin and his father. We have to do something and soon."

"What if they're holding him somewhere else?" Bella asked.

"Where else would they keep him?" Shelton said.

Elyssa held up a hand for silence. "The Exorcist ninja was there. She's the one who knocked me out. I'm positive they have him there."

"Maybe I can talk to Daelissa," Ivy said. She licked a grape lollipop. "I'll bet if I was really nice she might let my brother go."

Shelton shook his head. "Ain't gonna happen."

Elyssa's felt defeated. "If only I could contact Nightliss or Alysea," she said. "With them, I'm sure we could break through their defenses." Ivy was powerful, but alone, she wouldn't be enough.

"The Colombian Templar legion is still incommunicado?" Bella asked.

Elyssa nodded. "I don't know what's going on in Colombia, but it must be pretty bad. Even my father hasn't heard any news yet."

"I'm looking for images of the inside of the church," Cinder said. "Perhaps we could open a portal with the omniarch."

"That's a great idea," Shelton said, slapping the golem on the back.

"Thank you, Harry." Cinder flicked through holographic images projected by an ASE. "So far, I have been unable to locate anything, even in the city historical archives. Perhaps the Exorcists have never allowed pictures."

"Maybe I could destroy the doors," Ivy said.

"Not a good idea," Elyssa said.

"Please." The girl stood from her chair. "We have to do something."

"I just thought of something crazy," Shelton said, a worried look on his face. "This is probably a long shot, but maybe Ivy could convince Jeremiah Conroy to help us out."

"Are you insane?" Elyssa said.

Bella shook her head vigorously. "I'm certain the man won't be pleased to learn Ivy is here. He's not a person we can trust, and, in case you've forgotten, he's in league with Daelissa."

"He's not a bad man," Ivy said, sticking out her chin defiantly. "I just know I can convince him to help."

"Absolute insanity," Elyssa said.

"These are dire circumstances," Cinder said. "Perhaps radical action is called for."

"I can do it." Ivy put the lollipop into the side of her mouth and sucked. "Just give me the chance to help my brother. Plus, Jeremiah and Daelissa argued about a lot about things. Remember when I helped Justin keep your dad from being assassinated?"

Elyssa's breath caught in her throat. "I do, and I'm so glad you did."

"I didn't really sneak away. Jeremiah told me he wouldn't stop me if I wanted to warn Justin." Ivy switched the sucker to the other cheek. "Bigdaddy said what Daelissa wanted to do was wrong."

"I believe Jeremiah Conroy experienced what humans refer to as a moral quandary," Cinder said. "I still have had no success locating pictures of the inside of the church. Even so, the odds of sneaking into such a heavily fortified location are quite low."

They had no other options, Elyssa realized. They could either sit, wait, and hope Thomas Borathen's Templar forces pushed back the Synod, freeing up a few assault squads or they could risk everything and ask the most powerful and dangerous Arcane alive to help. She didn't know all the circumstances surrounding Ivy's raising by the Conroys. Alysea hadn't been very forthcoming with the details, and Justin only knew Jeremiah had taken her when she was just a baby.

"If Jeremiah threatens us, are you willing to do whatever it takes to get us away from him?" Elyssa asked Ivy.

The girl narrowed her eyes. "Anything."

89

Elyssa met her gaze. "Even if it means hurting him?"

Ivy crunched down on the lollipop with a fierce look. "Yes."

"Then let's do it."

"Please don't, Elyssa," Bella pleaded. "This is an awful idea."

Shelton shrugged into his duster. "I'll get my stuff."

Elyssa shook her head. "No. It'll just be me and Ivy. I won't risk anyone else." She turned to Ivy. "Where do they live?"

Bella's eyes flashed wide with alarm. "Elyssa, please reconsider!"

"I'll do anything for Justin." Elyssa took the other woman's hands. "Trust me. We'll be okay. I'm sure Ivy can handle any dangerous situations."

"You bet I can," the girl said, tossing her empty lollipop stick into the air and incinerating it with a narrow beam of white energy.

Shelton's eyes went wide as he watched the ash fall to the floor. "I think Elyssa will be fine."

Ivy took out her arcphone and supplied a picture of her bedroom inside Jeremiah's estate. "We can use this with the omniarch."

Bella put an arm on the girl's shoulder. "You're not leading Elyssa into a trap, are you?"

"How could you ask such a thing?" Ivy said, looking genuinely hurt. "I would never do that to her."

"I'm sorry," the petite woman said, looking pained. "But we still don't know each other all that well, and you've been a bit, um, naughty in the past."

"I was being used by Daelissa," Ivy said, blue eyes shining with anger. "Justin showed me how I could be good. He showed me I had a choice, and right now, I'm choosing to help."

Bella nodded her head. "I trust you, Ivy. Please be safe."

The girl pursed her lips and nodded. "I love my brother. I *will* help him."

The group made their way downstairs. Elyssa used Ivy's picture to open a portal into the girl's bedroom. The room was dark, but the light shining through the portal illuminated a four-poster bed

90

covered in stuffed animals. Elyssa swallowed a lump of apprehension and stepped through, Ivy close on her heels.

"Don't come through, no matter what," Elyssa said to the others. "If anyone besides us comes back, close the portal immediately."

Bella nodded. "Good luck."

Ivy turned on the light in her bedroom. She looked longingly at the stuffed animals for a moment, turned, and walked to the door. Taking a deep breath as if to steel herself, she opened it and stepped into a hallway. Elyssa looked up and down the corridor. It was the same one she and Justin had broken into to see Ivy when they were trying to save Alysea.

The door to the master bedroom hung open. It looked empty. Ivy motioned Elyssa to follow her down the master staircase. They walked down a hallway and to the door of a study. Jeremiah sat inside reading a book and sipping from a glass of amber liquid. He looked the same as ever, neatly trimmed gray goatee, spectacles, and a dark suit accented with a red bowtie. His eyes met Elyssa's, betraying not a hint of surprise.

"I expected I might see you again soon, Ivy." He raised an eyebrow. "I did not, however, expect Elyssa Borathen."

"I can assure you I never expected to be here either, Mr. Conroy," Elyssa said, trying to keep her voice calm even though she was screaming on the inside.

"It's obvious you've repurposed the arch in the cellar of the mansion." He steepled his fingers and rested his gaze on Elyssa's. "Ivy must have led you here."

"Yes," Elyssa said. *No sense in lying.*

"Furthermore, you must be here about young Mr. Slade."

"My brother," Ivy said, eyes flashing. "Big—uh—Jeremiah, we need your help."

Jeremiah gave her a sad look. "Do you no longer consider me your grandfather?"

Ivy looked at the floor. "You're not. Mom told me the truth."

"Eliza and I raised you from infancy, Ivy. I'd say that gives us as good a claim as anyone else." His gaze softened. "Come now, child. There's no harm in humoring an old man, is there?"

"You tried to make me do bad things, Jeremiah. You tried to kill Justin. You wanted me to let him die." She looked up, eyes locking onto his. "You have a lot to make up for if you ever want me to let you back in the family."

Elyssa felt a shock of surprise at the tone of command in Ivy's voice. The girl was unpredictable—one minute acting like a child, the next like a little dictator. Elyssa hoped Justin's sister was mentally sound, but considering her upbringing between Daelissa and the Conroys, her childhood had been far from normal or balanced.

Jeremiah chuckled. "I understand."

"The Exorcists have Justin," Elyssa said. "We need help freeing him."

He leaned back in his chair and took a sip of his drink. "It appears events have spiraled completely out of control. I was foolish to think I could ever direct the situation, no matter how much information I have."

Elyssa narrowed her eyes. "Did you have something to do with his kidnapping?"

Jeremiah stood. Elyssa blurred back, swords singing as they came free from her sheaths.

"I assure you, I intend no harm to you or Ivy," he said, motioning toward the door. "If you'll please step into the hallway, I have something to show you."

Elyssa put Ivy behind her, and backed into the hallway. It seemed rather foolish to put herself between Jeremiah and the one person powerful enough to stop him, but Ivy was still a young girl, and Elyssa's instincts overrode common sense. Jeremiah stepped into the hallway after them and walked to a set of oaken double doors across the hall. He traced a symbol over the seam. The outline of the symbol flashed white, and the doors slid into recesses in the wall.

Jeremiah stepped through the opening. Elyssa halted at the threshold, amazed at the sight beyond. A massive chamber filled with shelves spread out before her. The place was as large as an aircraft hangar—impossible to fit inside the mansion, no matter how spacious it appeared.

"Oh, we're going into the vault?" Ivy asked.

"How is this possible?" Elyssa asked.

Jeremiah raised a gray eyebrow. "I'm utilizing the same magic which creates a gateway into the Grotto, La Casona, and other pocket dimensions." He touched a foot to the threshold. "Once you step across, you are no longer in Atlanta, but in an underground bunker halfway around the world."

Elyssa stared at the vault. "I didn't think anyone knew how the pocket dimensions worked."

"Not many do." He stepped inside and walked down a long row of shelves. "It operates very much like the arch portals."

Ivy skipped after him, as if this was the most normal thing in the world.

Elyssa saw no choice but to follow. If Jeremiah was leading them into a deadly trap, they were in too far now to escape. The old man genuinely seemed to care for Ivy. Elyssa had to hope it was enough to keep him from killing them both.

Jeremiah stopped in front of a shelf and looked up and down it for a moment. Elyssa half expected him to make the hemming and hawing noises an old person made when searching for something, but the Arcane's vision seemed eagle sharp, and his hands betrayed not a single tremor of old age as he took a scroll from the shelf and turned to face her.

"Ooh, can I play with the snow globe?" Ivy asked, pointing at one on a shelf just out of her reach.

Jeremiah smiled. "It's not a toy, Ivy."

Her lips pouted. "I know, but it's fun making it snow in Sheboygan."

He chuckled. "Okay, you can make one snowstorm, but make it a good one, okay?" He gently handed her a large crystal globe attached to a silver pedestal. An intricately carved representation of a town resided within it.

"Does that really make it snow in Sheboygan?" Elyssa asked.

93

He didn't answer, instead unrolling the scroll and placing it on a table in front of her. "Long ago, I made it my sole mission to possess all foreseeances related to the Cataclyst."

"That's what Lornicus called Justin," she said. "A catalyst for a possible cataclysm."

"Indeed he is, despite all my attempts to blunt his effectiveness until I was ready."

Elyssa didn't like the sound of that. "Ready for what?"

"Foreseeance four-three-one-one supposedly came to pass when Justin and Ivy decided to protect each other, rather than fight," he said. "But there was more to the foreseeance than the scraps which I was unable to keep from circulation."

"So you're the one behind the cover-up."

"I am certainly one, but not the only one." He folded his arms. "Information about the future is sheer power, Miss Borathen."

"Doesn't take a genius to figure that out." It struck her that his trademark genteel southern accent was absent. She glanced at the ancient parchment on the table. "Am I supposed to read this?"

"Yes."

"Why are you showing this to me now?"

He remained silent for a moment. "Because my attempts to alter or resist the future have done little to delay the inevitable. Foreseeances are not set in stone. I have changed the path of others who were to play important roles in the battles to come. Mr. Slade has thus far overcome everything I and the others have thrown in his way."

A chill crept up her back. "You killed people?"

A nod. "I have done a great many things I regret, but I will not be stopped from my goal." He motioned toward the scroll. "Read it."

Elyssa looked at Ivy to be sure she was okay. The young girl was watching a thick snowstorm roiling within the globe. Ivy glanced at Elyssa and gave her a sly wink. She obviously wasn't as entranced as she appeared. *Sneaky girl.* Elyssa was starting to like Justin's sister more and more all the time.

94

"Fine, I'll read it." She looked at the scroll. It was written in what looked like Latin, but someone had scrawled an English translation beneath it.

The first decision determines who will be the Cataclyst. Once it is determined, the chosen must journey into the shadow of Eden. There will the final choice be revealed. The chosen must be wary, for there are more choices than three. Destruction, rebirth, stagnation— any alone will be the end of all.

Elyssa gasped and looked up. "I thought the choice had been made. I thought Ivy and Justin canceled each other out by not fighting."

"Mr. Slade is the Cataclyst." Jeremiah rolled up the parchment. "The final choice will soon present itself, and we have to hope he chooses the right path."

"The right decision probably depends on perspective," Elyssa said. "We all know whose side you're on."

"Things are not quite as clear cut as you think, Miss Borathen."

"What is the shadow of Eden?"

He placed the scroll on the shelf and turned back to her. "It is where Mr. Slade is right this very moment."

His statement didn't make any sense. "Eden was a mythical garden, a paradise. Are you telling me it exists?"

"You're thinking of a Biblical term for a real place." Jeremiah pointed toward a globe. "That is Earth. Earth is divided into many realms. Eden is the term for the mortal realm."

Elyssa blinked several times. "I've never heard that."

"I do not have time for history lessons, so I'll cut to the chase, young lady." Jeremiah took off his spectacles and locked eyes. "The shadow of Eden is the Gloom. Mr. Slade is there."

"The Gloom?" Elyssa felt her forehead pinch. "I don't understand. How—"

"The Exorcists banished him there. Daelissa hopes to use him for her own purposes."

"They did what?" Ivy asked, eyes wide with concern. "Why?"

95

"It doesn't matter why they did, only that they did," Jeremiah replied in a calm voice. "This is destiny carving a course through the present. Anything you do right now will only interfere or kill you. I suggest you sit back and let him follow the path to its conclusion."

"How did they send him there?" Elyssa asked. It took all her willpower not to grab the man by his fancy suit jacket and jerk him around.

"They have an arch within the church which enables them to enter the Gloom at will." Jeremiah motioned her toward the door. "You asked for my help; I have given it."

"How do you know where he is?" Elyssa asked.

Old man Conroy gave her a steely look. "Because Daelissa told me."

Chapter 12

I stood frozen in the face of a creature even bigger than the tragon from Arcane University.

"Go!" David shouted, shoving me to the right while the towering monster plowed through buildings.

I stumbled to the side as Timothy's maniacal shouts reminded me we had a much smaller but no less lethal problem right behind us. We ran down the sidewalk. Cars leapt from the ground as the giant monster continued its rampage through town. I looked behind and saw the raptor burst from the exit and leap over a car. It landed in the street and streaked after us. Godzilla's third cousin twice removed rumbled down the street behind Gloria, trashing buildings and cars as if they were toys.

"He's mine!" Timothy shrieked repeatedly over the roar and rumble of the rampaging beast.

"Through there," David yelled, pointing toward a tight alley between a neighboring apartment complex and another parking garage.

We dodged into the narrow space. David leapt. I ran right into the tin garbage can he'd jumped over and smacked into the sidewalk. The shotgun clattered from my grasp. I heard a hiss and spun onto my back in time to see the raptor reach the alley. It hissed and lunged. I scrambled backward too late. Sharp teeth snapped together inches

97

from my face. The raptor wriggled but its body was too large to fit into the alley.

"Get him, Gloria!" Timothy shouted.

The raptor's head swung forward, teeth clacking together as it tried vainly to reach me. I stuck out my tongue. "Guess Gloria needs to go on a crash diet, Timmy."

The vampire made a sound somewhere between a shout and the squeal a kid makes when throwing a temper tantrum. The building shuddered. Bricks rained down from overhead. One smacked into the concrete to my left while another caught Gloria Richardson right on her pointy noggin. It didn't even draw blood.

"Move," David said, his hand gripping me under the armpit and pulling me to my feet.

I stuck out my tongue at Timothy, grabbed the shotgun off the ground, and raced after my father. The building shuddered. Bricks crumbled. The wall caved in as we passed it. I looked back and saw the structure imploding.

"Run faster," I shouted above the din.

Brick and mortar dust choked the air, filled my mouth. We burst from the end of the alley and into a large grassy park. I didn't stop running until we were clear of all buildings. My eyes searched for Timothy. David pulled out his pistol and gripped it with both hands. I held the shotgun stock to my shoulder, aiming it like I'd seen in the movies.

The monster changed course and plowed through two more buildings before reaching into one and pulling out a female. I heard her screams, though. "Gee, let me guess," I said. "Some guy is gonna show up and save her."

The monster ate her.

I heard crazed laughter from nearby and assumed it was Timothy. Instead, I saw a short dumpy man dancing with glee near the foot of the lizard monster, shouting something about how women shouldn't ignore him.

"There are some creepy people in this world," David said.

"Let's worry about the vampire and not the misogynistic beast master," I said, surveying the area. Clouds of dust enveloped the apartment complex and the street nearby. I waited for the raptor to burst from concealment at any moment. "We're never getting to the Grotto at this rate."

"I'm more worried about evading a raptor when the fog closes back in." David trained the pistol sights on the dust and backed away a few feet. "At least now we can see him coming."

A vermillion unicorn trotted past with a woman riding on its back. I shook my head and looked north. "I say we make more time while the coast is clear. Maybe a brick hit Timothy on the head."

David snorted. "If only we could be so lucky."

A twisting funnel of gray reached into the sky on the nearby horizon. Veins of lightning flashed within the maelstrom, but I didn't hear any accompanying thunder. I wondered if someone was dreaming about being Zeus. The lightning storm lay in the same general direction we had to go, so I used it as a landmark and motioned my father to follow.

Keeping a careful eye as we went, we made our way down the road without seeing any sign of Timothy. The vortex of cloud and lightning grew larger and larger. We climbed a rise that gave us a good view of the road ahead.

"Look at that," David said, pointing out several more of the strange tornadoes. "I don't think those are dreams."

"Not unless someone is dreaming about the end of the world." I noticed some of the storms were larger than others. A monstrous tornado to the south had completely engulfed downtown Atlanta. A smaller whirlwind sprung up in the part of town we'd just come from. I noticed shapes within the clouds and peered at it before realizing what those shapes were. "The storm is full of minders."

"Definitely not dreams."

With great effort, I switched to incubus sight and immediately shielded my eyes from the light. "Those aren't clouds." I peeked between my fingers at the brilliant light storms scattered across the landscape. "It's aether. Lots and lots of it."

"Magical energy?" David said. "I thought it ran through ley lines in the ground."

99

"It does. I've never seen this much in the air." I looked down at the street and saw tiny ley lines like capillaries running through it. They faded to darkness over several seconds before pulsing bright white and repeating the cycle. I drew in aether like Shelton had taught me, and felt it gathering in my well—the reservoir where Arcanes held aether for casting spells.

Try as I might, I couldn't muster even a simple spell with all the magical energy I'd absorbed.

Why were the ley lines fading in and out? I'd never seen them do that before. A cold shock hit me in the chest. "What if they're draining aether from the earth?"

"And sending it where?" David looked skyward. "To aliens?"

I switched back to normal sight. "How come I can use my incubus senses, but I can't use my supernatural strength or speed?"

"That's a very good question," my father said. "It's a struggle just to use minor abilities. It's as if this place puts a bottleneck between us and our powers."

"That would explain why it's like sucking through a bent straw." I regarded the light storms, chewing my inner lip as I thought. I remembered the first time I'd used my incubus sight to look through the fog and sense minders. I remembered how bright the fog had been. *Gray fog.* "Holy crap."

"What?"

"The fog isn't fog. It's neutral aether."

David put a hand on his chin and seemed to mull it over for a moment. "So the Gloom is full of aether."

"It's invisible in the real world," I explained. "But here it's so thick you can't even see through it."

"The minders feed off dreams," he said. "What if the minders are creating aether from dreams?"

"Whoa." I let my brain process the thought. "You think dreams are the source of magic?"

"Maybe not *the* source but, quite possibly, one of many sources."

"Then why does the aether fog exist when people are awake and not dreaming?"

He shrugged. "I don't know. Maybe we're just jumping to crazy conclusions."

I turned my view back north. "We need to get moving."

David surveyed the area around us for a moment. "I'm trying to use my senses to find Timothy, but there are so many minders, it's impossible to single him out."

"Hopefully he gave up the chase."

He met my eyes. "I highly doubt that."

We headed northward. Within what I estimated was an hour, we reached the outskirts of Buckhead. The aether storm in the area had grown to such epic proportions, it claimed a huge chunk of the residential areas. Thankfully, the road leading through the business sector looked clear.

"I wonder what'll happen if we wander inside that," I said.

"Let's not find out."

We stopped at the top of an overpass and took another look at our surroundings. The scene looked like something out of an apocalyptic movie with magical tornadoes all across the landscape. Unlike real tornadoes, however, they didn't seem to cause physical damage. All the same, I didn't want to chance walking into one. For all I knew, the concentration of aether might short-circuit my brain.

While we walked, I saw dreamscapes popping up with greater frequency. Many of them lasted much longer than the ones we'd seen earlier. As a result we ended up waiting in safe areas for the Gloom to morph back to normal. I tried to use the free time to consider what the minders were doing with the aether, but it was hard to concentrate with the insanity going on around us.

I lost count of the number of women I saw frolicking with unicorns or riding on the backs of glittering vampires. For every one of them, there seemed to be a dozen men dreaming about saving women from danger. Zombies seemed to be the most popular theme.

"I don't know how much more of this I can take," I said after dodging a bipedal shark chasing a young boy down the street.

"Almost there," David said. He looked as tired as he sounded. It was as if the journey had drained all the smartass out of him.

101

My feet ached. My back hurt. It felt like I had blisters in places I never knew existed. Even though I hadn't possessed my supernatural abilities for that long, I'd obviously forgotten what it felt like to be a nom—a normal human. Despite all my aches and woes, hope glimmered in my heart as I saw Phipps Plaza just down the road. Beneath it lay the Grotto.

I heard a distant rumbling and looked up in time to see a flying saucer crash into a skyscraper, sending debris and glass billowing out in a dark cloud. Thankfully, it was far enough away to leave us unaffected. Gathering up my remaining willpower, I jogged down the road toward the mall. The parking lot was nearly empty, which made sense given it was nighttime in the real world. We walked down several ramps into the parking garage, and made our way to the far back where an illusionary wall hid the entrance down into the Grotto, except the illusion wasn't there, just an opening leading down the winding driveway.

I guess the illusion doesn't exist in the Gloom.

We exchanged looks, shrugged, and headed down the ramp.

Aside from the hollow echo of our footsteps, the place was quiet as a tomb and pitch black.

After several tries, I managed to flick on my night vision and gave thanks when it worked, revealing the descending corridor in a bluish tinge. We reached the vast cavern at the bottom. My night vision only granted vision about thirty or so yards out, so we headed toward the center where the arch should be. An Obsidian arch towered over us. Though it was black, something seemed off about it.

"Do you notice anything different about the arch?" I asked.

David looked it up and down. "There is something different about it, but I can't put my finger on it." He pointed in the direction of the doors leading into the Grotto pocket dimension. "I want to see something else."

We traipsed across the cavern. The ticket booth was there. The stable sat in its usual place. Cars even populated the parking lot, including a zebra-striped Ducati motorcycle with orange tires. The doors to the Grotto came into view. David walked over and opened them. Beyond, a niche ended in a rock wall.

"Very interesting," he said. "The pocket dimensions don't work here even if the landscape mirrors the mortal realm."

"The illusionary wall hiding the Grotto entrance wasn't in place either. Maybe the spells in the mortal realm aren't active here." I ran a finger down the wall to verify it wasn't an illusion, and sighed when I found cold stone. "What now? Do we just wait for Gloom fracture—or would that be reality fracture?—and hope we can get through?"

"It won't be quite that simple," David said. "When the Gloom opens in the mortal realm, it causes a vacuum to form. Without preternatural strength, it'll be very hard to push our way through it and into the real world."

"I could hardly fight the gale it created, even with super strength." I could chalk most of that up to not having a good handhold. Even so, we'd have to fight past the vacuum to establish a grip in the real world. Since I couldn't use magic or manifest into demon form, I really didn't see what we could do on the off-chance a Gloom rift formed.

"If a fracture forms," David said, "we'll need to signal people on the other side that we need help."

"Ah hah," I said, holding up a finger. "There's a sporting goods store across the road. Maybe we could grab some flare guns. Heck, maybe they have crossbows or something we could use to shoot a rope into the real world and anchor it on the arch."

"Great idea, Justin." He slapped me on the back.

I looked at his hand. "I'm going to have your handprint embedded on my back if you keep doing that."

He gave me an apologetic look. "Well, I suppose we should head over there now before the fog rolls back in."

"Yep."

We went back up the winding ramp, left the mall, and headed across the road for the three-story sporting goods store. We kept our guns at the ready, vigilant for any sign of Timothy, but he had either given up the chase or been squashed by bricks. Chuck's Sporting Goods was part of a complex of other stores, so we had to go through a parking deck to find the front entrance. I groaned when I saw it. A sliding metal barrier covered the glass doors behind it.

I knelt to examine the bottom of the obstruction. There weren't any latches I could see, but an electronic key lock set into the doorframe appeared to be the only way to raise the door.

"Crap!" I shouted. "How are we supposed to get inside now?"

David tested the metal door with a foot. "It's too thick to blast through with guns."

"Maybe we can pry it up," I suggested, looking at the bottom seam.

"Where will we find a crowbar?" he asked.

I stood in silence as I contemplated the problem. Finding a crowbar probably wouldn't be an issue, but it meant exposing ourselves to dangerous dreamscapes. I imagined most of the stores in the area were locked down as tightly as this one. I glanced across the parking deck and saw similar metal plating covering the entrance to another store.

I heard a faint clicking noise and looked at David. He seemed as lost in thought as I was. I heard another click, and another. I wondered if a dreamscape had formed inside the garage and looked around for the source. My search revealed nothing except a mostly empty parking deck. I was just about to give up when I realized how familiar the clicking sounded—like claws on concrete.

"Oh, crap," I said an instant before Gloria Richardson burst around the corner.

Chapter 13

Elyssa

Unsure what to believe, Elyssa glared at Jeremiah Conroy, fear and anger forming a poisonous mixture in her stomach. "Daelissa told you where Justin is?"

He nodded. "She called not long ago."

"You tell me not to go after Justin because he has a purpose in the Gloom, but admit you're still friendly with Daelissa." Elyssa's hand itched to draw steel, but she knew it would be a futile gesture. "How can I believe a word you say?"

Jeremiah closed the door to the vault and walked down the hallway. "My relationship with her is far more complicated than you could imagine." He entered his office and picked up the glass of amber liquid. "I have no intention of divulging more about the subject, so you'll simply have to take my word for it."

"How can I take the word of a traitor to the human race?"

His hand visibly tightened on the glass. "Traitor?" For once, emotion colored his voice. "I will have you know I've done more for Eden than you could dream."

"Like how you helped Daelissa sway the Arcane Council to her side? Or armed vampires with weapons enchanted to penetrate Templar armor?" She folded her arms. "The list goes on and on, Jeremiah."

He seemed to regain control of his emotions and waved his hand as though her words didn't matter. "As I said, you know nothing."

"It sure sounds like something," Ivy said. She stood in the doorway, eyes narrowed. "You seem to do a lot of bad things. I know you've sprinkled some good in there, but why won't you tell me the truth?"

Jeremiah chuckled. "The truth, my dear?" He sat down as if the weight of the world suddenly rested on his shoulders. "The truth is a very difficult thing to pin down."

The girl shook her head. "Not really. Either you did something bad or you didn't. You want me to be your granddaughter again? Well stop lying to me!" Her last sentence was the shout of someone desperate to be heard. "You and Bigmomma—Eliza—and Daelissa told me all this stuff and then I find out from my brother that you were using me! I hate the lies and I hate being used. I'll never be your little girl again unless you stop lying!" Ivy's fists clenched, eyes blazing with white fire.

Elyssa sensed a catastrophe might be brewing if Ivy didn't calm down.

Jeremiah nodded. "Very well, Ivy. The truth is Daelissa killed someone very special to me a long time ago. I have been treading a delicate line between pretending to assist her and plotting my revenge."

"Why did my parents give me to you?" she asked, the glow fading from her eyes.

"Your mother, Alysea, was nearly killed in the Desecration. Leyworms saved her, in a sense, rebirthing her as an infant."

"Like the leyworms in the El Dorado way station?" Elyssa asked. She'd seen leyworms swallow husked angels and spit them back out some time later as baby angels. Jeremiah had found out about it, or possibly knew about it all along.

"Precisely," he said. "I have something of a relationship with some of the leyworms. They delivered her to me, and I cared for her."

"That still doesn't answer my question," Ivy said in a stern voice.

106

"When you were born, Alysea still didn't have full control or knowledge of her abilities." He sighed. "Daelissa wanted to keep her in the dark, going so far as to white out Alysea's memories as they emerged. The two of them were once friends, but fought on opposite sides of the war."

Ivy nodded. "Mom told me that."

"Yes, well, as a result, Alysea couldn't teach you what you needed to know. Daelissa saw you as her protégé—her right hand." Jeremiah swirled the liquid in his glass. "She wanted to control you in the hopes you would one day be able to help her repair the Grand Nexus."

"What did you see me as?" Ivy asked.

He smiled gently. "My granddaughter. I wanted you to learn how to use your powers. With my guidance, I tried to keep Daelissa from completely controlling you."

"That's not the whole truth, is it?" Elyssa asked. "You wanted something else out of the arrangement."

He leaned forward. "It pains me to say this, Ivy, but I also had selfish reasons for raising you. I wanted you to help me avenge my beloved wife."

Ivy's forehead wrinkled. "But, isn't Eliza your wife?"

"She is, but it is an arrangement," he said with a sigh. "I'm sorry—"

"Sorry doesn't cut it!" Ivy shouted. "You used me. Daelissa used me. Everyone wants to use me but my Mom and Justin."

"The truth is painful," Jeremiah said, shoulders slumping. His eyes looked tired. "It is a terrible burden, child."

A tear ran down Ivy's cheek. "Do you know how awful it is to find out people you love are bad guys?"

A bell chimed. Jeremiah waved a hand at the wall, and the image of a limousine pulling up the long winding driveway appeared. "Why is Eliza back already?" he said, as if to himself. The limo reached the end of the driveway. The rear door opened.

Elyssa's heart stopped. "Daelissa!"

"You must leave this instant," Jeremiah said.

107

"The portal is upstairs," she said. "We have to pass the front door to get there."

Elyssa heard the front door open and shut. Jeremiah drew a symbol on the wall to his right and a small compartment appeared behind an illusionary panel.

"There's only room for one," he said. "Hide, Miss Borathen. Ivy will be fine. Daelissa doesn't know she isn't living here anymore."

Elyssa didn't have time to argue. She ducked into the small compartment.

Jeremiah made a motion with his hand. "The illusion is in place. She cannot see you." He turned to the girl. "Ivy, you must not tell her you've gone to live with your brother. Do you understand?"

Ivy looked a little stunned by the quick developments, but nodded. As if it were an afterthought, Jeremiah grabbed a lollipop from a jar on his desk and gave an orange one to Ivy.

She regarded it dubiously. "I don't like orange."

"They let him escape!" Daelissa said, coming into the office without so much as a by-your-leave. "I delivered him into their hands, and the fools could not find him."

"I assume you're speaking of Justin Slade," Jeremiah said.

"Of course I am!"

Elyssa was able to see Daelissa clearly through the illusionary wall. Having certain death only inches from her should have terrified her. Instead, she worried desperately about Ivy. The girl sat on the divan across from Jeremiah's desk, licking the orange sucker.

Daelissa suddenly seemed to realize Ivy was there, and knelt. "Your demon spawn brother is an evil little nuisance."

"What happened?" Ivy asked, her eyes flashing dangerously.

Please don't try to kill Daelissa, Elyssa thought.

"Is that not always the question, child?" Daelissa ruffled the girl's hair. "It is an important question to ask when someone has failed you. A good leader listens to their miserable excuses patiently. Once they have explained their incompetence, it is important to set an example for the others."

"Don't give them lollipops?" Ivy asked.

108

A girlish laugh escaped Daelissa. "You are precious as ever, my sweet." She shook her head, and flicked her forefinger out as if pointing at something. A thin blade of white light formed at the end. "I prefer severing their limbs with Brilliance." She smiled sweetly. "Sometimes, burning out an eye is also very useful."

"I think you told me this once," Ivy said. "Wasn't it when you were teaching me how to be a good leader?"

"Why, so it was," Daelissa said. The shard of Brilliance puffed away. She stood and turned to Jeremiah. "The Colombian front has engaged the rebel Templars."

"Do you think the vampires are up for the fight?" Jeremiah asked.

She pshawed. "Most of them are drug lords or slave runners, not warriors. They are rats, chipping away at the rebels, nothing more."

"Maximus certainly created quite a network," he said. "It was a great loss when the Slade boy took him out of the fight."

"It is almost as if the universe wishes to torture me," Daelissa said with pouting lips. "I had hoped I could use the boy."

"You told me that earlier," he said. "What is he helping you with?"

The angel smiled. "When Darkwater was clearing the husks from Thunder Rock, they made some most startling discoveries."

"To which discoveries are you referring?"

"Let us save it for a surprise," she said. Daelissa turned to Ivy again. "Darling, have you been practicing your singing?"

"Of course," she said, and began to sing. "Row, row, row your boat, gently down the stream."

Daelissa's smile flattened. "Still too young." She sprang to her feet. "We should find that horrible mother of yours. Traitor. Bitch. Demon lover!" Her eyes flashed to Jeremiah. "I need her now more than ever. I must task you with finding her."

"Why now?" Jeremiah asked. "Has something recently changed?"

The angel laughed. "Everything has changed, but I lack the tool to fix it."

"You realize I can't help you if you don't tell me what you're trying to fix." He rose and poured himself another glass of alcohol. "Besides, you don't need Alysea. All that tampering you did with her mind made her forget how to attune the Cyrinthian Rune, which, I might add, we still haven't found. Are you sure it wasn't destroyed in the Desecration?"

Daelissa stared vacantly for a long moment. She blinked slowly, as if waking up. "I lost myself again, Jeremiah. It is happening more frequently."

"You blacked out again?" he asked.

A tear trickled down the woman's cheek. "Yes. I was talking about something—was it singing?"

"You were telling me about a surprise Darkwater found," he said.

She snapped her fingers. "Ah, yes. I will show you when I'm ready." Daelissa looked down at Ivy. "You are the most precious possession I have left, child. Your mother abandoned me again. Promise never to leave your dear aunt."

Ivy visibly swallowed. "I promise, Aunt Daelissa."

The woman hugged Ivy tight and kissed her on the head. "The Synod has things well in hand here. Now, I must run to Colombia for a time. Continue your studies, and perhaps I will take you and your grandparents to see something wonderful."

"Be careful," Ivy said.

Daelissa burst into laughter. "You are too sweet, child." She kissed Ivy on the cheek. "Farewell." Without even saying goodbye to Jeremiah, she left as quickly as she'd come.

Elyssa didn't dare come out until Jeremiah gave her the all clear. "Is it my imagination, or is Daelissa absolutely crazy?"

Jeremiah's gaze settled on her. "She is quite insane at times, though lucidity returns after feeding."

"Why don't we just let her go insane then?" Elyssa asked.

"You do not want that," he said. "You might as well let a nuclear bomb go off."

"I think I understand why you wanted to kill the vampires now," Ivy said. She stuck out her tongue and threw the orange

110

lollipop in the garbage. "Daelissa is using them to build an army. You were trying to stop her."

"Yes," Jeremiah said, a smile creeping across his face. "Very insightful, my dear."

"Not all vampires are bad, though. Just Maximus and his master were bad." She frowned. "Justin fixed things so the vampires only lost their powers instead of killing all the good ones with the bad."

"To remove a greater evil, one must sometimes sacrifice the innocent," Jeremiah said.

"You're talking about killing dozens of innocents just to exterminate a few bad apples," Elyssa said.

"Daelissa would merely have found new leaders among these innocents you speak of," he replied.

"You're almost good," Ivy said. "I think you need to keep working on it, Jeremiah. When I think you're good enough, maybe then we can talk about you rejoining the family." She stood. "Let's go, Elyssa. I'm done talking with him."

As they left the room, Elyssa glanced at Jeremiah. For the first time, he looked old and very tired. She couldn't imagine how harsh a toll playing double agent exacted on someone, but it was very evident in his posture and voice.

"Remember, Miss Borathen, there is nothing you can do to stop the boy's destiny." Jeremiah drew in a long breath. "I would advise you to wait."

Elyssa didn't reply. She knew Justin and his father were at least not prisoners of Daelissa, even though being trapped in the Gloom was no laughing matter. Finding them would be nearly impossible, at least until she had a way into the Gloom. She needed the Exorcist church for that, but the Borathen Templars were too busy fending off Daelissa's advances in Atlanta and Colombia to help. It meant she had little choice but to wait, or search for alternate ways into the Gloom.

She would never rest easy until Justin was back.

Chapter 14

I shoved David out of the way as the raptor leapt. Pain seared across my back as the raptor claw raked my skin. Despite the pain, I managed to roll away as the dinosaur skidded to a stop on the concrete.

Timothy leered down at me. "Surprise."

"Surprise this, bitch." My father fired his pistol.

A bullet slammed into Timothy's arm. He spun off the back of the raptor with a shout of pain and surprise. The raptor stopped its attacks, freezing in place like a statue as the vampire writhed on the floor, screaming. David reached down a hand and pulled me to my feet.

"Turn around, son."

I was in too much pain to argue his use of the word, "son", and did as he asked.

He hissed. "We'll need to patch that up. The talon cut to the muscle."

I tried to nod, but a wave of nausea rolled through me. I leaned against a nearby support column and fought the urge to vomit. When I caught my breath, I looked up to see the velociraptor melting into gelatinous goo before my eyes. "What the heck?" I groaned.

David dropped to a knee, right on Timothy's chest. Air exploded from the vampire's mouth. My father gripped the vampire by the throat and shoved the gun to the other man's temple. "Well, well, well, Timothy Burkmeyer. Time to end your pathetic existence."

"No, please," the vampire begged, tears streaming down his face. "I'm desperate for fresh blood. Gotta have it. Don't kill me." He blubbered, saliva foaming at his mouth.

My father pistol-whipped him. The vampire's head lolled to the side. "I'm going to enjoy torturing you to death for what you've put me through, you pathetic germ. You puny speck. Do you have any idea who I am?"

Timothy shivered and drew in a deep breath. "N-no."

I sucked in a breath and spoke. "No torture."

David ignored me. "I'm the man who's going to give you a choice. Do you want me to torture you to death, or do you want to help us?"

A glimmer of hope shone in the vampire's teary eyes. "Help you?"

"Good idea." My father jammed the muzzle to the vampire's forehead. "One wrong move and I will end your insignificant life. Capisce?"

"I'll do anything," Timothy said.

By this point, Gloria Richardson looked like a wax statue left in the hot sun too long. Despite the haze of pain, I realized such a construct as this creature must require a great deal of concentration to keep intact. How much concentration, I didn't know. All I really wanted at that point was a painkiller. Gritting my teeth, I concentrated on the nearby stores, and spotted a pharmacy across the way as my father continued to talk to the vampire.

After a moment, he jerked the other man to his feet. Even without supernatural strength, my father seemed pretty strong. He also seemed a little psychopathic with all the talk of torturing the other guy to death. True, Timothy could have asked us nicely for blood instead of threatening us with disemboweling by dinosaur, and granted, I'd like to beat the guy to a pulp. But torturing someone to death was going a little too far for my tastes.

"I want you to tell your pet dino there to rip open the metal door," David said.

Timothy looked at his raptor and groaned. "Oh, Gloria, you look terrible."

"If the dino makes one false move, your brains will be all over the Gloom." David pressed the barrel firmly to the man's temple.

"It will take time for me to reconstitute her."

David shook his head. "Her claws look intact. If my reasoning is correct, all you need to do is tell what's left of poor Gloria to do what I say." He tightened his fingers around the vampire's throat. "Am I right?"

Timothy gulped. "Yes."

"Then do it."

The half-molten shape of Gloria Richardson firmed up and walked to the door. With a few quick slashes of the talons, the metal roll door crashed to the ground, and the glass doors behind it shattered.

"Pharmacy," I wheezed, unable to move my arm to point as fire seemed to burn in my back.

David directed the vampire's gaze to the store. "Have her open that one up as well."

The headless raptor loped across the parking deck and made short work of the entrance to the pharmacy.

My father looked at me. "Can you walk on your own, Justin?"

I nodded, unable to stop from wincing. Every step was agonizing. It felt as if my back muscles were tearing with every step. I let my father lead the way, his gun never straying from the vampire's head.

"How do you create things in the Gloom?" he asked the vampire.

"It's too difficult to explain."

David's grip squeezed the wound on the vampire's arm. "Tell me or I'll blow off a kneecap."

Timothy howled in pain. "Stop it! I'll talk!"

"Spit it out," David said, his hand releasing the wounded arm.

"The Gloom responds to dreams." Timothy looked at the flesh wound and winced. "You have to trick your mind into a lucid dream state."

"Daydreams don't work?" I asked, unable to keep the pain from my voice.

114

"I don't know how else to explain it. I used to put myself into a trance with meditation so I could switch on that part of my mind." Timothy shrugged. "Now I can do it without having to think about it."

"How long does it take to make something?" David asked.

"It used to take me a long time. Now I can do it in twenty minutes."

"What about a car or a tank?" I asked.

"I could make a tank, sure." The vampire looked adoringly at the raptor where it stood across the parking deck from us for safety. "But it wouldn't fire rounds. Whatever you make is basically just animated aetherplasm."

"Ah, makes sense," David said. "The aether condenses into a shape, and you simply pull the strings with your mind."

Timothy nodded. "Something like that."

We went inside the pharmacy. My father dug around until he found some pills and bottled water. I gulped down the medicine and hoped it worked fast.

David swept the counter clear of prescription bags. "Lie down on the counter. I'm going to treat the wound." David directed the vampire to pull supplies from the shelves. Once everything was gathered, the vampire helped me onto the counter.

Timothy drooled, his eyes gazing long and hard at the blood soaking my shirt. David slammed the butt of the gun into the back of the vampire's head, and Timothy went down in a heap.

My father shrugged. "Can't have him running around loose while I stitch you up."

A happy numbness crept over my entire body. I smiled back. "Vampires are mean."

"Indeed they are," David said, threading a hooked needle. "Hopefully, this won't hurt a bit."

I closed my eyes, and felt myself slipping in and out of consciousness. Aside from a tugging sensation on my skin, I didn't feel much else except a dark warmth.

I open my eyes and see three orbs rotating in the air above me, one of brilliant white, another dark ultraviolet, and the third a dull gray. "Make the choice," they seem to whisper. "Choose." They

115

repeat the words over and over again, but I don't know what to do, or how to choose. I try to respond but my mouth won't open.

My eyelids fluttered. I lay on a hard surface. Hands gripped me and helped me rise to a sitting position. I was in the pharmacy, I remembered. I felt pressure in my back, and tried to reach around to see what was there.

My father intercepted my hand and shook his head. "I sewed you up, but it won't take much to tear it back open. I used some medical tape as well, but you need to take it easy. No more heroics."

"Heroics?" I asked in a drunken voice.

"You saved my life."

"Oh," I said in a dull voice. My lips didn't seem to respond well to commands. I looked down and saw drool hanging halfway to the floor.

"It's not the first time you've saved my life," David said. I saw him move to pat me on the back and stop himself.

I remembered the strange dream with floating orbs. I felt too tired to speak, but forced out the words anyway. "I'm supposed to make a choice."

He tilted his head. "A choice?"

I told him about the vision I'd had upon first entering the Gloom and the one I'd had while he was patching me up. The painkillers made it hard to talk, but easier to remember.

"You're the Cataclyst," he said. "We've all been waiting a long time for this."

"How do I know which is the right choice?"

"You're a brave man. A good man. I think you'll know when the time is right." He rested a hand on my shoulder. "Can you walk?"

It was an effort just to nod, but I steeled myself. "I think so."

"Good." David reached down and grabbed Timothy by the foot with one hand, then guided me out of the pharmacy with his other arm while dragging the unconscious vampire unceremoniously behind.

"What are you?" I asked, the question slipping out.

"I hate to disappoint you, son, but I'm one of the bad guys."

116

I might have felt a shock of surprise if I hadn't been so doped up. Instead, I felt strangely calm. "Oh. I guess people think that about demon spawn."

"Yeah." He looked back at Timothy and smiled when the vampire's head bounced off the curb. "Technically, I'm not really demon spawn."

"Oh." My mind fumbled over this new information and failed to come up with a response. *I'm so stoned right now.*

My father laughed. "I could probably tell you I'm Satan himself right now and you'd have the same response."

I tried to raise an eyebrow and only managed to cross my eyes. "Maybe." I tried to clear the clutter from my head and failed. "Are you Satan?"

"Nope. Far as I know there isn't anyone by that name in the demon realm." We reached the sidewalk in front of Chuck's Sporting Goods. David jerked Timothy up over the curb and dropped his leg. My father regarded me for a long moment. "Maybe you're not ready for the truth, but I think you've earned it."

I tried to smile, or maybe I just imagined trying to smile. "Thanks."

"Don't mention it." David directed me toward the store entrance. "You're funny when you're high." He looked down at the vampire. "I don't feel like lugging him around inside. Maybe we can find something to tie him up."

We went inside and looked around.

I heard running footsteps and looked back to see Timothy sprinting with a staggered gait across the parking deck. My father didn't seem too concerned with the escape.

"Let's get our gear," he said.

"But—"

"Don't worry about him right now. Besides, I can't keep tabs on him and you at the same time."

"Oh."

He pursed his lips. "Probably should have killed him."

Any other time, his remark would have bothered me, but I chuckled instead.

117

I didn't do much shopping because it was hard enough for me to stay upright much less pick out trendy sports underwear. David grabbed some fresh clothes for me, and I just followed him around as he filled a shopping cart with equipment. He tossed in a grappling hook, flares, something that looked like a spear gun, and a wide variety of other items, including metal weight plates and rope. I wondered if the items would go missing in the real world, or if it was all replicated here.

"We should have just stolen a car," I mumbled.

"I never could find one with the keys in it," he said.

We headed through an emergency exit in the back of the building since it was shorter than going back through the parking deck. The alarm wailed for a moment before fading to silence. We crossed the road and made our way to the Phipps Plaza parking deck. I knew I should be concerned about an angry vampire on his raptor, but kept forgetting to be vigilant.

One constant on my mind was Elyssa. I really wished she was here. She'd know exactly how to escape from this mess. I could see her so clearly—her long black hair, fair skin, full lips, violet eyes. I knew every curve of her body. So clear was her image that I could literally see my girlfriend standing in front of me, the hilts of her signature sai swords poking diagonally up from sheaths on her back.

"Did you do that?" David asked me, looking at my imaginary Elyssa.

"Do what?" I asked.

"Make your girlfriend."

"Huh?" I reached out and touched Elyssa. She felt cold and waxy. I recoiled in disgust—the first genuine emotion I recalled since taking the pills. A shock of pain ran down my back. Apparently, the drugs were wearing off, and my girlfriend melted before my eyes. "No, Elyssa."

The melting stopped, and her skin began to reform.

"Whoa."

David chuckled. "Do you have the munchies? Should I get you some cheesy poofs?"

"Wow. I made my girlfriend in the Gloom." I reached out to touch her, remembered how icky the doppelganger felt, and pulled back my hand. "Wait 'til I tell her."

"She's a beautiful woman." He regarded her for a moment. "Maybe we should keep going."

I nodded and thought of Elyssa walking along side me. Her limbs jerked robotically. I imagined her grace and how she moved in real life, and the replica began to walk more naturally. "This isn't so tough," I said, and wiped my mouth. "I wonder if I can make her fight."

She and I had sparred plenty of times, so it wasn't difficult to direct the fake Elyssa into a flurry of quick moves. Her swords flashed and whirled. She spun, ducked, and did a forward flip, finishing with a stylish three-point landing, one sword raised high behind her.

"Having fun?" David said as he negotiated a tall curb with the laden shopping cart.

"This is so cool."

We walked back down the ramp into the Grotto way station, my replicated girlfriend walking by my side. Once we reached the bottom, David set up some battery-operated lanterns on tripods around the center of the ring where the Obsidian Arch loomed, and began unfurling the rope.

"I wish I knew the odds of a Gloom fracture forming."

I'd only seen them form on a couple of occasions, though that had been when Darkwater, a company owned by Jeremiah Conroy, had been experimenting with the smaller arches located in the hidden control room behind the stables. "I wonder if any of the other arches in the control room look different," I said.

"We should check," David said, and grabbed a flashlight.

I directed the clone of my girlfriend to follow us, and we went behind the stables. The illusion hiding the control room door in the real world wasn't there, so we simply went inside. The arches sat in their usual places, though something about each one seemed different. A large world map occupied the front wall above a platform. A pedestal sat in the center, and on it, a gray orb the size of my head.

119

"The modulus," I said, walking over to it. "Arch operators use it to activate the Obsidian Arch."

"I wonder if it's operational." David examined the orb. "Do you know how to work it?"

"I've used one before," I said. I approached the orb, and held a hand over it. A faint glow emanated from the surface, and the modulus rose from the pedestal. The stars on the map, each one indicating the location of an Obsidian Arch glowed faintly. Spinning the orb highlighted each star in turn. I selected the arch in the La Casona way station, located in Bogota Colombia, and flicked the modulus with a finger. The star pulsed in time with the star in the Grotto way station, indicating it was awaiting confirmation from La Casona. I highly doubted anyone was there to confirm unless the arches miraculously led back to the real world.

"Interesting," David said. "What now?"

I thought hard for a moment, fighting the haze in my mind, and remembered what a helpful arch operator had once told me. "If I place my palm on the modulus and raise it, it'll force the connection."

"I wonder what would happen," he said.

A nervous knot formed in my stomach. "No telling. Maybe nothing."

"Only one way to find out."

I nodded, put my palm on the modulus, and raised my hand. A klaxon sounded in the main way station chamber. I heard a deep rumbling hum and felt a rush of excitement. "It might be working." As if in answer, a thin beam of light arched between the selected stars on the map, forming a shimmering tunnel.

"Let's take a look."

We walked into the main chamber and saw a ghostly gray flickering in the center of the towering Obsidian Arch. An image of the destination way station formed in the portal—that of a large industrial warehouse since the La Casona arch wasn't underground like this one.

"Think it's safe to use?" my father asked.

I scrunched my forehead. "It looks like it, but what's the point if it only takes us to another location inside the Gloom?" I looked at fake Elyssa and considered sending her through, but decided it would be better to keep her around for protection should the need arise.

David folded his arms across his chest. "True." A sigh. "I guess all the smaller arches work the same way."

"Yeah, most likely." I couldn't deny I'd held some small hope of a miracle connection to the mortal realm. There were two different types of the smaller black arches. One version required the traveler to press corresponding numbered buttons on the world map. I called the other kind omniarches since they could open a portal anywhere without a destination arch. As far as I knew they wouldn't take a person to another dimension or realm, though I'd encountered some strange anomalies with them and accidentally ended up in places that most definitely weren't in Eden. Those arches required the user to magically close the silver circle around them and form a crystal clear image of the desired destination. Risking travel through one in the Gloom didn't appeal to me.

I explained the workings of the omniarches to my father. "Shelton, Adam, and I once accidentally created some kind of feedback loop by opening two omniarch portals next to each other. It sent us all over the place, including what looked like another realm." I remembered the strange siren beings singing an arch into creation. "But we could end up killing ourselves trying that experiment."

"You should test the omniarches anyway," he suggested. "Maybe we'll get lucky."

I grimaced. "Or end up trapped in some hellhole for eternity."

He chuckled. "I think this place qualifies already."

We went back inside the control room. I deactivated the Obsidian Arch so the klaxon would stop blaring. My stomach rumbled. "I think I'm getting the munchies." The pain in my back flared like hot metal pressed against my flesh. "I might need another painkiller too."

"We'll need to be careful with those. I want you ready to go if a Gloom fracture opens."

"I agree."

"Let's eat, and then we'll test the omniarches."

121

We went back into the main chamber and raided our satchel of provisions. I was so famished, the pasty granola bars tasted like heaven. I looked around for my clone of Elyssa and found a puddle of goop where I'd left her standing. "Oh, no."

"Can you remake her?"

I imagined her rising from the puddle and reforming. Nothing happened. After a few minutes, I gave up. "I don't understand why I can't do it now."

"The painkillers must have put you into a trancelike doze," David said. "It probably allowed you to use that lucid dream state to imagine her into being."

I nodded and winced as the skin on my back stretched with the movement. "I guess I can try it again after I take another pill."

My father finished off a bag of potato chips and sat cross-legged, eyes closed for a long moment. I almost asked him what he was doing, but figured he needed sleep as much as I did. As the food settled in my stomach, weariness crept into my muscles. It had been a long, trying day. We hadn't slept for probably close to twenty-four hours. I might be able to go into a dreamlike trance without any drugs.

I heard a clicking noise and looked up in time to see Gloria Richardson and her rider, Timothy, enter the circle of light. He raised a gun and aimed it at me.

"Let's finish this," the vampire said.

"Yes, let's," said David. He looked up with an evil leer on his face. A horrific screeching noise sounded from the darkness.

Timothy's eyes went wide. He looked around frantically. Something with more legs than I could count blurred into the light, tearing Timothy from his perch. The raptor went still as a statue as the vampire lost his concentration.

The creature on top of him looked like a huge spider, albeit with a lot more legs, and bristling with spiky black hair. Gunfire erupted, the muzzle flashing between the vampire and the spider thing. The bullets had no effect on the creature.

David rose, his face clouding with anger. "I've had enough of you, vampire."

122

"Please let me go," Timothy wheezed. "I'll leave you alone."

"Yes, you'll leave us alone," my father said with a sneer.

The spider monster opened jagged pincers and, with a savage chomp, took off the vampire's head.

Chapter 15

Blood spurted from the neck of the decapitated vampire. I cried out in surprise, flinched away, and groaned in pain as agony seared my back. The world faded for a moment and I felt faint. I looked away from the gore, breathing heavily. "You killed him."

"He was a nuisance," David said.

I looked up at my father and found a cold expression on his face. "We could have tied him up or knocked him out. Hell, we could have tossed the vampire through the arch."

My father touched a hand to his chin. "I didn't think of using him as our lab rat." He shrugged. "Oh well, the bastard deserved it."

I heard a scuttling noise, and looked over to see the spider thing dragging the corpse into the darkness, thick black blood trailing behind it.

"What is that thing?"

"One of the lower spawn of Haedaemos—a crawler." He booted Timothy's head into the darkness. It made a meaty sound as it rolled away. "The demon name for them is a bit harder to pronounce with a human tongue."

I tried not to think about how casually he'd kicked Timothy's head like a moldy head of lettuce. "Haedaemos?"

"It's what Daemos call the motherland." He placed a hand over his heart in a mocking salute. "The demon realm."

"Every time you speak of the demon realm you say 'we' or 'our' as if you're not part of the mortal realm."

"Because I'm not." He regarded the still form of Gloria Richardson as the raptor began to melt away. David took a seat across from me. "I said earlier you deserved some of the truth, even if you're not ready for it."

"Then tell me." I looked around the room. "We have plenty of time without Timothy chasing us down."

"I have...a problem. A serious condition." He took out a massive jar of cheesy poofs and flipped off the lid. He removed one of the orange balls into and gazed at it adoringly before tossing it into his mouth and crunching it. "I am addicted to cheesy poofs."

I rolled my eyes. "Don't deflect. Tell me."

He popped a couple more into his mouth, closing his eyes and moaning as they crunched. "I was not born in the mortal realm. I wasn't even born as demon spawn—as Daemos." Gripping a bottled water, he took a long drink and wiped his mouth with the back of his hand. "Our king—I guess that's the human equivalent—saw the Seraphim invasion of the mortal realm as a threat to him. Since we can't exist for long in the mortal realm without a corporeal body, he sent agents to possess humans so they could fight the Seraphim and drive them from the world."

"You're one of those agents?"

He shook his head. "Possession drives the human host insane after too long, at least in most cases. Even though the demons were chosen for their loyalty to the king, there were those who couldn't resist the temptation to do their own thing and wreak havoc in the general population."

"Guess I know where the Bible got its stories," I said.

My father made a noise like someone hawking up broken teeth.

"What in the world was that?"

"That's how you pronounce the king's name."

"Does he have an easier name in the mortal realm?"

My father thought about it for a moment. "I know one of his favorite names is Baal. He always got a kick out of creating fake religions."

"The name sounds familiar."

His lips tightened. "He also happens to be my father."

"Whoa."

David shrugged. "Let's just say the king of demons isn't the best father figure to have."

"I don't get it. If you're a demon, how haven't you driven your host insane?"

"Because I am not possessing this body." He massaged his temples with his fingers. "The greatest minds could not solve the problem of keeping a demon in the mortal world without a body. They finally realized only the permanent melding of human and demon would work."

I felt my forehead wrinkle. "Like fusing the souls together?"

David tossed a handful of cheesy poofs in the air and caught most of them in his mouth. "Something like that. They had to find a human soul and demon that were perfectly compatible. This meant the demon and human parts would need to be congruent, otherwise one would fall out of alignment and the human would go crazy."

"Sounds impossible."

"It very nearly was, and the tests took decades."

I cringed. "That was a long time while Seraphim were tearing up the world."

He nodded. "Hundreds of humans volunteered for the test, desperate to save their world from the Seraphim. Many were training to be Arcanes. I possessed several candidates without success. When I reached a young shepherd, I felt this very odd sense of wellbeing I hadn't felt in the others."

"You just naturally clicked."

He nodded. "Yeah. The man cried. I felt his emotions, all a jumble. He was happy because he knew the fit was perfect. He was sad because he knew he'd have to leave his wife and family behind. He knew he would seed a whole new race of beings."

"By having sex with humans?"

126

He nodded. "Truth be told, he was actually kind of excited about all the sex."

"I'll bet." I pursed my lips. "So is this other man still inside you?"

He waggled his hand in a so-so gesture. "We absorbed each other. Our original entities expanded into a new being. We were the first true demon spawn to walk the earth."

"So you're not the same dude who started this joy ride?"

David shook his head. "While we have some memories of our original lives, there is no division. We are now 'I'."

"Well, it still confuses the hell out of me." I grabbed another granola bar and chewed on it. "Was dear old dad proud of you?"

My father burst into laughter. "He was horrified. He said that our very existence now relies on the weakest among us."

"What a bastard."

David shrugged. "He referred to me as the Prince of Weaklings."

I grimaced. "Baal is the king of asshats."

He chuckled.

Another question occurred to me. "Why possess humans when you can possess Seraphim?"

He wiped orange cheese dust from his hands. "We tried that. They're just too powerful spiritually. Other Seraphim know when one of their kind has been spiritually compromised. It's like they can smell the demon presence."

"Nothing like brimstone-scented body spray."

"Yeah. Our attempts at possessing Seraphim ended with the annihilation of the demons who tried it."

"Seraphim sound like the perfect meld between physical and spiritual."

"Not perfect," he said, "but darned close. The only demons powerful enough to possess someone like Daelissa are afraid to try."

"So they decided to use humans and demon spawn as cannon fodder," I said.

"You hit the proverbial nail on the head, son."

I opened my mouth to protest his use of the word "son", but the word actually sounded kind of good right then.

I felt a tremble in my body, and thought it was fatigue at first. My mind ran in circles with the information I'd learned. My father was the first demon spawn. I already knew my mother was the first angel to set foot in the mortal realm. But to find out even demons were afraid of Seraphim scared the padooky out of me. I shuddered grimaced at the pain it caused in my back.

My nerves knotted. My stomach tried to twist into an origami swan. This wasn't just exhaustion or aftereffects of the painkillers. The future terrified me. Daelissa was gathering her old allies, the vampires. She wasn't stopping there. Now she was going so far as to draft the Arcane Council into her lineup through Cyphanis Rax, the man running in the special election to replace Shelton's late father, Jarrod Sager. If the demons were afraid of the Seraphim, what hope did the rest of us have for defeating them?

"You're right," I said. "I wasn't ready for this."

"And I haven't even told you half of it yet," David said with a rueful look. "I was the first demon to meld with humans, but I wasn't the last."

"Who are the others?"

His lips curved up. "You've already met two other originals."

"I have?" I hadn't met many Daemos in fact, the only ones I remembered were—I felt my eyes widen.

David gave me a knowing look. "Your sweet Aunt Vallaena and my soon-to-be bride, Kassallandra."

Chapter 16

I couldn't believe what I was hearing. "Aunt Vallaena and Kassallandra are originals?"

He nodded. "Mine and Kassallandra's mates were killed in separate battles during the war. Two other houses of Daemos were annihilated by Seraphim assassins. Kassallandra came to me and demanded I marry her to unite our houses or she would defect to the Seraphim."

Why would she do that when the Seraphim are a threat to humans and demons?"

"Kassallandra didn't merge with her human. She had the woman poisoned and took over the body at the moment of death." His lip curled into a snarl. "The melding of human and demon souls tempers our demon edge. Even after all this time, she doesn't have a shred of humanity in her, though she's good at hiding it."

"What did Vallaena think about this marriage proposal?" I asked.

"Like me, she is also a scion of Baal and my true sister, but he actually has some small respect for her." He looked away. "She told me it was my duty."

"Obviously you never went through with it."

"No. I met Alysea, fell in love, and the Desecration ended the war and tore her from me." He ran a hand down his face. "I thought she was gone forever."

129

"She's back," I said.

His eyes diverted from my gaze, and he spoke in a whisper. "I know."

I still didn't understand. "Then why do you insist on marrying Kassallandra?"

"When the war ended, House Slade was reduced to a handful of members. Vallaena and I decided it would be best to hide my identity as the Paetros, and assigned two of my offspring as the patriarch and matriarch of House Slade. I pose as their son." He chuckled. "You ask me why I'm marrying Kassallandra, and the answer is very simple. If I refuse her hand again, if I don't agree to unite the two most powerful Daemos houses and declare her my right hand, she will enter negotiations with Daelissa and create an alliance with the enemy."

His words sent a shock into my heart. "That's crazy! Why would she help Daelissa?"

"Power, Justin." He blew out a long breath. "She has no concept of love, nor does she care for others. All she wants is power."

"At any cost?" I couldn't believe how short-sighted she was. "Daelissa will betray her the minute the war is won."

David nodded. "Kassallandra's demon sire is second only to Baal in Haedaemos. She sees herself as having less power than me, and is obsessed with proving to her sire that she can be the most powerful spawn in Eden."

I face-palmed. "Good lord. Does everyone in the universe have daddy issues?"

He burst into deep throated laughter. "At least she didn't become a stripper."

A snort burst from my nose, followed by a chuckle, each jolt of laughter sending knives of pain into my back. "Oh, ow, ow, ow." I gritted my teeth to stop the laughter. "You're an asshole, but at least you have a sense of humor."

He knelt next to me, pulled up my shirt, and looked at my back. "The skin is red and swollen. Maybe I should get you some antibiotics."

"Some anti-bacterial cream would be nice."

"You should take a painkiller. You're pale as a ghost." He grabbed the bottle of pills, took out one and gave me a bottle of water.

I popped the pill and swallowed.

My father arranged some blankets on the floor. "Lie down, and I'll be back in a jiffy, okay?"

I nodded, lying on my side, and resting my head on a bundled blanket.

My father placed a hand on my shoulder. "You're going to be okay."

His words sent a calming comfort through me. The world blurred as the painkiller kicked in. I tried to say something, but my lips no longer wanted to move. *Thanks, Dad.*

Once again, strange dreams of floating orbs haunted my sleep. I woke up face-down on a small mattress. I felt a warm smooth hand caress my cheek. It reminded me of another amazing dream I'd been having. I looked up and saw Elyssa smile down at me.

"Hey, baby," she said, and kissed me, her lips soft on my skin. "Sleep well?"

I nodded. "I was having such a bizarre nightmare. My father and I were captured by these crazy Exorcist people, and then we had to run from dinosaurs and vampires through the Gloom."

"You're home with me now."

"I'm so happy," I said, and rolled over to pull her into my arms and kiss her. Dull pain raced up my back and snapped me fully awake. Elyssa's raven hair hung like a curtain over me.

"Baby?" she asked, as her face started to melt.

I stifled a shout of surprise as I remembered where I was. Wincing, I pushed myself upright, and told the dream Elyssa to give me some space. My eyes caught the face of my mother and the flash of blonde hair as she vanished into the darkness around our circle of light. David's guilty eyes met mine.

"You certainly dream of your girlfriend a lot," he said with a smile that failed to hide a hint of sadness in his eyes.

A lump caught in my throat. Here we were, two men trapped in purgatory, both dreaming of the women we loved. "You miss her, don't you?"

131

His lips pressed tight, erasing the smirk. "Every minute of every day."

"For the first time, I think I can say I know exactly how you feel."

A nod. "I think this is one of those father-son bonding moments. Maybe we should share a beer to commemorate the occasion."

I shuddered at the memory of the last time we'd shared a beer. "Maybe you should stop using humor to deflect real emotions."

"You took that page right out of my book."

I groaned, and with great effort, pushed to my feet. "Guess you could say I'm a chip off the old demonic block."

"More than you know, son."

A stab of pain hit me in the gut. "You can't just throw that word around casually. It used to mean something to me, you know."

"It still means something to me."

I shook my head. "Remember the whole, 'he will serve and die' convo?"

"Of course, but—"

"Yeah. I don't think the word 'son' carries any weight with you." I shrugged. "Then again, the universe is full of daddy issues."

"Don't forget dad jokes," he said.

"Like the time when I was five and you convinced me roaches were aliens, and when I tried to talk to one, you squished it and said we'd just started an intergalactic war?"

He beamed. "Gotta admit it was hilarious."

I pinched my eyebrows. "I lived in constant fear of roaches for months after that. I thought they were all out to assassinate us."

David roared with laughter. "Really?"

"Yes, really, you jackass. Worst dad joke ever!" I looked around for something to throw at him but a glimmer of light caught my eyes. I looked up as the space between the columns of the Obsidian arch rippled and undulated. A thin line split the air, and I saw people standing across the room.

"What the—" my father stood next to me. "Isn't that the Grotto way station?"

132

"Yes," I said. "And those are people. We can go home!" I watched as a man riding an elephant guided it toward us and the arch. "Let's go."

"Hang on," David said, and stepped toward the portal. He stopped in front of it, and reached out a tentative hand. His palm pressed against the air. "I don't think we can go through."

I limped over, each step sending sharp pains into my body from the slice across my back. My fingers probed the glimmering gateway to freedom, and found solid resistance. "No, this can't be."

"What a tease," David said, and pounded a fist against the invisible barrier. "Son of a—"

"Remember, use that dad humor to deflect the anger," I said, unable to resist curling my lip with frustration. I shouted out the worst curse words I knew, and started waving my arms at the man on the elephant. "Help! Send in the Templars, we're trapped in the Gloom!"

Neither man nor elephant seemed to hear a thing as they walked straight toward us. In fact, I couldn't hear them, even when the elephant curled its trunk upward as if trumpeting. Just when it looked like man and beast were about to hit us, they vanished.

"It's like looking through a mirror," I said.

The looking glass vanished, leaving the room in a still dimness. As if to put an exclamation point on the depression blooming in my chest, the aether fog rolled in on us, thick and suffocating.

A moment later, another portal winked into being, and we watched helplessly as a family of laughing people floated toward us on a flying carpet until they vanished. Judging from the line of people waiting across the room, I had a feeling the portal would be opening often. Sure enough, we witnessed everything from a pack of werewolves to vampires dressed in business suits go about their travel in the real world while we could only sit by and watch.

There was at least one positive to the torture. It was daytime in the real world. The Exorcists had tossed us in the Gloom in the late afternoon. We'd been here less than twenty-four hours, but it felt like days.

133

Once I got over the bitter taste in my mouth, I decided to be productive, and analyzed the situation. As a young girl wearing a sari rode a Bengal tiger the size of a car toward the arch, I realized something interesting. Each time the arch activated, the aether fog retreated, leaving a bubble of space around the traversion zone within the large silver circle.

A metal spear whistled past, bounced off the portal, and sent a ripple across it. I flinched, and grunted in pain thanks to the wound in my back. I looked back at David. "Did you really think a spear gun would work?"

He snarled, teeth flashing fiercely, picked up a ten-pound weightlifting plate, and hurled it at the portal. It bounced off and clanged to the ground. "This is really pissing me off."

"I'm not happy about it either," I said. "It's like the frigging Gloom is taunting us."

The faint echo of laughter reached my ears, followed by voices.

David and I looked at each other.

"Sounds like a group of real people," he said. "I don't think they're dreams."

Chapter 17

David's eyes ran over our little campsite and widened. "Go hide," he said, bundling my mattress and throwing it into the fog where it vanished from view.

"What are you doing?" I asked.

"We don't want them to know we're here."

"Why are they coming here?" I asked.

He jabbed a finger at the place where the arch usually stood. "What do you think?"

I grabbed a satchel with food and dragged it into the fog. My stomach rumbled nervously, or maybe it was just sick of all the granola bars and cheesy poofs. Locking down my nerves, I opened my incubus senses. A shock of delight ran through me the moment I found the newcomers—not because I knew them, but because two of them were female. I sensed at least five men. Most of them seemed in good spirits—all except for one woman who seemed immensely sad. Her mood matched mine. I couldn't imagine how anyone could be happy in this hellhole.

David suddenly appeared next to me.

"Is that dried blood?" a man said from the direction of the arch ring, he and his companions hidden by the dense fog. I realized with a shock, the man sounded like one of the two who'd come for us in the church right after we'd arrived.

135

"My god, I think you're right," replied one of the females in a disgusted voice. "It's real blood."

"Poor soul," said another woman, her voice soft and compassionate. "How awful."

Another man sighed. "Calm down, Theresa. Probably another newbie who killed himself with a dream apparition."

"Not the first time," suggested the first male voice.

"So much blood," said Theresa. "I hope they didn't suffer."

Someone shouted. "I found the body. Looks like something bit his head off."

"I don't want to see it," Theresa cried out.

"Enough of the drama," a gruff male voice said. "We've got a quota to fill."

"What's on the list, Jarvis?" the other female asked. Her voice sounded deeper than Theresa's.

"Two more Arcanes and a vampire," Jarvis replied, his rough voice easily discernible from the others. "Set up the ripper."

I heard scuffling and a squeaking noise.

"When are you going to learn to dreamcast a cart that doesn't have a bad wheel, Gavin?" the other female said in a chiding voice. "Do you know how annoying it is listening to that thing?"

"Carts always have squeaky wheels," replied one of the men whose voice I recognized from the church—presumably Gavin. He had a deep southern accent. "Besides, Pat, don't you always need something to complain about?"

"I knew you did it just to bug me," Pat grumbled.

I heard grunting and the clang of metal on stone followed by more grunts and a grating sound.

"It's ready," Gavin said.

"Test it," came the gravelly voice of Jarvis through the fog.

Ratcheting clicks and a low-pitched hum emanated from the direction of the arch. "As usual, it's working fine." Gavin sounded disgruntled.

"All right. Turn it off and get ready," Jarvis said.

Light suffused the fog from ahead. David touched my arm. "I'm going in for a closer look. Wait here."

136

"Are you crazy?" I whispered.

"We need to know what this ripper thing is, and what these people are doing." He moved forward in a crouch.

While I waited, I decided to experiment. As of yet, I hadn't had the typical demonic hunger pains that usually occurred when I needed to replenish the essence my infernal side required for supernatural activities. Either the Gloom repressed the hunger, or since I hadn't been able to use my super strength or healing, I simply wasn't hungry. Extending my essence like a snaking probe, I found one of the women about thirty feet away. I almost flinched when I realized how close she was. After calming my emotions, I gently tapped into her.

Immediately, I noticed something different about the way her soul essence felt. It was noticeably muted, as if something was damming up a portion of it. From what I could tell, she was a normal human, or nom, as the supers called them. She seemed sad and upset. If I had to guess, this woman was Theresa, and not Pat.

I also noticed a lack of response from my demon side. It usually jumped at the chance to feed, but now I could hardly sense it. Vallaena had taught me the souls of demon spawn had two halves—a fact which made all the more sense given what David had told me about how our species had come about.

The demon side resided in the Haedaemos while the human side resided in Eden. My demon side lusted for power and would try to overpower my control if I didn't work hard to keep it contained. This was usually a factor in feeding because unchecked, the demon half would arouse extreme lust in my targets. That half usually surged against my control every time I fed. That wasn't happening now, as if an extra barrier were separating us. Even so, I felt a very faint pressure deep inside.

I drew on the woman's energy. It felt weak, like watered down fruit juice. I felt the energy enter me in a trickle. Not daring to open the throttle wider, I fed slowly for several minutes. By this point, I should have felt a surge of energy. Instead, I felt only a mild boost. The pressure from my demon side swelled slightly, as if it could smell the soul essence but couldn't quite get to it.

137

David returned just as I disconnected from the woman.

"They're looking for particular people every time the arch opens," he said. "They have some kind of device right in the center of where the arch would be. It looks like a U with a wide, flat base, and two diagonal prongs with orbs on either end." He drew a shape in the air with his hand.

"What does it do?" I asked.

He shrugged. "They haven't reactivated it yet."

I told him about my attempt to feed. "Something isn't right with her soul," I said.

"Maybe she should go to church more often." He quirked an eyebrow.

"This isn't the time for dad jokes," I said. "I don't think it's her, though."

"What do you think it is?"

My mind ran over the oddities I'd encountered and settled on a theory. "I think the Gloom is causing it. It's like part of me and part of her is stuck behind a thin barrier and can't quite break through."

The glow from a forming portal suffused the fog. David pointed a thumb at himself and pointed ahead. "Be right back."

He crept away. I decided I wanted to see this strange device for myself and eased to my feet, gritting my teeth against the pain in my back. I couldn't afford to take another pill. Loopy as those things made me, I'd be a sitting duck. I moved forward, careful to keep my tread silent as possible. Without warning, I stepped into a bubble of clear space and saw the group of Gloom people staring intently at the portal. Before they could notice me, I stepped back behind the curtain of aether fog, and cautiously poked my face through.

"That's an Arcane," said a short woman with close-cropped red hair. She sounded like Pat.

"Duh, you think?" said a stocky man whose voice identified him as Gavin. "Maybe the robes gave it away?"

"I hate this part," said a willowy woman with long brown hair.

Gavin glared at her. "It's our job, Theresa. I don't know why—
"

"Shut your mouths," a pudgy man—Jarvis—said.

138

I paced the perimeter of the bubble of clear air until I could see inside the portal. A lanky man in dark blue robes, a compact staff hanging from a holster on his side, and a thick sheaf of scrolls bound by red ribbons beneath one arm, walked toward the group.

Jarvis drew a thick cigar from his shirt pocket, and put it in his mouth. "Grab him."

Pat and Theresa went to either side of the U-shaped device David had described. Two thick prongs with spheres at the end jutted upward at slight angles. Each woman stood to the side of the prongs, waiting as the Arcane approached. A few steps before he reached the portal in the real world, the women pulled the prongs like levers. The rods clicked apart at a wider angle. With a throbbing hum, silver light flashed between the orbs, coalescing into a ball of energy. The portal shimmered, rippled, and split.

Energy roared into me. I felt my demonic half jerk awake, as if the barrier between my souls had dissolved. A grim lethargy I hadn't even realized was there lifted from my shoulders. I sensed women on the other side of the portal. I felt their vital burning energies beckoning me. The burning pain in my back receded and strength swelled within my muscles. It felt like I'd just escaped a burning building and tasted sweet fresh air.

The Arcane stepped through the portal. He looked up from an arcphone and glanced at the group of grim people standing around him. The women pushed the prongs toward each other. The silver energy winked out and the rip in the portal closed and winked out.

My body felt like it turned to lead. The vibrancy in the air vanished, and my strength along with it.

"Where am I?" the Arcane said. "This isn't Queens Gate."

"Welcome to your new home," Jarvis said. "What's your name?"

"New home?" The man jerked away as two of the other men approached him threateningly. "Leave me alone. I'll have you know I'm not defenseless." He withdrew the compact rod at his side, and shook it out to a full-length staff. His eyes narrowed in concentration, then widened with confusion. "What are you doing to me? Why can't I cast a spell?"

139

One of the unidentified men chuckled. "I always love this moment."

The two men closed in and grabbed the man by his arms. One of them administered what looked like a hypodermic needle to the Arcane's neck. The prisoner slumped, and they loaded him into a cart. The portal in the real world vanished, and fog rolled back into the area, obscuring it from sight.

I made my way back around the perimeter and nearly ran into David. He gave me a confused look.

"Why didn't you stay put?"

"I had to see what they were doing."

He pulled guided me away from the portal staging area. "When they ripped open the portal, I felt normal again."

"Me too," I said, stretching my sore back. I paused, arms extended overhead. "My back isn't killing me anymore."

He pulled up my shirt and looked. "It's almost healed. I'd still take it easy for now."

I breathed a sigh of relief. "I felt normal too. That ripper thing seems to open the barrier between the Gloom and the real world. Do you know what that means?"

"It's our ticket out of this place."

Hope burgeoned inside me. The ripper was the answer to our dreams. *The way home.*

"They're getting more people," I said. "That means they'll be using it again."

David nodded. "We'll have our powers back when they open the window. We can overpower them and run back through."

I nodded enthusiastically until I remembered the captured Arcane and the menacing kidnappers lurking in the Gloom. Who were these Gloom people, and how many people had they abducted? I felt my smile fade.

David's eyes narrowed. "What's wrong?"

"We can't just leave that man there. We can't let these people continue to take people like this." I reached my arm around at an awkward angle to scratch my healing back. "We should follow them and find out what this is all about."

140

David put a hand on my shoulder and looked me directly in the eyes. "While that's very noble of you, I think it's also very shortsighted."

I poked him in the chest with a finger. "Maybe you don't care about saving people, but I do. I'm going to do this with or without you."

He rolled his eyes. "That's not what I'm saying, Justin."

It was my turn to narrow my eyes. "Explain."

"These are the people who came for us back in the church, and they're the same ones that kidnapped Timothy."

"Obviously."

"They're working for Daelissa." David pointed in their general direction. "We don't know what kind of operation these people have. We don't know their numbers or their capabilities. For all we know they're masters at dreamcasting creatures like Gloria Richardson and could quickly capture or kill us." He pointed his thumb over a shoulder. "Those people might be just the tip of the iceberg."

"I'm not suggesting we plow in without recon." Elyssa had, on occasion, accused me of leaping without looking, but I'd learned my lesson. "We'll follow them and watch."

"Again, you're being shortsighted. We aren't experts at extracting people from the Gloom. We're not equipped to take on these people. You, however, know Templars who are, and you have access to large numbers of them."

"Oh," I said, letting the O drag out a bit to indicate a light bulb had turned on inside my thick skull. "We should escape now and bring back the cavalry."

"Exactly."

I waggled my head side-to-side. "That could work. I guess all those centuries of wisdom are finally paying off."

He snorted. "Here's what we do. We wait at the edge of the fog bubble when the portal opens. Right when those women activate the ripper, we charge in, take out the group, and go through the portal. If possible, we'll bring the ripper with us so we can use it from the other side."

141

"Works for me," I said. "Maybe we can grab the prisoner on the way out."

He shook his head. "No. We can't risk getting stuck here." David sighed and pursed his lips. "Look, I know you want to save him now, but if we don't get through, we won't be saving anyone. For all we know, they have dozens of prisoners."

"Fine. Maybe he'll be okay until we get back."

The light of a portal activation caught our attention. David motioned me to follow. We walked up to the edge of the bubble, knelt, and waited. A group of men were herding a flock of sheep toward the portal. My father and I looked at each other with puzzled looks.

"Overworld people are strange," I whispered.

He nodded.

The Gloom people waited and watched through several more portal activations before deciding to kidnap a lone vampire. Even though I couldn't see fangs, the pallor of the man's face and his impeccable sense of style identified him right away. Apparently, torn and faded jeans were out of fashion if the skinny jeans he wore were any indication.

The women took positions on either side of the ripper and waited until the vampire was paces away from entering the portal. They pulled back on the rods and activated the device. The gateway shimmered and split. Strength poured into me. David counted down from three with his fingers. We raced into the circle.

The first two men didn't stand a chance. David flung one through the fog as if he weighed nothing. I ducked under a swing from the second and punched his lights out. Jarvis took out a gun, aimed, and fired at David. My father blurred to the side, leapt, and landed atop the man, delivering a vicious blow.

The women shrieked and jumped away from the disruptor. The vampire, still in the real world, stopped, looking around with a puzzled look.

"Did someone just scream?" he said.

"Go, Justin!" David yelled.

142

"Who the hell is Justin?" The vampire looked even more confused.

I ran for the portal at full speed, reached the split in the barrier. A blinding flash of silver energy crashed into me like a sledgehammer. My body rebounded from the portal and slammed into my father who was right on my heels. We skidded backwards across the smooth obsidian floor and landed in a heap.

"Doesn't work like that," Pat said. "It's set up for one-way, you morons."

"Get them," Jarvis croaked, pushing himself off the floor.

I looked up and saw the vampire backing away from the portal, alarm in his eyes.

Bullets pinged off the floor around us. David and I flashed to our feet, and raced from the circle of clear air, back into the fog. The further we ran, the weaker I felt. I estimated we hadn't gone more than a few hundred yards.

"Oh, no," I gasped. "We can't use it to escape."

We were still trapped in the Gloom.

Chapter 18

David bared his teeth and growled. Slamming a fist into the palm of his other hand, he paced in a compact circle. "Mother f—"

I grabbed his shoulder. "Look, I'm just as pissed as you are, but this isn't going to solve anything." Elyssa had taught me that raging rarely solved anything. "Maybe we can backtrack to the Gloom portal instead of wasting our time at the Grotto arch, and I'll try opening it again. The Exorcists might have removed whatever is blocking it." I highly doubted it, but it wasn't safe to remain here.

He sucked in a breath between clenched teeth. Nodded. "This situation is extremely annoying." Arms folded across his chest, he tapped a finger on his triceps and looked back toward the kidnappers. "We should follow these people and find out where they're based. The woman said the ripper was set to one-way. There must be a way to allow us to go through."

"You want to steal it?" I asked.

He nodded. "It's our best bet."

"Might as well come back," Jarvis called through the fog. "There's no way out of the Gloom. I promise we won't hurt you."

I almost yelled back a response, but David put a hand over my mouth and shook his head. "Don't give away our position."

I nodded, and he removed his hand.

"We offer safe refuge from the dreams," Jarvis said. "Safe lodging and human companionship."

144

David sat down, closed his eyes in concentration. I'd seen him do the same thing just before his crawler had torn poor Timothy's head clean off. I listened to Jarvis as he droned on about giving up, and kept a sharp eye out in case the Gloomies had spread out to look for us. A figure appeared out of the fog and nearly gave me a heart attack. It was a replica of David.

My father stood and inspected his handiwork for a moment. "It was harder than I thought imagining how I look. I guess I don't use a mirror enough." His doppelganger sprinted away into the fog. Several seconds later, I heard my father's voice ring out, though it was the clone speaking and not him.

"You're kidnapping people. Why should we trust you?"

Jarvis replied, voice smug. "You really have no choice."

"Tell me what you're doing with the Arcane."

"You can ask our leader. She's the one with the answers."

David's clone laughed. "You're kidnapping people and you don't even know why? There's no way I can trust you."

I heard sounds of scuffling.

"We found him!" someone shouted. "Where's the other guy?"

"Let me go," David's clone said.

"Tell us where your friend is, or I'll kill you," said the other man.

"He panicked and ran away into the fog. I don't know where he is," the clone said.

"What do you want us to do with him, Jarvis?"

"Is he a vampire?" their glorious leader replied.

"No."

"An Arcane?"

"Don't think so. I'm thinking werewolf or demon spawn."

Jarvis remained silent a moment before responding. "Knock him out and put him with the Arcane. I'll let Serena decide."

I heard a grunt, presumably as fake David was knocked unconscious. My father laughed quietly. "I love deceiving people."

"You're a demon. It's your job," I said.

He winked. "Can't deny it's a fun perk."

145

"The arch operators are shutting down the arch for inspections," Pat said. "That stupid vampire must have heard the commotion. I think we're done here for the day."

Jarvis shouted a volley of curse words. "Load up the equipment and we'll head back."

"I've got the mule ready," Pat said.

"Maybe you could figure out how to make us all horses so we could ride in style," Gavin said. "I'm sick of making the hike."

"I can only dreamcast one thing at a time, so you'll have to just walk."

"Shut your complaining trap," Jarvis said.

"Hope I can keep my clone from melting," David said.

I turned to my father. "You seemed to whip it up pretty fast. How'd you do it?"

"Meditation. It's a skill that's kept me sane over the years." He blew out a breath. "We'll have to use our senses to track these people through the fog, and keep a safe distance. We don't know how skilled they are at dreamcasting. They might have their own creatures guarding them."

I shuddered at the thought of bumping into a nightmare like the crawler. "True."

Within a few minutes, Jarvis and crew headed up the winding driveway leading from the Grotto and headed down a road I knew led to the southwest side of town. Even without my incubus senses, following the group wasn't too hard with Jarvis occasionally shouting orders, and the wheel squeaking on the cart they used to pull the ripper.

We walked for miles. My legs and feet ached. I found myself agreeing with Gavin's sentiment about conjuring a horse to ride on and put it at the top of my list of priorities when and if I had time. If Timothy could create a dinosaur, surely I could dreamcast a beast of burden. Dreamcasting Elyssa to give me a piggy-back ride seemed undignified, even if it wasn't really her. We crossed a wide swath of railroad tracks I recognized as the ones used by MARTA, the rail transport system in Atlanta. While I hadn't come this way before, I

146

remembered driving by while on the nearby interstate in the real world.

Once past the tracks, we crossed a road and headed down a street. The heavily worn asphalt was pockmarked with holes and laced with cracks. Bits and pieces of gray granite littered the surface, as if fallen from the back of a truck. We followed a curve in the road and suddenly stood in a huge clearing, free of fog. David and I hurriedly stepped back behind the curtain of gray, and poked our heads into the clear air.

A large gray fortress stretched before us on a landscape of dead grass and bare patches of red clay.

"A quarry," David said, pointing to a nearby sign which stated *Bellwood Quarry—authorized personnel only beyond this point.*

"Why is there no fog here?" I asked.

He shrugged. "No idea."

We examined the area from our hidden position, watching as the Gloomies wheeled their equipment inside. No fence guarded the perimeter, nor did there seem to be doors barring entry into the grim gray structure.

"This Serena must be a mad scientist," I said. "Because nobody in their right mind would willingly live in a place like this."

"This building doesn't exist in the mortal realm," he said.

"I've never been here," I said, "so I wouldn't know."

David ran his eyes up and down the length of the area. "I wonder if they dreamcasted it into existence, or built it."

I shivered. "I can't imagine how much concentration it would take to keep a building like this from melting away."

"I wasn't expecting anything like this." He rested his chin on a fist. "There's no way we could sneak in and steal the ripper."

"Is your clone still intact?"

His eyes narrowed. "I think so. I don't know if there's a limit to how far away it can go, but I'm not particularly worried about it."

"I wonder if we could use it to spy."

"It's essentially a puppet. If there's a way to have it transmit what it sees and hears, I don't know how to do it."

147

We watched the building for several minutes in silence. I didn't know what to do at this point. "Should we go back to the Grotto?" I asked.

"You heard those people. The arch operators shut down the Obsidian Arch for safety inspections." He folded his arms and stared into space. "It could be days before it resumes operations."

"We don't have many options at this point."

David seemed to mull it over. "Even if we steal a ripper, we'd have to hope they didn't notice it was gone. It's not like there's another Obsidian Arch to use it on."

The last thing I felt like doing was walking, but we had no choice. I extended my senses toward the fortress, hoping to get an idea about the number of people inside, but the structure lay too far away for me to reach.

An iron grip took me by the bicep. David grunted. Before I could look to see what had me, someone pushed me forward into the clear area. A humanoid creature without a face or other features on its pale white form held David in a similar fashion to me. He struggled, but the thing marched him forward without missing a beat. The one holding me pushed me along at a similar pace despite my attempts to resist.

"They're dreamcasted like Timothy's raptor," David said. He bared his teeth, but didn't resist the things herding us along.

I added in my optimistic two cents. "We're so screwed."

The guards took us inside the fortress and shoved us inside a holding cell along with the Arcane Jarvis and the others had captured earlier. The man was still unconscious.

"Guess we get the tour anyway," David said in a grim voice.

The windowless cell was constructed of smooth gray stone. I ran a hand along the surface and found it neither cool nor warm, much like the atmosphere of the Gloom. I sat down on the bare floor and looked at the door made of the same material as the cell walls. If the place had been dreamcasted, the creator hadn't used much imagination in the process. Then again, maybe simple construction made it easier to maintain.

After what seemed like an hour, the door swung open, and Jarvis appeared, flanked by two of the pale mannequin creatures. "Looks like you decided to join us after all," he said. "Clever trick with the replica, but you didn't hold its shape for long."

"Is this what you call hospitality?" David said, standing. "Or do you plan to show us to the guest rooms?"

Jarvis snorted. "Unless Serena has a use for you, ain't much chance of seeing the outside of this cell."

"Who is this Serena?" David asked.

"If you're lucky, you'll get to meet her." He took out a notepad. "Now, what are your names, and type?"

"I'm Bucky," my father said. "I like long walks in the park, and curling up next to a warm fire with a good book and a glass of wine. I guess my type would be hopeless romantic."

One of the mannequins stepped inside the cell and swatted a backhand at David. My father dodged back, narrowly avoiding the blow.

"What's the matter? Don't like romantics?"

"Shut your trap, or I'll have a sentinel break your jaw."

I shoved ahead of my father before he provoked Jarvis any further. "I'm Justin Slade. This is my father David. We were sent through an arch by the Exorcists."

Jarvis narrowed his small eyes then jotted the information down on his notepad. "So you're the two demon spawn that got away from Gavin and Stephan yesterday." He snorted. "Morons."

I decided not to pile on and changed the subject. "Did someone dreamcast this place?"

"How do you know about dreamcasting?"

"We overheard you talking about it," I said. "You're obviously the leader around here, so I assumed you'd know all there is to know." I figured stroking the man's ego couldn't hurt.

Jarvis nodded. "You're right I'm in charge and answer only to Serena. If you know what's good for you, you'll do as I say."

"I understand," I said. "Did you dreamcast this fortress? It's amazing."

149

A smug look came over his face. "No, but I designed it myself. The superstructure is constructed of granite brought in from the real world. Some parts of this place are dreamcasted while others are real." He patted the gray wall. "The trick is, only me and a few others know which parts are real, and which are dreamcasted."

"I'll bet you came up with the sentinels too," I said, looking the one in the cell up and down. "They scare the hell out of me."

"All mine," he replied, looking even more pleased with himself. "Not only are they physically perfect, but the built-in fear factor adds a psychological edge."

"Absolutely." I looked at the sentinel with fear in my eyes.

He crossed his arms and bared his teeth. "I run a tight ship here, just the way Serena likes it."

"You certainly caught us fast," I said.

"Look, I didn't mean any disrespect," David said, expression contrite. "It's good to find a man who knows how to survive in the Gloom."

Jarvis relaxed perceptibly. "We ain't got much use for demon spawn, but then again, neither do the Exorcists." He burst into rough laughter. "We could always use more help with manual labor. If you behave yourselves, I'll make sure Serena don't work you too hard."

Apparently, Jarvis didn't realize Daelissa had sent us through. The angel had mentioned Serena at the time, so perhaps she was the only one who knew what horrors lay in store for us here.

Jarvis continued to brag about how important he was before assuring us he was the only hope we had for living a comfortable life. "We'll make good use of you. How nasty the work is will depend on how well you obey me." Jarvis looked at the sentinel. It turned and left the cell. "And if you really piss me off, I can always throw you in the pit." The door slid shut with a dull thud.

David held a finger to his mouth. I extended my senses and detected Jarvis just outside the door, probably eavesdropping to hear if we were making escape plans.

"That's what a leader looks like," David said with a wink. "We need to make sure we do everything he says, because he's the one who can keep us safe."

150

"He seems really smart too," I said. "Can you imagine how much military knowledge it takes to build a place like this?"

Jarvis's mood switched from suspicious to pleased. I couldn't usually read men as well as women, but the man had a huge ego, and we'd just stoked it into a furnace. His presence faded. My father and I exchanged knowing looks.

"Good job, son. You have a bright future as a master manipulator."

I rolled my eyes. "Hardly my life's ambition." I regarded the door for a moment. "How do you think he opens the door? There's a handle, but no lock."

"I was wondering the same thing." He examined it. "It's either dreamcasted, or uses some kind of facial recognition spell."

I leaned against the wall and looked at the cell. "I keep thinking back to my Elyssa clone."

"My company not good enough?" David smiled.

I shook my head. "It's not that. I'm talking about how I controlled her simply by thinking about it."

"I'm following."

"What would happen if I'd made my clone of Elyssa fight Timothy's raptor? Dreamcasted beings seem impossibly strong, so which one would win?"

"Interesting question," David said, tapping a finger to his chin. "When you stop actively controlling a unit, it'll just stand there and eventually deconstruct. When we attacked Timothy, he lost control of the raptor. It seems to take a certain amount of willpower to create and control."

"So, if two dreamcasted beings fought, it would essentially be a contest of wills?"

"Yeah, I think so." He paused. "Your will would have to overpower the other person's."

"If these walls are dreamcasted, I could conceivably imagine a hole in one if I could overpower the will of the person maintaining it."

David shrugged. "Possibly. The problem is we don't know what's real and what's not."

151

"I just wonder if attempts to imagine a hole in a dreamcasted wall would alert the person who created it."

"It might." He ran a hand along the smooth wall. "Maybe we should see how this plays out before we attempt anything like that. Plus, we don't know how many of those sentinels would come running. We might be able to overpower one person's will, but not a team of them."

"Do you really think there's a team of people manifesting those sentinels?"

He mulled it for a moment. "I can't see any other way, unless they have some very gifted individuals."

"If only I could go into a dream state more easily." I felt the bottle of painkillers in my pocket. "Popping more pills isn't going to cut it."

"You're already capable of meditating if you know how to spawn to demon form or summon hellhounds at will," he said. "Reaching inside yourself and drawing out the inner demon takes a great deal of concentration."

"If you say so," I replied. "Maybe you could give me a few tips."

"I'd be happy to," he said. "Doesn't look like there's much else to do at the moment." He regarded me. "Vallaena said you learned quickly. She even admitted you beat her in a fight."

"She admitted that to you?" I said. "I find it hard to imagine someone with that much pride could admit defeat."

"Let's just say she's so proud of her accomplishments at teaching you, it overwhelmed her usual sense of self-importance." David chuckled. "I haven't seen that happen very often." He sat down, and patted the floor across from him.

I mimicked his cross-legged position. "Do I have to hum and close my eyes?"

"Nah," he said, batting the air with a hand. "But entering a lucid trance is a bit different than reaching for your inner demon. You have to enter a waking dream."

"Like hallucinating?" I said.

"Exactly."

"Get me some heroin and I'll be good to go."

His expression turned serious. "Let's keep the quips to a minimum, or you won't learn anything."

The look on his face sobered me. *Time to live the dream.*

Our lives could depend on it.

Chapter 19

"I want you to reach for your inner demon," David said.

I closed my eyes and reached inside. The barrier between me and the other half of my soul was still there, like a glass prison.

"I know you can't reach the demon, but I want you to maintain this concentration for a moment," David's disembodied voice said from outside the void.

Holding the emptiness wasn't hard. When I'd learned to summon hellhounds, I'd had to reach through the window of my soul to the demon plane and draw through lesser spirits which could be conjured in the real world as the huge demon dogs, though my first attempt had been outright embarrassing. Instead of a monster hound, I'd spawned a pipsqueak the size of a Chihuahua. Rather than banish him back to the demon plane, I'd kept the little guy as a pet and named him Cutsauce. Realizing my thoughts were running on wild tangents, I quashed them and settled back into the darkness.

"Pretend you are weightless, floating in water. You are numb to all outside stimulus."

The Gloom's neutral temperature made that easier than normal. The darkness drew me deeper and deeper into blank infinity.

My eyes flicked open. I stood on a precipice between two rivers. The rivers bubbled and churned like lava. One was blinding white, the other dark ultraviolet. The sliver of land I stood on was gray.

"Oh, crap. Not this again." This was obviously a different twist on the visions I'd had earlier. But the dreamlike quality was absent. This felt real. *Maybe because I'm in a lucid trance.* I took a breath and steeled myself as the weight of the looming decision pressed down on me. If previous visions were any indication, the choice I made here could determine the fate of the world.

No pressure.

I wondered if this was the universe prodding me to take matters in hand, or if some part of my consciousness knew my efforts to stop Daelissa had hit a standstill unless I claimed one side over the others.

Consider all possibilities.

In the past, Daelissa and Nightliss had been present in these visions. Now they were absent, and everything was boiled down to the two essentials—the Brilliance, or the Murk. As a Brightling, Daelissa represented the former. Nightliss, as a Darkling, represented the latter. If I was choosing on personalities alone, Nightliss's side won hands down. But the vision of the park flashed past in my mind, and I felt a deep certainty choosing either of those sides wasn't the right path.

Haven't I already chosen?

Foreseeance Forty-Three Eleven had supposedly been fulfilled when Ivy and I hadn't tried to kill each other. Was this still part of that prophecy, or something completely different?

Think, Justin, think!

I regarded the two rivers for several minutes and suddenly realized there was a third choice. Between the darkness and the light stood the gray. A Seraphim I'd aptly nicknamed Mr. Gray occupied that space. I'd only met him once, and even then briefly. Supposedly, he was manipulating events to prevent either side from winning because he wanted to maintain the status quo.

I hesitated to call him a neutral third party since his golems had tried to take me out of the picture on several occasions. Even with his position as the Switzerland of the Overworld, I wondered if choosing the gray was really a choice at all. Pressure built in my chest, demanding I do something to make known my affiliation.

155

Pushing back the desire to get this over with quickly, I stretched my back and looked at the roiling gray sky close overhead. I hadn't noticed it before since I'd been so intent on jumping in the correct river. As I stared at the sky, I realized it bubbled and frothed just like the light and dark rivers, except it was flowing in the opposite direction.

The third side.

I thought back to the vision of the park and remembered the gray statue of myself. All had been in order, and nothing ever changed. It sounded just as bad as the other alternatives. Did the gray represent balance, or something else?

Should I choose gray, dark, or light? I wondered why the other colors of the rainbow didn't have a say in this. Or was color just a meaningless detail? I looked at the horizon in front of me. A vortex of white and ultraviolet swirled upward from their respective rivers into the gray. Behind me, I saw a large gray vortex spinning down and splitting into white and dark.

One big endless cycle.

White and black came from gray. They combined again to form gray.

Does color matter or is this simply how my mind interprets it?

If aether really came from the dreams, nightmares, and thoughts of people in the real world, supers and noms alike, it meant negative and positive thoughts created the very source of magic. Our hopes, dreams, and fears formed those thoughts. I sucked in a breath as something of an epiphany hit me. I had things reversed. Dreams were a byproduct of our emotions and thoughts. Those all came from our souls. Dreams weren't the source of aether. Magical energy originated in our *souls*.

"Holy socks," I said, unable to come up with a proper Shelton expression.

I lacked a psychology degree and wasn't a religious expert, but my theory just felt right to me. Even if I was right, the knowledge didn't bring me any closer to making a decision. I had to make a choice.

156

I stared at the molten ultraviolet energy. Nightliss had always been there for me. She was a good person, and I loved her as a friend. On the other hand, my mother was a Brightling. Since rescuing her from the Conroys, I'd gotten to know her and learned a lot about her past. She'd made some poor decisions over the centuries, but she definitely wasn't an evil person. Daelissa, on the other hand, was crazy and evil. My mind returned to Mr. Gray. He seemed amoral to the point that he would do anything to maintain the balance no matter if it required murder or mayhem.

I didn't know any evil Darklings, but Nightliss had told me about plenty of her kind who'd joined forces with the Brightlings. Maybe that didn't make them evil, but it certainly didn't make them good.

I shouted in frustration and threw up my hands.

How could I make a decision when all sides seem to have their faults? In light of my wonderful vision of that awful park, none of them seemed the way to go.

Mr. Gray once told me the two primal forces in the universe were the Brilliance, destruction, and the Murk, creation. But if his theory of a middle place held true, it also meant there was a primal anti-force—stasis.

Thinking in terms of destruction, creation, and stasis removed the good-evil element from the equation. Each had their merits. Sometimes it was necessary to tear down something old and to create something new. A new creation could be used to tear down an old one.

I'm overthinking this, as usual.

My inner ramblings were only making a decision that much harder. It was so much easier to take a black-and-white approach, declare something evil, the other thing good, and make the decision based on absolute morals. Unfortunately, this wasn't a long time ago in a galaxy far away, and things weren't so clear cut.

Staring at the three possibilities, at the tornadoes of energy cycling the aether around and around and around, the correct decision suddenly hit me in the chest. It felt so right, I knew I had to make it immediately.

157

"Justin?"

Something stung my face. I jerked awake. David's concerned eyes hovered a few inches from my own.

"Ouch," I said, rubbing my cheek. I felt woozy and disoriented. Looking around, I saw the plain gray walls of our prison.

"Where were you?" my father asked.

"Wasn't I here?" I said.

He tapped a finger on my forehead. "Not exactly. Your mind went somewhere far away."

I told him about the vision.

"Sounds a lot like the other ones you told me about."

"It started the minute I entered the Gloom." I told him about the time Shelton and I had nearly been sucked into a Gloom rift. "It felt like something was calling me to come here." I shrugged off an uneasy feeling. "It's like I'm supposed to be here."

"Talk about lousy accommodations," he said.

"After looking at everything from all angles, I realized that maybe there's a fourth alternative."

His eyebrows pinched. "Really? What is that?"

I met his gaze. "I want to have my cake and eat it too."

His eyes brightened. "A man after my own heart. Must be your demon heritage."

I shrugged. "Why can't I choose all three? I feel like if I don't do something soon, I'll go crazy."

"Let me tell you a little secret," he said, looking at the snoring Arcane for a moment as if making sure the man wouldn't overhear. "As your mother may have explained to you, Seraphim naturally side with the light or the dark once they near a certain age. Your mother told me she often dreamed of diving into a lake of pure milky white, a clear indication her affinity was with the Brilliance."

"Mom had these dreams too?"

"From what she told me, all Seraphim dream about their affinity when the time is closing in and are driven to it."

I stared blankly for a moment. "In other words, they don't have a choice about which side they want to choose."

"Exactly."

158

"Then, why do I have a choice?"

"Here's another secret you might find interesting," David said. "Demons also have an affinity for either side."

"What?"

He nodded. "It's true. Our affinities are far more complex, however. Where the Seraphim see white, black, and gray, we see all levels."

"So color matters?"

He snorted. "Hell, no. Color is a way of translating a very complex subject into very simple terms."

"What other levels of creation and destruction are there?"

"How much power someone has."

I raised an eyebrow. "Like a level ten warlock versus a level one troll."

"Exactly. There are those who can create life itself. Those who can destroy worlds. And then, there's the vast majority of us in between who can do little things." He steepled his fingers. "Let's just pray the ones at either end of the spectrum don't ever come knocking on our door."

My stomach clenched at the thought. "Do you think I'm making the right decision?"

"I can't answer that. What I can say is you need to make a decision or your Seraphim abilities won't properly manifest."

"Is that why I can't channel?"

"You might want to ask your mother."

I blew out a breath. "Get me out of here and I will."

"If you'll remember, we were working on your dreamcasting skills when you decided to wander off into la-la land." He pursed his lips. "Ready to give it another go?"

"Yeah." I ran a hand down my face and made myself comfortable. "Let's do this."

It took some time to quiet my mind because I had trouble not thinking about my vision and the choice. When I finally got past those thoughts, I found the void again and pretended I was drifting weightless in space. It seemed like an instant later Elyssa came to me

159

in my dreams—her warm skin, her lips, the way she smelled when I pressed my nose to her neck and drew in her scent.

I'm dreaming.

I looked at Elyssa and sighed. Just a normal dream.

Open your eyes, my conscious mind commanded.

My eyelids felt heavy and unresponsive. They trembled and finally opened. Gray aether formed a ghostly figure in front of me. The shape took the hourglass form of my girlfriend. The gray paled until it resembled her fair skin. Smoky tendrils darkened to form black hair while her face and other features molded themselves. I maintained a crystal clear image of Elyssa until her doppelganger stood in front of me, every detail exactly as imagined.

"How do you feel, Justin?" David asked.

I looked at him, my sense of detached calm giving the scene a surreal quality to it. I wondered if that was a side-effect of the meditation, or of the concentration required to maintain a semi-dream state. "Weird," I said. My voice sounded hollow.

"It's natural to feel out of sorts the first few times." He examined Elyssa. "Can you make something besides your girlfriend?"

My head nodded, seemingly of its own accord. Aether fog gathered next to Elyssa, forming another figure. I felt my lips curl back in a snarl as the details took shape. Within minutes, Maximus stood next to Elyssa. He wore wraparound sunglasses. A close-cropped goatee hugged his chin. He smiled, revealing long fangs.

Another shape formed next to him, that of a tall thin man with unruly black hair.

"Vadaemos?" David said, stepping back.

Yet another form, and another, and another took shape until the cell was crowded with people. Shelton, Elyssa, Bella, Stacey, Maximus, Vadaemos, Maulin Kassus and more stared at each other from either side of the cell.

"Justin, you can stop now," David said, squeezing between the opposing forces and standing by my side. "In fact, you need to stop, or your imagination is going to kill us all."

I gazed dully at my father. His words made sense, but there were more people to create. Where was Underborn, the notorious assassin? Where was Daelissa?

"You son of a bitch!" The replica of my friend, Adam Nosti, gripped Maximus by the collar of his leather jacket. "You tried to turn my sister into a vampling. I'm going to kill you!"

Maximus shoved Adam. Adam whipped out a compact rod and flicked it into a full staff.

Maximus snarled. "How about I kill you next, Arcane?"

Adam shouted a word. Searing heat rippled from the end of his staff and charred Maximus's face.

All hell broke loose.

Chapter 20

Vadaemos roared. His body rippled, growing into a demonic beast. Cold steel flashed in Elyssa's hands as she met a thrust from the towering demon spawn. Bella took out her staff and blasted Maulin Kassus before he could throw a first strike at Harry Shelton who was busy combating Mr. Bigglesworth, the shape-shifter who'd killed his father.

"Justin, stop!" David slapped me so hard I staggered back and tripped over the unconscious Arcane on the floor. My dream state vanished. The replicas of my friends and enemies went still as statues. A beam of white light from the end of Shelton's staff hung in mid-air, inches from the face of Maulin Kassus.

"What—huh?" I said, feeling my eyes go wide at the bizarre sight in front of me.

"I knew you had an overactive imagination, but this is ridiculous." David walked around the clones. He peered at the beam of light coming from Shelton's staff. "For a minute there, I thought he was really casting magic." He reached a tentative finger toward the light, seemed to reconsider, and spit on it. It sizzled.

"Wow," I said. "It's real?"

"As real as it needs to be," David said. He whistled. "You are something else, son."

I couldn't stop a grin from reaching my face. "You mean that in a good way?"

"Heck yeah." He touched Maximus's sunglasses. "You need to learn control." A grimace crossed his face as the sunglasses began to dissolve into goop.

It was hard to watch my friends melt away even though I knew they were imaginary constructs. Maximus and the others could rot in hell for all I cared.

"Do you remember how you controlled them all at once?" David asked.

I tried to remember. "Everything kind of happened on its own. I didn't consciously control anything."

"Your dream took over." He walked away from the melting figures. "Still, it's a good start. You just need to practice switching into that lucid dream state and you're set."

"I'll keep practicing."

David nodded. "Good idea. No telling how long we'll be waiting in here, and you might as well keep trying."

Pushing back my excitement, I sat back down and went back through the exercise. It took longer this time thanks to my mind reliving the battle I'd started. Thinking of the fake spells I'd made the clones cast led to another train of thought. If I could make them do that, what kept me from using a similar method to cast my own spells?

After a time, I managed to slip back into the lucid dream state. This time, I maintained a firmer hold on my imagination to prevent the previous chaos. The detached, surreal feeling came over me. I forced my eyes open, and stood. This time, I imagined a fireball. An orange sphere formed in my hand. I let it grow to about the size of my head and directed it to fly across the room.

It streaked across the small space and poofed against the wall, leaving a black mark where it hit, though it didn't otherwise damage the surface. A small voice in the back of my head told me it wasn't powerful enough to break through. My conscious voice tried to override my subconscious, explaining that a fireball could indeed damage the wall. Concentrating, I imagined another fireball. This one *would* destroy the wall. It *would* leave a huge hole in it.

163

My subconscious slipped from my grasp, and with it, my lucid dream state. I let out a frustrated grunt.

"What happened?" David asked.

"If I try to control my dream state too much, it fades."

He nodded. "Just like a typical lucid dream. The subconscious mind is sometimes more powerful than we give it credit for."

"Then I'll have to convince it."

He chuckled. "Good luck with that. It's a primal force all of its own." He examined the stain on the wall. "That was still very impressive."

I yawned. Grogginess weighed down my brain. Putting a part of myself to sleep and waking it back up sure was tiring. I paced around the room in an attempt to stay awake. I heard a snort of surprise and looked back to see the Arcane waking up. His eyes filled with fear when he saw us.

"Who are you people? What do you want with me?"

David held out his hand in a placating gesture. "Easy there. We're prisoners too."

"Prisoners? What did I do? Am I accused of a crime?" The Arcane pushed himself up and looked around the room. By now, the clones I'd made earlier were nothing but goop on the floor. A foggy gray steam rose from them as they presumably turned back into aether. "What is that stuff? Where are we?"

"We're in the Gloom," I said, stifling a yawn. "There are people who live here and have a device that allows them to kidnap people who are traveling via Obsidian Arches."

"Impossible," he said, eyes hardening with disbelief. "There were no Gloom cracks when the arch activated."

"It doesn't work like that," I said. I gave the man a brief rundown of the ripper and our experiences thus far.

"The Gloom is a place where dreams take shape?" he said. "Inconceivable."

"You'd better believe it," David said, his patience obviously wearing thin with the man's obstinacy.

I couldn't blame the Arcane. It was a lot to take in. Heck, I still had trouble believing half of what we'd been through.

164

"I'm Justin, and this is David. What's your name?"

"You've probably heard of me. My name is Gregory Wax."

His name didn't even sound remotely familiar to me. "Uh—"

The Arcane reached to his side and found his staff. "They're going to regret not taking this from me." He flicked it out to full length, aimed it at the door, and—his brow scrunched.

"Remind you of the time you came through the arch and you couldn't cast any spells?" David said.

"Casting doesn't work in the Gloom," I said.

"No, this cannot be." The Arcane tried again and again to produce magic and failed miserably. He even withdrew a wand—as if the staff might be defective—and tried it. Same results. "Margaret will be so upset when I don't show up with the new spell scrolls I promised her." His wand clattered to the floor, and the man buried his face in his hands.

"I tried to tell you," I said.

I watched the poor man groan in misery and wondered what Serena could possibly want with Arcanes and vampires. Supernatural abilities barely worked here, and casting spells seemed downright impossible. That pretty much made Arcanes and vampires useless. Then again, I might be thinking along the wrong lines. Dreamcasting was the big thing here in the Gloom. If there was anything I knew about casting spells in the real world, it required the ability to concentrate.

Shelton and Bella made me run through meditation exercises when I was just learning how to fill my aether well. Simply filling my well had been difficult to learn. Once I got over that hump, I had to actually cast spells. Although I could blow things up real good, my fine control was awful.

Any Arcane worth his or her salt wouldn't even have to think about those basic things. They'd simply flick a mental switch, draw in aether, and cast the desired spell, or start the ritual for a spell of more complicated design. This meant Arcanes could possibly adapt to dreamcasting much faster than other supernaturals. From that standpoint, kidnapping them made sense.

But why vampires?

165

Timothy hadn't demonstrated any supernatural abilities, which drove me to the assumption vampires wouldn't have preternatural strength in the Gloom. While he had been able to create a velociraptor and ride it—something any nerd could appreciate—the vampire hadn't conjured an army or done anything to dazzle us with amazing dreamcasting. Timothy had also been trapped in the Gloom for quite some time and hadn't developed his dreamcasting much beyond Gloria Richardson.

Maybe his ex-girlfriend had put him through too much psychological trauma. Maybe other vampires exhibited excellent dreamcasting skills. I had a feeling if we survived long enough, we'd eventually find out what Serena wanted with blood-suckers.

I explained my theory to David.

"Makes sense," he said. "She probably brainwashes them into serving her, then adds them to an army of dreamcasters."

"But, why," I asked, "in the world would anyone in their right mind want to build an army of dreamcasters in the Gloom? Not only is it more depressing than Seattle, but the population of real humans can't be very high. If this Serena person wants to rule the Gloom, she can have it."

"Did you say a woman named Serena is running things here?" Wax said, looking up from his pity party.

"That's what Jarvis told us," I said.

"Is she short and blonde with a sharp tongue?"

"We haven't met her," I replied. "Why?"

"I was on a research team assigned to the Gloom Initiative. Jarrod Sager put an Arcane named Serena Thain in charge. When he pulled the plug on the project, she and a handful of loyal researchers vanished into the Gloom and were never heard from again." He shuddered. "This place is driving me insane, and I've been here less than a day. I can't imagine how insane that woman is." He groaned. "She was already difficult to deal with, even under the best of circumstances. She used to steal my yogurt from the cooler though I'd clearly marked each container with my name." He blew out a breath. "The nerve of that woman."

166

"Do you think she'll recognize you?" I asked. "Maybe she'll take it easy on you."

His eyes flashed wide. "I certainly hope she doesn't recognize me. My negative evaluation of the way she handled the project was instrumental in causing Sager to pull the plug."

"Actually," I said, "Sager had to pull the plug because he was using his own Arcane consulting company to run things, and Cyphanis Rax found out about it. Apparently, it made for a huge scandal."

The Arcane's distant gaze told me he hadn't heard a word I'd said.

The cell door slid open, and one of the pale sentinels walked inside. The Arcane screamed as the thing came for him.

"Help! Help!" Wax backed into a corner until he had nowhere to go. "The Gloom monster is going to get me!"

Jarvis guffawed, holding his belly and crying with mirth as he watched the poor Arcane possibly soil himself. "It isn't going to hurt you if you shut your trap, moron."

"Calm down," I told Wax. "Do what Jarvis says and you'll be okay. He's the man in charge around here."

Jarvis's chest puffed out. "That's right."

"His name is Gregory Wax," David said, sidling up to Jarvis like an informant.

The stocky man nodded sagely and sneered. "Keep showing me this kind of loyalty, and things will go good for you."

The sentinel dragged the gibbering Wax from the cell and the door closed behind him.

I extended my senses to be sure Jarvis had left and made a gagging noise. "If I have to suck up to that man for much longer, I'm gonna barf."

"I might conjure up another crawler and have it bite his head off," David said.

I gave him a pleading look. "No more decapitations, please."

Several minutes later, the door opened, and the willowy form of Theresa entered. She placed trays with bread and cheese on the

167

floor. I thought about making a break for it, but noticed a sentinel standing outside.

She stood and regarded us with sad brown eyes. "How long have you been in the Gloom?"

"A day or so," I said. During the kidnapping, the woman had seemed uncomfortable with the Gloomies' mission. I wondered why and if we might exploit it. "How about you?"

Her lower lip trembled. "So long I can't remember. I was abducted while leaving the Grotto to visit my family."

"Sounds like you don't want to be here," David said, a note of caution in his voice.

She glanced back at the sentinel, knelt, and whispered, "I want to go home."

I knew entrusting this woman with any escape plans might be foolish. I extended my senses and found her brimming with sadness and hope. She seemed genuine. Maybe we could use that to our advantage. "Can the ripper be used to allow us back through the arch?"

She nodded. "Yes. It's a simple calibration. I tried to do that once, but Pat stopped me." A tear formed in one eye. "Jarvis put me in solitary for so long I thought I'd go insane."

"Why do they allow you to operate it if they know you don't want to be here?" David asked.

She made a whimpering sound. "I think Serena enjoys seeing my pain." She took my hand and squeezed it. "If I free you, can you help me get home? I'll do anything, just please help."

Empathy swelled inside me. I covered her hand with my other one and nodded. "We'll do what we can."

She took back her hand, wiped away a tear. "I don't know how yet, but I'll figure out a way. Jarvis won't let me go anywhere without a sentinel following."

"Why does Serena want Arcanes and vampires?" David asked.

Theresa grimaced. "They're hardier than most supers. Arcanes are good at dreamcasting, and vampires last longer when Serena feeds them to the brain." She shuddered. "Just do what they tell you, and I'll figure something out." She looked behind her toward the door. "I have to go, or Jarvis will be suspicious."

"Theresa?" called a male voice. "What the hell are you doing?"

She wiped her face frantically and stood, backed out of the room. "I'm feeding the prisoners." The door slid shut behind her, and her voice and that of the male faded in the distance.

David gave me a look. "Our ticket out of here. I hope she has the wits to free us."

"Without getting herself killed," I said with a grim note in my voice. "Serena sounds like a monster."

"I agree." He settled back against a wall. "Time to wait and hope."

"Yeah." I wasn't feeling too optimistic. If Theresa hadn't been able to escape after all this time, what made her think she could free us? "Well, it's not the first time I've been held against my will."

David sat down, back against the wall, and gave me a serious look. "You've been through a lot in your short life."

I snorted. "I've been through more in the past year than in the previous seventeen."

"You've grown in ways I never thought possible." He sighed.

"Why did you sigh?"

A shrug. "I feel like I've missed out on the majority of you growing into a man. You were so different than the, um—"

"Chubby nerd kid who played live action role-playing games?" I chuckled. "C'mon. You can say it."

He chuckled. "I honestly thought you were never going to change."

"It sure came as a shock to me." I thought back to the exchange between David and Montjoy. How my father had said he didn't care about Ivy. A question rose in my throat, but I hardly dared ask it. *Wimp.* I took a deep breath, and asked the dreaded question. "Do you really not care about me and Ivy?" My voice sounded small and timid.

David looked at the floor for such a long time, I thought he wasn't going to answer. When he looked up, his eyes looked troubled.

169

He looked tired, like a man who hadn't slept in days. "I didn't want to care. I didn't want to feel something for someone who might die." His voice trailed off.

I remained silent, hoping he would continue.

After a moment he did. "When we had to give up Ivy to the Conroys, it was the hardest thing I ever did in my life. When I knew you had to go into danger to save me, it tore me apart. I tried to suppress my emotions. I lied to myself, convinced myself I didn't care. But the truth..."

"The truth, Dad."

His eyes flicked to mine, and he swallowed hard. "I'm proud. So very proud to be your father, Justin. I love you and Ivy. You're my children, and in my quest to end the Seraphim threat, I lost sight of what's important." A tear glistened in my father's eye. "Family."

My throat went dry, and for a moment, I couldn't speak past the swelling in my chest. "I love you too, Dad. Even if I die in whatever horrors are to come, I want you to know that. I'm still angry for everything you've put us through. For what Mom has put us through. But in the end, I'm doing it all so my friends and family can have a good life."

His lips compressed together. He nodded. "That's what I want too."

"What do you intend to do about Kassallandra?" I understood why he felt he had to make the sacrifice and marry her. If her house defected to the Seraphim, it would make the battle that much harder. But I wanted our family to be together, damn it.

He shook his head. "I don't know."

I decided now was the time to ask another burning question. "Why did you and Mom give Ivy to the Conroys?"

He picked at a piece of the bread. "Your mother felt Jeremiah was the best person to train her." He shrugged. "When Alysea was reborn from the mouth of a leyworm, Jeremiah found her. He raised her. But her powers remained weak even by the time I reconnected with her. When her abilities began to manifest in earnest, she decided to live with Ivy and assist in her training."

"But Jeremiah was working with Daelissa." I scrunched my forehead. "You gave her to the enemy."

"And Daelissa taught Ivy well." David's mouth quirked into a smile. "As I've said, demons are masters of manipulation. What better way for Ivy to hone her Seraphim skills than with the enemy we thought she was destined to one day defeat?"

"I suppose Mom benefited from Daelissa's training as well."

His smile broadened. "Keep your friends close and your enemies closer."

I frowned. "Your plan almost didn't work, though. Ivy could very well have killed me and turned into Daelissa's puppet. Jeremiah practically brainwashed her."

His grin faded. "Your mother saw the danger signs. When we realized Jeremiah was using Ivy for his own agenda, she knew it was vital she take a firm hand in Ivy's development."

"Jeremiah is one twisted old man."

"The truth about him might surprise you." He opened his mouth to speak but the cell door opened.

Two pale mannequins entered, Jarvis behind them. "Well, looks like I don't have to throw you in the pit just yet. Serena wants to see you."

David and I looked at each other. We stood and headed out the door for whatever fate awaited.

Chapter 21

The sentinels walked just behind us with Jarvis leading the way. As we proceeded, he pointed out signs of his genius intellect, such as chokeholds in the fortress, and traps set to contain any would-be invaders. We entered a circular room with eight passages extending in all directions.

"This place right here is the hub," our kidnapper said. "If anyone gets this far, the doors seal them." He clapped his hands together as if squashing a fistful of roaches. "Then we annihilate the bastards from up there." He pointed to a second floor where inert sentinels stood like statues. "Not that they'd get this far, of course."

"This place is a certified deathtrap," David said. "You must have studied military strategy."

The man nodded, a smug look on his face. "Ain't nobody storming this castle."

"I'd bet you even have the doors locked down with some kind of complex recognition spells, too," I said.

"Nah, we have something even better."

"Better?" I asked.

He returned a smug smile. "You'll find out soon enough." Jarvis motioned us onward.

I memorized the corridors we took just in case the information came in handy later.

After a few more twists and turns, our guide led us through a wide doorway. I stopped listening to Jarvis as we entered a large rectangular room filled with all sorts of odd apparatuses. One device on the far right was composed of rings within progressively smaller rings. A silver orb the size of a cantaloupe rested in the center. Each ring had an independent axis, presumably so they could spin in different directions. A Tesla coil hung from the ceiling above, a thick metal rod with a pyramid of discs spaced down its length with the smallest at the top. I noticed several more of the coils arranged in a hexagonal shape on the floor around the ring device. None looked active.

We passed a large silver box a little larger than an old-school phone booth, something that looked like a seesaw with circular saw blades along its length, and even an iron coffin filled with metal coils. There were so many bizarre contraptions, I couldn't take them all in.

This place is a certified mad scientist's lab.

David nudged me. I followed his gaze and gasped. A ring of at least five minders circled around our former cellmate, Wax. The man stood frozen, eyes wide as the tentacles of the disgusting creatures writhed around his head.

"What are they doing to him?" I asked.

Jarvis chuckled. "You remember when I said we had something better than spells controlling the doors and sentinels?" He nodded toward the creatures. "Meet the brain."

"The brain?" David asked.

I remembered Theresa's comment about feeding the brain and would have recoiled in horror if not for the sentinel holding me.

"That will be all, Jarvis," said a hard feminine voice. A short blonde woman appeared from behind a contraption that looked like a huge metronome constructed of brass pipes.

Jarvis's eyes went a bit wide. "I was simply showing—"

She cut the man off with a wave of her hand. "See to your other duties."

Jarvis backed away, bowing as he did. "Yes, Serena." He turned and left, glancing over his shoulder as if the woman might set his pants on fire any minute.

173

"What's happening to Wax?" I asked Serena.

She smiled sweetly. "Perhaps you'll find out, young man. Follow me."

Despite feeling like a lamb being led to slaughter, I did as she asked. Near the back of the room I saw a low, stainless steel table. A white articulating arm hung over it. An array of smaller hinged arms protruded from a metal ball at the end, each one bearing horrors straight out of a dentist's office.

"Lie down, please," she told me.

I looked at the table. My knees went weak as I remembered my time as Maximus's prisoner. He'd kept me bound to a metal table while his pet Arcane, Dash Armstrong, experimented on me.

"No," I said, backing away. "I can't." Two sentinels gripped me by either arm. Dragged me toward the table. I struggled and fought like a cat on a leash. I couldn't lie on that table. I felt sick to my stomach, like I was going to throw up. "I can't!"

"Stop," David said. "I'll lie on the table."

"I only want to examine him," Serena said, still smiling.

"We're both demon spawn," he said. "I assure you the results will be the same."

She turned an understanding gaze my way. "Of course. Perhaps once he sees it's quite painless, he'll have the courage to follow." She clenched a fist. "Buck up there, young man."

I slumped to the floor as the sentinels released me, my limbs weak with relief. But as I looked at my father taking my place, guilt quickly swelled to replace any joy at being spared.

Serena opened David's mouth, inspected his teeth and throat like one might look at a horse for sale. She held a scope to his eyes, looking intently into them. She checked his pulse, and took his blood pressure as well. My father looked as confused by the process as I was, and I began to think maybe she didn't plan to drill into our skulls with one of the wicked instruments on the articulating arm.

She wrote something on a notepad, clicked the pen, and looked up. I turned my head and watched as one of the minders circling Wax detached itself and glided silently over, its translucent tentacles gliding over various apparatuses as it passed them.

"Are you still running the Gloom Initiative?" David asked, his eyes uneasily regarding the minder.

Serena turned her smile on him. "How do you know about the initiative?"

"I work with Jarrod Sager's son," I said.

Her gaze turned to me. "Jarrod abandoned the initiative a long time ago. The poor man let politics overrule the need for arcane research and discovery."

"What exactly have you discovered?" I asked. "You have quite an operation here."

"Well, aren't you sweet?" She clasped her hands. "I've dedicated my life to discovering the origin of the relics like the Obsidian Arch network, the Grand Nexus, and so forth."

"Are you about to feed me to the minder like Wax?" Dad asked.

She tutted. "Of course not. I'm simply extracting information. It's much easier this way than having to perform something as crude and unpleasant as torture." She nodded at the minder. "Now, if you'll just relax, let's get started." The minder's tentacles lifted languorously, brushing against my father's head. His eyes went blank.

One of the tentacles wrapped around Serena's head. Instead of freezing, she seemed to be fully conscious. Her eyes widened and flicked to David. "How interesting."

"What?" I asked.

She didn't answer but stood there for so long, I wondered if she would ever move. I thought about diving for the minder and ripping it away from my father, though the attempt might simply put me in the same state he was in.

"Very informative," she said after a time, and nodded. The minder's tentacles retracted from David's head.

He sucked in a deep breath like a man who'd just leapt into an ice pond. He propped himself on his elbows and looked at the woman. "Did I make the team?"

"While I find your heritage very interesting, you are only of secondary concern to me," Serena replied. She turned to me. "Now, are you ready to be a big boy for me?"

175

This woman's motherly tone was creeping me out. Knowing I wouldn't be strapped down to the table made it easier for me to lie down. I wasn't looking forward to the minder digging into my skull but had no choice. Once again, she went through the physical tests. I was just glad I didn't have to give her a stool sample. When she looked at the minder, I tensed, waiting for the cold grip of the tentacles. I closed my eyes, and willed myself to float free in a sea of pitch black.

There's nothing to fear.

A cold numbness settled over me, and I realized the minder must have me in its grip. I'd managed to slip into the lucid dream state just before it touched me. It was a very strange feeling. I sensed the minder as something not quite sentient in the same way humans were. It was like part of a mind, but missing certain elements that would give it full autonomy.

Autonomy?

The question echoed in the void, and I realized it must have come from the minder itself.

Free will, I sent back.

It seemed to have no response to that, and went silent. I felt its psychic probes tightening around my head, as if that would help it break past the barrier of lucidity I held against it. The tentacles looked like tunnels of light to my mind's eye. I wondered what would happen if I traveled through one.

I floated in the still waters of the void, wondering if I should chance it when a gentle wave caused me to bob. Another wave broke over my face, making me sputter. I heard a roaring, like a massive volume of water falling over a cliff, and fear overwhelmed the calm.

What's happening to me?

Unknown, said the calm whisper of the minder.

I felt a wave cresting beneath me, picking me up, and hurtling me through the invisible ocean. Barely keeping my head above water, I saw a beam of light shining on something at the base of the huge wave as it crested through darkness. "Crap!" I shouted. The wave broke. I slid across rough wood and came to a stop against a pile of rope. Pushing up on my knees, I coughed water from my lungs.

Double shadows appeared beneath me as two sources of light hit from either side. I looked up and watched twin suns rise in the sky. One glowed a deep violet. The other pulsated like a white dwarf star. Between them hovered a huge gray moon.

"What is this?" asked Serena.

I spun and saw her standing next to me on the deck of a large galley ship. "A choice," I replied.

Her eyes widened for an instant. "She was right. You are the Cataclyst."

"Who was right? Who said that about me?"

She made as if to write something in an notebook, but seemed to remember this was all in my head and stopped herself. "Let us simply say it is vital you decide. You are the progeny of Alysea and have a very important task ahead of you."

I blinked in confusion. "Does that mean you want me to succeed?"

"Of course I do." She took my hands and smiled. "As the son of Alysea, you can help me in a way no other can."

I couldn't tell if her smile was sincere or not. "How can I help you?"

"Once you awaken from this, I will show you."

I felt an odd sensation, like something cold sliding away from my head, and Serena vanished. Water lapped at the sides of the ship. The suns pulsed overhead, their erratic orbits carrying them closer and closer to the gray moon. The three orbs met. In the center of their juxtaposition, I saw nothing but clear sky. It was like they were eating each other, or turning invisible where they hit.

As I stared into the empty space where the suns and moon met, I felt a sudden tugging on my chest. A great urgency to make the decision.

As I'd told David, I already knew the right choice wasn't any one of the three, but all of them. How exactly I could announce my decision to choose all sides at once wasn't apparent.

Once again, the three heavenly bodies merged into one another leaving nothing more than a shimmer in the air, though the

177

light never dimmed. The pull on my consciousness grew stronger. I felt heat rushing into my blood, and with it, strength.

What's happening to me?

I saw the crescent shapes of the suns and moon appearing as the orbs drifted out of perfect alignment. Within what seemed like seconds, they once again stood apart fully intact, just in opposite positions. The moon was now at the top of the triangle with the bright and dark stars reversed. The pull on my mind vanished. The sky and everything else melted away, and I jerked awake on the table.

Serena smiled down at me. "Did you decide?"

"I—I almost had it," I said. "But, no, not yet."

"You can still help me." She waited as I stood. "I will show you."

"You okay, son?" David asked, watching from a distance. A sentinel held him immobile by both arms.

"I'm fine," I said. I still didn't trust Serena, despite her sudden interest in me.

"This way," Serena said, and moved toward a large double door at the back of the room.

I looked back and saw the sentinel remaining still with David. "Isn't he coming?"

"There is no reason for him to see this," she said.

"I'd feel more comfortable if he came along."

She frowned, head tilting like a curious puppy. "If it will make you feel at ease, then of course." She took out her notepad and wrote something down, tapped the pen to her chin, and then added, *Possible daddy issues.*

I groaned. "Everyone has to be so judgmental."

She moved on, though I noticed the sentinel guiding David behind us. I followed her through the door. We emerged in a huge room with a domed roof. While the room itself was impressive, what nailed my guts to the floor was the huge Alabaster Arch in the center—or at least it closely resembled one. Instead of a black arch veined through with white, this one was white veined with black. Large granite pylons shaped like pyramids stood in a circle around the arch just outside a thick silver ring.

"Did you build this?" I asked.

She shook her head. "A research team recently discovered a cache of large stone cubes in Thunder Rock."

My heart skipped at beat at the mention of the abandoned relic. When the rebellion against Daelissa and her minions had removed the Cyrinthian Rune from the Grand Nexus, the shockwave had gone throughout the Alabaster Arch network, draining the light from anyone caught in the blast. Thunder Rock had an Alabaster Arch. In that accursed place I'd encountered my first husked angel. I called the infantile little creeps cherubs.

Serena continued. "At first, we thought the cubes were building blocks for another city like El Dorado. By accident, we discovered they were merely packaged arches."

"Packaged?" David asked.

She nodded. "Whoever constructed the arches built them elsewhere and shipped them here as stone cubes. A specific series of frequencies will activate a cube, causing it to grow into an arch. The arch roots itself in the ground, latching onto the largest available ley line. If there are no ley lines, it will stunt the growth of the arch and the structure will not function." She grimaced. "We wasted two cubes in such a manner."

I was tempted to ask if she asked for a refund, but restrained myself. "So you brought one into the Gloom and grew it here?"

"Yes." She motioned us closer to the arch. "As you can tell, it was supposed to be an Alabaster Arch—a gateway to other realms."

"Would it even work with the Grand Nexus disabled?" I asked.

"As you may or may not know, the Gloom Initiative was about discovering why and how the Gloom functions in relation to Eden." She motioned toward the arch. "As you can see, it has an interesting effect on arches."

"Does the arch work?" I asked.

"It does, but is rather erratic." She smiled again.

I heard the sound of chains dragging on the stone floor, and looked around. A creature, humanoid, but walking on all fours appeared from behind a granite pylon. Chains hung from its neck, and

179

manacles on its arms and legs. A mass of sharp crooked teeth jutted from its lower jaw and mangled gums while a single serrated tooth shaped almost like a saw blade protruded from beneath its upper lip.

"Master," it hissed in a gurgling voice. "What will you have of me?"

"I did not call you." Serena looked at the thing with disgust. "Return to your den."

It bowed ever so slightly, though its solid red eyes burned with what looked like hate. "As you wish, master." It crawled away, the chains rasping on the floor.

"What in the hell was that?" I asked.

Her smiled returned. "The arch opens upon the plains of the Nazdal realm."

"That thing was a Nazdal?"

She nodded. "Justin, you were sent here for a reason."

"I'm starting to realize that," I said, thinking she must be talking about the choice.

Her hand rested on my shoulder. "I hope you will help us."

I gave her an uneasy look. "How so?"

"Alysea attuned the Cyrinthian Rune on the Grand Nexus." She pointed to a small sphere in a socket on the arch. "Inside you resides the ability to attune the rune on this new nexus—the Shadow Nexus. That is why she sent you to us."

I was even more confused. "Are you saying my mother sent me here to help you?"

"Of course not, young man." Another motherly smile. "You are here to help Daelissa."

Chapter 22

I already knew the answer, but hearing this woman speak the truth as if Daelissa were some wonderful woman who needed help getting her groceries out of the car, jolted me.

"This is insanity," I said. "You want to help Daelissa rule the world?"

Serena kept on smiling. "I have no interest in who rules, but Daelissa has offered me full access to all the realms I desire so I can advance the cause of magic."

"Wait, I have a counteroffer," I said. "How about you help us against Daelissa, and I'll grant you the same thing. I'll make you the Minister of Magic. How's that for a snazzy title? I'll even throw in a new diamond-studded magic wand with a fine Corinthian leather carrying case."

She sighed. "There is no way to prevail against the Seraphim. Whether you want to or not, you will be helping Daelissa's cause. You will help me calibrate this new Grand Nexus to allow us access to Seraphina."

"First of all, you're bat-poo crazy woman. Second, I don't know the first thing about fixing arches."

Her smile faded to a sad frown. "But you have the answer inside you. You're the son of Alysea, the Seraphim who attuned the Cyrinthian Rune on the Grand Nexus." She pointed to a small glowing orb set in the side of the arch. "You may not know how just yet, but you have the ability to attune this rune."

I backed away and felt the hard bulk of a sentinel behind me. "Why don't you just take that rune and use it on the Grand Nexus in the real world?"

"We cannot simply remove the rune without attuning it. To do so might cause another Desecration."

I felt might eyebrows pinch. "Why did you build this arch here instead of Eden? You would have had another Grand Nexus."

"Unfortunately, one of my former assistants took it upon himself to use the cube here," she said. "I was very distressed about his poor decision."

"Lucky for the world," I muttered.

Serena didn't seem to hear me. "Nevertheless, it functions as the Grand Nexus does." She touched my arm. "You are the key to a wonderful future full of discovery. Does that not appeal to you?"

"Oh, I'm all for discovery," I said. "But not if it means helping a maniacal tyrant like Daelissa use it for her own gains."

"You misunderstand her," she said, not seeming to take offense. "She will bring enlightenment to a world of chaos."

"This woman is as crazy as Daelissa," Dad whispered.

I agreed. "Boy and how."

Serena moved toward the arch. The sentinel took me by the arm and dragged me after her until we stood closer to the rune. I'd never gotten a good look at the Cyrinthian Rune. We'd found it hidden inside an omniarch beneath the mansion in Queens Gate, but Jeremiah Conroy had plucked from beneath our noses. From what I remembered it was white with an intricate pattern of glowing lines in it. This one was black with glowing lines.

Serena held out a hand toward the rune as if to reverently touch it, seemed to realize something, and jerked her hand back. "As I said, we have no safe way of removing this rune without possibly causing a backlash like the one during the Desecration."

Maybe that's what needs to happen. Sure, it would husk all of us, but at least it would prevent Daelissa from achieving her goals.

The Arcane seemed to sense my thoughts. "Let me give you a little more information about the Gloom before you decide on heroics."

182

"I wasn't thinking about being a hero," I lied. *More like a suicidal maniac.*

"The Gloom is a mirror of the real world, but it lacks true natives."

"What about the minders?" David asked.

A smile curled her lips. "As you've noticed, the Gloom is a realm where dreams and thoughts from Eden become something of a reality. Psychic emanations from the beings in that realm reach the minders. The minders enact the dreams."

"Makes sense," I said. "They eat dreams."

Another smile. "Every time a new life enters Eden, a version of itself appears in the Gloom."

"Like ghosts?"

"Nearly so." She raised an eyebrow. "We call these shades minders."

I reeled back. "Wait, everyone in Eden has their own minder?"

"Yes."

"What happens when someone dies?"

"Those minders will eventually fade and die unless given a live host to feed from." She tapped her pen against her chin. "Darkwater takes orphaned minders and repurposes them for guard duty in the mortal realm where they can feed on the living. The minders that comprise the brain feed from live subjects we bring from Eden."

A sick feeling came over me. "You're feeding Wax to those things? You've got serious issues. Why bother keeping the minders alive? Is that your perverted notion of fun?"

She waved a hand at the room. "The minders who comprise the brain are the ones who maintain the dreamcasted parts of this fortress. They control the sentinels. I'm sure you noticed the bubble of clear air around this fortress. They are the ones keeping the aether fog at bay."

"Why are you telling me this?" I asked.

"If you risk another desecration, the aether fog may carry the blast wave like magical conductor to all corners of the world." Her eyes lit with horror. "You might husk every minder in the Gloom."

183

My chest tightened. "What happens to the people in the real world if their minders are husked?"

She shrugged. "I have no idea, but I imagine it would be catastrophic."

"No doubt."

She nodded. "Well, please keep that in mind should you think of causing a Desecration here."

I've got to kill this woman.

"Come along, dear," she said, and started back the way we'd entered. The sentinels pulled me and David along behind her. We took a right through Serena's laboratory and walked down a long corridor before exiting the fortress through twelve-foot-tall double doors in the rear of the facility. The granite quarry curved around the back of the fortress. The part of the pit to our left touched the far corner of the fortress. The large circular structure of the domed arch chamber ran from the center of the fortress up to the very lip of the quarry.

The ledge we stood on was nice and wide. It led down a slope, presumably into the quarry depths. A quick scan of the far side revealed a rugged cliff face without any obvious trails or ways out without rock climbing gear. I had to hand it to Jarvis—this place was a tough nut to crack.

Serena led us down the slope and onto a winding path about five feet wide which led to the bottom of the gaping hole. I figured out immediately this must be the pit Jarvis had referred to. Murky water filled one corner of the quarry. The rest was filled with rubble, granite, and something else—Nazdal. The chained creatures occupied nearly every square inch from what I could tell, even though part of the quarry disappeared around the bend, presumably curving toward the other side of the fortress.

I grimaced. Hopelessness wrapped a cold hand around my stomach as I considered the army lurking in these depths. Serena stopped on a ledge about fifty feet from the bottom and I saw the horrors close up. Some of the Nazdal had no chains while others wore even more than the first one we'd seen. They varied in size, from toddler, all the way to a couple boasting the bulk of small bears.

184

I recoiled at the sight of a bipedal form shambling into view. A band of metal plating covered its eyes. Green drool hung from purple lips and liver spots covered its pale skin. One of the smaller Nazdal bumped against the walker's leg. The thing roared, spraying green spittle and grabbed the crawling creature, savagely chomping into it. The Nazdal screamed and wriggled, but was unable to break free.

Blood spurted from bite wounds. The Nazdal cried out again and again with the most horrific screams I'd ever heard while its people watched, red eyes glowing with unholy light. None of the chained beings lifted a claw to stop the slaughter. Some of them moaned in ecstasy as if drawing strength from the agony and gore.

"Is that thing from the same realm as the chained people?" I asked, referring to the walker.

Serena gave me a sad look. "The creature eating the Nazdal was formerly a human, an Arcane if I recall. This is what they become after the minders are done feeding from them."

"You're sick!" I said. I wanted to break the Arcane's neck, or push her into the pit to see how much she liked it when one of her monsters tore into her throat. The sentinel gripped my other arm, as if sensing I might try something stupid.

"The ghouls are a rather interesting side effect, I must say." Serena jotted something on her notepad, and then waved an arm at the vast quarry. "We have hundreds of them here."

"And they eat the Nazdal?" I asked.

"Sometimes."

"How do you keep all these monsters fed?"

"The Nazdal steal life force from the weaker ones among them, whether by inflicting harm, or killing them." The woman spoke as if it were a sad fact of life. "We also bring supplies from the Gloom. Whatever exists in the mortal realm eventually appears here."

"And it doesn't vanish?"

"No. The Gloom mirrors the real world. Despite the destruction occurring here during nighttime in Eden, when the sun rises, the Gloom rebuilds itself. Anything out of sync is replaced."

185

I wrinkled my forehead. "So if I eat a loaf of Gloom bread, if that bread still exists in the real world, it's recreated at sunrise?"

"Precisely. The food doesn't taste nearly as good as what we import from Eden, but it supplies the required nutrients." She regarded the blood-spattered rocks as the ghoul crunched the bones of the dead Nazdal.

I gagged at the noises from the gorging ghoul. "You realize you're a bad guy, right? You're a traitor to the human race." I motioned my head toward the army of monsters. "Have you ever been to the movies, or read an epic fantasy novel? These are the kinds of creatures the bad guys use!"

"I'm afraid this is not fantasy, dear." She gave me a sad look. "This is cold hard reality." Serena headed back up the path. The sentinels pushed us after her. "You must accept that defeating Daelissa is also fantasy."

We entered the fortress. The sentinel with David took him down a corridor leading away from us. "Where is it taking him?" I asked, unable to stop thanks to the faceless mannequin pushing me along.

"A holding cell." Serena headed left from the door. "You will remain at the arch to help us."

"I don't know how to attune the rune," I said.

"Then you must learn. Time is of the essence." She entered the laboratory. About a quarter of the way across the room the minder brain swirled around Wax.

I couldn't help but look at the man. The poor Arcane looked pallid. I couldn't imagine what sort of tortures the minders were putting him through. If the minders were truly shades of people in the real world, what was happening to Wax's minder right now? I wondered if Daelissa had a minder in this crazy shadow dimension, or if Seraphina had its own mirror universe complete with their version of minders. I wondered if a floating jellyfish with my name on it was drifting around aimlessly at this very moment.

So many other pieces didn't fit in this bizarre puzzle. If the Gloom was a mirror or shadow version of Eden, could the reversed Alabaster Arch really open to Seraphina? I'd always expected a mirror

186

universe to be filled with evil people sporting goatees. Yet again, the universe had no problems disappointing Justin Slade.

Serena took me back to the cavernous arch chamber. A sentinel appeared bearing a tray of food. "Please eat," the Arcane said. "A full stomach will help you determine how to attune the rune so it will open in different realms."

"How am I supposed to do that?" I had absolutely no clue.

A minder drifted into the room and stopped next to the sentinel. Serena produced a blank notepad and pen for me. "The minders can often help someone discover hidden secrets in their minds. This one will assist you."

I wondered if it was the same one who'd probed me and my father earlier. My stomach grumbled at the sight of the food. I decided I might as well stall for time by eating first, and tore into a hunk of bread. "Do you seriously think I'll be able to crack this thing?" I asked.

"I have faith in you." Serena regarded the arch almost reverently. "I hope to someday meet the true creators of this marvel. They are the ones who can answer all my questions."

"I used to think the same thing about the Seraphim," I said. "I used to think that about the demons." I brushed the crumbs from my hands. "None of them have all the answers. I have a feeling even the beings who made the arches will disappoint you."

She shook her head. "No, they won't. Think about it, young man. Every realm is a step closer to the truth."

Or a step closer to nightmare. The Nazdal came to mind, not to mention the siren people who created the arches.

"I have others duties to attend," Serena said. "Please do your work, and I will ask Daelissa to reward you."

"Yeah, with negative karma out the wazoo," I grumbled.

I finished eating and stared blankly at the rune and arch for a long while. No epiphanies struck, so I took a walk around the room. A sentinel followed me at a short distance while the minder remained floating in place.

As I walked around one of the tall gray pylons, I nearly tripped over a chain in my path. I glanced to the left and almost

187

screamed like the lead singer of a boy band. The Nazdal I'd seen in here earlier regarded me, its grotesque mouth gaping open, red beady eyes looking me up and down. The creature bore a human resemblance, but stood on all fours. Slight deformations in the spine made its posture seem almost natural. Aside from chains, it wore little else in the way of clothes except, thankfully, rough leather pants. Its bony spine bulged unevenly beneath its pink skin. Though its hands and feet had as many digits as a human's, they bore claws instead of fingernails.

"Master," the Nazdal said, and bowed its head. Long strings of drool hung from the cluster of sharp teeth jutting from its lower jaw.

"I'm not your master," I said, and backed away a step.

"Then, you are food?"

"No, I'm not that either," I said, backing away several more steps.

It said nothing, but continued to look at me, as if curious. Finally, it spoke. "You are not like the others the master's servants feed to the brain." It spoke slowly, its voice slurred as if it had great difficulty speaking English, or maybe just because it needed some serious dental work.

I didn't know what to say. "Why do you let her command you?"

"She works for the gods," he said, as if that should answer everything.

"The Seraphim?" I asked.

"That is what she also calls them," he said. A puddle of red-tinted drool formed on the floor beneath his jaw.

"They aren't gods," I said. "They just like to pretend they are."

The Nazdal sniffed. "I sense the god in you. Why do you not command the small one called Serena?"

I couldn't help but chuckle. "Must be my body spray," I said. "It's god-scented."

The Nazdal tilted its head, shifting the string of saliva to the other side of its mouth. "Your insides reek of the god."

188

I decided he must be sniffing my Mom's genetic contribution to little old me. "Will your people follow me?" I asked, wondering if I might be able to use this army.

"If you are mightier than the bright one."

I raised an eyebrow. "Daelissa?"

"The very same."

Beat up Daelissa, rule an army. I didn't need a therapist to tell me how crazy it sounded. I had a better chance of defeating an army of Nazdal than I did beating Daelissa's punk ass. But I didn't let that stop me from lying to this guy. "Sure. Next time she comes around, I'll kick her ass and show you who's boss."

"That will be acceptable," the creature said.

"Do you speak for your people?" I asked. "Are you their leader?"

A sound like air bubbling through phlegm came from its throat. I wondered if it was a laugh, or if the thing had contracted pneumonia. "I am a low one of the upper ranks. I gather information for the leader."

"Do you have a name?"

It made a horrendous noise, like a man hawking up a goober the size of an Olympic ice skating champion's left buttock. It looked at me for a moment then made the bubbling laugh noise again. "You cannot say my name with your words. Call me Maloreck."

"Ooh, that's a cool name," I said. "Is that how in translates from your language to mine?"

"No. It was the name of a man they threw in the pit." The creature gurgled. "I was the one who life drained him. I absorbed his knowledge and power."

I gulped. "Is that how you feed?"

Maloreck nodded. "When you wound the prey, its life drains with the blood. It is an honor to drain mighty prey."

"At least his name wasn't Bob."

Maloreck tilted his head. "Is that a glorious name in your tongue?"

"Yeah, it means 'slayer of gods'."

"Then I am not yet worthy of the name Bob."

189

I stifled a snort.

Maloreck tilted his head slightly. "I will return to"—he made a god-awful rasping noise—"and inform him you plan to dethrone the bright one. If your powers are greater than hers, we will follow you." He crawled away.

Pressure squeezed my chest as I thought about what I'd told Maloreck. *Beat Daelissa? That's crazy talk!*

Unless I figured out how to open my Seraphim abilities, Daelissa would tear me to shreds.

Chapter 23

I walked back to the minder and stared at it for a while. The thought of using it sent cold shivers down my spine. Unfortunately, I had little choice in the matter. The only question remaining was how to use it. When I'd been in a lucid dream state, the minder hadn't been able to control my thoughts. Earlier, when my father and I had been touched by the minders, memories had surfaced. With everything that happened between then and now, I hadn't given much thought to the dreams.

The part about my father telling Mom that I would serve and die had kind of overwhelmed everything else. As I remembered it now, I also recalled the song Mom sang to me. I'd heard that melody before, or at least part of it when Mom was explaining how she attuned the Cyrinthian Rune with her gift of perfect musical pitch. Considering the arches were created by sirens who sang them into being, it made perfect sense.

If Serena wanted me to serenade the rune, though, she was in for a huge disappointment. Mom had a beautiful, unearthly voice. In short, she sang like an angel. My singing voice flat out sucked. Elyssa would turn off the radio if I started belting out my favorite power ballads. She told me I must be studying necromancy because my voice could wake the dead.

Why did Serena have so much faith in me? *Maybe my post-pubescent singing voice will improve.*

"*La, la la,*" I sang in an off-key croak. "*Hey, baby, baby. It's Friday.*" Even I could hear how out of tune my voice was. I was likely to create another Desecration just by singing. I looked at the minder. "Let's do this, but let me have the controls, okay?"

Its tentacles swung toward me.

"Whoa, hold up!" I said.

The tentacles froze in place.

"Let me lie down first." I lay down on my back. Took a deep breath. "Okay, now let's—"

The world blinked away.

I stood in a void. "You don't waste any time."

What is free will? The whispery voice sounded like the one that had spoken to me the last time.

"It means you choose to do what you want. Other beings don't tell you what to do."

This is possible?

"Yes." I waited for another response, but none came. "Can you identify other minders?"

Yes.

"Do you have names?"

Not names. Associations. Feelings.

"Can you identify my personal minder?"

At first there was no answer. *It is possible. The notion will be put forth into the thought stream.*

I didn't bother asking for clarification since that sounded like a yes to me. "If you find him, can you send him to me?"

If the idea carries, so it will be.

Sounded like another affirmative, so I didn't pepper the thing with questions. I wondered if Serena carried on conversations with the minders.

She does, in a fashion.

Obviously, the minder could read my, um, mind. *Creepy.*

Agreed, in the context provided.

I tried to stop thinking about how unsettling its response was, and forced my thoughts to the matter at hand. "I need to remember the song my mother sang." I concentrated on the tune.

192

I look up at Mom as she sings to me. The song delights my little body. I open my mouth and coo at her.

I'm older. Mom is singing to a newborn baby. I peek into the room. She looks at me and smiles. The baby stares at Mom. It's too young to be able to see yet, but it seems to understand everything.

Several months have passed since seeing the newborn. Mom sings to my sister, Ivy, every day, and lets me listen. Though the song is simple, there are some parts I can't hear, as if my ears are incapable of detecting the notes.

"Mom, why do you sing the same song?" I ask.

"You might need it someday," she says, brushing a hand through my hair.

"They're coming," my father says from the doorway.

Tears run down Mom's face. "I hate this idea. What if he perverts the mind of our little girl?"

David takes Mom in his arms. She buries her face in his chest. "I'm sorry, my love. This is the only chance we have for her to attain her full abilities." My father looks at me. "Go to your room, son. I don't want you in here when they arrive."

I do as asked. As I play in my room, I hear Mom singing the song over and over again. I hear other voices. I look down the hall and see the man in the top hat. Jeremiah Conroy sees me. His eyes tighten, but he says nothing. Eliza Conroy exits Ivy's room, a bundle in her arms. Mom is sobbing. David holds her tight, his own eyes filled with tears.

"She will be mighty," Jeremiah says.

"Be careful with our daughter," David replies. "Are you sure there's no other way?"

Jeremiah shakes his head. "I am sorry, but no. The girl shows all the signs she is the one. The boy has no powers. He is useless to me."

After Jeremiah leaves, Mom comes to me, eyes red from crying. "Don't worry, sweetie. I'll protect you." She presses a hand to my head, and everything blurs away.

I sucked in a breath and looked around. I was back in the void. Pain swelled in my chest, and tears gathered in my eyes. Mom had

193

blurred many memories from my mind. I'd had some recollections of the Conroys taking away my sister before, but nothing like that.

Sadness. Grief. Pain. If you have free will, why do you allow the pain?

"We don't always have a choice in what we feel," I said. "Free will doesn't mean you can control every aspect of your life, but you can make choices that will make you happy sometimes, and sad others."

A great burden.

"Tell me about it," I said.

You feel responsible for that which is beyond your control.

"What do you mean?"

Other entities. Loved ones. You wish to prevent harm to them.

"Yeah. That's why I want to stop Daelissa," I said.

Great responsibility.

"I know, I know." A sigh burst from my lips. "I've got to stop her though."

The minder didn't respond.

I took the time to hum the tune Mom had sung. The tune itself was simple except for the missing notes. I understood immediately why I hadn't heard those notes. Until just before my eighteenth birthday, my hearing was as normal as a human's. There was no way I'd know those frequencies because I'd never heard them. It meant without her, I'd never know the tune.

"You can let me out," I said. "End the dream."

I awoke on the floor of the arch room, and pushed myself up to a sitting position. *We're so screwed.* How was I supposed to figure out the tune if I didn't know all the notes? Maybe I could convince Serena to send me back to Eden so I could talk to Mom. Then I'd return with the cavalry, rescue Dad, and beat the snot out of Serena.

Except, there was no chance in hell Serena would let me go. More than likely, she'd somehow use me to trick Mom into entering this hellhole. If I discovered the song, what then? I'd have to attune the arch and possibly unleash Armageddon. There had to be a way out of this mess. I wondered if anyone could do the singing ritual, or if it required someone specific. Lornicus, the most lifelike golem Mr.

194

Gray had made, told me my mother was the only one who could perform the ritual since she'd been the first to attune the Grand Nexus and the rune.

When I'd asked her about it, she told me she was able to do it because she had perfect pitch. I wondered if Ivy had the same control over her voice or if she was still too young.

Unfortunately, all the speculation in the world wasn't going to teach me the song. I paced back and forth, thinking furiously. Mom once told me she could feel the tuning of the Cyrinthian Rune, and it allowed her to feel what lay on the other side of the portal. She'd discovered the mortal realm that way. If that were true, it meant the Grand Nexus could conceivably lead to other realms besides Seraphina. This Shadow Nexus had obviously led to the realm with the Nazdal. Could I possibly attune it so it would take us back to Eden instead of Seraphina?

We could escape.

I knew what my goal was. I would learn how to change the destination of this arch. Another problem occurred to me. The song Mom sang in my memory might unlock the way to only one destination. Or it might be the song to remove the rune from the nexus. Why would Mom have taught us the song to open the gate to Seraphina? It didn't make sense, because the last thing she'd want was to reopen the gateway to her home world. It made a lot more sense to teach us how to remove the rune.

"Ugh, I'm never going to figure this out." I paced some more, trying to figure a way out. No one except Mom knew the songs. Nobody but me and Ivy had heard her—I suddenly realized that wasn't true at all. Someone else had heard her sing. That someone else might know more about the tuning.

Dad.

I walked to the minder and said, "I need my father. He has information I need."

The phantom creature didn't so much as twitch.

"I'll also need some way to tune my voice." I had no idea what device could actually hit all the notes I needed, but at least it would make Serena think I was doing something.

195

The minder still made no move to indicate it heard or cared about my requests.

"Look, I really need my father. Ask Serena for permission if you need to." With that, I spun on my heel and walked to the arch.

The rune gave off a benign glow, but I didn't dare touch the thing. I also saw no way to activate the arch. Alabaster Arches had a symbol in the arch control runes. Pressing it would activate the arch, which would then open a portal. There were no buttons in this room. The Obsidian Arches had a modulus for choosing destinations on the map. Admittedly, I'd never used the Grand Nexus. The only Alabaster Arches I'd activated had malfunctioned since the nexus didn't have the rune.

I examined the rune again. Hoping I didn't blow off my hand, I held it toward the rune. The glowing patterns brightened. Gritting my teeth, and offering up prayers, I reached my palm toward the small sphere.

It sprang from the socket and hovered an inch from the surface. I yelped and jumped backward. The tiny orb reset itself back into the slot. I took deep breaths and waited for my heart to stop pounding.

Maybe it's supposed to do that.

I sure hoped so. I paced back and forth for several minutes, working up the courage to try again. Steeling myself with a deep breath, I reached my palm toward it, as if activating a modulus. The orb sprang free. I willed it to activate.

The silver ring around the arch flared bright. I felt a sudden rush of magical energy building around me, washing past like static electricity. The arch hummed. Black and white sheets of light flickered between the columns. The thrumming grew louder and louder. The alternating light pulses quickened. With a bright flash, the portal opened and a window to another world appeared.

A great open plain of red sand and craggy rocks ran into the distance. A blood red sun hovered low on the horizon. Scrub brush with shimmering thorns grew in scattered clumps, and something that looked a lot like a huge, horned coyote streaked past.

I saw movement. Heard the susurrus of gravelly voices and the gurgling of gullets with too much phlegm. The sand moved. No, it wasn't the sand moving, but creatures—Nazdal—their skin camouflaged perfectly to match the environment. Jaws open and drooling, they lunged, intercepted the coyote, and brought it down. The creature yipped.

More and more of the sub-human crawlers phased into view until the plain was dotted with what had to be thousands upon thousands. I felt my eyes go wide at the sight, and my heart went tight as skinny jeans. The Nazdal swarmed toward the portal, their voices gurgling in excitement.

"Close!" I shouted, and willed the portal to shut.

The gateway flicked off, and the only other sound besides my beating heart was the throbbing hum of the arch winding down. I backed away a few steps. My knees felt weak. I turned, and saw my father standing outside the ring. A sentinel held him. He looked as pale as the guardian.

"This is not good," he said.

I couldn't agree more.

Chapter 24

I looked at the minder. "Can you make the sentinel release my father? It's not like we can escape."

The pale guardian's hand opened, and David stepped away from it.

"Thank you," I said, wondering if good manners made a difference to the ghostly brain creature. "Let me show you something." I motioned my father toward the arch. As we walked, I noticed the sentinel didn't follow. I wasn't sure if the minder could hear me. The thing didn't have ears, but it obviously knew what I wanted when I spoke to it. Unfortunately, I had no choice but to relay my theories to David.

I told him what I needed.

"You want to pick my brain using the minder to find out if I remember any songs your mother sang?" he said.

I nodded. "Look, here's the deal. From what Mom told me, I think the arch can be attuned to open into different realms. The Cyrinthian Rune adjusts the destination, but it requires a ritual." I explained how the siren-like beings had grown an arch from solid rock. Shelton, some others and I had accidentally caused a glitch by opening two portals right next to each other and briefly ended up witnessing the sirens building an arch.

"And your mother's songs are like the ones the sirens used to grow the arches?" he said.

"Exactly. So, it makes sense the Cyrinthian Rune responds to those musical frequencies."

"Why don't all the arches work that way then?" he asked.

I shrugged. "I think the Seraphim were able to build their own versions of the Obsidian Arches, or at least modify them. Or, maybe the builders specifically made them simple to use."

He nodded. "All except for the Grand Nexus, in case a hostile race decided to use it to take over a few worlds."

"Hmm." I pursed my lips. "I hadn't thought about it that way, but you could be right." While the builders might be fine with beings using the Obsidian Arches for travel across their own realm, they might have issues with a race like the Seraphim using the Grand Nexus as a means of invasion.

David tapped his temple. "It might just work."

"I hope so. We activate the arch, dash through, stick out our tongues at Serena, and run for the hills."

"If we do escape, we can't just leave her here to build an army of Nazdal."

I felt my eyebrows rise. "Aww, you do care."

"Of course I care about an invasion," he said with a sigh. "I didn't go through centuries of grief and longing to give up the ghost now."

"Then why did you act so nonchalantly when we met in the graveyard?" I folded my arms across my chest. "And you were such an asshole to me after the Exorcists banished us here."

David looked away. "I didn't want to feel what I was feeling, Justin." His eyes met mine, and he placed a hand on my shoulder. "I didn't want to care. I didn't want to feel pain if something happened to you."

"All that smart-assery was you deflecting emotion?"

"Yeah."

I rolled my eyes. "Man, we're both gonna need therapy after this."

He chuckled. "I hope our healthcare plans pay for it."

We walked back to the minder. "Can you link us?" I asked it.

Tentacles reached for us and paused, inches away.

199

"Ah." I nodded. The thing remembered. "Let's lie down first."

My father and I laid down next to each other. One of the minder's tentacles reached for me, and I was suddenly standing in a dimly lit room.

Dad looked at me. "Man, this is weird."

"Tell me about it," I said. "Let's start."

"Here goes nothing," he said, and the room vanished.

I walk through a forest. A beautiful voice echoes through the trees. I'm entranced. I have to find whoever is singing. I see sunlight painting a green meadow through the trees. A shimmer of golden blonde hair catches my eye. A woman is sitting on a boulder, looking at a deer as it looks back at her. It seems as taken as I am. I approach as silently as possible. A branch crackles beneath my feet.

The woman turns. Her eyes widen when she sees me, but she doesn't seem frightened.

"Who are you?" I ask.

"I might ask the same of you," she says.

"You might." I grin, and approach. This woman's eyes shine like sapphires. Her skin is fair. Dimples form in her cheeks when she smiles. She will be a fun conquest. "What is that song?"

"Oh, it's not a song," she says. "More of a tune."

"I've never heard it before." I switch to demon sight and am taken aback by how brightly her halo of soul essence shines. It's unlike any I've seen before. "You're not like any human I've met."

"Nor are you." She smiles, displaying her cute dimples. A stray lock of hair falls across her face, and I want to tuck it behind her ear.

She is so confident. Power radiates from her. Something tells me she will be much harder to bed than any woman I've met before.

The scene flickered back to the room. I realized with a start I had seen the past through my father's eyes, when he and Mom had first met. I looked at Dad. His mouth hung open slightly, and his eyes seemed full of longing. "Are you okay?" I asked.

He nodded. "That was...intense."

"Yeah." I'd felt his emotions. Felt the lust burning in him when he'd seen Mom. I hoped the minder avoided any sex scenes, because I did *not* want to see them.

"I remember more now," David said. "I met Alysea in the meadow every day. She sang to me."

"Let's revisit those memories," I said.

I sit on the boulder next to Alysea. She refuses even to kiss me. It's maddening, but so alluring all the same. "Where is your homeland?"

"Far away," she says, looking into the distance.

"As is mine."

Her blue eyes fix on me. "Why do you continue to come to me when you know I won't bed you?"

"I find your company enjoyable."

"Enjoyable?" She laughs. "I hardly think you a man who idles time away with frivolous pursuits."

"I am David," I say, finally telling her my name. "I am not exactly a man."

She raises an eyebrow. "Truly?"

I sigh, and tell her of my demonic origins. How I am here to stop the invasion of the mortal realm by those we call the Seraphim. Her eyes grow troubled as I speak. "What's wrong?"

"David, I am Seraphim."

I jump from the boulder and look at her. "You are one of the invaders?"

She gives me a sad look. "I am the one who allowed them here. All this destruction is my doing."

The scene flickered.

Alysea and I sit in our usual place. She sings the melody which attuned the Cyrinthian Rune to this realm.

"Is there a way to close the Grand Nexus?" I ask.

She nods. "I am attuned to the rune. I can remove it from the arch and close the gateway."

"Will you help us?" I ask.

"Do the demons plan to invade if we drive away my people?"

I shake my head. "No. We only wish to protect our own realm."

A lovely smile graces her lips. "I don't know why, but I trust you, David. I will help."

A warm feeling blossoms in my heart. To have the trust of this woman means more to me than anything else before. I don't understand why. She could die in our quest to disable the nexus. The thought of her death, of her absence fills me with such pain I can hardly bear it.

I reach my hand to her hair and tuck a golden lock behind her ear. My thumb traces her cheek, her dimples. Every part of my being aches when I'm apart from her. I don't understand what is happening to me.

Each day we meet and speak. She sings the melody which aligned the Cyrinthian Rune to Eden, and those aligning it to other realms.

"I can usually sense what lies on the other side of the nexus before opening it," Alysea says. "Sometimes there is nothing but void. In this case, I sensed life, but when I opened it, there were horrific creatures there."

"Were you attacked?" I ask.

She shakes her head. "They wore chains and crawled like animals. One made it through before I could close the gateway. It lunged at me, but I killed it."

"Were you afraid when you opened a gateway to Eden?"

"I was more careful," she says with a smile. "I was shocked to discover beings so much like us."

"How many realms do you think there are?"

"Does not your sire, Baal, know the answer? Is he not the most powerful demon?"

"If he knows, he does not tell me. He thinks me a failure."

Alysea's hand goes to my face. Her touch sends wonderful chills down my back. "You are no failure, David. Moses trusts you, and so do I."

Flicker.

Alysea sings the song of Eden to me. We speak of finding others who may have the perfect pitch needed to remove the Cyrinthian Rune in case something happens to me and Alysea when we attempt it. So far, we have found no one who is capable of the task. We are meeting with Moses tonight to hear his plan. Though we outnumber the Seraphim, most of our soldiers are only human. We have the Darklings as well, but most aren't nearly as strong as their Brightling brethren.

Moses thinks engaging the Brightling forces with our army will give a small group a chance to slip through and disable the nexus. I will go with Alysea and Nightliss. My heart swells with fear for Alysea's safety.

The vision ended. Dad and I stood feet apart in the dream room. He wiped at his eyes.

"So vivid," he said in a whisper. "I'd forgotten so much. The way she made me feel. The way she touched me."

I placed a hand on his shoulder. "Dad, I know it's hard."

His eyes met mine. "You're calling me Dad again."

I felt a smile tug my lips. "Don't get sentimental on me now, old man."

"I'll do my best." He squeezed his eyes shut, pinched the bridge of his nose then opened his eyes. "Did you memorize the song to Eden?"

"Yes, but we have another problem."

"You can't sing it, can you?"

I shook my head. "I'm a terrible singer. There's no way I could get the perfect pitch I need."

"Damn." He rolled his shoulders, as if loosening tension. "It was a great idea, Justin, but I don't know how to fix your voice."

"I don't either." The grim realization hit me in the gut like a fist.

The room vanished, and I jerked awake. The first thing I saw was Serena's smiling face as the diminutive woman looked down at me.

"How are things progressing?" she asked.

I blinked a few times and sat up. "Figuring out how to fix the nexus."

"Wonderful." She looked at David. "The minder said you needed him to help. How?"

"My mother is the one who tuned the Cyrinthian rune," I said. "My father is the one who knows more about her than anyone else here."

"Ah." She pursed her lips and regarded the arch for a moment. "Very clever. I knew you could do it." Her gaze returned to me. "What did you discover?"

"I have to sing to the rune to align it with another realm." I hated telling her the information, but she already knew a lot about me and my mom, so I had to assume she also knew about the singing part. "I just don't have the voice for it."

"Perhaps you can practice," Serena replied.

"You don't understand," I said. "Some of the notes are so high, I'd need supernatural hearing to hear them. I probably need a supernatural voice to go along with it." I knew for a fact my voice was just awful, supernatural or not.

"I'm confident you will succeed," the Arcane said. She gave me a sweet smile. "Feel free to use your father's help." She tilted her head slightly. "Do you require more food?"

I wanted to tell her I didn't believe this nice act for a minute, but decided to play along. "No, thanks."

"Very well, I will leave you." She turned and left, writing in her notebook as she walked.

I stood, and walked in a circle. How in the world could I crack this nut? I couldn't hit the notes. Hell, I couldn't even hear them if I did. Hearing them in a dream was obviously different since Dad's hearing was supernatural at the time of the memory. There had to be an answer.

"I know why Daelissa wants Ivy," I said. "She might be the only other person besides Mom capable of attuning the Cyrinthian Rune. She must have developed her abilities much faster than I did. If I'd had supernatural hearing when I was little, I might be able to sing it now."

"Possibly," Dad said. "But Ivy's voice is too immature to handle it."

"Who actually removed the rune from the Grand Nexus during the battle? Who caused the Desecration?"

He shrugged. "We never even made it close enough to find out."

"Where is the Grand Nexus?" I'd been there during the portal glitch that had sent me, Shelton and some others to the realm with the siren women. The control room was so full of cherubs, we hadn't dared go back.

"Chernobyl."

I felt my eyes widen. "The radioactive place in Russia?"

He returned a wry smile. "Actually, it's in Ukraine."

"Oh." Geography had never been my strongest class. "Why am I not surprised?"

"The Soviets nearly stumbled upon it several times, so those few of us who knew what it was decided on drastic measures and caused the nuclear plant meltdown."

"All this time, you've known where the Grand Nexus is, and you never told me?"

"Believe me, it was best we kept the secret." Dad folded his arms. "Daelissa doesn't even seem to remember, thanks to the Desecration."

"Somehow, your memory has remained intact all this time?"

"Not exactly," he said. "We may be immortal, but our brains don't have enough room for every memory. Only the important ones remain."

"Like how you met Mom?"

"Yeah." He sighed. "I remembered, but the dream memory brought it all back with such clarity. It was like being there all over again."

"Nothing quite like falling in love is there?"

A smile touched his lips. "No, there isn't."

An odd sensation tugged on my senses. I turned as another minder drifted into the room. Dad and I looked at it with

205

apprehension. The first minder reached a tentacle for me. I flinched, but allowed it to touch me.

Yours, came its whispery presence.

"Mine?"

Your minder.

Chapter 25

I looked at the creature floating before me. Like the other minders, it resembled a brain with jellyfish appendages. In other words, I couldn't tell the difference between it and the other one floating next to me. I wondered if it was an actual representation of my psychic emanations in the Gloom, or simply a minder who was in charge of enacting my dreams.

The image of a minder taking another of its kind under one tentacle and explaining the job popped into my head. "Look here, Bob. It's your job to stalk this guy's dreams, and recreate them here in the Gloom so we can fill the world with magic. The pay might suck, but the benefits are amazing."

Something about this situation felt right, as if I'd been waiting my whole life for this moment. "Hello, Minder Justin," I said, not sure how to greet it.

It reached a tentacle for me and touched my forehead. *You look shorter in real life.*

"Shorter?"

And you really need to lay off the erotic dreams about Elyssa.

This minder was a complete smartass.

"Something wrong?" Dad asked.

I chuckled. "Not at all. This is definitely my minder."

Yes, unfortunately.

"Fine, you don't have to lay on the sarcasm so thick, buddy." I took a deep breath in an attempt to put my thoughts back in order. "Why do you have such an attitude, but this other minder is so short on words?"

His human is dead. We lose our minds when that happens, or at least the personality.

"Is that why he doesn't understand free will?"

We don't have free will like you do. We are extensions of those in the mortal realm.

"You seem to know a lot."

Only because you do, and because I'm connected to you. When I disconnect from you, I won't have nearly the spark I do now.

"That stinks."

It's better this way.

"I have a silly question—"

You think I can help you sing?

"That wasn't exactly what I was going to ask." I noticed Dad giving me a strange look. He couldn't hear Minder Justin's side of the conversation, so it looked like I was talking to myself. "I need your help with something else."

The decision.

The second I heard the word, everything suddenly felt right. "Exactly."

It's odd, but I feel like this is destiny taking shape.

Calm settled over me. "I think you're right."

Lie down, and we'll get started. I'm curious to see what happens next.

"You and me both." I lay down on the floor. "Here goes nothing," I said to Dad.

"With what?" he asked.

"The decision."

A look of concern flashed across his face. He knelt and touched my arm. "Good luck, son."

The world vanished.

I stood on a small island. The black and white suns hung halfway down the sky with the gray moon above them, forming a triangle. Something caught the corner of my eye. I looked right and saw a copy of me standing there. His eyes glowed white instead of my normal blue.

"Weird," said another voice.

I looked left and saw another clone of me on the other side. His eyes burned ultraviolet.

You have the freakiest visions, said the voice of my minder.

"Tell me about it," my two clones and I said at the same time.

We looked at each other, our brows scrunched with confusion.

I backed up and bumped into someone behind me. I spun and saw yet another copy of myself, this one with gray eyes. "Oh, I get it," I said, refusing to be surprised again.

"You do?" the other copies asked, eyes hopeful.

"Yeah, your eyes are the same colors as the two suns and the moon."

They looked at each other, and then up at the sky. "Oh," they said, dragging out the O the way I did when finally grasping the obvious.

I felt somewhat pleased I'd been the first me to figure it out.

Any idea which one to choose? my minder asked. *I kind of like you with the gray eyes.*

You don't know how to make the choice? I thought back to the minder, to avoid confusing my clones.

Look to the eclipse.

I looked up and noticed the two suns moving behind the moon as they had in the other vision. As before, the heavenly bodies vanished where they aligned with each other until only an invisible shimmer remained in the air.

Why are you waiting? You already know the answer.

"But, what if I'm wrong?"

I don' think you are.

"I hope you're right." One last look at the sky, and certainty filled me.

I'd say the choice is clear. The minder laughed in my head.

"Very clever." The heavenly bodies separated once again, this time with the moon beneath them, and the white and dark on reverse

209

sides. "Now I understand the vision from the park." It all made such sense. "Mr. Gray told me neither the Murk nor the Brilliance is evil or good. They merely represent different kinds of change."

"Sounds right," my clones chimed in unison.

I continued. "His idea of balance is gray. I mistakenly thought balance meant stasis. But there's no such thing as true stasis. If something tries to remain exactly the same, it almost always ends up deteriorating and falling apart."

Different states of being, Minder Justin sent.

"Exactly. Paper comes from a tree. Is it still a tree, or something new? Was the tree destroyed to make the paper, or was it simply recreated?"

Creation and destruction are the same.

"They are simply two different ways of looking at changing state," I said. "To build a house, you must first destroy the original state of the trees."

In other words, the choice wasn't between the light, the dark, or the gray. The choice was how I decided to use the power associated with them. Combine the light, the dark, and the gray, and the result was colorless, neutral. In other words, the choice was clear.

I joined my left hand with my dark-eyed clone and my right hand with my light-eyed clone. The three of us stepped forward into the gray-eyed clone. My body expected a collision. My mind felt certain something else would happen.

The clones vanished. I stood alone on the island. Pressure built in my chest and an invisible shockwave radiated out from me, consuming the suns and the moon. A calming light suffused the air around me.

Warmth flared in my hands. I held the suns in either palm. Almost by instinct, I cast a white sphere of energy into the air. It orbited around my chest. I sent the ultraviolet orb chasing its brother around me. With both hands, I conjured a gray orb and sent it circling as well.

This is so awesome! My minder shouted in my head.

"Totally."

I channeled magic through the orbs. A shimmering beam of invisible light speared into the sky. Fireworks of every color bloomed overhead, their explosions shattering the silent landscape. I channeled through the white orb, aiming a destructive beam at the water. Steam rose from the ocean where it touched. I channeled through the dark sphere, and turned the steam into a cloud shaped like an elephant.

"I got this!" I shouted, pumping a fist into the air.

Now you need to do it in the real world.

My heart sank. In the Gloom, I'd have no way of doing magic. *I might as well enjoy it while I'm here.* I channeled through the gray orb, and the elephant cloud held its shape instead of drifting apart.

I felt so different. So alive. Something stirred inside me, and I felt the demonic part of my soul for the first time since the ripper had torn a hole in the portal from the real world. It seemed somewhat happy to sense me again. But there was something else there as well, as if another presence had suddenly found me for the first time.

Great, now you have another voice inside your head, my minder said.

"No, this is different," I said. "It's like a window opened, and a fresh spring breeze hit me in the face. I don't know what it is."

It's your Seraphim side finally connecting with you.

I felt my jaw drop. "At last."

Tell me about it. How do you think everyone else feels about you taking so long to grow some hair on that chest of yours?

"Welcome home, Seraphim Justin." I smiled from ear to ear, and tried not to think about how powerless I'd be when I woke up from this dream. Right now, it felt like I'd opened a window to the various parts of my soul, and we were all meeting and greeting for the first time, sans name tags. If only I could do that in the Gloom.

Maybe you already are.

I jolted to an upright sitting position. The island was gone. I was back in the arch room of the fortress.

Dad was sitting up and staring at me, white faced. "What was that?"

"What was what?"

211

"It felt like a wave swept over me." His eyes went wide. "You did it, didn't you?"

"I did it," I said, beaming from ear to ear. "I did it!"

He gripped me in a firm hug and we whooped like we'd just won the Superbowl.

I had made the decision. Now I just had to survive to play my part with destiny.

Chapter 26

Elyssa

The forecast had been for a sunny day, but thick stormy clouds rolled in over the Templar compound in Decatur, blotting out the sun, and obscuring what little of the Atlanta skyline Elyssa could see from the top deck of the house. She'd been waiting and hoping her father's campaign would go well against the Synod Templars as they attempted to chip away at her father's forces.

So far, she'd heard no word.

Ivy had returned to Jeremiah's to find out more about Daelissa and her plans. Elyssa hoped she could squeeze more out of the old man than she had.

She sighed. Her heart felt heavy. *Where is Justin? Is he still alive?* She had no answers and no obvious way to go after him until the Borathen Templars could spare soldiers to take the Exorcists' church. She'd even offered to help her father, but he'd consigned her to guarding the compound along with about a hundred other Templars at the horse ranch which served as headquarters.

So far the Synod had raided only safe houses and other assets held by the Borathen Templars, but it might be just a matter of time before they attempted a strike here at the seat of power.

A wolf howled. Elyssa tensed at the sound. It was one of the lycans assigned to patrol the perimeter. Using a pair of binoculars, she scanned the area. Her arcphone dinged as security wards around the outlying area warned of intruders. She looked at the map and saw the location of the wards in question. Multiple icons blinked red to the

213

east, behind the house. She redirected her gaze to the area in question. The skeletal branches of the trees allowed her to spot movement rustling the bushes.

Dark forms rushed toward the compound. She zoomed in and saw the face and fangs of the enemy. *Vampires!*

Vampires wouldn't usually be effective during a daytime assault, but the thick clouds overhead prevented the sun from weakening them and burning their vulnerable skin. Elyssa swiped a finger, setting off the general alert. The vampires emerged from the trees, heading across the open pastureland around the buildings. Gloating leers flickered across their faces as they saw an enemy fortress unguarded. She counted about fifty intruders. As they closed in, Elyssa pressed another icon on her arcphone and sprung the trap.

Templars burst from illusion-concealed trapdoors in the ground behind and in front of the enemy in the east pasture. Silver darts flew from lancers attached to soldiers' wrists, immobilizing dozens of vampires before they could react. Vampires leapt at defenders. Some aimed pistols, no doubt using cursed ammunition, which penetrated Templar armor.

Bowmen atop the chapel to the side of the house rose from behind the crenellated walls, nocked arrows, and let them fly while Templar Arcanes aimed bolts of energy at the gun-wielding enemies.

Steel flashed as Templars swordsmen engaged the vampires who hadn't fallen from lancer darts. Elyssa itched to be down there in the thick of the action, but knew her role as coordinator was far more important. Within minutes, the vampire force was neutralized with minimal Templar casualties.

The soldiers bound the unconscious forms of vampires and checked for signs of life from those who hadn't been incapacitated in the first volley. A crew of Custodians, Templars who usually served to keep noms unaware of supernatural events, emerged from within the house with floating platforms designed to carry heavy loads. They helped the soldiers pile the vampires on the platforms so they could carry them to underground holding cells until Commander Borathen decided what to do with them.

Elyssa breathed a sigh of relief. *That was easy.* She took out her phone so she could reset the perimeter wards when she noticed something strange. There were blank spaces where several icons for wards had been. Another icon vanished, followed by another, this one on the west side. As the wards disappeared, a realization suddenly hit her. The first wave had been a feint to see what the Templar response would be.

She scrolled through a list of names on her phone and touched one. "Lieutenant Hutchins, perimeter is not secure. I repeat, perimeter is not secure."

"What's the situation, Coordinator Borathen?" he asked.

She told him.

"I planned for a contingency," he said, and shouted something to someone.

"Explain," she said.

"Watch the map on your arcphone," he replied.

Elyssa did so and noticed icons appearing, indicating a tighter perimeter around the compound. "You had the Arcanes set up more wards?"

"Yes. They just activated the secondary line. Let me know when they're tripped." He barked another command and then returned to her. "My wife and the other healers will have the wounded inside soon. We've loaded up the first enemy wave, and they'll be out of the way shortly."

Elyssa spotted Healer Hutchins and her group of Arcane medics moving a floating platform of injured Templars off the field. The woman usually worked at Arcane University, but had taken a leave of absence to assist the Templars.

"Are the secondary wards your contingency plan?" Elyssa asked.

"Part of it—" Elyssa heard someone speaking to Hutchins in urgent tones and took the time to look back at her arcphone. The secondary wards to the east and the west blinked red.

"Hutchins, rally your forces," Elyssa said. "The enemy has breached the second perimeter."

"On it," he said, and disconnected.

215

As if the oppressive cloud cover wasn't bad enough, even more gathered overhead, almost as if summoned to further underscore the stormy situation on the ground. The Templars gathered in ranks, several neat rows facing the east and west against the oncoming danger. Those on the front lines readied long shields designed to repel even cursed bullets while the back rows readied long swords to attack anyone attempting to breach the defenses.

Attackers arrived at the edge of the woods. The sounds of guns firing punctuated the air. Templar Arcanes on the roofs aimed their staffs at the lines of enemies and cast large balls of fizzling static electricity. The spheres hit the ground, flattened, and released waves of jagged energy. Cries of surprise rang out as guns were wrenched free from the grasps of the shooters. The weapons stuck together in clumps as the electrical pulses magnetized them, rendering them useless.

A few vampires broke from the tree line, trying vainly to recover their weapons, only to fall to lancer darts or blasts from the Arcanes. They quickly reformed ranks and marched from the trees. Elyssa gasped at their sheer numbers. There were hundreds—far more than the defenders. Even with their defensive lines, Elyssa knew there was little they could do to stop them all.

She saw sneers on the attackers' faces as they advanced on the Templars. The soldiers stood their ground. A cry went up from the attackers and they raced to sandwich the defenders between their masses.

Howls pierced the cold air. Dozens of lycans in wolf form raced from the north. The vampires turned to face the new threat, but even with the werewolves added to the defenders, they still vastly outnumbered the Templars.

The vampires attacked. Steel flashed. Bolts of arcane energy blasted into the attackers, sending them flying. Lycans bit into the flanks of the eastern line. The wall of Templar shields buckled and broke under the mass of bodies.

Elyssa felt useless watching from above. There wasn't anything more she could do from her observation platform, so she raced down the stairs and into the fray. A vampire came at her from the right. She shot a lancer, and his body went limp, crashing to the ground. Another attacker swung a sword at her neck. The vampire lacked proper training, she realized as she parried the clumsy attack, disarmed him with another stroke, and ran him through.

Enemies on the west had flanked the line. She raced in to counter their attack, ducking a sword thrust, and taking off the legs of the attacker. Her body flowed in and out of parries, thrusts, and kicks, disabling and killing vampires with a practiced ease she barely noticed thanks to years of training. Even so, a part of her realized their lines were crumbling, and the number of Templar bodies on the ground grew faster than those of the vampires.

She felt a strange sensation pressing against her and wondered if she'd been run through with a sword. Others nearby seemed to feel it as well, some pausing in mid-attack and backing away from their opponents. A wave passed over her, leaving a pleasant but odd feeling. She felt sunlight on her back and looked up to see the clouds clearing, as if a great wind had carried them away. But the gentle breeze had not been the cause.

The sun turned the battle. Vampires cried out as the rays hit their sensitive skin, burning many like fair-skinned people in the sun too long. Some collapsed. Others ran for the woods, but the winter had stripped the trees bare of leaves, offering no cover from sunlight. The Templars roared. The vampires, weakened by daylight, fell in droves, and before Elyssa could catch her breath, the battle was over.

A sense of well-being settled into her, as if something very important had just happened. Hope welled deep inside her. Templars straightened and looked into the sun as if they too felt it.

Hutchins came up to her, a grim look of satisfaction on his scarred face. "What happened?" he asked, looking around. "Was that a spell?"

Elyssa shook her head slowly. "I have no idea. But it feels...good."

He nodded. "We'll clean up the mess and get casualty numbers." His lips pursed. "We lost a lot of good people today."

"If the Synod is using vampires, that means Daelissa is giving her full backing." She looked at a vampire writhing on the ground, his

217

blistered face turning purple from sunburn. "Let's subdue them and get them underground. No sense letting them suffer."

Hutchins bared his teeth. "I'd as soon let them burn, but I'm tired of hearing them scream."

Elyssa turned her face to the sky again. This battle was just a taste of what was to come. But whatever had just happened gave her one of the most important things a warrior needed to be effective.

Hope.

Chapter 27

After Dad and I finished celebrating my victory, a gurgling noise caught my ear. I turned slowly and saw Maloreck watching me from a position near one of the pylons outside the ring. If the size of the drool puddle beneath his mouth was any indication, he'd been there for a while. I shuddered, and felt grateful he hadn't eaten me.

"I felt the surge as well," he gurgled, red eyes glowing. "I felt your power radiate. But are you stronger than the bright one?"

"I am," I said. "Join me."

He looked at me a moment longer. "Perhaps you will be our new master, but first, you must defeat the bright one. You must prove yourself."

"Tell your leader I will."

He nodded. "I will do so." Maloreck crawled away.

Creepy, Minder Justin noted.

I rocked back and forth on my heels with glee, and realized with a shock how strong I felt. Gravity no longer pinned me down. I felt as if I could fly.

You opened a window to your soul, said the voice of my minder.

"I did it," I said in a quiet voice. "I really did it." I still felt the connection to my demon half, but another strong presence also filled me.

Dad clapped me on the back. "I knew you could do it, son."

219

I looked at the other minder and the silent sentinels. "Now we have to figure out how to get out of here. Let's take a look at the arch."

"Lead the way."

Can I come? Minder Justin asked.

Of course. I paused. *Can you convince other minders to help us defeat Serena?*

It might be possible, but without their humans present to give them autonomy, breaking us out of our dream duties is almost impossible.

I nodded. *Do what you can.*

The three of us went to the arch, and I made a show of inspecting it. *Can the other minder hear me?*

Not over here, my shade replied.

I told Dad everything I'd experienced in the vision.

"The choice is clear, huh?" He glanced with amusement at my minder. "Sounds like you two are peas in a pod."

Boy and how, my minder and I thought at the same time. I think we looked at each other, but since the minder didn't have eyes, it was hard to tell.

Dad bit his lip. "I guess the only question remaining is can you sing?"

I tried a few experimental notes and felt the equivalent of a cringe from my minder.

Don't quit your day job, he said.

Dad grimaced. "You might be part angel, but you sure as hell can't sing like one."

I sighed. "No." I kicked at the floor. "What are we going to do?"

"So close," Dad said. "I can remember Alysea singing it so vividly."

"Me too," I said. The recalled memories burned bright in my mind. "But I don't have the voice for it."

You two are clueless, my minder said. *If you can remember it, you can dreamcast it.*

I felt my jaw go slack, and followed it up with a facepalm. "We can dreamcast her singing it," I told Dad.

He groaned. "Why didn't I think of that?" His eyes gazed into the darkness. "I can't stop thinking about her, Justin. Every time I close my eyes, she's there."

I put a hand on his back. "That's a good thing. You seem to be better at the dreamcasting, do you want to try it?"

He looked back at the sentinels. "I wonder if they'll notice."

"I don't know how much longer we have before Serena tightens her demands on us. We're all here, so let's do it now."

He nodded. "Let me get ready." He sat cross-legged on the floor and closed his eyes. After a few moments, a ghostly figure formed to his right. The nebulous figure sharpened into a feminine shape. Details formed, the hair, face, and a long white dress. The process seemed to take forever. I kept looking over my shoulder, hoping Serena didn't decide to make an appearance. The other minder stayed put as well, which I hoped was a good sign.

Dad rose from his sitting position and wiped sweat from his forehead. He looked with longing at the statuesque form of his wife. She looked at him and smiled. He caressed her jaw, and ran a thumb over her dimples. "Sing for me," he said.

She opened her mouth, and the haunting melody flowed forth. There were no words to accompany the chilling highs or alternating cadence. Her voice rang long sonorous notes one moment only to race through hundreds of staccato tones the next. Goosebumps ran up and down my spine at the sound of a true angel singing while memories from my childhood flooded my mind. I couldn't wait to see Mom again.

I looked at the rune. The glowing lines flickered a multitude of hues. I concentrated on it, trying to sense what was happening, but felt nothing. Alysea's voice held the last note, and faded to silence. There was one thing I hadn't considered. Even if the rune was now linked to the mortal realm, *where* in Eden would it open? I hoped it wasn't linked to the Grand Nexus, because going there wasn't an option, not with all the cherubs infesting the place. Darkwater had been clearing the relics of the husked angels, but I didn't think even they could clear the sheer number of shadow creatures haunting that place.

I reached out a hand to the rune. It floated from its socket and glowed.

I hope this works, Minder Justin said.

"It has to," I said.

I'm going to go before you activate it. I don't want to be around when Serena comes back.

"Probably a good idea," I said.

In the meantime, I'll see what I can do about rounding up minders to help you tear this place apart. When and if you return, just think real hard about me, and I'll come.

Thanks for the help, I thought back.

Just don't do anything stupid. And, good luck, dude. It floated away and vanished through the door at the far end of the chamber.

Serena practically ran into the chamber a moment later. "I felt something," she said, her excited voice echoing in the cavernous chamber. "It shook the fortress to its foundation."

"Sorry, just a little indigestion," I said, trying to stand in front of the effigy of my mother.

Serena's eyes widened. "Brilliant. You dreamcasted Alysea. Were you successful?"

"Now or never, son," Dad said.

Grinning, I said, "As a matter of fact, I think so." I held a hand to the rune. It sprang from the socket, rotating beneath my fingers, tickling each one with static. I willed the arch to activate. The silver ring in the floor flashed bright. Aether filled the air around us, and sheets of black and white energy flashed across the center of the arch. I sensed the arch questing for an Alabaster Arch in the real world, since that was the only way for it to open a portal to another realm. It connected, but I sensed dark, deep cold all around the unseen destination.

For all I knew, the sensation was perfectly normal. On the other hand, I didn't want to die the instant the portal opened, so I willed the connection to shift to another Alabaster Arch.

222

"What are you doing?" Serena shouted over the hum of the arch. "I promised Daelissa she would be the first one to open the arch to Seraphina!"

"Why does she get first dibs?" I said, stalling as I felt the arch continue to search for a suitable destination. Impressions of a dark room filled my mind. I heard Serena shouting commands.

"Sentinels," Dad said. "They're coming into the circle."

We couldn't wait any longer. I sent the command to the arch. *Open!* A wave of white static crossed the arch. An image flickered and stabilized. It looked like an arch control room. I didn't see any cherubs waiting and felt a flood of relief. I looked at the rune. *I can't take it without causing a backlash.* I didn't like leaving it in the arch, but unless Serena could attune it, she couldn't remove it either. For now, the rune was linked to Eden, and the Shadow Nexus couldn't be used to connect to other realms.

"Go," I said, risking a look over my shoulder. A dozen sentinels raced across the space between us.

Dad ran through. I followed. The sentinels were almost upon us. I turned to close the portal. A sentinel ran through and puffed into vapor the instant it crossed into the real world. It was followed by another and another, but their dreamcasted forms couldn't survive outside the Gloom.

"Na-na na-na boo-boo," I stuck out my tongue at Serena. "Stick your head in doo-doo!"

The door behind her burst open, and a horde of Nazdal loped into the room, their crooked gait deceptively fast. Their voices gurgled with excitement, their eyes glowed red with hunger.

"Goodbye, creepazoids," I said, and willed the portal closed.

The gateway vanished. We had escaped.

Chapter 28

"Holy Mary," I shouted. My legs were shaking, and sweat dripped down my face.

"I need a drink," Dad said.

We looked at each other and burst into crazed laughter. When the laughter died down, I took stock of our location. It was definitely an arch control room with an Alabaster Arch. Judging from the size of the structure, it was not the Grand Nexus.

"I have no clue where we are," I said.

"I don't care." Dad made a fist and bared his teeth. "I feel strong again. I guess that means we're really back in Eden."

"Well, we're certainly not in the Gloom."

"Can Serena use the arch to send Nazdal after us?" Dad asked.

I'd been so busy celebrating our escape, I hadn't given it much thought. "Yikes. We better go now, just in case."

"What about these other arches here?" He waved a hand at the rows of black arches in the control room. "Can we use one to get out of here?"

I glanced at the rows of other arches. "Possibly, but I don't want to chance using a damaged one and end up dead." I jogged toward the front of the room and out the door. "All we need is a phone so I can call Elyssa. She'll be able to open a portal using the omniarch in the mansion."

We ran up a long tunnel with a ramp. It only took me a few seconds to realize where we were. "We're in Australia at the Three Sisters control room," I said. "I was just here not long ago."

"What brought you here?"

I told him the short version of how I'd rescued Mom from Maulin Kassus and his band of battle mages as we ran up the tunnel.

"I don't know how you do it, Justin." Dad shook his head. "All this time you've been saving the world, and I thought I was doing my duty by keeping the Houses of Daemos glued together by any means necessary."

"I understand why you're marrying Kassallandra, Dad." My stomach knotted. "I don't like it, but I understand. If she goes to the Seraphim, there's no way we'll win. It'll be tough even with her support."

"Especially if Daelissa uses the Nazdal," Dad said.

We reached the top of the ramp and pushed through a thicket of vines. A jungle waited outside. I groaned, because it wasn't a short walk back to civilization. Elyssa and I had chased Kassus on a flying carpet for several miles before reaching the Three Sisters, a popular tourist attraction in these parts.

"Let me get my bearings," I said, and scrambled up the trunk of the tallest tree in the vicinity. From the top, I looked across the green canopy and spotted the trio of towering cliffs known as the Three Sisters. It was nearly impossible to use the sun for direction because once I was back on the ground, the trees would shield much of the light. It was good having my supernatural powers back, though. They made climbing the tree a cinch.

I slid back down to the bottom, and brushed the bark off my clothes. "We need to go that way," I said, and pointed.

Dad was looking back toward the concealed tunnel mouth leading back down to the arch. "While you were up in the tree, I could have sworn I heard sounds coming from the arch cavern."

"Serena might have reopened the gateway," I said.

Dad looked around. "Let's get out of here."

I hadn't taken more than a couple of steps when something leapt from behind the vines covering the tunnel. The sound of

225

bubbling phlegm quickly told me it was a Nazdal. Its skin blurred from the color of the tree to a normal pink hue just as it slammed Dad in the chest. I flashed toward him, and kicked the creature hard. It flew off and smacked into a tree. Several more of the creatures jetted from the tunnel after us.

"Run!" I shouted.

Before I could move, red vapor shot the mouth of one of the creatures. I held my breath, but it didn't matter. The vapor dragged on my limbs, weighed them down like lead, and it was all I could do to move. Dad seemed to be in similar shape.

"No more Mr. Nice Guy!" Dad roared, and morphed into demonic form. His muscles exploded to humongous size. His clothes ripped and tore, and horns as thick as my arms grew from his forehead. He caught the first Nazdal leaping at him, and crushed the creature with one hand. His giant foot lashed out at the next, and sent it ricocheting off the trunks of several trees before coming to rest in a lifeless heap.

It occurred to me I had more than my demonic origins to rely upon now, and instead of manifesting, drew upon my Seraphim side. I hurled a ball of sizzling white at a Nazdal, catching the thing in mid-air. The creature's gurgling scream cut off as searing flames consumed it. Another Nazdal lunged toward me. Its claws nearly reached my throat. I caught it by the neck at the last second and summoned more destructive Brilliance.

The Nazdal howled, its crooked body flailing as the heat cauterized its throat shut. I flung the body away. The disfigured creatures prowled around us, eyes glowing brighter than ever. They seemed to be growing in size, their muscles swelling with every death of a comrade.

"Are you stronger than the bright ones?" said Maloreck as he crawled from the shadows.

"I am," I said. "How many of you do we have to kill to prove it?"

"We take the life of the fallen," Maloreck said, his bones cracking as his body stretched and grew. "The blood pact is an honor with any who fall before us. To waste the life is wrong."

"Not good," Dad said, his voice deep and guttural in demon form.

I did a quick headcount and estimated about twenty more Nazdal. Those remaining had all grown, though not as much as Maloreck. If they'd been absorbing life force from their dead, it meant each survivor would be that much stronger.

"What happens if you kill one of us?" I asked.

"We will not waste your life, honored one." Maloreck panted, as if his desire to sample my life force would be the sweetest thing he'd ever tasted.

"My life force tastes like soot and poo," I said. "You won't like it at all. I think it's a genetic deformity."

"Soot and poo?" Maloreck asked.

I saw the other Nazdal closing in from the other sides. My limbs lightened, and I felt the effects of the red vapor wearing off.

"Let me explain," I said. "It's like—one, two, three, run!" I said the last part really fast, but Dad caught on without hesitation.

We needed a clear path. I summoned dark energy and imagined what I wanted. A shockwave burst from my hands, knocking the Nazdal in our way to all sides. One of them hissed the red vapor, but the cloud narrowly missed us as we streaked past.

Dad's feet sounded like the pounding of timpani drums. His stride was absolutely monstrous thanks to the extra few feet he'd gained as an infernal creature. I didn't have the time to manifest into demon form, but managed to keep up thanks to the path he cleared through the thick foliage. I glanced back. The Nazdal loped after us. Their stride looked ungainly, but the mere fact they were keeping within sight meant they were faster than they looked. Dad crushed a sapling, and leapt up an incline. I jumped atop a boulder, slipped on the mossy surface, and scrambled back to my feet. Roots and muddy ground made the terrain slick and treacherous. The Nazdal with their claws were having no such issues.

Then again, neither was Dad with his big demon feet. I knew if I paused to manifest, the Nazdal would be on me. Then again, why couldn't I just use magic to help me out? Channeling Murk, I shot strands of dark energy from my hand. They latched onto trees. I willed the energy to contract, and it shot me forward like a rubber band.

Before my feet hit the ground, I shot more strands of Murk, swinging myself along much faster than when I'd been on the ground. I caught up with Dad. He gave me a surprised look.

"You've read too many comic books," he said, breathing heavily.

"Hey, it works doesn't it?" I yelped as my next swing nearly carried me into a low-hanging branch. "Guess it could use a little more work." I risked a glance back. The Nazdal were nowhere in sight. Either we'd outdistanced them, or the trees and foliage were hiding them. I hoped they'd given up because we were closing in on the cliff wall ahead. We reached the base. I looked up the sheer vertical wall of rock and a wave of vertigo made my knees go weak.

Dad dug his claws into the rock and climbed. I shot a strand of energy, and slingshotted myself upward. Just as my upward momentum slowed, I shot another strand. Before long, we were halfway up the cliff face.

I looked down and saw Nazdal climbing the cliff behind us, their claws making them nimble as squirrels.

"I don't know if I can make it," Dad said. His huge muscles trembled with fatigue. "Something in that red mist drained my endurance."

I felt my own endurance flagging but wasn't ready to give up. "I'll carry you, but you'll need to shrink to normal size."

One of the Nazdal closed in and hissed out more red vapor. The fringe touched my father's legs.

"Go, Justin. You're the important one." His eyes rolled into the back of his head, and his body toppled backward.

"No!" I shouted. I shot a strand of Murk around his waist. His demon form was huge, and with my waning super strength, it was all I could do to hold him up. In one hand I held onto the rope of energy attached to the cliff. In my other hand, I held my father's life.

The Nazdal lunged for him. I jerked my arm, and swung Dad just out of reach. David's body shrank rapidly. His weight diminished drastically. The Nazdal swiped at him again as his body swung like a

228

pendulum. I jerked up, and Dad just barely sailed over the outstretched claw.

This wasn't going to work well, not with the speed of our pursuers. Magic was wonderful, but I had to use physics as well. I might be able to muscle Dad up to me, but I'd need all my remaining strength to make it to the top of the cliff. "Please help me science," I prayed. Holding the energy rope anchored to the cliff, I ran sideways along the vertical cliff face as fast as I could. I managed to run until I stood at a forty-five degree angle from where my magical rope anchored me to the cliff. Dad's body swung below me. Using the momentum, I jerked forward the arm supporting him. His body swung perpendicular to mine. As it swung back down, I timed, it, and pushed off the cliff. Our bodies flew back the other way. The Nazdal had changed direction and were coming for us. I extended my feet and booted the first one off the cliff. One of the creatures grabbed the Murk rope connecting me to my father.

My forward momentum slowed. Dad's body swung up at a sharp angle, and the Nazdal lost its grip on the cliff. I willed the energy strand to vanish, and our attacker plummeted down the face, its gurgling wail fading. The other Nazdal watched it fall, their eyes gleaming. Some of them raced down the cliff face like roaches toward their fallen comrade. I imagined they wanted to absorb the life from it.

Dad's body reached the apex of its upward trajectory. I shot another strand at him, and snatched him from the grasp of another Nazdal. I didn't have any choice but to burn more energy, so I jerked the aetherial rope upward and caught Dad around the waist. At the same time, I saw Maloreck, bigger than ever, scampering up the cliff wall, his claws digging gouges in the rock.

My body cried out with pain. My magical muscles were ready to give out. We had so far to go. I felt raw hunger tearing at my stomach. I needed to feed. I considered firing a volley of energy at Maloreck, but knew it would cost me too much. Every ounce of strength left had to go toward getting us up the cliff. I climbed past a chunk of rock jutting from the cliff wall. It shuddered when I put my

229

foot on it. I wondered if I could kick it loose and take out a few Nazdal below.

I could make a giant magical slingshot and take them out.

A slightly less suicidal idea ricocheted off the original thought and gave me a much needed dose of hope. Balancing Dad on my aching shoulder, I attached a strand of energy to the boulder, and kicked it. It shifted from its precarious perch. I heard the crumbling of rock and felt the small ledge holding the big rock give way. "Here goes nothing." I willed the strand of energy anchoring me to the cliff wall to become elastic.

The boulder fell and we were in freefall. I heard a screech as the boulder knocked loose a Nazdal. Its claws grasped at us but fell just short. Air whooshed when we passed other pursuers climbing the cliff. I felt tension in the rope anchoring us to the rock face. The falling Nazdal's gurgles faded as he continued his plunge. The tension in the anchor grew tighter, tighter, and tighter still. We slowed to a crawl as the weight of the boulder carried us at least a hundred feet below our attackers.

I released the rope connected to the boulder. We flew up like a shot. I felt the anchor go slack as we passed the point where it connected to the cliff. I saw the railing atop the cliff beckoning, and shot another rope of Murk toward it. It connected just beneath the ledge. With all the strength I had left, I jerked hard on the magical rope and gained another twenty feet.

Still holding Dad in one arm, I jerked hard on the rope with the other, climbing a few inches at a time until we were just below the ledge. I looked down and felt sick with vertigo. We were so far up, the Nazdal looked like insects below us. Holding onto my father, I couldn't reach the railing, so I connected him to the cliff with another rope. Muscles burning with fatigue, I pulled myself over the ledge. Tears formed in my eyes as I fought the pain. I looked below and saw Dad dangling in free air like a spider's next meal. I gripped the cord and pulled him up. I heard murmuring and cries of surprise as I pulled him over the railing.

I staggered backward. Felt someone catch me.

"Are you okay?" I heard someone ask with an Australian accent.

"Where did they come from?" someone else asked.

I heard someone else cry out in fear. I looked as a Nazdal crested the rise and leapt on a man taking a picture. The man screamed as the disfigured creature dug a claw into his stomach and ripped out his intestines.

Chapter 29

Pandemonium erupted. People scrambled to escape as more Nazdal clambered over the railing and set their sights on an all-they-could-eat buffet. A Nazdal leapt on a woman as she tried to video the event on her cell phone. Her scream cut off abruptly as the attacker tore out her throat with jagged teeth. The phone slid across the pavement and stopped near my feet. I was too tired to fight. My muscles were fried. My magic was fizzling. I had only one thing left to do.

I took a picture of a kiosk, and texted it to a number I'd long ago memorized. The phone rang.

"Who is this?" asked Elyssa.

"Baby, I need your help now!"

"Justin? Oh my god, I've been—"

"No time. I'm about to die. Take the portal and get me!"

"I'm not at the mansion. Hold tight, baby, I'll save you." The phone went dead.

I looked as Nazdal tore into tourists left and right, not differentiating between man, woman, or child. I felt sick. I'd led these creatures here, and I couldn't stop them.

I have to try.

I lay Dad on the ground, drew in a breath to steady myself, and channeled aether. A Nazdal pounced toward a screaming child, his short legs pumping in vain to escape. I directed a jagged pulse of

Murk. It knocked the predator off course, causing it to smack into a large metal map display.

Another Nazdal hissed a cloud of red mist toward a group of teenage tourists who were taking as many pictures as possible. One of the girls shrieked as the disgusting spray blew across her face. Everyone it touched dropped to their knees. They tried crawling away, but the poison, or whatever it was, seemed to inhibit muscle movement. The attacker's eyes gleamed. I directed another pulse of energy toward it. It was just enough to send the creature reeling backward as if it had been sucker punched, but that only delayed it.

My target glared at me. I noticed the other Nazdal focusing on me as the greatest threat.

"Come get me, you ugly sons of bitches," I growled. I aimed another blast at the closest Nazdal. Instead of blistering heat, a beam of light about as powerful as a flashlight momentarily blinded it. I had plenty of aether to use, but something inside me was weak from the overuse. My knees felt like gelatin. I wobbled. Maybe I could manifest. Maybe I could scream like a girl and run, possibly lead these things away from the other people and Dad.

Maybe I can die.

My future looked shorter than a midget in a meat grinder.

A Nazdal leapt for me.

Goodbye cruel world.

A fireball caught the creature in midair. Charred remains hit me low in the legs and knocked me on my butt. A spear of violet sliced the head off another Nazdal. A blazing meteor the size of a car crushed a group of them. Screams and cries went up from the injured and dying Nazdal.

I caught sight of Maloreck. He was huge, muscles swelling larger with every death. He leapt to the railing and looked at me. "You have given me many lives today, warrior. If you defeat the bright one, we will be your devoted."

"You have a funny way of showing it," I said, trying to shout, but managing only a hoarse whisper.

"I go now to become the master of my tribe," he said. "We will see each other again." With that, he vanished over the side.

I gave up trying to regain my feet and flopped onto my back. I saw Shelton and Bella looking down at me.

"The Australian government must hate you," Shelton said with a shake of his head. "This is the second time you've torn up their country."

"What, may I ask, was that thing?" Bella asked.

I was too tired to respond.

"Is that your Dad?" Shelton knelt down and felt my father's pulse.

"Help the poor boy stand, Harry." Bella lifted my father, tossing him like a sack of potatoes over one shoulder. Despite her petite frame, she was pretty freaking strong, due to her being a dhampyr.

Shelton, on the other hand, was a plain-Jane Arcane. Hs slung my arm over his neck and help me stagger next to him.

"This is horrific," Bella said, tears forming in her eyes as she looked over the massacre. The photographers had managed to get away, but there were at least a dozen people dead. It was hard to tell with all the body parts and internal organs strewn around. I felt sick. Dad and I could have led the Nazdal away from people. Instead, we'd led the creatures right to helpless noms.

"Let the Custodians handle it," Shelton said. "We need to get these two back to the mansion, pronto."

"Okay," Bella said. They headed behind a kiosk where a portal shimmered in the air. Through it, I saw the mansion cellar. They stepped through, hauling us with them. The portal within the omniarch winked out.

"Where is Elyssa?" I asked.

"She's at The Ranch," Bella said.

"The Templar compound in Atlanta?" I asked.

"Yes. Things have been quite eventful since your disappearance." She shifted Dad to the other shoulder. "Meghan is gathering supplies so she can look at you, but I need to come back down here and open portals for her and Elyssa."

"I can't wait to hear the story behind this," Shelton said with a grim sigh. "First thing I heard you were going to talk to your dad.

Next thing I know, Elyssa's got us tracking down the long-lost tribe of Templar Exorcists and paying visits to Jeremiah Conroy."

"What?" I said, nearly losing my feet at the shock of his last statement.

Shelton chuckled. "Sounds like we have some good stories to swap."

"Can't wait." At the moment, it was all I could do to stay awake. My knees gave way and Shelton grunted as he struggled to keep me upright.

"I'm an Arcane, not a vampire, man. Use your feet." Shelton gripped my waist and jerked me from my knees.

We reached the second floor. Bella took Dad to another room, and Shelton dropped me into my own bed. The room was a mess. Elyssa usually kept everything spotless, probably thanks to her Templar military upbringing, so I knew her mental state was way out of whack if she'd allowed the room to deteriorate like this. I couldn't wait to see Elyssa. Couldn't wait to kiss the real her instead of a dreamcasted clone. I closed my eyes and imagined her walking through the door.

And promptly fell asleep.

I woke and saw an arm across my chest. Elyssa lay next to me, her head pressed into the crook of my arm, her leg tossed over mine. I didn't know how she'd fallen asleep because I had some serious body odor going on thanks to not showering over the past two days. I kissed my girlfriend's forehead.

She moaned and blinked open her eyes. Before I could say a word, she pressed her lips to mine and took my breath away. She pulled back and leaned over me, a curtain of raven hair hanging around her face. "I missed you."

"I missed you too," I said, and kissed her again. "Sounds like you've had some adventures while I was gone."

Elyssa smiled. "You did it, didn't you?"

"Did what?"

"Made the choice."

I raised an eyebrow. "How do you know about that?"

235

"Jeremiah Conroy told me it was why you had to go into the Gloom."

I sucked in a breath. "You really went to see him?"

"Ivy went with me."

"Do you realize how dangerous—"

She pressed a finger to my lips. "He told me you had to go into the Gloom, and showed me part of Foreseeance Forty-Three Eleven I'd never seen before."

I felt my forehead scrunch. "But I thought the foreseeance was done and over with."

"It is now," she said. "I didn't realize it at first, but when you chose, I felt it—everyone felt it."

"Dad said something similar," I said. "Geez, I didn't realize it was such a big deal."

Elyssa smiled. "We were fighting vampires at the compound. Whatever weirdness sent that wave, cleared the sky and let the sun shine. Your choice won the battle."

I felt my eyebrows rise. "I saved you and wasn't even in this plane of reality? I am a badass."

She snorted. "You certainly smell like ass."

"Hasn't stopped you from kissing me." I winked. "Why don't you help me clean up."

"Whatever his awesomeness requires." She bit her bottom lip, eyelids heavy. "Just tell me where you want to get clean…or dirty."

After a much-needed "shower", Elyssa and I went downstairs. It was midafternoon, though it felt like morning. I'd completely lost track of time in the Gloom, but apparently we'd been gone a little more than forty-eight hours. Meghan Andretti, an Arcane healer and friend, saw me coming down the stairs, and motioned toward a chair.

"I need to give you a checkup," she said.

"How's my dad?" I asked.

"Much better," he said, emerging from the kitchen bearing plates piled high with pancakes, bacon and eggs. My little hellhound, Cutsauce, jumped around his feet, yipping like crazy. "I know it's not breakfast time, but my stomach doesn't care."

"Me want pancakes," I said, mouth watering.

"Grab the orange juice, and it's a deal." He winked and dropped a piece of bacon. Cutsauce caught it before it hit the floor, and raced away with his prize.

Grinning like a school boy, I ran into the kitchen and grabbed two glasses filled with orange juice. When I came back out, I caught a confused look from Elyssa. The last she'd known, I was furious with Dad.

Meghan took out a wand and waved it down my body. Numbers floated in the air to the side. I tried to ignore them and made short work of a stack of pancakes. I couldn't stuff them in my mouth fast enough.

"Well, my readings make absolutely no sense," Meghan said after a moment. "I suppose that's to be expected from the Cataclyst."

I groaned. "I wish everyone would stop calling me that."

"Well, well, well. Look who decided to wake up," Shelton said as he and Bella walked down the stairs. His eyes lit on the pancakes, and he rubbed his hands together. "Ooh, breakfast for lunch? Count me in."

Bella rolled her eyes. "You're such a terrible roommate, always eating what other people cook."

He snatched a piece of bacon and crunched down on it. "Mm, crispy. Just the way I like it."

I looked at the group. "Why isn't Mom back yet? Where's Ivy?"

Dad stiffened, but quickly recovered with a smile.

Elyssa took in a breath as if she was about to say something I wouldn't like. "When your mom went to Colombia to help Nightliss, it was just supposed to be a day trip, but either the Synod, or vampires allied with Daelissa put on an offensive. The Colombian Templars went into communications blackout and we haven't heard from them yet."

My chest went cold. "And Ivy?"

"She's at Jeremiah Conroy's."

I jerked to my feet. "Say what?"

Elyssa's eyes wrinkled with worry. "When Ivy decides to do something, there's nothing anyone can do to stop her, and you know

237

it. I don't think Jeremiah can keep her against her will even if he wanted to."

"No, this isn't good. We have to get her."

"Justin!" cried a girlish voice.

I looked across the room and saw Ivy racing for me, arms outstretched. She gripped me in a tight hug. I grunted at the impact.

Ivy looked up at me. "I'm sorry you were worried, but it was so cute watching you show brotherly concern."

I kissed her on the forehead. "Visiting Jeremiah wasn't a good idea."

She shrugged. "It worked out. He knows a lot about Daelissa, so I figured it wouldn't hurt to grill him."

"Did he tell you anything?" I asked.

"He said we're not ready to fight her." Ivy backed away, her face serious.

"Why is Jeremiah being so helpful all of a sudden?" I asked.

Dad cleared his throat. "Conroy has his own agenda. He's got his finger in nearly as many pies as Daelissa does."

"It is good to see you again, Justin," Cinder said, walking from the direction of the planning room.

I stood and shook his hand. "Good to see you." I looked around. "Looks like the gang's all here—at least most of us—and we have a lot to catch up on."

"Man, is that an understatement," Shelton said. "But first, we have something for you."

Bella burst from the kitchen with a white frosted cake on a plate. A candle in the shape of an angel sat on top of it with a burning wick for a halo. "You did it!" she shouted.

Shelton stood and started a slow clap. Meghan rolled her eyes but joined in. Dad barked a laugh, and stood as everyone clapped faster and faster.

I stood and waved off the applause. "I don't know whether the slow clap is a good thing or not, but yes, I finally made the decision." Looking at the angel candle, I couldn't help but smile from ear to ear.

"Welcome to the big leagues," Ivy said, giggling.

I flicked a finger, and the candle poofed out.

"Holy Mary, did you see that, Bella?" Shelton said. "The kid finally put out a candle without destroying everything around it."

"I'm so proud of you," Bella said, walking over and giving me a hug. "We all are."

Elyssa kissed me on my cheek. "Happy angel day, sweetie."

Dad met my eyes. He seemed to be beaming as wide as I was. I noticed Ivy staring at him, apprehension in her eyes. Dad's gaze shifted to her, and his smile faded somewhat. She'd never really known her father. Maybe he'd faked a lot during my childhood, but at least I'd seen him almost every day, from childhood to adolescence. Ivy hadn't seen him since infancy. This new family life wouldn't be easy for either of them. Then again, Dad had to marry Kassallandra. If the good guys were going to beat Daelissa, we absolutely required a united Daemos.

"Enough of the congratulations," Shelton said, interrupting my thoughts. "I want to hear everything."

I put a smile back on, and sat down. "Let me start from the beginning."

After I finished, Elyssa relayed her adventures. I couldn't fault her for anything. If roles had been reversed, I would've torn the world apart to find her.

Standing up, I put on my game face. "The next order of business is shutting down Serena's army."

"And stopping the Exorcists," Elyssa said.

"Sounds like more than we can chew at the moment," I said.

"We should go to the planning room," she said. "I've discovered a lot of interesting things about the Exorcists while you were gone."

The group migrated down the hall to the room. I took a slice of cake and a glass of orange juice with me. Shelton grabbed the tray of breakfast food and took the whole thing with him.

Once inside the room, I closed the door and Shelton activated the anti-eavesdropping wards.

Elyssa placed her arcphone on the table and projected a holographic image above it. A pyramid of pictures appeared with

Montjoy at the top. "This is Albert Montjoy, the man in charge of the Exorcists."

"Justin and I can confirm that," Dad said.

"During my hunt for information, I interrogated several Exorcists," Elyssa said. "The organization keeps their initiates in the dark, but I discovered some very frightening facts."

"Like what?" I asked.

"There are thousands of Exorcists. Maybe tens of thousands. They've infiltrated branches of government, religious organizations, and corporations worldwide."

I felt my eyes widen. "They're even more dangerous than the Synod Templars," I said.

She nodded. "Daelissa knew she needed the Exorcists when the Templars disbanded them. She gave Montjoy resources to take the organization underground and he grew them like cancer into a massive organization that answers to him and Daelissa."

"Holy crap in a cupcake," Shelton said. "I thought we were already behind the eight ball just because the Synod has more Templars than we do. But if this is true, we're even more screwed than I thought."

"It's true," Elyssa said. "And we simply don't have the resources to fight them."

Chapter 30

"We still have a chance," Dad said after a moment.

Hopeful eyes turned to him.

"What do you mean?" I asked. "If we kill Montjoy, would that remove the threat?"

He shook his head. "The Daemos knew about the Exorcists and their secret mandate, so we devised a plan to counter them. We infiltrated nom politics, social organizations, companies, and so forth, placing our people in high places in case we ever needed help."

"I didn't realize there were enough Daemos to occupy so many positions," Shelton said.

Dad raised an eyebrow. "There aren't. Do you really think the masters of seduction would have any problems recruiting noms?"

Shelton whistled. "That's a lot of pillow talk."

"You realize that's against the Overworld Covenant," Elyssa said with a tiny smirk.

Dad shrugged. "The vampires and other factions do the same thing. Our 'human'"—he made air quotes—"resources are much more limited. House Slade and House Assad partnered this effort centuries ago, and it has proven to be quite profitable."

"You said we have a chance" Shelton's lips pressed together. "What is it?"

"Houses Slade and Assad can activate their agents. We might be able to purge the Exorcists from high positions, or at the very least counteract them."

"What happens if Kassallandra goes over to the dark side?" I asked.

Dad's troubled gaze met mine. "She could expose our entire network."

"I don't like this Kassallandra woman," Ivy said. She'd been very quiet during the proceedings. "I can do something about her if you want."

Dad held up his hands. "No, sweetie, that won't be necessary."

Ivy narrowed her eyes. "Why not? If she goes away, you can take over House Assad."

"It's not that easy." Dad pursed his lips, and gave her a very serious look. "There are others in her house who want to take everyone into hiding at the first hint of war. She is the only one with the power to keep all of House Assad in line."

"Bunch of scaredy-cats," she said. "They're so scared of Daelissa, they won't fight." She wound a strand of blonde hair around a finger. "Maybe I should make them scared of me. Maybe Daelissa is right—"

"Ivy," I interrupted. "Daelissa is wrong. Fear will make people obey you, but it doesn't command respect or loyalty. Someone who believes in you and respects you will fight harder and with more courage than someone fighting out of fear."

"But Kassallandra doesn't believe in you," she said. "She doesn't fear you. All she cares about is herself."

"Well, maybe we can change her mind," I said. "But now is not the time."

She sighed. "I still think we should blast her."

Shelton snickered. I shot him a warning glare. Ivy was still a danger. Her impressionable mind was filled with Daelissa's lessons.

"Now that we've covered the Exorcists, what about the Nazdal?" Shelton said. "Seems like our favorite insane angel has been busy."

"A finger in every pie," Dad said.

242

"The Nazdal might join me," I said.

"But first you have to beat Daelissa?" Shelton said. "She'll eat you like a chicken burrito."

"Thanks for the vote of confidence." I pursed my lips. "When I re-attuned the nexus in the Gloom, I exclusively linked it to the Alabaster Arch in the Three Sisters control room. She can't connect it to any other Alabaster Arches in Eden, and she can't use it to bring more Nazdal from their realm. That means she only has the Nazdal from the pit."

"From what you described, there are hundreds of those monsters in the quarry." Shelton shuddered as he snatched another piece of bacon. "If Maloreck got fat from the humans they killed in Australia, imagine how big those things will grow once they start a wholesale slaughter."

"It sounds to me as if the Nazdal must wound their prey to steal its life," Meghan said. "The poison cloud they secrete temporarily slows or disables the prey and drains endurance."

"It drops humans pretty fast," I said. "If Maloreck decides to attack a city, it'll be a massacre."

Elyssa's phone buzzed. She snatched it off the table and answered. "Commander Salazar?" She got up and left the room for a moment. Upon returning, she looked excited. "The Colombian legion has completed its operation. They're off communications blackout."

"What about Mom?" Ivy asked.

"Once they finish tying up some loose ends, she and Nightliss will be back."

I noticed Dad's eyes flash with something akin to alarm, though he said nothing.

"This means we have the manpower to do what needs to be done," Elyssa said. "We can take a legion into the Gloom and wipe out the Nazdal and the Gloom Initiative once and for all."

"Uh, you're overlooking something huge," Shelton said. "Arcanes can't cast in the Gloom, and you'll be cut off from your supernatural strength."

243

"Not necessarily," I said. "If I can reopen the Shadow Nexus, the window to the real world should allow us to operate at full power."

"What's the range?" Shelton asked. "How far can you go from the arch before you weaken?"

"Maybe a few hundred yards." I shrugged. "It's a gradual weakening, not a total cutoff."

"You can't open the Alabaster Arch in the Three Sisters control room from this side," Dad said. "The Grand Nexus doesn't have a Cyrinthian Rune, so the Alabaster Arches in Eden can only receive portal transmissions from other realms, not send them."

"We could use the Gloom arch in the Church of the Divinity," Bella said.

Elyssa made a face. "That arch is tiny. I'd have to send an entire legion through it in single file. Can you imagine how long that would take? Not only that, but we'd have to march across the city to the fortress, and fight our way through it to the arch chamber. From the way Justin described the place, our forces would be massacred."

"Serena obviously activated the Shadow Nexus again to send the Nazdal in pursuit," Dad said. "Maybe she left it open. The Alabaster Arch is big enough to send a legion through in no time."

"We could check it out using the omniarch," Shelton said.

Dad nodded. "Good idea."

"Let's do it," I said, rising from my chair.

"I'm calling my father." Elyssa took her arcphone off the table and made a call. She stood and walked away from the group as she talked.

"Justin, my biography of you is growing quite large," Cinder said, showing me a thick sheaf of bound parchment.

"Why are you writing it instead of recording with an arcphone?" I asked.

"Shelton told me real books are written with quill and parchment, and it would be—how did he phrase it?—ah, an artistic travesty to use technology." Cinder tucked the massive tome under an arm. "I believe this history will be important in the future."

244

"I'm sure," I said, wondering who in the world would believe half the stuff I'd been through. "Thanks for keeping a record."

"It is my pleasure," he said, managing to look proud despite the somewhat disturbing toothy grin on his face.

Elyssa took me by the hand and led me away from the group as they went downstairs. "My father is coordinating with Commander Salazar and his Colombian legion to see how many people they can spare. Our battle with the Nazdal and the Exorcists will have to be a joint effort."

"Sounds like a logistical nightmare," I said.

"Yeah, we're working on that." She squeezed my hand. "Your mother and Nightliss are coming."

I felt my stomach clench.

"What's wrong?" she asked. "Your family will be mostly together again."

"Dad has to marry Kassallandra," I said, feeling sick to hear the words come out of my mouth. I winced at the pain. "The part of me that is his son hates it and doesn't want it. But the part of me that has to fight Daelissa and her army understands that he has no choice."

Elyssa hugged me tight. "Duty and family don't always go hand-in-hand." She kissed me and drew back. "I should know."

"I know it'll be hard on Mom, but it sounds like she's already accepted the inevitability," I said. "Ivy will be a challenge."

Elyssa grimaced. "Considering her offer to blast Kassallandra, I think you're right." Her eyes met mine.

I squeezed my eyes shut and pinched the bridge of my nose as regret threatened to overwhelm me. "I want my family together one last time before Dad has to marry Kassallandra."

"I'll make it happen," she said. "After we take out Serena, we'll have one last party before your father has to leave."

My heart swelled with love and hope, nearly overwhelming the sadness. I wrapped my arms around Elyssa and buried my face in the crook of her neck for a long moment. Her scent, like flowers and cold steel, always seemed to reassure me. She was beautiful and soft, but deadly and hard as nails when she needed to be. She was mine, and I was hers.

"I'm so lucky to have you," I said.

"I know." A sudden sob shook her.

"What's wrong?"

Elyssa pressed her face to my chest. "I thought I'd lost you, Justin. I thought I'd never see you again. I felt sick to my stomach and couldn't stop crying." She looked up at me with tear-stained eyes. "It felt like the end of the world."

"I'm back." I wiped a tear from her cheek.

"And I feel like the luckiest girl in the world." She smothered me with a fierce kiss. "Let's go kick Serena's ass." Elyssa wiped away the tears. Her stern Templar exterior took over.

Yep, that's my ninja girl.

I smiled with pride.

We went down a long flight of stairs to the arch room. The room connected with a corridor that went through the old dungeons beneath Arcane University, offering a back way out of the mansion should we ever need it. Thankfully, the omniarch could open a portal to just about anywhere in Eden, provided we had a clear image of where we wanted to go. Unfortunately, it couldn't open a portal to another realm—at least not on purpose. I wasn't counting the accident that sent me, Shelton, and Adam on our journey of discovery and near death into the Siren realm.

Shelton had opened a portal to the Three Sisters arch control room in Australia. The Alabaster Arch was off, and the room was silent. He looked back at me and Elyssa. "I sent through a couple of ASEs to patrol the place in case Serena sends troops through. You're sure this is the only Alabaster Arch the Shadow Nexus links to?"

"I'm positive," I said. "She can't change the attunement of the rune, so it's locked onto one destination."

ASEs, or all-seeing eyes, were marble-sized devices that magically recorded their surroundings. Templars used them for spying and remote patrolling.

Elyssa glanced through the portal. "Good." She took my hand. "Justin and I are going through. I'll need to scout a staging area for the troops."

246

I looked at the small omniarch and the small portal between its columns. Three people abreast could fit through it. Maybe four if they were scrawny. Most Templars were anything but scrawny. "You're planning on moving the troops through that?"

She pursed her lips. "The aperture is not much larger than the Gloom arch. That's why I hope the Obsidian Arch in the Three Sisters way station works. Then I can send troops through the La Casona Obsidian Arch in Colombia straight through to the Three Sisters."

"How many soldiers are we talking about?" I asked.

"Nearly a thousand." She sighed. "I hate logistics." Still holding my hand, she stepped forward through the portal and into the Three Sisters arch control room. After surveying the area, we stepped outside into the main way station. An Obsidian Arch loomed in the center. Despite the yellow light suffusing the air in the chamber, the place felt spooky. Darkwater had cleared the place of cherubs, and for that I was immensely grateful.

Elyssa regarded the arch for quite some time before turning to me with a thoughtful expression. " So, can you make that thing work?"

"Maybe." I walked back inside the control room and stepped up to the modulus pedestal. I pressed my palm to the modulus and raised it. Stars on the map highlighted as I rolled through them. The world map showed an Earth with landmasses far different than the ones we knew now. The creators had likely designed it before the dawn of man. Even so, the continents were similar enough to recognize. It also explained why some arch stations were in the middle of nowhere. When they were made, no cities or points of interested had existed. Other cities had grown around arches, quite possibly due to Overworld influences.

I settled on the Obsidian Arch in the Grotto way station just to see if I could connect to it, and flicked my finger to select it. The star in Atlanta pulsed, but there was no corresponding star to indicate this arch. Most way stations with Alabaster Arches didn't show on the world map. The arch builders must have intentionally left such way stations off the map to prevent the natives from discovering a way to travel to other realms.

At least, that was my theory.

For over a minute, nothing happened. I could force the connection, but was hesitant to do so since the Grotto way station usually hummed with activity. A klaxon sounded from the way station, and a thin beam of light arced from the Grotto to a blank spot on the continent resembling Australia.

We jogged outside into the chamber and watched as an image of the Grotto way station stabilized. A man in black-and-yellow-striped robes peered curiously through the portal. He caught sight of us and his eyes flicked wide.

"I thought Darkwater activities were officially shut down," he said. His eyes narrowed and he looked us up and down. "You don't look like Darkwater employees."

"We're not," I said. "This is official Templar business."

"Which way station is this?" he asked.

"Weren't you able to see it on the map?" I asked.

"No. The traversion indicator didn't light up." He pursed his lips. "Which Templars are you with?"

Elyssa and I looked at each other. She apparently decided to play dumb. "I'm sorry, but what do you mean?"

The man, still standing on the Grotto side of the portal took a step back. "You're not a Templar if you don't know what I'm talking about. Cyphanis Rax ordered us to cease all cooperation with the Borathen renegades."

"Commander Borathen is not a renegade!" Elyssa stepped forward, a snarl on her face.

The arch operator yelped and leapt back. The portal shimmered, rippled, and winked off.

I groaned. "This isn't good."

"Since when did Cyphanis Rax take over the Arcane Council?" Elyssa asked. "This is even worse than I thought."

Cyphanis Rax was an ally of Daelissa. The former Arcanus Primus, Jarrod Sager, had also been Daelissa's stooge, though not willingly. He'd died to protect his son, Harry Shelton. Rax seemed to be entirely devoted to Daelissa. Last I'd heard he was running in a special election to take over as primus. Somehow, another giant roach had just taken power. The odds were stacked even higher in favor of Daelissa.

Chapter 31

"At least they don't know which way station we're in," Elyssa said as we jogged back to the portal which would deliver us into the mansion.

I growled. "As far as I know only Alabaster Arch way stations don't show on the map. It won't take them long to narrow down which one we're using."

"We have to take a chance and use it," Elyssa said. "The regular control rooms can't select this arch anyway, right?"

I shrugged. "I don't think so. That won't stop someone from taking one of the omniarches and opening a portal here."

"When my father tried to arrest Maulin Kassus, he decided to severely cripple Darkwater, so he sent a team of Arcsys experts to download all of the data from their network and erase everything Kassus and his people had collected over the years." Elyssa sniffed in satisfation. "That should keep this place safe for a while."

We stepped through the portal and back into the arch room beneath the mansion. Shelton wasn't there anymore. Elyssa turned to me as I deactivated the omniarch. "Commander Salazar took control of the La Casona way station. He's in control of the minders and the Obsidian Arch there. We can use it to transport his Templar legion directly to the Three Sisters way station."

"See?" I said, brushing my hands together. "Logistics aren't so awful."

Shelton rushed down the stairs. "Holy crap, man. I just found out Cyphanis Rax just took over as the new primus via secret ballot."

"What happened to holding a special election?" I asked.

Shelton shook his head. "According to council bylaws, in a state of emergency, they can replace the current primus with a new one by secret ballot and bypass the special election." Shelton made a face. "They claimed the rebellion in the Templar ranks constituted an emergency and put Rax in command without so much as a by-your-leave from the Arcane community." His jaw tightened. "They're already posting bounties on Arcnet and the aethernet." He flashed an image on his screen. It was my face. "Folks, we're wanted men."

"That's nothing new for me." I blew out a breath. "We need to mobilize immediately and take out Serena. If we can prevent her troops from entering the mortal realm, it'll be that much easier when the war starts."

"It'll be an uphill battle no matter how you cut it." Shelton made a fist. "But we'll make them pay for every inch."

"What if Serena never reopens the Alabaster Arch at the Three Sisters?" Elyssa asked. "So far, that's our only way back into the Gloom and the fortress."

I'd already mulled the possibilities and come up with one answer. "We'll have to secure the Exorcist church and use the Gloom arch inside. We can send a small, covert force through the Gloom arch to infiltrate Serena's fortress and open the connection between Shadow Nexus and the Three Sisters Alabaster Arch. Then we send in the troops and mop the floor with her."

Elyssa pressed her lips together. "Not bad. It might just work."

Unfortunately, one major detail stood in the way. "Before we start the battle, we'll need to kill the brain."

"The minders who control the sentinels and fortress defenses?" Elyssa asked.

"Yeah. Otherwise, the sentinels will crush our troops." I folded my arms. "Unfortunately, I don't know how to kill a minder."

"I'll bet Cinder could figure it out," Shelton said.

I headed upstairs and went in search of the golem. As usual, he was in the planning room just off the main hall on the first floor.

"Hello, Justin." Cinder looked at the holographic display from an ASE hovering over the table. "The Darkwater database is full of interesting facts. Did you know they tracked major figures in the Overworld and human political systems? It appears many of them engage in illicit affairs. Darkwater apparently used this information to extort—"

"Yeah, yeah," Shelton slashed a hand through the air. "We don't care who's spreading their wild oats. We need more practical information."

"I would be delighted to help." Cinder tilted his head slightly. "What would you like me to find?"

"Can minders be killed?" I asked.

"I will search until I find something," he said.

"The Colombian legion deals with the minders at La Casona," Elyssa said, taking out her phone. "I'll ask Commander Salazar what he knows." Elyssa stepped outside the room.

"Searching now," Cinder said. "Unfortunately, the information acquired from Darkwater is scattered within these ASEs. It may take some time to parse them all."

"Do what you can, please." I turned to Shelton. "I highly doubt Serena is going to reopen the portal between the Shadow Nexus and the Three Sisters any time soon. Elyssa and I think a small team can enter the Gloom through the arch in the Exorcist church and infiltrate the fortress."

Shelton's forehead wrinkled. "That's the arch the Exorcists used to banish you in the first place, right?"

I nodded.

"Sounds like sweet irony in the making." He tapped a finger to his chin. "Didn't you say the sentinels nabbed you the second you got close to the place?"

"Yeah." I bit my lip. "We have to figure out how to sneak inside their perimeter without the minder brain knowing."

Shelton mulled it over. "Could you dreamcast something to fight the sentinels?"

"Maybe." Dad and I hadn't tried it. "The minders rule the Gloom, so they might be more powerful than we are when it comes to that sort of thing."

"Mind over matter."

"A fight we probably won't win against creatures that look like floating brains." I pondered the problem. "Maybe my minder could help."

Shelton's face brightened. "Yeah, it could even the odds."

Dad stepped through the doorway. "If you need a team, count me in."

"Are you really that eager to go back?" I asked.

"Hardly." He snorted. "You and I have the most experience with the Gloom. It makes sense for us to lead the way."

Elyssa entered the room. "I spoke to my father. Commander Salazar will be on standby to attack the fortress once the Shadow Nexus is opened either by us or by Serena."

"What about the Exorcist church?" I asked.

"Borathen Templars will help us secure the church."

"Justin, I believe I've found something," Cinder said, displaying the image of a familiar contraption on the screen.

"Is that a picture of Serena's lab?" I asked.

"Yes," he said. "This device is called a psionic disruptor."

A hexagonal arrangement of large Tesla coils surrounded a device composed of interlocking rings at the very center. "I saw that thing when we were there," I said. "What does it do?"

"It was created so they could experiment on minders." Cinder retrieved the image of a control panel with glowing symbols on it. Next to the control panel was a legend with various combinations of symbols. One combination had the word *terminate* next to it. Cinder highlighted the word. "I believe entering this combination will kill any minders within the perimeter of the disruptor."

"You're amazing," I said, patting him on the back. "Can you send this image to my phone?"

The golem nodded. "Right away."

I turned back to Elyssa. "What do you know about the church?"

Elyssa displayed a holographic diagram of the Exorcist church. She touched a finger to an area on the front and the back of the structure, marking them red. "These are the only two ways in."

"What about the windows?" I asked.

"Magically reinforced." She shifted the view to the side of the building. "They use the same kind of spells the windows on the mansion use."

I'd found out how tough those windows were when trying to dive through one. The material stretched and repelled attacks. Even demons summoned by the Black Robe Brotherhood hadn't been able to smash through them. "Are the doors warded?"

"Magically locked," Elyssa said. "We'll need someone to crack the spell." She scrolled the image and pointed at rows of cross-shaped holes in the sides of the church. "When we tried to get in, the Exorcists shot at us from these holes. We may need someone to shield whoever is cracking the wards on the door."

"Adam Nosti can crack the wards," Shelton said. "I should be able to shield him while he does it."

"What's the plan once we're in?" Dad asked.

"Templars will secure the sanctuary," Elyssa said. "Justin, didn't you say the Gloom arch was blocked when you tried to come back through?"

I nodded. "We'll need to remove that before we can use it."

"Adam again," Shelton said.

"Justin, this information may be useful." Cinder whirled an ASE and brought up a holographic display of a Gloom arch over the table. "Darkwater acquired some of the Exorcist training videos."

"Videos?" Shelton laughed. "I gotta see this."

"They are quite informational," Cinder said. "As explained in the video, The Gloom arch does not open to a remote destination, but creates a portal to the Gloom in the same place as the arch."

"The Exorcists used a singing ritual," I said.

"The singing ritual is unnecessary, according to the video." Cinder flicked the image of the arch. It vanished and was replaced by the video of a man dressed in the monk-like robes of the Exorcists.

Awful easy-listening music sounding like a duet between a pan flute and an organ played in the background. The man spoke to the camera.

"During your time as an Exorcist, you'll see many amazing things. The Gloom arch is one such wonder." He touched the gray structure. "Since exorcism is successful in most cases, banishment isn't used very often. However, you may come across tough cases every once in a while." He offered a reassuring smile as another man in a robe appeared on camera. "Remember, always ask your backup buddy to help you move the possessed into the containment circle." He pointed to his eyes. "Keep a sharp eye out for any silver objects that may have fallen across the circle and might prevent it from closing." The man touched his ears. "Listen for signs of danger from the possessed subject, and don't be afraid to ask your coordinator for more help." The two men smiled vacantly. "Remember, look, listen, and ask."

Shelton roared with laughter.

I sighed. "Cinder, can you fast-forward to the important parts?"

"Of course." Cinder waved his hand over the video and advanced it.

"...the ritual is just for show," the man said, and pressed a finger to the silver circle in the floor around the Gloom arch. "You seal it like any other arch, and will it to open." A portal flickered on in the arch. "If you simply will it to open, it won't rupture the veil between realms and cause the vacuum usually associated with Gloom fractures. The Exorcist ritual leaders typically use the slashing method when opening the portal. This tears through the veil and causes the vacuum between the mortal realm and the Gloom." The man smiled. "This is often used to demonstrate power to prisoners. Don't be afraid to use intimidation. Remember, the possessed are dangerous, and the Gloom is no place you want to end up on accident, right, Phil?" He turned to his partner.

"That's right, Roger. Know your surroundings. Know how to operate equipment. Know how to handle the possessed. Remember the three Ks" Phil turned to Roger. "Now you know."

Roger smiled. "And knowing is half the battle."

255

Cinder stopped the playback as the two men clasped hands and raised them overhead in some sort of victory pose. The golem turned to us. "This means you can safely enter and exit the Gloom via the arch."

Shelton slapped Cinder on the back. "Nice job, buddy."

The golem regarded Shelton for a moment. "Thank you for your non-aggressive show of appreciation, Harry."

Shelton rolled his eyes. "You sure do have a way of ruining the moment."

"This is perfect," Elyssa said.

The new knowledge encouraged me. "It also means we'll be able to cast spells, at least within range of the arch."

"Will magic carpets work in the Gloom?" Shelton asked.

I shrugged. "I think so. Their levitation spells are self-contained."

"There's a great deal of speculation in the Darkwater database about the Gloom effect on supernatural abilities," Cinder said. "So far, I have found no definitive answers."

"I should be able to use my abilities," I said. "My Seraphim side seems to help me overcome the Gloom limitations."

"Can you draw us a diagram of the Gloom fortress?" Elyssa asked me.

I hadn't seen the entire structure, but remembered enough of Jarvis's tour to sketch the basics. Using my finger, I drew a map on an arctablet and displayed the image above the table. "Here's the pit," I said, drawing the quarry. The pit extended like a semi-circle around the back of the fortress like a barrier. Next, I drew a long rectangle in front of the pit and another large circle behind the complex. "This is the fortress"—I touched the rectangle—"and the circle is the arch chamber." I marked the front entrance and outlined the corridors as best I could. Each bottleneck resembled a roundabout where the sentinels could eliminate any threats. Near the back, I drew Serena's lab, marking the location of the minder brain on the left. Behind the lab, I sketched the round chamber with the Shadow Nexus inside. I drew an X on the back wall of the fortress to the left of Serena's lab. "I think that's where the rear exit is."

Elyssa studied the diagram for several minutes. "The pit provides plenty of incentive not to come through the back." She narrowed her eyes. "Unless flying carpets work. Then we could fly across it and enter via the back."

"The minder brain controls the doors," Dad said. "We'll need to open them somehow."

"What about an invisibility spell?" I asked. "We could wait near the door until someone opens it."

"You're talking about a major power drain," Shelton said with a shake of his head. "Even if an Arcane could cast inside the Gloom, they'd be too tired to do much else after maintaining an invisibility veil."

"We can use Nightingale armor," Elyssa said. "It has rudimentary camouflage, but it won't last long."

I raised an eyebrow. "How long?"

"About ten minutes before it needs to recharge."

"That's not very long," Dad said.

I sighed. "It'll have to do."

Elyssa looked over the holographic diagrams of the Exorcist church and Gloom fortress floating side-by-side above the table. She drew circles, lines, and squares of different colors on both of them. Grunted, and erased them before starting again.

Adam Nosti and his girlfriend, Meghan Andretti, entered the room. Adam gave me a wave and walked over to Shelton. "Got your text," he said.

Dad pulled me to the side. "Why don't you fill me in on the plan later? I'm going to take a walk or something."

I felt my forehead crinkle. "Um, okay. You look a little pale. Are you feeling okay?"

"I'm fine. I just need some fresh air." Dad headed for the door.

I gripped his arm. "What's wrong? Why are you acting so antsy all of a sudden?"

The door to the war room opened. Dad stiffened. A petite woman entered. Nightliss was the spitting image of her sister, Daelissa, though her dark hair, green eyes, and olive-toned skin were in sharp contrast to Daelissa's blue eyes, blonde hair, and fair skin. I wasn't sure there was a term for the kind of twins they were—identical mirror twins?

"Justin!" Nightliss said, and gave me a firm hug. She kissed me on both cheeks. "It is so good to see you." Her eyes grew troubled as they gazed at Dad. "David?"

He grinned, reminding me of the smartass with whom I'd entered the Gloom. "Good to see you again, Nightliss."

"I have not seen you since Vadaemos," she said. "But lately I have begun to remember things from the far past about you and—"

"I was just leaving," Dad said, tipped his head, and headed for the door.

Nightliss shot me a puzzled look. I shrugged.

Dad headed through the door, and plowed right into someone rounding the entrance. He grunted. Blonde hair flashed, and a bundle of parchment paper flew apart and scattered across the floor.

My father's face went white. He recovered quickly with a smile. Alysea, my mother, looked at him in surprise.

"David?" Mom paused a heartbeat before bending down to retrieve her parchment papers.

"Here, let me get that for you." Dad leaned down to help her at the same time. They bumped heads so hard I heard the *thunk* from across the room.

"Ouch," they said, standing up and rubbing their foreheads in unison.

"I don't know if they're a match made in heaven or hell." Shelton barked a laugh.

Elyssa was suddenly at my side, hands gripping mine. "Are we about to have family drama?"

I suddenly understood why Dad had been in such a hurry to leave. He'd known Mom was on her way.

I felt someone grip my other hand and looked down at Ivy. Her young face looked troubled. "Should I go say hello to Mommy now, or wait until she kisses David?"

I wasn't sure what to tell her. "Maybe wait a minute and see what happens."

She squeezed my hand tighter. "Justin, I don't remember David, but now that all of us are here together, I just realized how much I want us to be together forever."

I squeezed her in a hug. "Me too, sis. Me too."

Mom and Dad seemed oblivious to the rest of us as they finished picking up the paper. Mom regarded my father with liquid blue eyes. He cleared his throat nervously and handed her the documents. "Hello, Alysea." He said her name so tenderly it was as if he'd just told her he loved her and missed her, all wrapped up into one word.

She smiled. "David." Affection filled her voice. A tear trickled down Mom's cheek.

Dad gently wiped away the tear with his thumb. "There, there, now." He caressed her cheek, and tilted her face up. "I'm sorry. I shouldn't be here."

Mom took his hand and squeezed it. "I'm glad you are."

I looked around and saw everyone else watching the scene like it was the best reality show ever. I steeled myself as conflicting emotions washed over me. Seeing how much they still loved each other filled me with happiness. Knowing Dad had no choice but to abandon Mom and marry Kassallandra drowned my happiness with intense regret.

This was torture. If it was bad for me, I couldn't imagine how bad it was for my parents. "Hey, Mom," I said.

She turned her solemn gaze on me. "Justin! Ivy!" Mom ran over and squeezed us in a big hug, kissing each of our cheeks. "I'm so happy to be back." She looked over at Elyssa. "Sorry we're late."

Elyssa offered a gentle smile for my mother. "Given the circumstances, it's perfectly understandable."

Mom looked at the diagrams Elyssa was working on. "What's the plan?"

A fierce look came over my girlfriend's pretty face. "It's time to start a war."

259

Chapter 32

Elyssa enlarged the diagram of the Church of the Divinity. "Two squads of Templars will accompany our infiltration team to the church. The Gloom infil team will consist of me, Justin, and David." She indicated circled areas on the roofs of neighboring buildings. "Alpha Squad will take up positions across the street. Beta will cover the rear entrance of the church. Gamma will occupy and secure the interior once we're inside." Elyssa turned to Shelton. "I'd like you and Bella to accompany Adam while he cracks the shield spell guarding the back entrance."

"You got it," Shelton said.

Elyssa circled the rear entrance with a finger. "I'm allowing a twenty minute window for opening the shield. Is that enough time?"

Adam nodded. "I doubt the spell is even half as complicated as the one we had to break in the arch room, plus I've optimized the spell code."

"Good." Elyssa shifted to an inside view of the church. "Once inside, Justin will activate the Gloom arch."

"I want to accompany your team," Mom said.

"Inside the Gloom?" Elyssa asked.

She nodded. "I have some experience at dreamcasting."

"I don't think that's a good idea," Dad said. "Arcanes can't cast spells in the Gloom."

"The Gloom dampens abilities, but Seraphim are strong enough to still channel magic at a diminished capacity," Mom replied, eyes flashing the same way Elyssa's did when she'd made up her mind and nothing would stop her. "I'm coming."

Dad seemed to know better than to argue. "Great. Let's have a family outing. I'll bring the picnic blanket."

"What about me?" Ivy asked.

Elyssa paused. "I'd like you to accompany Nightliss and the Colombian legion when we activate the Shadow Nexus. You'll be protecting our defenses." She glanced at my mother. "If that's okay with you, Alysea."

Mom looked uncertain. Ivy might be powerful, but she was still a little girl.

"I can do it," Ivy said, defiantly sticking out her chin.

"I will protect her," Nightliss said.

It was Ivy's turn to look uneasy. She'd once thought Nightliss evil due to her being a Darkling. Hopefully, that was a thing of the past. Ivy smiled sweetly. "Maybe I'll protect you." Nightliss laughed.

"Please take care of my little girl," Mom told Nightliss.

The Darkling nodded. "I will protect her with my life."

Elyssa exchanged a look with me. I returned an uneasy nod. She looked back at my mother. "Looks like the infil team will consist of the four of us then. I'll procure an extra set of camouflage armor."

She switched to the diagram of the Gloom fortress. "The Colombian Templar legion will take the Obsidian Arch at the La Casona way station to the Obsidian Arch at the Three Sisters way station. They will then form up inside the control room and wait near the Alabaster Arch for our infiltration team to reach the Shadow Nexus inside the fortress and open a portal to the Alabaster Arch." Elyssa traced a line from the Exorcist church to the fortress. "Once our team has entered the Gloom arch in the Exorcist church, we will infiltrate the fortress by taking flying carpets across Bellwood Quarry, landing near the rear exit of the fortress, and waiting for a target of opportunity to open the door."

"What happens if the camouflage charge on the suit runs out?" Shelton asked.

261

"We'll have to hope no one sees us," Elyssa said. "The flying carpets also have camo spells. We can cover ourselves with them to buy some time."

"Smart thinking." Shelton looked at me. "Thank goodness one of you knows how to plan."

Elyssa folded her arms and turned a questioning gaze on my mother. "How limited will your channeling be inside the Gloom?"

"Half power. Maybe less. It's been a long while since I've been inside the Gloom." Mom shrugged. "I plan to rely more on dreamcasting than channeling if at all possible."

"How does the Gloom keep Arcanes from casting?" Shelton asked.

Mom strode to stand beside Elyssa and turned to address the group. "When I first experimented with the Grand Nexus in Seraphina, I learned how to sense what lay on the other side of the portal without completely opening it. Seraphina has a shadow realm similar to the Gloom, as do many of the major realms I discovered."

"Seraphina has a shadow realm full of minders?" Shelton asked.

"I'm not sure what's there," she said. "Seraphina, Eden, and Haedaemos are full realms. The Gloom is essentially a shadow cast by Eden. The minders—to the best of my understanding—are shades of the people who live in Eden."

Shelton raised an eyebrow. "We all have our very own ghosts floating around the Gloom?"

Mom nodded. "In a sense, yes. Because the Gloom is not a full realm, entering it dampens your abilities. It's like placing a translucent barrier between you and your soul. While it's not impossible to penetrate, it is very difficult."

I turned to her. "Mom—Alysea, are you saying it's possible for Arcanes to cast spells in the Gloom?"

"It is possible, but extremely unlikely." She held her hand flat. "Imagine my hand is a sponge. Water can flow through the sponge, but only in a trickle. Most Arcanes don't have enough raw power to saturate the barrier enough so it can seep through."

"But the Gloom is chock full of aether," Shelton argued. "From what Justin described, they make the stuff there."

"Yes, but you're still out of phase from the real world." She shrugged. "I don't know how else to explain it."

"I think I got it." Adam's face brightened. "When we're physically in the shadow world, we're essentially shadows of our usual selves. Those who are very powerful in the real world will still have some abilities. The rest of us normal schmucks who don't have the raw power of a Seraphim can't cast spells."

"An excellent explanation," Alysea said. "Much better than mine."

"Kind of like someone trying to physically enter the demon realm," I said. "Our bodies aren't made to be there, and it screws us up."

"Exactly," Adam replied.

I turned to Elyssa. "When do we start?"

"Just as soon as the squads involved in the church assault arrive," she said. "That should be any minute now."

I swallowed a ball of nerves. "Alrighty, then."

"Are we late to the party?" said a sultry feminine voice.

I turned to see Stacey and her boyfriend, Ryland, enter the room. "Couldn't resist?" I said with a broad smile.

Stacey strolled to me with cat-like grace, and pressed her soft curves against me. "It's so bloody good to see you, my lamb."

"She's sitting this one out," Ryland said. The lycan stroked one of his mutton chops. "You want to tell them, babe?"

Stacey pursed her full lips into a sulky pout. "Bloody hell. You know I'd be perfectly fine."

I gave her a confused look. "What's going on? Are you injured? Sick?"

"You could say I'm sick," she replied, offering me a sly wink. "Unfortunately this particular sickness lasts nine months."

The women's eyes went wide with delight.

"You're pregnant?" Elyssa said.

"I'm so happy for you," Mom said, embracing Stacey.

"What wonderful news," Nightliss said.

263

"Oh, you're having a baby?" Ivy asked. "They're so cute. How do you make them?"

The women exchanged uncomfortable looks. Mom stroked Ivy's blonde hair and said, "Perhaps we should save that discussion for after we save the world."

Laughter broke the tension, though Ivy seemed a bit befuddled.

The conversation immediately devolved into discussing whether they knew what gender the baby was, whether it would be a felycan, lycan, or a kid who could switch between wolf form and feline.

Shelton conjured a case of cigars from somewhere and handed the first one to Ryland, slapping him on the back. I congratulated Stacey and walked over to the men along with Dad. My father took a stogie and lit it up. Adam took a cigar, but declined a light.

"These things give me the runs," he said with an apologetic simper.

I declined a proffered cigar, and shook Ryland's hand. "Congrats, man. When is the baby due?"

He shrugged. "Few months, I guess. Stacey didn't get morning sickness. I figured out she was pregnant when I started hearing two heartbeats when we went to sleep at night."

"Wow, what a way to find out," Adam said with a nervous laugh. "I, for one, am nowhere near ready for kids." He looked at his girlfriend, Meghan. She produced a wand and began checking Stacey's vitals and those of the fetus.

I looked at Ryland. "I appreciate you offering to help out on the mission, but you kind of missed the briefing."

He chuckled. "Meghan told Stacey what was going down, so I already have an idea what to expect." His expression turned serious. "You goin' up against the Exorcists?"

"Yeah. Are you familiar with them?"

"Only 'cause I'm a Templar." He took a puff on his cigar. "I've been busy rounding up my old pack over the past few months. I brought a dozen friends with me. We'll patrol the church perimeter and take out any threats coming your way."

"That'd be awesome," I said. "Why have you been gathering your people? I thought there was bad blood between you and them."

"We've smoothed things out." Ryland dug into his pocket and withdrew a folded bit of parchment. He smoothed it out to display barely legible handwriting. "One of my old betas sent me this message. It appears our politicians on the Overworld Conclave are secretly working to create an alliance with Cyphanis Rax and the Templar Synod."

A cold spike nailed me in the stomach. "Are you telling me the lycans are looking to join Daelissa's side?"

He shook his head. "Not all—some. Blasted politicians. From what I've heard, she's guaranteeing each faction their own independent country if they join her."

Shelton grimaced. "This ain't good."

Ryland chuckled. "When is it ever good when lowlife, self-serving, political hacks get involved?"

Dad took a puff on his cigar and looked at the parchment. His eyes flicked between it and Mom. I could tell he was uneasy despite the easy smile he wore on his face. "I hope the bulk of the lycan packs realize Daelissa isn't going to keep her word."

Ryland grunted. "Your average ordinary lycan pays more attention to pack politics than what goes on at the top." He shrugged. "Even so, you put a powerful enough alpha in charge, and people obey."

"You really think there's an alpha the packs would unite under?" Dad said. "He'd have to be one hell of a guy."

"Ain't but one I can think of," Ryland said. "He went lone wolf a long time ago, and he hates politics, so I don't see him getting involved. I'm getting back into the game so I can bring him over to our side."

Elyssa appeared at my side. "It's time to suit up. The squads joining us for the church operation just arrived and are waiting in the arch room. They brought our camouflage armor."

Mom and the others had finished making a scene about Stacey's delicate condition and headed downstairs. Dad and I looked at each other, shrugged, and followed along with the other men.

The omniarch portal was open. Through it, I saw neat rows of Templars jogging from the Obsidian Arch at the Three Sisters and lining up in formation. Every soldier wore black Nightingale armor which covered them from head to toe. They looked like ninjas in skin-tight material, but a lot cooler. Each Templar also wore a red armband enchanted with a friend or foe spell, a precaution they took to differentiate themselves from Synod Templars.

Elyssa handed me a belt of dark gray cloth. I raised an eyebrow. "Isn't Nightingale armor usually black?"

"Camouflage isn't standard issue," she said.

I lifted my shirt and fastened the cloth around my bare waist. It felt light and silky to the touch. I pressed a finger to the lower seam and the cloth extended down my legs and over my feet beneath my jeans and shoes. Touching the top seam caused it to cover my torso, forming a crew neck at my throat.

Elyssa took off her civilian clothes, revealing toned curves beneath her armor.

"Nightingale armor is the next best thing to yoga pants." I leered and waggled my eyebrows.

She rolled her eyes and graced me with a kiss. "Keep your mind on the business at hand, Casanova."

I saluted. "You got it, hot stuff."

Mom and Dad put on their armor beneath their clothes.

"Lose the clothes," Elyssa said. "Otherwise the camouflage is pointless."

Mom smiled shyly and took off her dress. Dad dropped his slacks and unbuttoned his shirt. I felt my face grow warm even though I knew the armor concealed them beneath the clothes. There was something very uncomfortable about seeing the two of them in such form-fitting outfits. A lopsided smile slid over Dad's face, giving the impression none of this fazed him one little bit. Judging from all the sideways looks he gave Mom, I could tell she affected him in ways he didn't want to admit.

She looked up at him with demure eyes. "Thank you for helping us, David."

"Ah, it's no biggie," he said with a casual flick of the hand.

Elyssa stepped inside the silver ring surrounding the omniarch and closed the portal leading to the Three Sisters. She consulted an image on her phone. It showed the view of the Exorcist church from the roof of a nearby building. She closed her eyes for an instant, and a new portal flickered into place with the same view visible through it. My girlfriend motioned us through.

Ryland stepped in after us. "My people are already patrolling the streets around the church," he said, and headed toward the stairwell door on the roof. "I'm going to join them."

"Good luck, Ryland."

He winked. "You too, cowboy." He went through the door.

Adam and Shelton came through the portal a second later and joined our group.

A familiar Templar approached Elyssa. I realized he was the same one who'd led a special ops division and helped in the capture of Maulin Kassus. Hutchins nodded at me. "Good to see you again, Mr. Slade."

"Same to you." I shook his hand. "I feel better about the odds already, knowing you and your men are on the job."

"What's the sitrep?" Elyssa asked.

Hutchins pointed out the rooftops of several nearby buildings. "Every angle and approach is covered. We've been monitoring the building for the past twenty minutes and have detected no signs of Exorcists outside."

"Any occupants?" Elyssa asked.

"Unknown. The windows are covered from the inside, and the building is protected against thermal spells or infrared equipment." He cast an almost admiring look toward the church. "The Exorcists take their security very seriously."

"Has Beta reported in?"

He nodded. "The rear entrance is secure. No OPFOR vehicles present."

It took me a moment to remember that OPFOR stood for opposing force, a term the Templars used generically to indicate their adversaries.

267

"We should get started on the shield," Adam said. "I hope it won't take long, but, well, best laid plans and all that."

"Agreed," Elyssa said. "Carry on, Hutchins."

He nodded. "Good luck in the Gloom."

We made our way downstairs and took several side alleys to covertly make our way to a thin belt of trees at the rear of the Exorcist church. Elyssa greeted the Beta Squad leader for a brief report.

"We removed detection wards from the rear perimeter," a Templar Arcane said in answer to one of Elyssa's questions. "Everything is clear up to the back door. No resistance or signs of life."

Elyssa turned to Adam. "You may proceed."

We went to the edge of the trees and stepped through a neatly sliced hole in the iron fence around the parking lot. The group jogged to the rear door.

Adam took out his arcphone and held it close to the door. He whistled. "Wow, this is a nasty shield. It'll knock you out if you touch it. Looks like someone threw this spell together a few hours ago."

"Thank goodness I didn't touch it when I was here earlier," Elyssa said.

Shelton scanned the door with his arcphone and grunted. "Amateurs. The shield ain't bad, but they should've used separate wards instead of combining them all into one big messy spell."

"Will that make this easier?" I asked.

"It should. It's hard to optimize spell code when you combine several functions together." He shoved the arcphone back in his pocket. "Messy code means more exploits in the matrix."

"Here's hoping." Adam flicked through a list of spells programmed into his arcphone and activated one named *Spell Cracker 5.2*. A timer began counting the seconds while a wide beam of light swept up and down the door, revealing an azure glow in the spots it highlighted. He released the arcphone, leaving it hovering in the air just before the door. "Now, we wait."

Elyssa made a signal with her hands, and a squad—presumably Gamma—emerged from the trees bordering the iron fence around the parking lot and took positions near the door. I

268

counted a dozen silent figures, each clad in standard-issue black Nightingale armor.

She looked up at the cross-shaped holes, as if expecting an attack at any minute. "I don't know why they haven't responded unless they abandoned the church."

"Do you really think they'd leave it?" I asked.

She shrugged. "I haven't been back since the first time. Maybe their guard is down."

"Or, it's an ambush."

"I've already considered the possibility. We'll have to be ready for anything."

Adam's phone beeped. He raised an eyebrow. "Wow, that was fast."

"Yeah, thanks to the contributions I made to your spell." Shelton flashed a self-assured smile.

Adam chuckled. "You go on thinking that, buddy." He snatched the hovering phone and read what looked like a report log. "Whoever spliced this crappy shield spell together left tons of exploits." He flourished a hand toward the door. "I believe the Templars can take over from here."

Elyssa motioned toward one of the Templars. The masculine figure knelt in front of the door and produced a set of lock picks. I looked at Shelton. "Can't you pick the lock with your wand?"

He snorted. "How many times I gotta tell you it ain't as easy as it looks?"

It didn't take the Templar long to click open the lock. He twisted the handle, and opened the thick iron door to reveal the hallway into the sanctuary. Without a word, he and the other Templars filed through, vanishing inside. Elyssa held up a fist.

"Does that mean to wait?" I asked.

She threw me a disapproving look. "You still haven't memorized the hand signals."

"He's a terrible student," Shelton said with a laugh.

Dad peered inside the door. "I'd like to burn this place to the ground after we're finished here."

269

"I can't believe Montjoy is still after you," Mom said, eyes full of concern.

"The man has a one-track mind." Dad smirked. "But, he makes life interesting sometimes."

She frowned. "As usual, you and I have far different definitions of interesting."

Elyssa touched a finger to her ear and nodded. "Gamma gave the all clear. Let's proceed."

We walked inside. A glowball hovered high above even the massive chandeliers, casting the sanctuary in a pale light that almost made it seem not as spooky as before. The cages where they'd kept the possessed inmates were empty. Rows upon rows of pews ran the length of the large rectangular sanctuary. Icons of mosaic glass ringed the domed ceiling. I assumed they represented religious figures— which ones I couldn't say since my family wasn't exactly the church-going type. About fifty feet up, a thick wide ledge ran along the walls. Statues of angels with bowed heads were spaced along it.

The place looked abandoned.

"Something doesn't feel right," Elyssa said, looking around the empty church. "Why would they leave it completely unguarded?"

The light from the glowball hit a nearby angel from the side, casting a long shadow against the wall. I was just about to turn away from the angel, when I realized something odd about the shadow. Instead of one head, it had two. I felt my eyes widen as I realized the angel on the other side of the apse was also casting dual shadows.

I turned to ask Elyssa if Templars had taken positions up on the ledge when I saw a shadowy figure behind one angel raise a staff.

"Watch out!" I yelled just as a spear of light slammed into a nearby Templar, throwing him across the room.

I jerked Elyssa behind a stone column as another deadly spell blasted a divot in the stone floor where she'd been standing.

"It seems only death will remove you from this world, Mr. Slade," said Montjoy from somewhere above us. "And I will be the one to do it."

Chapter 33

"Montjoy, when I kill you, I plan to mount your head over the fireplace," Dad hollered back.

"Subdue him!" Montjoy shouted.

Elyssa took out her phone. "We need more troops in here now!"

I peeked from behind cover. "You were right. It's an ambush."

My girlfriend's eyes went wide. She flicked her wrist. A silver blade blurred through the air and slammed into a hooded figure as it emerged from the space behind an angel on the ledge above and across from us. A man cried out and plummeted over the side, his body bouncing off the pew below.

"Secret passageways behind the angels if I had to guess." Elyssa threw another knife. Her target on the ledge brandished a staff. An azure shield sprang up, deflecting the blade.

A bolt of white light speared past my head and gouged a hole in the stone column behind me. Elyssa and I dove in opposite directions as more spells blew stone to dust. Elyssa's arm blurred. Knives flashed in all directions. Two more Exorcists screamed and fell from the ledge. A man bellowed in agony. I turned my head toward the sound in time to see jagged bolts of magical energy tearing a Templar's armor to shreds. Bloody mist sprayed from exposed flesh.

I ran toward Elyssa. A blast threw me to the side. I crashed into the hard stone of a support column.

More yells and shouts erupted. Another Templar went down as one of the stone angels fell from the ledge and crushed him. I saw Shelton and Adam near the front of the apse. Shelton roared and sent a meteor of fire slamming into the ledge. The stone collapsed, sending hooded figures screaming to their deaths. Their bodies thudded into the floor far below. As if that wasn't enough, tons of stone and debris landed on them. Mom and Dad stood back-to-back, fending off a flurry of spells.

Something slammed me in the back and threw me headlong into the pews. Heat washed over my skin even through the Nightingale armor. The pew to my right exploded into splinters. I rolled, ignoring the burning pain in my back, and dodged several more lances of searing light. Another explosion sent me tumbling to the side. I scrambled to my feet and dove toward an alcove, seeking some cover from the enemies above.

In my desperate dash to escape death, I'd lost sight of Elyssa. I finally saw her across the room. She ran up a wall, flipped backward, and skewered an Exorcist with a thrown knife. I'd rarely seen her use knives. She usually preferred non-lethal methods unless left with no choice. Since these wackos were trying to kill us, I didn't particularly mind. I saw a group of Exorcists emerge from behind an angel across the room. One of them pointed in my direction. I ducked behind a nearby column, but knew it wouldn't cover me for long. Besides, I'd had enough.

Time to bring out the big guns.

I gritted my teeth, stepped from behind the stone column, and flicked my hands open. A statue against the wall to my right made a grating noise and slid to the side. Another group of robed figures poured from it, their staffs glowing with deadly light. One of them flung his hood back and regarded me with a wicked leer.

"I remember you," he said. "The demon spawn child."

At least half a dozen staffs pointed at me, their glowing ends bathing hooded faces in light.

I suddenly recognized the Exorcist as one of the men who'd guided me into the church while I was paralyzed. He was the one who'd made me watch as Montjoy tried to exorcise my father. I smiled. "I'm going to give you one chance to surrender peacefully."

The man laughed. "Your Templar friends are dying, boy. There's nobody here to help you."

I showed my teeth. "I don't need protecting." I felt the window in my soul open wide as I connected with my inner Seraphim. The palms of my hands blazed with heat. "I'm no ordinary demon spawn, jackass. My mom is an angel."

The Exorcists' eyes went wide as spinner hubcaps.

With a roar, I thrust my left hand forward. Violet light coursed from my palm and splintered the staff of the gloating Exorcist. With my right hand, I formed a blazing white sword of light and slashed it across the other staffs, slicing off their ends. The Exorcists shrieked like little girls.

One of them pulled a knife and slashed at me. I kicked him in the chest. He crashed against the wall. Another Exorcist drew a sword and hacked at my arm. I ducked. Grabbed his wrist, and twisted. Bones cracked. His body flipped forward and slammed into the floor. I heard several quick whirring sounds and felt impacts explode all across my body. Iron shafts with smoking packets at the end littered the floor. I turned in time to see the man I recognized fire what looked like a crossbow with a rotating auto-loader like revolver pistols used. Before I could move, the shaft slammed into my head and exploded like a huge firecracker.

The Nightingale armor stopped it from penetrating my brain, but the impact knocked me silly. I staggered back.

"Use the sacrificial knives," one of the Exorcists shouted. "They'll go through the armor."

My vision blurred. I heard movement and felt something slash against my shoulder. Pain seared my skin. I heard crossbow bolts explode again. An impact against my chest knocked me onto the floor.

Rage and bloodlust surged like fire through my blood. The heat in my palms blazed as I felt my demon and Seraphim sides connect.

They tried to kill us. They sent us to the Gloom. Never again.

273

A guttural roar burst from my throat and the world went red.

I rolled backwards and sprang to my feet. I saw hazy shapes before me.

Enemies.

A white streak blazed across my field of vision as I slashed my right arm at the nearest dark blur. I heard a gurgle and the figure went down. Another explosion rocked me on my feet. My left hand flew up on instinct. A shield of ultraviolet sprang up and caught another exploding arrow. Two more indistinct figures slashed at me. I felt their knives hit the shield.

I blinked a few times, and the blurriness faded to clarity. I saw a man jamming more shafts into the crossbow.

Kill.

The shield and sword vanished. Orbs of malevolent energy filled my palms.

I saw the whites of my enemies' eyes as fear replaced certainty. I hungered for their blood. A guttural laugh emerged from my throat. "You are mine."

The Exorcists ran.

Before they were a dozen paces away, I clapped my hands together and sent a shockwave racing down the aisle. The energy blasted a column to rubble, burying two of my enemies. I raced after the survivors, leapt high, and pounced one of them.

"Die, puny mortal." Saliva drooled from my mouth and onto the face of the terrified man beneath me.

"Please, no!" he screamed.

Before he could utter another word, I picked him up by the neck and threw him high into the air. A beam of white energy speared from my hand and burnt a hole through his chest before his body hit the ground with a meaty smack. Movement caught the corner of my eye. I saw the familiar man running for the door. I sent a pinprick of Brilliance into his ankle, slashing his Achilles tendon.

He screamed and tumbled forward. I raced toward the downed figure. I smelled his burnt blood. Sensed his fear. His pain. I swept him off the floor with one hand and held him aloft by the neck. He squirmed in my grasp, his hands prying at mine. I squeezed his throat

274

slowly. Felt his windpipe collapse. Heard the gurgle of his last breath as it wheezed through his constricted throat. I felt a smile spread my lips.

Death. Destruction. The world is ours now.

"Justin!" cried a familiar voice.

I turned in time to see a figure in black flip off the back of a pew and nail me in the face with a foot. The dead body fell from my grasp. Another kick to my chest sent me sprawling across the floor. I saw the Exorcist ninja's foot a third time as it slammed into my face.

The red in my vision cleared. I gasped, and rolled to the side to avoid a fourth kick.

"Try to take me in a fair fight, bitch!" Elyssa shouted as her body flashed before me in time to block another attack from the ninja.

Their arms and feet blurred with speed as they fought. My eyes locked onto the body of the man I'd just killed, and horror swept through me. *What have I done?* True, I'd really wanted to kick their asses, but I'd actually reveled in killing them. I sensed pleasure emanating from my demonic side. It had taken control after the bullets stunned me.

Swords clanged.

I sprang to my feet. Elyssa's sai blades caught a vicious blow from the ninja. My girlfriend's foot swept at her attacker's feet. The ninja flipped backward, avoiding the attack with ease, and threw a shuriken from a belt at her waist. Elyssa batted the projectile with a sword, sending it flashing right back at the attacker. The ninja ducked. The throwing star embedded itself into the stone wall behind her. Her masked head turned toward the star and back to Elyssa.

I imagined Elyssa's fierce grin crossing her face since I couldn't see it beneath the Nightingale armor mask. The ninja flicked her sword in a circle and assumed a defensive stance. Elyssa took a similar stance, and the two faced off.

Something exploded near the front of the church. I turned and saw Shelton and Adam exchanging fire with more Exorcists.

"I've got to help the others," I said.

"Go," Elyssa said. "I've got this."

I hesitated, unsure for an instant. The ninja sprang toward me. Elyssa's sword stopped the blow from taking off my nose.

"Go, Justin!" Elyssa growled. "You're only distracting me."

I streaked toward Shelton. Anger filled me as I thought about the Exorcist ninja. I had so much power but still couldn't beat her.

We are powerful, my demon side said. *Turn and kill her.*

I stopped in my tracks, watching as the ninja flipped through the air to avoid Elyssa's thrusts. I could use the same trick I'd used on the other man. I could cut her tendon. I could slice her in half. Anger built in me like a rising tide of lava.

Kill her.

"Son of a biscuit eating buffalo!" Shelton shouted. "We need help!"

I turned as another explosion sent chunks of stone raining down on his and Adam's position. My head cleared and the anger faded. I had to help Shelton.

Before I could take another step, two of the attackers sent blasts of energy at the ledge behind my friends. Chunks of heavy stone collapsed toward them.

"No!" I shouted. But I was too far away to stop it.

The stone slammed into an invisible barrier before it crushed my friends. I saw Mom straining, as if holding up a heavy weight. Dad showed his teeth and made a punching motion with his hand. The ground beneath the Exorcists trembled. A fiery hand reached from within the earth and gripped two of them, squeezing their bodies. Blood sizzled from their pores, and their eyes boiled in their sockets. Their awful screams of agony cut off within seconds.

The remaining attackers looked stunned. A fleeting second passed, and the Exorcists turned tail and ran.

I looked to the left and saw Mom make a swiping motion with her hand. The debris above Shelton and Adam slid to the side. A fierce smile came over Dad's face as he watched the remnants of the Exorcists flee for their lives.

"Who are you?" Elyssa yelled.

I spun and saw her and the ninja facing off, swords locked as each one tried to throw the other off balance.

"I am the one who guards the light!" the other woman cried out.

"Daelissa wants to rule the world," Elyssa said in a strained voice. "Don't do this. Join us."

"Lies!" the woman cried. "Lies!"

"The Exorcists have fled. We have you surrounded." Elyssa dodged back as the ninja aimed a kick at her feet. Sparks flew from their blades as the two women disengaged and leapt back from each other.

The woman shook her head. "I was abandoned by the Templars long ago. Thomas Borathen, my own father, left me and my brothers for dead when he could have saved us!"

Elyssa literally staggered beneath the weight of those words. "Your father?"

"I will never join you," the other woman said. With that, she threw something to the floor. Smoke exploded.

I raced to Elyssa's side where she stood staring at the dissipating smoke. The woman was gone.

Elyssa lowered her mask, revealing wide eyes and a pale face. She looked at me. "It can't be true."

I remembered Thomas Borathen once mentioning something about another family in one of his rare slips of the tongue. "Are you okay?"

She bit her lip, staring blankly.

I took her by the shoulders. "Elyssa, are you okay?"

Grim resolve melted the look of confusion. "After this is over, I'm having a long talk with my parents." She made a growling noise. "Can't think about it now. We need to complete the mission."

"Hey, Montjoy, want to come out and play?" Dad yelled.

There was no answer.

Elyssa's jaw tightened as she looked around the room at the debris and bodies scattered across it. "Montjoy knew we'd be coming back."

"He must have known who you are and assumed you'd be back with reinforcements," I said, taking a guess.

277

She slammed her swords into the sheaths across her back. "I wonder if this means Serena knows we're coming."

"We'll have to assume so," Dad said. Shelton, Adam, and Mom walked by his side. "I also don't think this was the last Exorcist attack."

"What do you mean?" Elyssa said.

Dad swept an arm around the church. "This isn't just some place they use on an occasional basis to purge demons. I'd bet it's their headquarters." He pointed at the ground. "Churches like this have crypts and all sorts of secret passages. We're probably standing right on top of an anthill."

I remembered Maximus's old hideout. It had once been a church. I'd learned more about the crypt beneath the place than I'd ever wanted to since the vampire had kidnapped Dad and held him prisoner down there.

"If you're right, we have less time than I thought," Elyssa said. "Montjoy might be on his way to warn Serena about us."

"Either her or Daelissa," Dad said. "There might even be an army of Synod Templars hiding below."

"This gets better and better," Shelton said, his dour expression heaping more sarcasm onto his words. "Is the mission a bust?"

"No." I shook my head. "It means we go into the Gloom with the expectation that the only way out will be through the Shadow Nexus."

"Can't you ever do things the easy way?" Shelton said with a groan.

I gripped his shoulder. "You and Adam need to leave. We'll take it from here."

"My spell cracker took down the barrier blocking the Gloom arch," Adam said. "You're good to go."

Elyssa looked grimly around the room. "Someone needs to look for Templar survivors and get them out of here ASAP."

"We'll inform your people outside," Shelton said.

She nodded. "Make sure you give them the details of the engagement and—"

278

Shelton waved her off. "Don't worry. You don't have time to waste telling me what to do. Now go!"

The four of us raced toward the large silver circle surrounding the arches near the apse. Shelton and Adam broke off from the group and headed toward the corridor leading to the rear exit. Dad shoved a large chunk of stone away from the Gloom arch. Mom waved a hand, and a breeze cleared the dust from the silver ring. Elyssa jogged to the door and returned with a bundle of rolled-up flying carpets.

"Ready," she said, and stepped inside the circle.

Mom and Dad joined us. I knelt, jabbed a thumb against the silver circle and willed it closed. I looked at the Gloom arch and willed it to activate. With a slight hum, a portal flickered on within the arch showing a foggy mirror image of the church. I stepped through first. Elyssa followed close on my heels.

"Hang on," Dad said. "Are there any Templar reinforcements coming to guard our backs?"

"Yes," Elyssa said. "The plan is to completely take over the church, but my father said he was finishing an operation against the Synod and couldn't spare enough men." She took out her phone and sent a quick text. "I just let him know to expect a lot more resistance than the Exorcists." She looked up. For now, our flank will be wide open. There's no way around it."

An amused smile spread Dad's lips. He nodded. "Nothing spices life like knowing you're gonna die."

"David," Mom said in a disapproving tone.

He held up his hands in surrender. "Just making an observation."

Elyssa looked at me. "Close the portal."

I willed the portal closed. It vanished.

My girlfriend gasped and drooped.

I touched her shoulder. "You're cut off from your supernatural talents."

She flexed her fingers and stared at her hand. "I don't feel right."

279

"I know the feeling." Even though my newfound abilities granted me more power in the Gloom, the dampening effect was profoundly noticeable.

"Oh, by the way, I got you something," Dad said. He tossed me a clear plastic bag.

I caught it and looked at the contents. "My phone!" I said. "Where did you find it?"

"Storage room near the entrance of the church," he said.

I grabbed my wallet, eighty-two cents in loose change, and my beloved phone, Nookli, from the bag. "I may be stuck in the Gloom, but at least I can tell the time."

Elyssa wrinkled her forehead and looked around. "I didn't realize how dense the fog was. Piloting the carpets is going to be a nightmare."

We made our way outside to the back parking lot. I noticed a hole in the iron fence where the Templars had cut one in the real world. I checked the time on my phone. We still had three hours until the fog cleared, assuming the Gloom kept to the same schedule. That was a lot of time to be flying blind, especially when we might have Montjoy and his people close on our heels.

Elyssa seemed frustrated. "I didn't account for crappy visibility." She huffed an angry breath and stared into the foggy surroundings. "This was a huge mistake on my part."

"It's not your fault," I said. "I should have emphasized just how bad vision is in here during the day, but it didn't even occur to me."

Mom made a fanning motion with her hand. The fog cleared in all directions by about twenty feet. She stopped fanning, and the fog rolled back in. "I don't think this will help much while we're flying."

"All we need to do is fly in the direction of the quarry," Dad said, aiming a finger in the general direction. "If we take the carpets high enough we won't have to worry about running into trees."

"What about buildings?" Elyssa asked.

"We'll need to fly high enough to avoid them as well," he said.

"How will we know if we're high enough?" she asked. "We can't see the ground."

I fiddled with my phone. "The GPS works. Maybe I can use 3D mode to help us avoid buildings."

Elyssa nodded. "That might work."

An even better idea occurred to me. *Minder Justin, I need you, buddy.* I concentrated on instant messaging my shade using brainwaves and hoped for the best.

Elyssa gasped. "I feel strong again."

"Oh, crap," Dad said.

A surge of strength flowed into me. I opened my eyes. "What's going on?"

"Someone opened the Gloom arch." Dad looked behind us. "We're not alone anymore."

Chapter 34

"Montjoy is sending in the troops," I said.

"We don't know for sure," Elyssa said. Something whistled through the air. Her hand blurred and caught an arrow inches from her face. Her eyes went wide. "Then again, maybe we do."

Another arrow whistled inches from my head and clanged off the iron fence. I ducked. "How can they see us through the fog?"

"With the portal open I'm at full power," Mom said. "Maybe I can do something." She made a sweeping motion with her hands. A gust of wind cleared the parking lot all the way to the door where a group of figures in gray uniforms were aiming more arrows our way. Each wore what looked like glowing spectacles.

"Magic glasses." Elyssa made a frustrated noise. "Why didn't I think of that?" She slid through the hole in the fence. "We've got to get out of here."

Another volley of arrows deflected from an invisible barrier Mom had apparently thrown up. She looked at Dad. "David, go through the fence while I hold them off."

Dad shook his head. "I'm not—"

"Go!" she said in her parent voice.

He climbed through the hole after me.

Mom backed up as more arrows bounced off the shield. I heard one of the uniformed soldiers shout a command. Mom turned, and dove through the hole. Once outside of the fence, we didn't dare run. There were trees everywhere and fog concealed them all. We hadn't gone more than a few paces when I felt my strength dissipate.

"They shut down the Gloom arch," Dad growled. "Looks like we're back to being normal."

We reached the other side of the trees and found a clearing. Elyssa unrolled the bundle beneath her arm, and tossed two flying carpets on the ground. "No choice. We have to fly." Her eyes went to me. "You still have the coordinates on GPS?"

I nodded. "We'll need to fly the carpets close to each other. If we lose sight, it'll be tough to find each other."

Mom and Dad hopped on one of the carpets while Elyssa and I took the other. Using a nearby tree to judge our height, we floated up until we lost sight of the top.

"Going high!" someone shouted from below. Arrows whistled past. One punched through the bottom of our carpet. The tip barely missed nailing my rear end.

I willed the carpet forward at a modest pace. The GPS showed buildings ahead, but I didn't know how high we were in relation to them.

"I can't believe I didn't think of magic glasses," Elyssa said. "We wouldn't be running blind like this."

"You can't think of everything" I said, peering intently into the fog for any obstacles. "I didn't think they'd be following us so soon after we kicked their butts."

"They must have realized we didn't have reinforcements." Her eyes went wide. "Watch out!"

I swerved left and barely missed hitting the tip of an antenna atop the roof of a building hidden in the fog below. "Whoa, that was close."

"Justin?" Mom called from somewhere in the fog.

"Over here," I shouted back.

We called back and forth a few times before finally drawing close to my parents.

"Distance?" Dad asked.

I checked the phone. "A few miles." I blew out a frustrated breath. "It's going to take forever at this rate."

283

"Let's go higher," Elyssa suggested. A shadowy shape flitted past. "What was that?"

I shook my head. "I didn't get a good look."

"I think it was a minder," Dad said.

I pointed up. "We're going higher."

He nodded. "Good idea."

Our carpets rose a distance made undeterminable by the thick fog. I'd decided to keep going up for at least another minute to be certain we were above any nearby buildings, but a shout of alarm from Elyssa caused me to halt.

"Look," she said, pointing straight up.

Even through the fog I saw lightning streaking in horizontal bursts across the billowing fog close overhead.

"Reminds me of the aether storms," Dad said, his carpet holding steady next to mine. "I think we're as high as we're gonna get."

It was hard to judge the distance to the lightning storm, but given the dense aether fog, it had to be close. I imagined a bolt of magical lightning frying the spells on the flying carpets and sending us plummeting to our deaths. "Hopefully we're high enough to avoid any buildings," I said. I didn't feel terribly confident about my statement since so much construction on the west side of town involved high-rise condominiums.

A crowd of minders flew past our position without a sound except for our collective gasps. I looked up and saw shadows appear in the fog with every lightning strike.

"This place is seething with minders," Mom said, looking all around with dismay.

"Must be social hour," Dad said. "Maybe this is how they spend their off time."

"Justin, your phone." Elyssa pointed at the screen. Static flickered across it every time lightning threaded through the fog. The GPS signal blinked in and out.

I cursed. "We need to drop lower. The aether storm is playing havoc with my phone."

Dad nodded. "Lead on."

We had to descend for nearly half a minute before my phone decided to work again. We went forward a few feet and nearly ran into the side of a red brick building. I slapped the hard surface. "Son of a—"

"Justin!" Mom said with a stern look.

"—bad person," I finished with a contrite smile. "We're never getting anywhere at this rate."

Something clattered off the wall a few inches from my head.

"Arrows!" Elyssa dropped low on the carpet and looked behind us. "The Exorcists must have carpets too."

"How are we supposed to outrun them in this pea soup?" I said with a growl. "I should've taken them out earlier." Something cold touched my head.

You rang? said a familiar voice in my head.

I didn't have time to properly greet my minder. "We need help!"

I just read your mind, he said. *Come with me if you want to live.*

I saw Minder Justin floating a few feet to my left. One of his tentacles rested on my head. "Lead on."

I have a better idea.

My vision blurred and sharpened back to normal. As I looked around, I realized my vision was much improved. I couldn't see clear as day, but shadowy shapes of buildings and other obstructions filled the fog.

That should help you run from those homicidal maniacs behind you.

I glanced over my shoulder and saw the shadowy outlines of the pursuing Exorcists maybe fifty yards away. "Dad, get behind us and overlap the carpets. We're about to go a lot faster."

He nodded and lined up his and Mom's carpet so the edges overlapped, and gripped the edges. "Go."

Mom wrapped her arms tight around his waist. "Never a dull moment," she said.

I willed the carpet forward. It went from zero to turbo in three seconds. Apparently the Templar flying carpets were a lot better than

285

their civilian counterparts. I zoomed down to street level, flying just high enough to skim over empty cars. The Exorcists shouted and dove after us. I saw a volley of arrows shoot toward us, but our forward velocity was too much for them to overcome.

"Why don't they just use guns?" I said.

"The Exorcists shun technology," Elyssa said.

I threaded between a city bus and a semi-truck. "I guess that explains the weird crossbow that dude in the church used."

Elyssa gripped my waist tighter. "Just pay attention to where you're going and be glad they aren't shooting assault rifles."

Through there, Minder Justin said.

I felt a tug on my attention and saw the unfinished condo complex he referred to.

"It's terrifying not being able to see where we're going," Elyssa said.

The carpet wove between two concrete pillars. I took us into a nearly vertical climb up several stories of the skeletal superstructure before straightening out and flying through a maze of plywood and steel beams in the center. Only the magic bonding our bodies to the carpet prevented us from flying off.

"I should probably be grateful I can't see very far," Elyssa said, her grip growing even tighter as we whooshed past a row of support columns.

Dad laughed. "It's the only reason my underwear is still clean."

"Don't you ever get tired of poop jokes?" Mom said.

"Never."

They're falling behind, Minder Justin said.

I didn't risk a glance back. "Let me know when they can't see us." I wound through a narrow alley, and took a sharp right around a corner.

Now.

"Hang on!" I shouted above the wind even though it really wasn't necessary. I gripped a lamppost and took the carpets into a tight turn.

286

"Maybe I shouldn't have eaten before I left," Dad said in a strained voice.

The building ahead appeared to be a combination apartment and commercial complex. I took the carpets to the sidewalk and jerked open the door to a restaurant. Everyone jumped off the carpets and ran inside.

Are they still following us? I sent to Minder Justin.

See for yourself, he said.

The Exorcists appeared as blue outlines against the black shadow of the building. There were three carpets with two people on each one. The people on the rear of the carpets had bows. They streaked past the building and slowed. I saw one of them pointing in the direction we'd been heading while another shook his head.

"What's going on?" Elyssa asked.

I explained the situation. "We'll have to wait."

"They only sent six?" Dad said. "Maybe we can ambush them."

"They have bows and arrows," I reminded him. "With their magic glasses we wouldn't make it close enough before they skewered us."

The Exorcists spread out, apparently combing the nearby area for us. There weren't many other tall buildings in this section of town, or my ploy might have worked better.

Which way to the fortress? I asked my minder.

A tug on my brain told me without him saying a thing. *You want to kill minders?* he said in a disgusted tone.

It took a few seconds to process the question before remembering he could read some of my thoughts. *Just the brain Serena uses to control the fortress and the sentinels.*

He made a pshawing noise in my head. *That's easy. Just jerk out their tentacles.*

That's not what Cinder told me."

Yeah, I was just joking about the tentacles, Minder Justin informed me. *Cinder might be right. I don't know.*

Can you convince the minders to enter the psionic disruptor? I asked.

He paused. *I don't think so. They'd read my intentions. You'll have to lure them in some other way.*

I suddenly spotted a flying carpet hovering outside with shadowy shapes resembling Mom and Dad. I was about to yell in alarm when I saw my parents still inside.

"I'm dreamcasting that," she said. "I can lure them away."

Already, my minder vision helped me spot one of the Exorcist duos on a carpet swooping down to investigate. "How far away can you lure them before you lose control of your clones?"

She shrugged. "I don't know."

I narrowed my eyes. "I have a better idea."

I wondered if the magic glasses allowed them to see our heat signatures through the concrete. If they looked through the windows, they'd see us for sure. The restaurant was built like a loft with a high ceiling. Even though I couldn't see the details, my mind seemed to know what my eyes were seeing thanks to the link with my minder.

"Back on the carpets," I said.

Everyone stepped back on without question.

"Crouch low." I took us to the ceiling, set the carpets against the front corner where the concrete would hopefully block us from sight from their thermal goggles.

"Lure them inside," I told Mom.

She nodded. The dreamcasted versions of my parents got off the flying carpet and ran inside."

"Down there," I heard a man say.

My fake parents ran to the bar, ducked behind it, and peeked over the edge enough so their pursuers could clearly see them.

I looked down and saw the archer and his companion rush inside the restaurant. They were only ten feet below us. One look up, and it was game over. I felt Elyssa squeeze my hand as the two men spoke in low tones.

The archer nocked an arrow and aimed. "Come out now, and I'll spare you."

The other man drew a sword and held it at the ready.

Elyssa pointed down and made a motion of hitting a palm with her fist.

I nodded. Gripping the edge of the carpet, I slid off it and hung over the men's heads. Elyssa performed a graceful forward flip off the carpet so she was hanging next to me.

The cloned version of my parents stood from behind the bar, arms raised. The archer laughed. "Actually, I lied." He shot my father in the chest. The arrow bounced off harmlessly.

"What the hell?" the archer said.

Elyssa mouthed the word, "Now" and dropped. I let go at the same time.

I landed atop the bowman. He grunted. A knee to his stomach and blow to the head put him out of commission. Elyssa put the other man in a chokehold and squeezed until he passed out. She ripped the magic glasses off the man's head and tried them on.

"Perfect," she said.

Dad took the other set from the archer. "We're golden now."

"There are still four more Exorcists out there," Mom reminded him.

"I have an idea," Elyssa said. She grabbed the bow from the floor and slid the quiver over her shoulder.

"We going wabbit hunting?" I asked.

She blew me a kiss. "You know it."

Our girlfriend is hot, Minder Justin said. *Especially with those nerdy magic glasses.*

She's mine, not ours.

A guy can dream, can't he? Chagrin filled his voice.

I felt kind of bad for him.

Oh, don't feel sorry for me. I'll just live vicariously through you. Oh, wait, I already do.

I smiled. *You can help us put down some bad guys.*

Dude, I am so in.

"Their carpet is a little larger," Elyssa said. "We'll need to use it so they think it's their buddies."

I looked at my parents. "We'll be back."

"Son, be careful," Mom said.

I pecked her on the cheek. "I'm always careful."

Liar, my minder said in a smug voice.

289

We went outside and hopped on the Exorcist carpet. I told Elyssa how the archer had stood behind the carpet driver. She mimicked the position, and we shot upward. Thanks to my minder vision, I spotted the other two carpets quickly. They were circling over opposite sides of the area, one of them scouting through a parking deck, and the other combing nearby alleys.

I told Elyssa their positions and directed the carpet toward the pair in the alley first. Since I knew they couldn't see us through the building, I used my unfair advantage to its fullest, and swooped down from above as they passed below. Elyssa put an arrow through the archer. He shouted and fell off. Before the driver could react, an arrow sprouted from his back. He slumped forward, and the carpet coasted to a halt. We dropped next to the carpet. Elyssa hopped to it and landed it on the ground. We stripped the gear from the men. I noticed the arrows had hit the men in virtually the same exact spot even though one was taller than the other.

"I didn't know you could shoot a bow," I said.

She stuffed the extra magic glasses into a duffel bag one of the Exorcists had strapped to the carpet. "I've never shot a person with an arrow before." Her voice sounded sad. "I didn't want to take a chance by just winging them."

I squeezed her hand. "Hey, I understand. They're trying to kill us." I kissed her cheek just beneath the rim of the thermal goggles. "You did what you had to do."

"Let's take out the others," she said.

I heard a shout of alarm and turned to see they'd already found us. An arrow streaked right at me. Before I could react, I felt Elyssa slam into me and we hit the ground with a grunt.

I heard shouts of alarm and rolled to my back in time to see my parents slam their flying carpet into the Exorcists. The men plummeted to the ground bellowing in terror.

The impact of carpets didn't even faze my parents. When their doubles pulled up to us a moment later, I realized why. Mom had used their dreamcasted clones to take out our attackers.

"Very clever," I said to my Mom.

She looked at the bodies of the fallen with sad eyes. "Hopefully that's the last of them."

We went back inside the restaurant we'd used for cover to get our Templar-issued carpets since they had the camouflage spells. I saw the men we'd ambushed slumped against a wall, their necks bent at grotesque angles. "What happened?" I asked.

Mom looked at my father. He looked at the bodies. "We couldn't let them report back to Montjoy so I took care of the problem."

I felt a little nauseated even though I understood his reasoning.

Man, our dad is sick, Minder Justin said with awe.

I looked away from the corpses. *Tell me about it.*

No, I mean he's wicked sick, dude. This is a man who does what needs doing.

I looked at the floating brain and blew out a disgusted breath. *If you say so.*

"Let's get moving," Elyssa said. "We've lost a lot of time."

Dad had gathered magic glasses for everyone. I elected to stick with minder-enhanced vision since it was so much better. We took a couple more bows and quivers of arrows though I figured they wouldn't do much good against sentinels or Nazdal, and hopped onto the carpets. At full speed, we reached the outskirts of the quarry and the bubble of clear air within minutes.

Are there any flying sentinels guarding this place? I asked Minder Justin.

Hang on. He vanished into the fog, and I was suddenly blind again. My chest tightened at the claustrophobic sensation. Relief swept over me when he returned and latched onto my head again. *All clear. I guess they didn't think anyone would come by air.*

We dropped beneath the fog cover and into the clear bubble of air around the fortress. The others took off their magic glasses. I looked straight down into the quarry pit and saw rubble and water. Something was missing. A lot of something. "The Nazdal aren't in the pit."

"It's empty," Mom said in a quiet voice.

291

"They must have sent them through the Shadow Nexus," Elyssa said.

Dad looked at me. "Oh, crap."

The battle had already started.

Chapter 35

"We've got to get down there," I said.

Dad grimaced. "A better question is how we're supposed to get through the back door if nobody is left inside to open it."

"Before we jump to any conclusions, maybe we should observe the situation." Mom peered over the edge of the flying carpet and looked at the fortress and quarry for a long moment. "If the Shadow Nexus is inside the domed building and the arch is open, shouldn't we feel at full strength?"

Elyssa nodded. "I still feel puny."

"Me too." Dad lay down next to Mom and poked his head over the edge of the rug. "Then again, they could have sent through the army of Nazdal and closed the arch behind them."

Despite the dampening effect of the Gloom, coming into my new powers seemed to have helped quite a bit. For one thing, my vision remained sharp even from this distance. Movement caught my eye. I zoomed in on it and spotted one of the formerly human ghouls shamble a step or two before stopping. Its skin was so discolored, it blended in with the moss and algae on the rock near the quarry pond.

The granite near the creature's feet seemed to move. I looked long and hard for so long, I thought it might have been my imagination. The ghoul dropped to its haunches. The rock beneath it leapt and scurried away. I suddenly realized why the quarry looked empty. Thinking back to when I'd opened the Shadow Nexus to the Nazdal realm clarified my confusion.

"The pit isn't empty." I looked at the others. "The Nazdal are camouflaged."

"Just like in their realm," Dad said. "They blended perfectly with the terrain."

"Why now?" I asked.

"Either they know we're coming, or maybe they're sleeping." He shrugged. "Let's assume the worst."

Elyssa blew out a breath. "Good idea."

"I just hope there aren't any Nazdal surprises hidden near the door," Dad said. He slipped on his magic glasses and surveyed the area. "I don't see any heat signatures near the door. Looks like we're clear."

"Good idea," Elyssa said, putting her glasses back on. She stared at the pit. "I can't tell how many Nazdal are down there. It looks like they're clustered in groups."

I activated the camouflage on the carpet. The spell concealed us, the bows, and other stolen gear while allowing us to still see each other. Once we stepped off it, we'd have to rely solely on the Nightingale armor to conceal us. "Let's set up near the door."

I'll wait here, my minder said. *Good luck. Don't let anything happen to our hot girlfriend.*

I sent him the mental image of me rolling my eyes. *Did you ask any other minders to help us?*

I tried, but like I told you, they're locked into minder duties unless... Minder Justin trailed off.

Unless what?

Maybe if their owners think really hard about summoning them, they'll come. Minders can sense the people they're connected to, but only if the intent is strong.

I raised an eyebrow. *You mean Elyssa and the others can ask their minders to come?*

It's worth a shot.

Hope bloomed in my chest. *Great idea.*

You'll have to figure out a way to get us inside, though. We can't phase through walls.

I nodded. *I'll think of something. Is there anything else we need to worry about with the brain? Can they detect us by our thoughts?*

Minders whose owners are dead can't sense thoughts unless they're touching you. They can hear sound when you're near them, though.

That much I knew from talking to Serena's minder.

"Ready?" Elyssa asked.

I told her and the others my minder's plan, including the limitations of the brain minders.

"I hadn't thought about the possibility they could sense our thoughts. Thank goodness they can't." She pursed her lips. "The help of our own minders could be crucial."

Elyssa gave a signal. We descended slowly until we were only twenty feet off the rubble-strewn ledge next to the rear door. Elyssa held up a fist, indicating a full stop. We inspected the area, looking for anything out of the ordinary. I figured that included just about everything in my life, but opted to keep the smart remarks to myself.

After convincing ourselves nothing hidden lurked below, we landed near the gray door and waited. Elyssa activated the camo on her armor. She didn't so much vanish as she blurred into a very hard to see smudge on my vision over several seconds. When I tried to look directly at her, it was as if the camouflage deflected my eyes somewhere else. She touched my head, and suddenly I could see her again.

"I activated the squad spell that'll allow us to see each other," she explained, activating the camouflage on my parents' armor.

I traced a circle with a slash through it on my chest to activate the camo. Even though I could see the others, it was like looking through a slightly distorted window. "Weird."

Elyssa took the rigid flying carpets and bent them into semi-circles so they'd stand on edge, and aligned them next to the fortress wall so we could duck behind them in case the aether charges on our armor ran out. If that happened, the armor would recharge, but we'd be exposed for a long time.

"Why don't we keep the camo turned off and hide behind the carpets?" Dad said.

Elyssa nodded. "Good idea."

We hid behind the carpets and deactivated the spells on our armor, lowering the face-concealing masks as well.

Elyssa examined the door, but there wasn't a handle to be found. Like the others, it slid into a recess in the wall when opened. "Justin, you told me the doors open and close without anyone actually touching them, right?"

I nodded. "The minders must respond to whoever is walking through them."

She hugged the wall to the right of the door. "When it opens, we'll have to wait for whoever is coming out to clear enough space for us to slip through. We'll have only a few seconds to get inside. From what Justin told me, we can't just hold open the door. It'll probably crush anyone who doesn't make it all the way through."

Mom nodded. "If this place is dreamcasted by minders, anything could happen if they detect us."

"Like the walls crushing us?" I asked.

"Or spikes shooting from the floor and impaling us?" Dad added.

I widened my eyes. "Or the floor falling into a bottomless pit?"

Dad grimaced. "Or into a lake of burning lava?"

Elyssa and Mom turned highly disapproving looks on us.

"Jarvis said only parts of the fortress are dreamcasted," I said. "But that doesn't mean they can't conjure traps wherever they want them."

"I need silence," Elyssa said in a harsh whisper. "We can't afford any distractions." She motioned toward the side of the wall the door opened away from. "Everyone line up and be ready to go on my signal. Remember, once we're inside, no talking. The brain might detect us."

296

I just hoped it couldn't detect us merely by our stepping foot inside.

We did as commanded with Elyssa standing closest to the edge of the door. The wait dragged on and on, making it difficult to keep my guard up despite the dangers of invisible Nazdal sneaking up on us from the pit. Their nifty camouflage trick must have been how Maloreck was able to get into and out of the fortress so easily. Either that, or Serena had granted him access. Somehow, I doubted the woman allowed him free reign inside the complex. The Nazdal had proved himself too clever and too strong to trust.

Then again, it wasn't as if the creature had lied. In fact, he'd been pretty straightforward about wanting to kill me and take my life essence. I shuddered. Elyssa glanced back at me. Her alarmed looked turned questioning. I didn't have time to answer the unspoken question because, at that moment, the door grated open.

We quickly activated our camouflage and raised the masks on the armor.

A slobbering ghoul shambled through the door. It looked dazed. A string of saliva hung from its slack lower jaw. The skin was as green and mottled with liver spots as the others of its kind I had seen. A thick iron collar bound its neck. I realized with a shock I recognized this ghoul. It was the Arcane, Wax. The minders must have drained the poor man already. My fists tightened as two sentinels walked through the door behind Wax, each one gripping a thick metal pole attached to either side of the iron collar.

Elyssa looked through the door and jerked her head back just as Jarvis strolled through, a smile across his face.

"Should have eaten more vitamins, Wax," the chubby man said. "You might have lasted longer in the brain."

Wax was obviously far past understanding anything. Elyssa jerked my arm, dragging us through the door as it grated closed. We whisked past just in time.

My girlfriend said nothing as she moved forward. I didn't think the walls had ears, but in this place, there was no sense taking any chances. We crept down the corridor. Going by our memories, Dad and I directed the group through the grid of hallways.

Thankfully, it was almost a straight shot to Serena's lab. Voices echoed down the hall. Elyssa held up a fist. We halted. She pointed to her eyes and made a circling gesture. Once again I wished I'd studied Templar black ops signals a little more, but Elyssa didn't stick around to elaborate before disappearing inside the lab.

"They attacked the church," hissed an angry female voice. "My church!"

My heart almost stopped. Daelissa was here.

"Why did they attack it?" Serena asked.

"Perhaps they thought the Slade boy was still there," the Seraphim replied. "I do not have all the details yet, but there will be suffering."

"The Cataclyst—"

"Do not call him that!" Daelissa screamed. "He is a speck compared to me."

"The speck," Serena said, "was indeed instrumental in showing me the way to realign the Shadow Nexus to Seraphina."

"His sister is still too young. Her voice still unsuitable," the angel said.

"It wasn't his voice that showed me the way," Serena said. "He may have escaped, but he unwittingly gave me the key. I can attune—"

"My church, my church, my church!" Daelissa sounded as if she were losing her mind.

"The church doesn't matter," I heard Serena say. "I have already—"

"Doesn't matter?" Daelissa shrieked. "This will not stand. I will personally erase the Borathen scum from the face of Eden."

"Please reconsider, Daelissa." Serena's voice sounded sweet and soothing, much like the one she'd used in her attempt to con me. "You have still not rested or fed after the battles in Colombia. Please return to Eden via the Gloom arch at Kobol Prison. Regain your strength. When you are ready, we will open the way to Seraphina, you will have your army, and we will march an unstoppable force into Eden."

298

Elyssa returned from scouting the room, and pointed toward a large silver box to the right of the door. She made some hand signals which I assumed meant she wanted us to follow her lead.

"It is happening again, and so soon," Daelissa said. She actually sounded scared. "I'm losing myself."

"Replenish your energy. You must be completely stable to open the gateway." Serena's voice was soothing. "Seraphina will heal you, but it will take time, and you must be ready in case there are unforeseen dangers waiting on the other side."

I will return in two hours," Daelissa said in a low voice. "Be ready by then."

Elyssa motioned us inside and pointed to a large silver box about ten feet away.

"Of course," Serena said. "Let me walk you out."

Elyssa flattened against the wall and pressed me alongside her. Mom and Dad mimicked us just as Daelissa and Serena appeared from behind a row of bulky devices.

The pair walked toward the door we'd just entered. I saw beads of sweat on Serena's forehead as she closed to within a few feet of us. Despite the armor veiling our presence, any movement would be detectable standing this close. I didn't dare breathe.

Daelissa's face contorted with rage one moment to an odd vacuous expression the next, as if a war were being waged in her mind. She suddenly stopped, nostrils flaring. "They're here." Her eyes went wide. "How dare they come against me?"

My heart went cold as ice. My knees felt like jelly. It was all I could do not to run.

Serena looked confused. "Who's here?"

"The leyworms dare to side with Moses against me?" Daelissa raised a hand, and a bolt of searing white melted a metal table with glass vials on top of it. The vials spilled to the floor, shattering when they hit. She stopped her attack, staring at the mess on the floor. "That will hold them for now."

What in the hell is she talking about? This woman was out of her ever-loving mind.

White as a sheet, Serena seemed to muster some courage and took the angel by the hand. "Daelissa, you must feed." She led her towards the door. "You must regain your strength."

The Seraphim blinked and flinched. She looked at the Arcane as if suddenly realizing where she was. "Get me to the flying carpet. I will return to Eden and feed. I expect to see my homeland when I return."

"Of course," Serena said, wasting no time in escorting Daelissa from the room. Their voices faded as they went down the hallway.

I noticed Elyssa's chest deflate at the same time I let out the breath I'd been holding. *That was way too close.* I also noticed Elyssa's camouflage veil fading in and out. The charge in our armor was running low. She led us to the far end of the room where we hid behind crates of equipment and lowered our hoods.

"This room is empty except for the brain at the other end of the room," Elyssa whispered. "Keep your voices low."

"For a minute I was thinking we could take Daelissa's crazy ass out," Dad said. "Then she blasted that table."

I shivered. "If that's how powerful she is with the Gloom dampening her abilities, I'd hate to face her at full strength."

"We need to plan our next moves carefully," Elyssa said. "Hopefully we can sneak past the brain."

"How long until our armor recharges?" I asked.

She traced a pattern on her sleeve. A meter appeared showing only a sliver of red. "We need at least twenty minutes."

I groaned. "Someone needs to make longer-lasting aether batteries."

"I can make them charge faster," Mom said. She gave me a meaningful look. "You should be able to as well. Remember how you told me you charged the flying carpet when you were chasing Maulin Kassus?"

"And set it on fire?" Elyssa asked. "I don't want to catch on fire."

"Give me a break," I said. "I got a little excited and overcharged it."

300

Mom pressed a hand to my armor and Dad's. "Our powers are muted here, son. Even at full strength there shouldn't be any danger of spontaneous combustion."

Dad barely repressed a snort.

I frowned at him. "You have a sick sense of humor."

"Can you truthfully tell me you didn't find it funny?" he whispered.

I imagined him screaming as he threw off burning armor and was forced to run around the Gloom naked. I held back a laugh.

He winked. "See? Sick minds think alike."

I pressed a hand to Mom and Elyssa's armor and concentrated on charging them. It took me a moment to remember how to rejigger my thinking so I could become a walking, talking charger. Once I managed that, I felt aether channeling through me.

A surprised look came over Elyssa's face as she watched the charge indicator creep up at about one percent every few seconds. I pushed harder and was rewarded by a slight increase in speed.

"I wonder how Serena can attune the rune without me," I said. "She seemed pretty confident."

"I don't know," Dad said. "And I don't want to give her the chance."

Elyssa knocked my hand off her armor. Apparently it had reached full charge while I was busy talking. Mom's armor was also at full charge. Mine and Dad's were only about halfway. I joined my efforts with Mom's and strained to listen in case Serena came back but heard nothing.

After our suits finished charging, we slipped into camo mode and followed Elyssa across the lab. I saw the minder brain drifting lazily without any victims caught in tentacles. We stayed behind cover until we reached the arch room doors and peeked through. Again, I was amazed at its size. The circular chamber was at least a hundred yards in diameter. The domed ceiling looked about seventy feet at the highest point. Something about the ceiling looked different, though I couldn't quite put a finger on it. We made our way across the room.

Mom sucked in a breath at the sight of the Shadow Nexus. "It looks just like the Grand Nexus, though the colors are off."

Earlier, I'd told the others about how Serena had grown it from a cube left by the mysterious builders of the arches. "It seems to work just fine," I said, looking from side to side in case any stray minders or Nazdal were wandering about. "Which is why we need to capture it and shut this place down."

Mom nodded and walked up to the arch. "I still only remember bits and pieces of how I activated the original arch," she said. "But I do remember how to remove the Cyrinthian Rune without causing another Desecration."

"That's exactly what we'll need to do after we shut down Serena," I said.

"What about the minder brain?" Dad asked, jabbing a thumb in their general direction.

"We can't invade with the minders still in control. The sentinels will tear us apart." I looked at the large room and wondered how much of the building was real, and how much was dreamcasted. I didn't want it collapsing on us. "While Serena is gone, I'm going to see if I can draw the minders into the psionic disruptor."

Elyssa made a quick circuit around the room and returned. "Looks empty." She deactivated her camouflage, and we did the same.

Mom hummed a few notes as she inspected the rune in the arch. Her eyebrows pinched. "The rune isn't attuned to Eden."

"It was when we left it," I said.

Mom's eyes widened. "This arch is set to open in Seraphina. Serena must have already done it."

My stomach twisted into a jumbo-sized knot. Somehow, Serena had attuned the arch to the angel home world. Daelissa really didn't need the Grand Nexus anymore.

Chapter 36

"How is that possible?" Dad asked.

Mom shook her head. "Serena said she had the key."

"Why would Serena have kept this from Daelissa?" Elyssa asked. "She could have opened it for her already."

"I think she wants Daelissa in full control of her faculties when she opens it," Mom said.

My mouth suddenly felt very dry. "How long will it take you to realign it with Eden?"

"Several minutes." Mom held her hand out to the rune, eyes closed in concentration. "I can't tell if the arch was used. It feels cold which probably means she hasn't actually opened it yet."

"That's good, right?" Dad asked. "It means we don't have a horde of Seraphim in the fortress."

"It's not good any way you look at it." Mom bit her lower lip. "Perhaps we should take the rune and find another way out of the Gloom. We can't risk losing the battle with Serena and leaving her with a fully functional nexus."

Elyssa swatted the idea out of the air. "Absolutely not. We have enough assets waiting on the other side of the arch to shut Serena down once and for all. Then, and only then, will we deactivate this arch."

"I don't think you understand, child." Mom regarded her with soft eyes. "If we lose this battle, we lose the war. But if we take the rune, Daelissa will still be shut off from Seraphina and reinforcements."

"What makes you think Daelissa still has the political capital to command a Seraphim army?" Dad said. "For all we know your current leaders will kick her to the curb if she shows up after being gone for so long."

"That was exactly what I thought would happen when Daelissa and inner circle conspired to overthrow our political system thousands of years ago," Mom said. "Feeding off humans made them incredibly strong. They overpowered all resistance and wiped out the government. Daelissa and the others established a regency with her closest advisor, Skazaeleus as the regent."

"Sounds like a monarchy by council," Dad said, a sour expression on his face. "I assume what's-his-face stayed in power even after the Desecration."

"It's likely, though we've been cut off for so long, anything's possible," Mom replied. "If Skazaeleus is still in power after all these millennia, Daelissa will have her invasion."

I decided to toss my own two cents in. "Maybe they got tired of his crap and overthrew him."

Mom shrugged. "We have no way of knowing until we open the portal."

Elyssa shook her head. "I understand your concerns, Alysea." She placed a hand on Mom's shoulder and looked her in the eye. "I need you to hear me out. Serena has multiple ways to ferry troops into and out of the Gloom. The arch ripper Justin told me about is probably a small sample of the devices she has at her disposal. This means Nazdal could pour into the mortal realm from any Obsidian Arch. They could surprise attack us anywhere around the world. Imagine what they could do to people living in one of the pocket dimensions like the Grotto."

"It would be a massacre." Mom shuddered. "I hadn't thought of that."

"I have a plan that should prevent Daelissa from controlling this arch in case we do lose this battle." Elyssa looked up at the black-veined structure. "Once my troops are through, I want you to remove the rune."

Mom's eyes flashed wide. "But that means—"

"We'll all be trapped here. No retreat, no surrender."

As if my stomach weren't already one giant iron ball of stress, the idea of being trapped in this place with Daelissa's imminent return added a thick layer of heart attack gravy to the mix. Unfortunately, I couldn't disagree with Elyssa's idea. "Mom, you remove the rune and escape."

Mom shook her head. "I'm not leaving. I will remove the rune and hand it off to a Templar who can hopefully take it somewhere nobody will find it in case we lose the battle."

"I can agree to that," Elyssa said. She motioned toward the arch. "Let's get started. We've wasted enough time already."

Dad nudged me on the shoulder. "Ready to go slaughter some minders? We need to get rid of that thing before it dreamcasts an army of sentinels."

"Wish I'd gone potty before we left the house," I replied. "But unless you can dreamcast a port-a-potty, yeah, killing the brain sounds like a good plan."

Elyssa kissed me. "Be careful, and kick ass."

I flashed her a confident look. "I'll see you soon, babe." The room fell quiet as the weight of the situation sunk in. I was about to offer up one last witty comment when a faint noise caught my ear. "Do you hear something?"

She tilted her head. "No."

I held out my hands. "Everyone be quiet."

Again, the sound. Like a very faint gurgling. My heart froze solid. My eyes wandered up the wall of the domed room. When they reached the curving ceiling, I realized something was definitely off. The surface looked lumpy and uneven in spots. "Mom, get started on the arch right now."

She backed away toward the rune. "What's wrong?"

The ceiling swarmed with movement. The gurgling, wheezing sound grew to a susurrus. Camouflaged Nazdal revealed themselves, clambered down the walls, and moved across the floor towards the

305

arch. Their red eyes glowed with hunger and bloodlust. The urge to drop a load vanished as my sphincter shrank to the size of a molecule.

Maloreck appeared at the head of the pack. He was big as a lion. Raw muscle showed through parts of his skin, and drool still hung from his gaping jaw. Unfortunately, it seemed the worse a Nazdal looked, the healthier they actually were. "She knew you would return." His chest heaved with a heaving laugh. "You are brave to come with such a small pack."

"Maloreck, join my pack," I said, extending a hand. I heard Mom begin singing in the background. *Stall for time.* "Together, we will make the mightiest tribe ever." My words sounded incredibly lame, but I didn't know what else to say under the circumstances.

"You have not proven you can beat the bright one." He took a step forward, long yellowed claws clacking against the stone. "I am still hers to command unless you defeat her."

"I haven't had time to challenge her to a duel," I said. "Maybe we can wait a few minutes and see if she shows up."

"She comes as she wills," he replied, taking another step forward. "Her underling told us to kill any who came into this room." Wet gurgling, like sick cats trying to purr, grew louder as Nazdal closed in from all sides.

"There must be at least a hundred," Dad whispered in my ear. "Unless Alysea opens the portal, there's not much I can do."

I reached through the window in my soul and found all the power I could muster. I summoned orbs of burning Murk and Brilliance in each hand, and faced my palms toward the encroaching creatures as if I might give them a bear hug. "I am greater than the bright one," I said in as loud a voice as possible. "I will destroy any who step closer."

Mom's voice rose in pitch before diving deeper in a series of notes so quick I could hardly follow. I felt a tremor in the air, a vibration touching my back, and sensed what lay on the other side of the nexus.

Seraphina. Home.

I shook off the feeling. That place wasn't my home. Eden was.

"You look strong," Maloreck gurgled. "But appearance is not always truth."

"Take one more step and you'll find out the truth," I said, plastering a fierce grin on my face, and hoping it really looked fierce and not stupid. *I have to protect Mom at all costs.*

Two smaller Nazdal advanced past Maloreck. One dropped its lower jaw almost to the floor, making its mouth wide enough to swallow a dog whole. It and its companion crawled forward.

I wasn't sure if they were independent thinkers or testing the waters for their boss. At this point, it didn't matter. I had to act or look weak. Pushing as much power into the Brilliance as I could, I shot a white hot beam at the closest interloper and sliced its lower jaw clean off. It let out a scream that could have peeled the polish off a woman's fingernails. Its buddy leapt at me. I spun and roundhoused it out of the air, sending it crashing and skidding through its comrades.

Maloreck crunched down on the neck of the screaming Nazdal, and the room went silent except for the purr-gurgles from the horde around us. His lids went heavy with pleasure as he drank in the life force of the fallen.

Crap. Killing these things would only feed Maloreck. I wondered if there was an upper limit to what he could hold, or if I'd have to deal with a titanic version of him in the near future. I looked him in the eyes. "Do I need to kill more?"

Maloreck wheezed out a laugh. "Always."

Mom's singing continued behind me. I hoped she didn't have much longer to go, because things were about to get real. There was only one thing I could do, and I'd have to do it fast to keep us from being overrun with Nazdal.

The arch sat at the center of the huge chamber. As with most arches, a silver circle surrounded it. When the arch was activated, it formed a closed magical circuit designed to keep magic from escaping. But circles could be used for a lot of things, especially when they were made from silver.

Most of the Nazdal still remained outside the silver circle. Only Maloreck and a dozen or so of his underlings were inside it. A plan formed in my mind. Before more Nazdal entered the circle, I

307

acted, shooting a wall of murk in front of me, pushing away the Nazdal in my path. Before they could react, I darted forward, bit my thumb hard enough to draw blood, and pressed it down on the silver band. With an act of will, I created a physical barrier with the circle to keep the rest of the enemies out.

Maloreck leapt outside the circle before it flashed closed, leaving his buddies trapped inside with me, Dad, Elyssa, and Mom.

It was better than facing all of them at once. I heard gurgling growls and looked into the eyes of the trapped Nazdal. Metal flashed, and one of the creature's heads bounced onto the floor. I leapt back, hit the floor, and rolled as another dove at me. Elyssa skewered the next attacker, but its body slammed into her and pinned her to the floor. Without the open arch, she didn't have the extra strength to save her.

Dad raced over and pulled the dead weight off her. Three more Nazdal raced for them. I channeled Murk in both hands and threw up an invisible wall. The creatures slammed into it with bone-breaking impact. That, however, didn't stop them. They felt their way along the barrier, jaws hanging open, their clusters of jacked-up teeth glistening with drool. The first one around the edge of the barrier shot out the weakening red mist.

Dad got the body off Elyssa, but not before the poison found them. I tried to conjure a breeze, but was too flustered to manage anything more than a puff of air. The trio of Nazdal leapt for them, claws extended. I ran and dove, crashing into Dad and Elyssa, and carrying them out of harm's way. By the time I rolled onto my back, a Nazdal leapt on my chest. I caught its open jaws inches from my face. Its tongue ran along my face. Another Nazdal chomped down on my foot. I screamed.

I heard hacking, and saw Elyssa throwing up. I couldn't turn my head far enough to see Dad. I clenched my teeth and growled. Anger burned through my veins. "Die," I hissed, and channeled Brilliance into my hands. The Nazdal's flesh smoked, steamed, and burned. It gurgled horribly. I roared and filled my hands with destruction. The white light enveloped the creature's head. Its body shuddered and collapsed on my chest.

The other two Nazdal were tearing at my legs. Only the Nightingale armor had saved them from being shredded. I sat up, aimed a palm at each of them, and sent twin beams spearing into their heads. Brains and other gunk boiled from their noses and mouths. The stench made my eyes water.

I turned and saw the rest of the trapped Nazdal encircling Mom. They lunged at her, but their claws drew azure sparks from the air around her. *She must have thrown up a shield.*

Dad and Elyssa were still barfing, but all the nearby attackers were dead. Nazdal outside the circle threw their bodies against it and bounced off. The closed circle would hold off physical and magical attacks for now, but even a magic circle bound by silver wouldn't hold against so many bodies for long.

Somehow, Mom was still singing away, despite the horrors intent on breaking through her shield. I could only imagine the concentration it took to do both things at once. I drew on the aether around me. Despite the sheer volume of magical energy building in the enclosed container, it was like sucking the ocean through a straw. I took aim, and sliced the arm off one attacker. The other four turned toward me. One made a heaving motion as if it was about to spew the crippling red mist. I speared it in the chest, dropping it. The others fought over its body, each one apparently trying to take the life essence for themselves. I took advantage of the infighting and smoked another Nazdal. Elyssa ran past, still coughing, and slashed at an attacker. It intercepted her blade with a claw.

"Careful!" I shouted, but she was already in the heat of battle, spinning, ducking, and lancing her sword through the Nazdal's throat. It spurted blood and crashed to the floor.

"I have it!" Mom shouted. She waved a hand, and the arch hummed.

I felt the physical barrier I'd thrown up around the arch blink off as the arch reset the magical containment circle. An instant later, the silver circle flashed, closing itself to magical energy. When it reset, it removed the barrier, replacing it with one that would only stop magical energy, not physical bodies. The Nazdal had already realized this and were crossing inside the circle in droves. Neat rows of Templars appeared through the portal in the middle of the arch.

Strength roared into me. Elyssa straightened, and her coughing stopped.

The clacking of claws and gurgling of Nazdal throats grew closer as the small army swarmed toward us. Elyssa held an arm straight up and slashed it forward. With a roaring battle cry, the Templar force rushed through the portal. We leapt out of the way, joining Mom at the side of the arch.

Mom took in a long breath. "That was exhausting."

Dad appeared at her side, and wrapped an arm around her waist. "Alysea, are you okay?"

She smiled up at him. "I'm much better now."

"Rest up," I said. "We'll take it from here."

Elyssa's full lips spread into a wicked smile. "Let's show these nasty effers not to mess with us."

We turned and watched as Templars crashed into the much smaller force of Nazdal. It was time I put an end to Maloreck before he grew any bigger.

Chapter 37

Maloreck tore into the Templars.

His huge clawed hands tossed them to the side like sacks of feathers. Elyssa engaged the first Nazdal leaping our way. She dispatched it with two quick slashes from her swords. Another dropped from the ceiling above, claws extended. I incinerated it with a blast of Brilliance. Ashes rained down.

Elyssa gave me a look of surprise before diving into a fray to save another beleaguered Templar fending off two Nazdal. Before I could charge in after her, another group of the creatures pounced from the side. I ducked, rolled, and grabbed the one closest to me. Its back faced me thanks to the missed lunge. I twisted its head savagely and heard bones crack. The next one slashed at my legs. Its claw connected and knocked me off my feet, though the armor once again saved me from a nasty wound. Without wasting a moment, it pounced on my back. I felt teeth stab into the armor around my neck.

Even though the armor saved me from severe bite wounds it couldn't stop the pressure. I gasped as my air supply cut off. I pushed hard against the ground with my hands. We flipped backward. I felt the Nazdal's body shudder with the impact as its back hit the floor. The attacker's grip around my neck loosened. I reached back with my hands, gripped its disgusting slimy mouth, and yanked hard as I could. I heard a scream. Felt its jaw crack and break. I rolled free and

311

watched the injured Nazdal squirming, its lower jaw hanging loose, blood pouring from tears in its flesh.

With a savage stomp to the head, I ended its suffering and turned to look for Elyssa. She was lost in the crowd of black-clad Templars. Swords flashed, and claws slashed. One side of the Templar formation still held. They held shiny black shields with the Templar symbol emblazoned on it while those behind stabbed encroaching Nazdal with swords.

I looked left. Maloreck swiped a Templar and the man crashed into me, bowling me over. I shook my head, clearing the fog, and dragged the dazed man out of the fray. A Templar with a healer symbol on her uniform took the man from me and pulled him to the back of the line. Another wave of Templars came through, these bearing staffs. They took up positions behind the shield line and blasted the Nazdal with beams of light every color of the rainbow. Flesh charred and smoked. The enemy screamed and died.

It looked like we had things well in hand, except for Maloreck. I swore the creature had grown even larger, thanks to the deaths of his comrades. One of the Templar Arcanes blasted him with a spear of light. It had little effect on the huge Nazdal. He sprayed a cloud of red mist, and the Templars in front of him fell back, choking and gasping for air.

I saw more crimson poison falling around me and looked up. Nazdal on the ceiling had joined their leader, huffing clouds of the stuff down on the Templars below.

"Up there!" I shouted to the Arcanes. "Kill the ones up there!"

Arcanes looked up and redirected their deadly spells on the creatures above. Bodies rained down as they raked the ceiling with searing light. I dodged away as a Nazdal crashed on the floor where I'd been standing, the crunch of bones audible even over the battle. I generated a ball of Murk in my hands and imagined it gusting like wind across the room. The wave of ultraviolet whooshed overhead, carrying red poison with it and clearing the air.

My efforts weren't enough to clear the battlefront where Maloreck waged war, a pile of Templar and Nazdal bodies at his feet. He didn't seem to care who he killed as his body stretched and grew.

312

How large can that bastard grow?

I couldn't ignore him any longer.

I rushed through the sea of bodies, dodging swords, claws, and flying bodies. Only the surefooted Nightingale armor kept me from slipping in the puddles of blood all over the floor. I noticed several Templars with wounds visible through tears in their armor. The material hardened to prevent punctures, but apparently had its limits. Maloreck's huge arm reared back for the death blow on a fallen Templar. The man's mask was in tatters, and blood streamed from his wounds. Even so, he stared defiantly at the beast, holding his sword in an offensive posture that might allow him one last strike.

I dove. Grabbed Maloreck's arm, and twisted. I heard a loud crack. The beast roared. Spun to face me.

"You have come at last," he said, eyes glowing with bloodlust. "I would test myself against the strongest."

"What's one plus one?" I asked.

He looked puzzled. "I do not understand."

"It's two, you moron. You just failed the test."

Laughter boomed from his throat. He absentmindedly batted aside a charging Templar and lunged for me. I shot a blast of Brilliance at his chest. His flesh blackened, but seemed to heal just as quickly. I ducked beneath him and performed an evasive somersault, just like Elyssa had taught me. Maloreck landed in a group of Nazdal, sending his smaller minions scattering.

I noticed that several of them had grown larger and sensed if we didn't stop this fight, there would be a lot more like Maloreck beating the snot out of us. He lunged again. I funneled a solid wall of Murk and slammed him backward. He landed on all fours, claws digging gouges in the floor as I pushed with all my might, trying to crush him against a wall several feet behind him. He bellowed and pushed forward. The wave of magic began to warp and flow around him.

"Why won't you just go away?" I shouted. I felt sweat dribbling down my face and knew I couldn't press this attack much longer.

313

The beast's huge jaws widened in a malevolent sneer. "The lives I have reaped give me strength. They grant me magical resistance, young one."

It was time to switch to Plan B. I didn't actually have such a plan, but there was at least one more ace to play in my deck. I manifested into demon form. The armor bulged to accommodate muscles as they coiled around my frame. I felt my flesh swell against the fabric as my inner demon roared forth.

As usual, it made a power grab for my very mind, seeking to submit it to its pure bloodlust and ravenous desire to destroy and take everything. I felt weak from using so much raw magic and nearly lost control as my demon side surged for every last ounce of me. I grew until I rivaled Maloreck himself. I felt my tail lash behind me, felt it make contact with something attacking my rear and sweep it away.

The world began to fade. I fought back, straining to close the cage and keep my demon soul from consuming me. If it took me, no one would be safe from what followed.

Don't be so damned greedy!

With a final effort of will, I slammed it back into its cage and resumed control. I hardly had time to breathe a sigh of relief before Maloreck was on me. One of my huge hands caught his throat. My tail wrapped around a claw coming for my face, and my opposite hand gripped his other wrist. Maloreck hissed a cloud of red vapor.

I blew as hard as I could and sent it right back down his ugly throat. Then I reared my head back and slammed him in the face with my horns.

Maloreck grunted, the first sound of pain I'd heard. He bellowed and snapped his jaws at my face. I held him at bay by his throat and squeezed, roaring so loudly it overcame the cacophony of battle. For a brief moment, everything went silent.

Maloreck laughed. It sounded like a man with third-degree pneumonia at the bottom of a pool of slime. "You are more impressive than I knew."

"Surrender or die," I said in a deep guttural voice. If I could beat this thing, maybe he would acknowledge me as his master. "Join me!"

"You have not defeated the bright one," he wheezed. "I cannot submit."

I squeezed his throat. "Then die." Something slammed against my back. I heard the phlegmy breath of a Nazdal at my throat. More bodies impacted me, throwing me forward. Maloreck snapped at my face. His teeth caught on the armor and tore it loose. I felt stabs of pain as more Nazdal on my back tore at the armor.

I threw Maloreck against the wall. He slammed into it, sending a crack up its face. I gripped the Nazdal on my neck and crushed its throat with a brutal squeeze. My tail gripped another by the arm and flung it at Maloreck as he gained his feet. He swatted his minion out of the way. More claws and bites stung my legs. I gripped two more of the disfigured attackers and smashed them together. Blood and gore spattered into my eyes.

Maloreck slammed into me while I was blinded. We rolled across the floor, tearing at each other with abandon. Chunks of his flesh tore loose as my clawed hands dug in. He didn't seem to feel the pain, his own claws tearing at my armor and stabbing into my toughened skin. Somehow, I stopped the roll while I was on top. I gripped his neck and slammed his head into the floor. He spat a stream of red liquid into my eyes. A bellow of pain erupted from my throat. I'd never been sprayed with pepper spray, but imagined it couldn't feel as bad as this. My eyes burned like a thousand suns.

Teeth like razor-sharp spikes clamped into my bicep. I swung my other fist blindly and missed. His jaw clamped down on my other arm. I tried to grab him but he slipped away before I made contact. His next attack stabbed savagely into my leg. This time, I tried to retreat, backing away. I felt the wall and knew I was trapped. I couldn't see, and the agony was overpowering.

Maloreck seemed to know he had me. "You fought well, but you are not strong enough."

"You couldn't take me one-on-one," I shot back. "Your little pals are the only thing that saved you, you lily-livered pansy." As insults went, it certainly wasn't my best work, but I was in absolute searing pain. My eyes felt like miniature volcanoes. The places where

Maloreck had bitten me stung like a swarm of mutant bees had made me their own personal pin cushion.

"Your insults will not win this fight," he said, sounding closer than a moment before. "Nothing will, now."

I braced for his next attack and fervently wished I'd trained with a blindfold like Elyssa had often suggested. I had no way to see this creature, and from the sounds of battle, it didn't seem anyone was coming to my aid anytime soon. If only I had Minder Justin with me to show the way.

An answer slapped me in the noggin. I didn't need eyes to see this jackass. I had incubus abilities. Despite the searing agony in my eyeballs, I managed to extend my senses. I still couldn't open my eyes, but I felt the presence of Maloreck nearby. He was a few feet in front of me, pacing back and forth. I felt a burst of glee from him and his clawed hand slammed me in the side of the head.

I staggered left. Another surge of manic joy pulsed from him and I braced as another blow punched into my gut.

"Your life will add to mine," he gurgled. "I will be mightier than the bright one."

"You sure enjoy playing with your food," I said. "Admit it. You're afraid to fight me even while I'm blind."

That remark triggered what I could only describe as hurt pride. I sensed a surge of emotion and knew he was coming in. This time I was ready. I ducked and charged forward. My shoulder met what felt like his stomach. Maloreck grunted. A shock of surprise emanated from him. Using my momentum, I leapt forward and slammed him earthward. Air burst from his throat. I guesstimated where his throat was, and managed to find it on the first try, gripping it with both hands and squeezing.

He flailed, hissing and gurgling. His claws dug at my face. I held my head back, and squeezed my eyes tighter. I felt more Nazdal leap onto my back. This time, I ignored them. The pain they caused was nothing like the infernos in my eyes.

How long does this stuff take to wear off?

I squeezed with all my might, desperate to end the fight fast. Maloreck's claws raked against my stomach. I knew the armor had failed when I felt my flesh ripping. At this point, I didn't care. I had to kill him or die.

"I'll save you, Justin!" I heard Ivy shout. The Nazdal on my back screeched. I smelled burning flesh. The load on my back lightened and the attacks stopped. Something wrapped around my midriff and tore me loose from Maloreck, depositing me on the floor.

A tremendous roar sundered the air. "*Xhi kaklni xhe*," bellowed a demonic voice. *I will kill you.*

I felt tender hands press against my face. "Hold still, Justin," Mom said. "I'll make you better."

Cool, cold liquid splashed down my face and the agony subsided. I blinked my eyes open and saw Mom's face through a haze. She trickled more of her miracle fluid into my eyes, and the haze faded until my sight was once again clear. I stood, looking desperately for Maloreck. When I found him, I saw I had hurt him. Blood poured from multiple wounds. Even so, he still looked as dangerous as ever, though not as dangerous as the towering red-skinned demon facing him.

"Leave my son alone," my father said, his voice deep and booming. "I think it's time you died."

Mom grunted. "I concur, David."

Ivy stood next to Mom. "You hurt my brother," she growled. "Let's finish this!"

"You are not as strong," Maloreck hissed at my father. "If he had not injured me, you would have no hope of winning."

"Now look who's crying foul," I bellowed.

Maloreck seemed to know the gig was up. Faced with the four of us, even he didn't have a chance. He turned to run. Ivy threw out a hand. A net of blinding white shackled him to the floor. Dad made a fist and punched upward. His hand opened wide. A fiery hand ripped from the ground and clenched the Nazdal's midriff. He screamed as his flesh steamed and burned. Dad squeezed his hand tighter. Bones crunched. Gouts of blood spewed from the creature's mouth.

Dad looked at me. "Finish him off, son."

I roared and charged the trapped Nazdal. Using all my strength, I karate-chopped him in the throat. Maloreck gurgled. I

317

chopped again. Breath rattled from his mouth. Gripping his head in my large hands, I twisted and yanked. With a sick, wet pop, his head dislocated and hung loose by the flesh. Maloreck wheezed his last breath.

I saw several of the larger Nazdal racing for the body. I knew if they took his life essence, we'd have another huge problem on our hands. Mom came to my side and pressed her hands together. She drew them apart, displaying a roiling ball of white light. She thrust her hands forward and a beam of Brilliance sliced through the first Nazdal. Mom swept it left and right, shearing off limbs and heads.

"Ivy, get rid of the body," I said.

Still maintaining the net of Brilliance around Maloreck's corpse, she swung her arm and hurled the body far back behind our defensive lines.

Looking across the room, I caught sight of Elyssa and a group of Templars finishing off the remaining Nazdal.

"We did it," I said, hardly able to believe it.

"We sure did, bro," Ivy said, wiping her hands and scowling at the remaining force. She looked me up and down. "You actually look kinda cool as a demon. Maybe I could learn how to—"

Mom grimaced. "Ivy, find Nightliss and help her."

Ivy pouted. "But she doesn't need—"

"*Ivy*," Mom said in a stern voice. "She needs you."

My sister sighed. "Fine. But I want to learn how to be a demon too." She looked across the chamber and sprinted where Nightliss was helping Templars fend off flanking attackers.

I shoved the demon back in its cage, resuming my normal form.

Dad also shrank back to normal size. "We still haven't finished off the brain," he reminded me. "I can't believe Serena hasn't shown up—"

The words had hardly left his mouth when dozens of sentinels burst through the door. I caught sight of Serena through the open passage, eyes glittering with what could only be anger. The sentinels weren't the only thing coming through the door. I saw ghouls shambling close behind. After them came more Nazdal. I remembered

Serena saying there were hundreds of ghouls and god only knew how many more of the crawling sub-human Nazdal.

The light of victory vanished from Dad's eyes as he looked at the oncoming horde. "Okay, now I'm pissed."

Chapter 38

"We're outnumbered," Mom said.

I heard Elyssa shout a command and saw the Templars reforming their ranks. Bodies littered the floor. How many Templars lay dead, I couldn't tell, but at least the dead Nazdal seemed to outnumber our people. Elyssa spoke with two other Templar squad leaders, and then ran over to us. "We're going to hold the line."

Mom's eyes flashed wide. "Impossible. We need an orderly retreat." She glanced at the arch. "I can remove the rune, but it will take several minutes. Once the last Templar is through, I'll remove it and shut down the arch."

Elyssa shook her head. "There's no escaping this room once the portal is closed. You'll be trapped and Serena will still have it."

"We can blast a hole in the back wall." Mom seemed to measure the distance. "If you take care of that and provide me with a flying carpet, I can hide until we find another way out of the Gloom."

"These walls are incredibly thick, not to mention magic resistant." My girlfriend clenched her jaw and looked at the encroaching force. "They have a numbers advantage, but not all of them can fit in this room."

"That door is a bottleneck we can take advantage of," Dad said, pointing to the narrow opening.

A Nazdal and ghoul squeezed through the door at the same time. The ghoul roared and grabbed the Nazdal. With a savage swing, it slammed the creature against the floor like a sack of flour until it hung limp. Another ghoul shambled through while the first subhuman snacked on the body of its victim, seemingly oblivious to anything else around it. Other Nazdal crowded around the body, probably taking what little life essence they could.

"They're not a coherent fighting force," Elyssa said. "Just a bunch of monsters. Maybe we can use that to our advantage."

Even as the ghouls and Nazdal bumped and crowded through the door, more infighting erupted. By now, the Templars formed a solid wall. Those in the front held their shields in an overlapping pattern while Arcanes and swordsmen stood behind.

Dad took Mom by the arm. "Before you go trapping yourself in the Gloom, let me try something else."

She looked up at him. "But, David—"

"You remember the Battle of the Sand Canyon?"

She nodded.

"We beat impossible odds then. We can do it again."

Mom smiled. "Just like old times, isn't it?"

He chuckled. "Never a dull moment when you're around, Alysea. Besides, you know me; I always have another card up my sleeve." He gripped my shoulder. "Come on, Justin."

He and I jogged through the Shadow Nexus portal and into the Three Sisters arch control room back in the real world. Racing from beneath the Alabaster Arch, we took the aisle to the front of the chamber. A Templar manned the modulus. Dad pulled out an arcphone and dialed a number. I heard a female voice answer. "Looks like I'll need you after all." He handed the phone to the Templar. "Please do as she says."

Before I could ask who he'd called, Dad turned and raced back toward the portal to the Gloom. Through the portal, I saw Mom and Elyssa looking toward the wall of Templars—a thin black line standing between Serena's forces and the rune. My stomach sank as I thought of how close we were to losing this battle and how close Daelissa was to realizing her dream of world domination.

We stepped back through. I opened my mouth to ask Dad who he'd contacted when Elyssa raced up to me. "We're trying to push enemy forces back toward the door. The Arcanes are at a disadvantage because they're at floor level."

I raised an eyebrow. "I don't get it."

She pointed to what looked like a large pile of ebony lumber. "Those are self-building mage platforms, but I can't spare anyone to set them up." She looked at my mother. "Alysea, I need you, Nightliss, and Ivy on those platforms. We need all the help we can get."

A bloodied Templar jogged from the front line. "We're unable to stop the dreamcasted sentinels. Our attacks have no effect on them."

"The brain," I said, looking at Dad. "We have to destroy it." I suddenly remembered something. "Elyssa, remember what my minder said?"

Her eyes widened. "We can try to summon our own minders." She looked at the only entrance to the chamber. "But how will they get in?"

"We'll figure something out," I said.

"Do it," Elyssa said. She pulled out her phone and issued commands, explaining how to call the minders.

"Soon as we figure out how to get them in, I'll give you the signal," I said.

"I'll get Ivy and Nightliss," Mom said, and raced away.

Dad and I dashed over to the pile of unconstructed mage platforms and took several. Each one looked like an ordinary chunk of lumber. I touched a symbol on the surface, and tossed it on the floor. With a loud clacking noise, the wood unfolded itself, shooting upward until a square platform with a ladder balanced atop a tripod. It stood no more than twenty feet high, but that was probably all the height someone with a staff needed.

Dad grabbed a handful. The two of us ran behind the line, throwing up platforms until we were out of them. Arcanes on the ground climbed the structures. From their height advantage, they were able to easily pick off targets from a distance. I saw Mom, Ivy, and Nightliss mounting platforms behind the center of our line.

Some of the Nazdal had taken to scaling the walls, probably hoping to drop behind our lines. The Arcanes picked them off as they tried, sending charred corpses falling back into the midst of the monsters below. But the Arcanes were already tired. No matter how many monsters they killed, more popped out of the woodwork.

I climbed to the top of one of the platforms and looked down at the battle. Some of the ghouls and Nazdal were still fighting among themselves. Others tested the Templar line only to be hacked to bits. I quickly saw the biggest problem—the sentinels. As the Templar messenger had mentioned, the dreamcasted warriors had no problem crushing any resistance. Swords did nothing to them. Arcanes blasted the faceless mannequins with all forms of magic to little effect.

Even though the sentinels numbered less than fifty, they formed a coherent line that was cleaving through our forces like they weren't even there, and the Nazdal were taking full advantage of the breach.

"We need our minders," I said to Dad. "But how will they get through?"

He joined me atop the platform. "We'll make a hole."

"How?" I nodded toward the only way into or out of the arch room. "It's more crowded than a strip club on payday."

I heard a blood-curdling howl and spun around. At least forty people appeared through the portal in the Shadow Nexus. With them were the biggest nastiest-looking dogs I'd ever seen. No, not dogs—hellhounds. I recognized the shapely blonde woman leading the group, my dear Aunt Vallaena.

"That was fast," Dad said. He waved his sister over.

"Hello, nephew," she said to me in her usual reserved tone.

"Howdy." I looked at the horde of hellhounds tagging along behind the other Daemos.

She raised an eyebrow. "So, how may we serve the cause?"

I suddenly realized she was asking me. "The Nazdal are breaching our lines right behind the sentinels." I pointed them out. "We need help holding the line. The problem is nothing we've done can contain those things."

323

Dad explained to her about how they were dreamcasted. "Don't even waste your time with them. If you can control those crawling freaks, that would help even more."

She nodded. "Very well." She raised a fist, and the Daemos manifested into demon form, bodies bulging with muscle, horns and tails sprouting. Some of them had blue-hued skin. One of the females looked almost purple. All of them looked badass. "Onward!" Vallaena shouted. The hellhounds howled, and they charged the hole.

Some of the Nazdal looked at the oncoming demon spawn, and something like surprise or fear finally registered on their ugly faces. The Daemos mowed through the enemies who'd poured through the breach in the line slashed by the Sentinels. Templars roared and cheered. But the line wouldn't hold long unless we did something about the sentinels. Even now the dreamcasted soldiers were harassing another part of our lines. The Daemos could help, but they couldn't be everywhere at once.

I spotted a large Nazdal racing up and down the line of his troops, probably rallying them. He wasn't as huge as Maloreck, but between him and at least three others I spotted organizing their ranks, we were about to have another big problem on our hands. The sentinels had effectively stopped the Templar push. Nearly twenty yards filled with enemies stood between us and stopping up the entrance to the chamber.

Vallaena and the Daemos raced up and down the line, shoring up the weak positions, but for the Templars to push forward, the sentinels needed to be gone for good.

A light bulb lit in my head. I clambered down the ladder and stood next to my father. "Remember your earthquake trick back when Montjoy banished us? Think you can use that to break a hole in the wall?"

"These walls look thick, but we can give it a try."

The two of us sprinted across the open ground to the back of the chamber. I saw Elyssa rallying the troops where the sentinels had broken and scattered the ranks.

"How did you do that fiery hand out of the ground trick?" I asked as we ran.

324

"It's like summoning hellhounds. Instead of forcing a minor demon into a hellhound form, I give a more powerful demon a chance to reach out and touch someone." We reached the back wall. He tapped on it and frowned. "Elyssa was right when she said the wall is thick and magic resistant. It's going to be a hard nut to crack."

Dad knelt and braced a hand against the obsidian floor. "Hope this works." He closed his eyes. For several seconds, nothing happened, or at least it seemed that way. I felt a tremor in the earth behind me and spun. A thin crack in the rock ran from the portal and grew in our direction. I stepped to the side as the anomaly raced past me and beneath Dad's kneeling form.

The fissure met the wall. A tremendous grating noise overwhelmed my ears. Chunks of rock burst from the ground. It sounded like a giant sledgehammer striking rock over and over again. I clamped both hands over my ears. After all this racket I'd be lucky if I didn't need hearing aids. I fought to keep my feet as the ground trembled and shook.

Sweat poured off Dad's face. A grimace peeled his lips back to reveal clenched teeth. "C'mon, damn it." Chips of granite fell from the wall, but so far only a hairline fracture ran up its surface. Just because the walls were magic resistant didn't mean they were magic immune.

I drew upon Murk and channeled a thin wedge into the hairline crack. Ultraviolet energy flashed along the tiny rift, filling it. I imagined the energy solidifying and expanding. A tremendous weight settled onto my shoulders and dropped me to one knee. It was like trying to break a mountain in half by prying it open with my fingertips. I heard the straining and cracking of rock. The infernal forces Dad employed slammed into the wall again. The crack widened an iota.

Once again his underground battering ram slammed into the weak point. The instant it made impact, I sent a burst of energy into the breach. Dozens of cracks formed a spider web across the surface. Ultraviolet Murk flooded the small fissures, straining and pushing. I drew upon Brilliance and as Dad slammed the wall, fired a burst at the center of the damaged wall section. Most of the energy splashed harmlessly away, probably due to the magical resistance.

325

It didn't matter. With a snapping groan, a section of the wall collapsed into rubble. Dad panted. Whatever magical force he'd employed raced back into the portal, leaving a small fissure behind.

"Whew." He wiped away sweat with the back of his hand. "I didn't realize summoning an elemental demon would be so hard here."

"An elemental?" I asked.

"They're more like spirits, really, but you do *not* want to mess up when you summon them." He stepped toward the hole in the wall and whistled. "This thing must be ten feet thick."

I shoved some of the larger chunks of rubble out of the way to reveal a hole large enough for a horse to walk through. "What happens if you lose control of an elemental?"

"In the case of an earth spirit, you might just get buried alive."

I shuddered. "I don't know if I want to learn how to do that."

He slapped me on the back. "We're part demon. We have it a little easier than human Arcanes."

I stepped outside and felt my butt cheeks clench. The wall of the arch room faced the quarry pit. Only a ledge about a foot thick offered room to move. Thanks to the pounding we'd given the wall, a good portion of the ledge outside had crumbled into the quarry. Pressing my back firmly to the wall, I edged along the ledge to the left. "Hopefully we can go in through the quarry entrance."

Dad gripped my sleeve. "No way. All the Nazdal and ghoul reinforcements are coming from the pit. That door will be jammed with enemies."

I looked at him and tried not to look down. "What do you suggest then?"

He motioned his head to the right. "The front door."

"We'll have to run all the way around the building."

"Better than forcing our way through an angry mob of monsters." He sidled to the right.

I sighed and followed. It took several minutes of pant-wetting ledge walking to reach the part where the arch room curved back to wide-open ground.

326

The fortress stretched into the distance. It would take twenty minutes just to race around the perimeter. I aimed a hand at the surface and shot a strand of Murk far up the wall. "Take my hand," I told my father. "Whatever you do, don't let go."

We locked grips. "What now?" he asked.

"Jump off the cliff on the count of three."

"You sure know how to have a good time," he said with a grin.

We counted down and jumped. I willed the aetherial rope to stretch as we plummeted toward the bottom of the quarry. Ten feet off the ground, we slowed and stopped. With tremendous force, the rope shot us upward. We flew up the wall and landed on the ledge.

Dad was beaming. "Can we go again?"

"Let me clean my pants first," I said, surveying the top of the fortress.

Large turrets with huge crossbows occupied the flat roof, forming a grid. Jarvis obviously took his fortress building way too seriously. We picked an aisle leading to the front and ran between rows of turrets. Unfortunately, the further we ran, the weaker we became thanks to the distance between us and the open arch. By the time we reached the front of the massive building, Dad was puffing. I had less problem thanks to my newfound abilities, but picking up my father and running wasn't an option.

When we reached the front edge of the fortress, Dad gripped my shoulder. "Look up there," he said, pointing to the sky.

At first I thought I saw a small cloud descending on the fortress. As it grew closer, I realized it was a flurry of minders swooping down toward us. One of them detached and floated toward me. A tentacle reached out and touched my head.

The cavalry is here, Minder Justin said.

I almost whooped but didn't want to draw the attention of any enemies that might be lurking nearby. *The sentinels are tearing us apart. Can you and the other minders dreamcast something to keep them at bay? We made a hole in the rear of the domed building.* I pointed toward it.

327

You got it. My minder detached and led the others toward the opening.

I dared to hope we might actually survive this.

"They're here to help?" Dad asked.

"We have a chance," I said. "Let's go."

I found a stairwell leading down. We quietly made our way to the ground floor. The main entrance lay a few yards to our left. We went right, racing through the maze of kill zones Jarvis had shown us. No sentinels manned those positions now. Since the threat came from inside the fortress, Serena apparently hadn't bothered to fortify the approach.

As we ran through and gained proximity to the Shadow Nexus, Dad and I grew stronger. I was thankful Jarvis had given us such a thorough tour of the facility. Even though the layout was sterile and monotonous, we managed to take the same path our imprisoner had led us through and arrived outside Serena's lab. Ghouls and Nazdal packed the back left side of the huge room, their numbers flowing in from the corridor that led to the quarry door.

The right side of the room looked mostly empty, though we spotted a few ghouls and Nazdal wandering through the maze of contraptions as if they had nothing better to do while a battle raged. I heard the din of battle emanating from inside the arch room. I heard a huge cheer erupt and wondered if that meant the minders arrived and were locking down the fortress sentinels.

I heard a stern female voice nearby. Dad and I ducked behind a large silver box and peered around the corner. Serena was speaking with Jarvis and some of the other humans who Dad and I had seen during our first escape attempt from the Gloom. "...do you understand?"

Jarvis nodded. "We'll take care of it. The Templars will never know what hit them."

The others in his group hefted bulging duffel bags. I strained to get a look at them, but could only make out rectangular forms pressing against the fabric. Jarvis and his gang ran toward us. Dad and I ducked around the other side of the box. I peered around and watched as they left the same way we'd come in.

328

"What do you think they're up to?" I whispered.

"Nothing good," Dad replied. "We have another problem." He slid his back to the opposite corner of the box and nodded toward the front of the room. "What do you see?"

I shrugged. "Nazdal and ghouls."

"That's right. The minders are gone."

"Serena must have moved them." The fortress was massive. It would be like finding a needle in a haystack, and we had no time to spare.

Chapter 39

"Why would she move them?" I asked.

Dad shrugged. "Maybe to get them out of the way of her army."

I blew out a frustrated breath. I felt at a complete loss as to what we should do next.

"They might still be in this room," Dad said.

"What makes you think that?"

He nodded his head toward the arch chamber. "They might need to be close enough to the battle to dreamcast the sentinels."

"Maybe." I hadn't thought of that.

Dad's eyes lit up. "We're being dumb about this. Let's use our incubus abilities. The minders have a pretty distinct aura."

"Of course." I resisted the urge to snap my fingers as was usually appropriate when a bright idea hit me. I probed the area with my senses, extending them further and further. They drifted over a nearby Nazdal. I recoiled and felt as though the mere contact had drained a little life from me. An odd tingle sent a shiver up my spine.

"I found the minders," I said. "Not too far from here."

"I feel them too." Dad, looked around, and then dashed to cover behind what looked like a steel coffin standing on end. I followed him. We made our way across the room, hugging various contraptions along the way until we found our targets.

The minders hovered close to one another, tentacles drifting. They were so tantalizingly close but impossibly far away. We couldn't simply drag them inside the disruptor. The second they touched us, we'd be immobilized, caught in their waking dreams.

"How are we supposed to move them?" I asked.

Dad hissed out a breath between his teeth. "We need bait."

I felt my eyes widen. "That would be suicide."

"No, not suicide, just a very risky gambit."

"I'll do it," I said. My insides writhed at the thought.

He gripped my arm. "No, Justin, I'll do it."

"But—"

"Listen to me," he said in a stern voice. "I'll present myself to them, lure them into the disruptor. They'll know I'm not with Serena and should come after me. You activate the control panel. At the last second, use one of those magic ropes you used to scale the building and jerk me out of there."

"I don't like this plan."

"Neither do I, but it's our only shot." He bit his lower lip. "Get to the control panel, and be ready."

A lump formed in my throat. "Look, I know we didn't get off to the best start, but I kind of like having you around."

He grinned and put a hand on my back. "I'm proud of you. No matter what happens, never give up."

I took his hand and shook it. "Good luck, Dad."

"Good luck, son." He released my hand and nodded toward the hexagonal ring of Tesla coils comprising the disruptor. "Time to pull off a caper."

We sneaked to the closest Tesla coil and hid behind it. The control panel sat atop a platform against the wall just outside the ring of pylons.

"Any idea if the minders can see me sneaking up behind them?" Dad asked.

I shrugged. "Your guess is as good as mine."

"Here goes nothing," he said, and made his way toward the targets, hiding behind crates and other contraptions spaced around the

331

room. The bulk of the Nazdal army swarmed far enough away I hoped they wouldn't spot him.

I turned and crept to the control panel and waited as Dad sneaked to the brain. When he closed to within a few yards, he stepped from behind a crate. As one, the minders turned toward him, tentacles writhing. He backed away a step, the creatures closing in, drifting almost languorously after him. I pressed the symbols on the control panel in the order Cinder had shown me. Each one stayed lit as I touched it. Holding my finger above the final symbol, I ducked behind the control panel, breath locked in my throat, and peered over the edge.

Dad walked backward, leading them until finally he reached the perimeter of the disruptor, his position about fifty feet from me. The minders stopped, seeming to realize his intent. He waited for a moment, but they didn't advance. David took a cautious step forward. Tentacles strained for him, stopping just short of his face.

I wanted to shout at him, tell him to come up with another plan, but a calm look of resignation came over his face. He looked at me and said, "Get ready." With that, he stepped forward. The minders swarmed him.

A cry swelled in my throat. Clenching my teeth, I cast a strand of Murk at Dad. It caught his waist. I jerked him inside the disruptor, his body trailing the minders with it. Then I pressed my hand on the final symbol.

Static crackled. A whining noise like a jet engine powering on vibrated the air. The Tesla coil on the ceiling glowed blue. The whining sound grew louder and louder until it overpowered every other sound in the room. I knew it was only seconds away from discharging into the structure with all the rings directly below it.

I had no idea if the disruptor would kill my father. I only knew I had to pull him out of the ring before it engaged. To do that, I'd have to pull him out at the last second without dragging the minders with him. Unfortunately, the minders seemed to realize their peril and released their prey, making for safety outside the perimeter of Tesla coils.

Dad slumped to the floor, unmoving. I remembered Minder Justin telling me minders couldn't phase through solid objects. I channeled Murk and threw up a wall around the creatures, trapping them. Dad pushed himself unsteadily to his knees. His unfocused gaze met mine as the whining noise reached a fever pitch.

In my panic to block the minders, I'd released the Murk rope. I shot another strand at him. Something pounded against my back. I crashed face-first onto the platform. The raspy breath of a Nazdal warmed my ear. On instinct, I reached back and flung the creature off, throwing him inside the perimeter of the disruptor. I still held the lifeline to my father. I saw the Nazdal preparing for a lunge at Dad and pulled the rope with all my might, but the creature pinned him to the ground.

A brilliant bolt of blue energy blasted from the Tesla coil on the ceiling. It pulsed into the sphere in the center of the rings. They spun to a blur. Dad threw his attacker off. Azure beams lanced out from the rotating orb in five directions, each one intersecting a pylon. I gave another pull on the rope, but a kinetic barrier whirled around the pylons and sliced the bond, trapping my father inside.

Dad looked at me. A devilish smile curled his lip just before a blinding flash sent me reeling backwards. I squeezed my eyes shut saw the shadow of my father in the afterimage. The disruptor wound down, fading to silence.

Dad lay on the floor, eyes closed. The minders drifted down, brainy heads shriveling like deflating balloons, tentacles limp and unmoving. They settled onto the floor and started to fade. The Nazdal trapped inside the disruptor lay on his back, all fours straight up in the air, twitching.

"No," I said in a whisper, looking at Dad's still form. "No!" I staggered to my feet and raced across the space between us. I knelt and shook his shoulders. "Wake up, Dad. Wake up!" I peeled back his eyelids. I saw just from looking at him, the light was gone from his eyes. I'd failed to save him. I'd killed my father.

I heard a huge cheer from inside the arch chamber, probably because the sentinels were decomposing with the minder brain defeated.

"We did it, Dad." I choked back a sob. "We did it."
But the cost had been staggering.

Chapter 40

More Nazdal appeared, apparently drawn by the noise from the disruptor. I roared and shot a beam of Brilliance, severing limbs and incinerating them before they drew close. Slinging my father over a shoulder, I raced from the lab, back the way we'd come until I reached the stairwell near the front. I paused, panting, and listening for anything following me, but heard nothing.

The mission wasn't over yet. Not even close. Dad had killed the brain, but Jarvis and his people were up to something. My lips trembled with grief as I looked down at Dad. I couldn't just leave him here. I had to get his body back to Mom. The fighting had weakened me. Supernatural strength or not, I was tired as hell.

I climbed the stairs and sat down next to one of the large turrets. Fumbling my phone from my pocket, I called Elyssa to warn her about Jarvis.

"You did it, Justin!" she said. The sounds of yelling and fighting nearly overwhelmed her voice.

"It's not over." I almost told her about Dad, but decided now wasn't the time. "Some of Serena's men are up to something, I don't know what. I suspect some kind of sneak attack."

"I don't know how they could sneak in here unless there's a secret entrance," she said.

"There's the hole Dad and I made to get out."

"They won't be getting in there," she assured me. She shouted a command to someone else. "I have to go. You and your father be careful coming back."

I swallowed a lump. "Okay."

I bent down and picked up Dad. Just as I took my first step, I heard running footsteps from somewhere ahead. Someone cursed. I set down my human cargo as carefully as possible and ducked behind the block.

"Send me running like his errand boy, will he?" someone growled as he approached.

I looked and saw Gavin with two empty duffels slung over either shoulder. His shirt was soaked with sweat. As he passed the turret I was using for cover, I jumped out, grabbed him, and knocked him out with a swift punch to the jaw. He went limp. I dragged him down the stairs and left him on a landing. When I ran back up to the roof, I peered toward the domed roof of the arch building. I saw silhouettes climbing around on it. From this vantage, the Atlanta skyline stood against a gray sky. It had to be nighttime in the real world for all the fog to be gone. I figured with the brain minders dead, the fortress would once again be filled with fog during the daytime.

I made sure Dad was lying comfortably on his back and looked toward the dome. Whatever Jarvis and the others were up to, I would put a stop to it. I'd already gotten Dad killed today. I wouldn't allow anyone else to die.

Mom will be heartbroken.

I choked back a sob. Mom was still in love with him as much as he was with her. It was so obvious when they were together. Every time he said her name, he sounded so vulnerable. I couldn't imagine the pain it had caused them to decide he should preserve the alliance and marry Kassallandra. I'd hated him for that. My god, I'd even told him he was dead to me. And now he really was.

My eyes watered with tears and the world blurred. I wiped them away with the back of my hand. Now wasn't the time to turn into a big crybaby. I had to protect the others. There was no way I could ever atone for what I'd let happen to Dad—*Stop dwelling on it!*

I knew I wouldn't get close to the dome without Jarvis and the others seeing me. Gavin was a little shorter than me, but he had black hair. Mine was slightly longer, but I hoped they wouldn't notice from a distance. I ran back to Gavin's unconscious form, took off his T-shirt and put it over my tattered Nightingale armor. Grimacing, I pulled off his shoes and pants and stuffed them into a duffel bag to make it look full as possible. Then I raced back toward the dome, focusing my supernatural vision on the people there.

They were placing what looked like gray bricks all along the edge. Two of the men wielded rifles. Between the back of the flat roof and the dome was a long stretch without cover. I slung the duffel over my shoulder and headed toward the dome, keeping my head down. If Jarvis or his people saw my face, they'd instantly know I wasn't their comrade.

"About time," I heard Jarvis shout as I came into view. "Hotfoot it over here. We need to hurry."

I jogged forward, keeping my head low as I dared, looking at the others from the corner of my eye. I realized with a shock the bricklike objects his men were placing were explosives. They planned to bring the roof down on the Templars. If they succeeded, tons of granite would crush our people like bugs.

They were planting the explosives all along the ledge bordering the dome and the dome itself. Jarvis turned to look up the structure and said something to a woman I recognized as Pat. She seemed to be adjusting something on one of the brown packages, probably an igniter module. I didn't see anything resembling a detonator on Jarvis. He began to turn toward me. I lowered my gaze to hide my face and saw a bag near his feet. I wondered if the detonator might be inside it.

"Who the hell?" someone said.

The gig was up. I turned toward the voice in time to see one of the men on the ledge levelling a rifle my way. I ducked. Blurred forward, and gripped the barrel of the rifle just as he fired. I tore the rifle from his grasp, swung it, and slammed him in the side of the head. He bounced off the curvature of the roof and fell over the side with a fading scream.

The other man with the rifle stood ten feet up the dome. With his precarious balance it took him longer to aim. I didn't give him time. With a shout, I shot a web of Murk at him and jerked, sending him the same route to hell as the first guy. Pat pulled a pistol and shot me.

The bullet slammed into my shoulder, penetrating the damaged armor beneath Gavin's shirt. Searing heat bit into my flesh as the impact drove me back a foot. Unfortunately, I didn't have a foot of ledge behind me and found open air.

Gravity took me in its unforgiving embrace toward the hard, stony ground below. I tried to move my arm. Pain blinded me.

Mom. Elyssa.

I couldn't let them down. Using my other arm, I shot out an aether rope and snagged the side of the building. Willing the coil to stretch, I let myself fall as if on a bungee cord. As I felt the rope go taut, I willed it to collapse. The effort threw me up twenty feet. I shot out another web and caught the lip of the ledge. My injured shoulder slammed against the side of the building. Agony tore through me and I lost my concentration. The rope remained, but without allowing it to stretch, I couldn't slingshot myself upward.

It was time to get creative. I willed the coil to shorten, concentrating my efforts on the center of the rope, lest I accidentally loosen it from the side of the building and send me falling again. The rope dragged me up the side of the building.

As I neared the ledge, I heard Jarvis shouting. "One more row of satchels. Hurry!"

My injured arm was so stiff I could hardly move it. I needed to feed on soul essence to enable my supernatural healing. Despite the searing pain caused by moving my arm, I swung it up and caught the ledge. It hurt so bad I thought I might black out.

Releasing the aether rope, I reached my other arm up. All the weight on my injured side sent consciousness fleeing as black dots danced across my vision. I choked back on a scream and flailed with my other hand. Somehow it found the ledge. Using every last iota of willpower, I pulled myself up. I heard a gasp and saw Pat draw the gun.

"No," I said, and held out my hand, fingers splayed, as if that would stop her from killing me. Instead, something entirely unexpected happened. Her eyes went blank and the gun dropped, clattered down the roof and went over the side. Her left hand rose straight up in front of her. Ultraviolet light spilled from her fingers and into mine. I felt the urge to raise my other arm. Despite the pain, I did so. Her right arm rose in time with mine and milky white essence poured from her other hand and into mine.

Strength roared back. I felt an odd pinching sensation and looked at my right shoulder as the flesh pushed a dented bullet from within the bloody T-shirt. The wound healed. I felt flush with life and ablaze with power.

Pat groaned. Veins strained against her skin. Darkness and light pulsed beneath her skin. I cut off the connection. Her body toppled toward the ledge. I caught her and threw her over a shoulder. There had been too many deaths today. I spotted Jarvis standing on the flat roof adjacent to the dome. He leered and held up a red trigger.

"Too late, boy. You lose."

I opened my mouth to speak but it was too late. His fingers tightened. I had nowhere to go so I leapt the gap toward him, expecting to feel the burn of an explosion behind me. Nothing happened. I landed on the roof, dropped the woman to the surface.

Jarvis cursed like a sailor. I dashed across the open space toward him. He looked up, saw me coming and flicked something on the device. With an evil sneer, he pressed hard on the trigger.

"No!" I sent a beam of destruction. It incinerated the trigger and punched a hole through the man's chest. He went down without a sound as steam boiled from his mouth and nose.

I heard dozens of simultaneous beeps and turned to face the roof. Red LEDs atop the explosives blinked. I simultaneously thought there was nothing I could do, and did something about it anyway. I channeled Murk, scraping explosives off the roof and into a huge bubble just as they detonated. Pressure swelled in my hands as the shield blossomed with fire.

It was too much to contain. Like a boy flinging a live firecracker, I shifted the entire shield. It warped into a sphere boiling

339

with contained energy. I swung it down at the mass of Nazdal and ghouls standing outside the building, and released it. The shield hit the wall of the building below, warping like a soap bubble. The ultraviolet surface cracked. Orange flames spilled from inside like a dying sun. With a tremendous boom, the shield shattered. The explosion demolished half the wing of the fortress and sent remains of monsters scattering like ghastly rain. The side of the quarry caved in, and cracks ran beneath the fortress. I felt the dome shake beneath me. Saw the earth shift a fraction and realized with horror the cliff beneath the arch chamber was crumbling.

If that happened, everyone inside would still die. I hadn't saved anyone, I'd just killed them all.

Chapter 41

I ran to the back edge of the fortress and was about to leap off it when I remembered Dad.

He's gone. I can't save him, but I can still save everyone else.

I had to leave Dad's body. I knew coming back for it later would probably be impossible. His tombstone would be this cursed place.

The ground lay far below. It didn't matter. I jumped. Just before I hit the ground, I shot a coil of ultraviolet Murk at the wall and rode it to the ground.

Not allowing fear to control me, I raced along the back ledge and through the hole in the back of the arch chamber. Two Templars flashed steel at me, then checked themselves when I shouted Elyssa's name.

"She's over there," one said, pointing toward the battlefront. I raced in her direction. A chasm had formed near the front of the cavernous chamber. Nazdal scurried away from the widening gap, trying to get through the exit, but it was jammed with bodies. The creatures fell to their deaths as the ground vanished beneath them. Any enemies trapped on the side with the Templars were quickly dispatched with swords and spells.

A circle of minders hovered near the back of the army. Faceless black warriors—our very own dreamcasted warriors—helped the Templars squash the remaining enemies.

A horn sounded and Templars retreated at a steady pace toward the arch. Arcanes climbed down from their platforms, and joined in the general retreat. The minders broke their loose formation and floated toward the hole in the back of the chamber. One drifted over to me and touched me with a tentacle.

We saved your asses, Minder Justin informed me in a smug voice.

I appreciate it.

Any time. He flashed the mental image of a grin. *We're getting out of here before this place collapses. If you're ever in the Gloom again, look me up. We'll grab a beer.*

I would have laughed if not for the trembling ground signaling imminent death. *I'll be sure to do that.*

By the way, Elyssa's minder is hot. I'd totally hook up with her if I didn't lose my free will once you leave the Gloom. With that final pronouncement, my minder drifted after his retreating brethren.

I spotted Elyssa and ran over to her. "This entire place is about to fall into the quarry."

She gripped me in a tight hug. "Oh, Justin. I tried calling you but you didn't answer." She wiped away a tear. "I thought—"

"I'm fine," I said in a brusque voice. *But Dad's dead.* I told her Jarvis's plan to drop the roof on them.

"I should have known the explosion had something to do with you," she said, sounding proud.

"Yeah but now this entire place is going to take everyone with us." As if to underscore my point, the ground buckled beneath us, and a large chunk dropped into the earth.

"We'll be out of here before that happens," she said.

Templars streamed at top speed through the arch, moving with such order and precision, I dared to believe her. I spotted blonde hair and saw Mom standing next to the arch. Her hand extended toward the rune. It spun from its socket in answer.

"Where are Ivy and Nightliss?" I asked.

"Through the portal already," Elyssa said. "Your mother has prepped the rune for removal. Once everyone is through, she'll remove it."

"And trap herself here?" I shook my head. "Not without me."

"Justin, she has a flying carpet. Even if this entire place collapses—"

"The building will fall right on top of her!" I shouted. "She doesn't have time."

"Alysea!" A woman screamed in a voice that overpowered the sounds of destruction. "Betrayer!"

I spun and saw something right out of nightmares flying across the collapsing chasm. Daelissa had returned.

Mom looked up at her former BFF, and her face blanched.

Daelissa glowed with unholy light. "I'll kill you and your family, you filthy whore!" White hot beams speared from her fingers and into retreating Templars, reducing some to ash. She raked the streams of Brilliance across the back line.

Without thinking, I threw up a wide shield of Murk and blocked her attack. Light washed across my barrier. I felt the heat traveling down my hand and into my arm with a painful jolt. Blazing blue eyes settled on me.

"You insignificant speck!" Daelissa screeched. She pointed a finger and bolt of lightning speared toward me. My shield blocked part of it. A loud crackle nearly burst my eardrums. The blast threw Elyssa and me back onto the floor.

She pointed her finger again. I willed a bolt of my own. Brilliance burst from my finger and met hers. The two forces exploded, sending a disc of destruction shearing into the floor and ceiling. The shockwave shook the chamber and knocked me backwards. A huge chunk of earth near Elyssa dropped into the ever-widening chasm. I saw the dome above Daelissa crumble as she crossed to our side. I aimed a bolt of Brilliance and punched through the weakened structure. It fell toward the crazed angel. Insane as she was, though, she had the presence of mind to throw up a shield and deflect the massive debris.

She couldn't stop it all. A huge curved section of roof slammed to earth right on top of her. A roar went up from the retreating Templars.

"Did you kill her?" Elyssa asked. "I can't believe—"

343

A scream of pure rage echoed from beneath the section of roof. Granite shrapnel exploded in all directions. Daelissa burst from within, a halo of bright white glowing all around her. I grabbed Elyssa's hand and raced for the arch. The ground tossed and shook. A bolt of lightning blasted the ground just in front of us.

"Hurry!" Mom shouted. "Hurry!"

I made a snap decision as I ran toward her. Another beam of Brilliance nearly turned me to burnt toast. I threw up a shield of Murk behind us, channeling enough energy so it would self-sustain for a few precious seconds. As I raced through the arch, I grabbed Mom and dragged her through after me. The other Templars were already through. I spun. Daelissa streaked toward us on wings of cloudy white. She raised both palms and sent a meteor of Brilliance toward us.

The ground just outside the arch fell into the chasm. The deadly pulsar streaked toward us. Before I could deactivate the portal, chunks of the Shadow Nexus fell to the ground and the gateway winked off. The arch must have broken apart or fallen into the quarry. Daelissa wouldn't be able to follow us.

"I didn't take the rune!" Mom said. "Daelissa—oh god no. She has it. She has it."

"Maybe it fell into the chasm with the arch," Elyssa said.

Ivy raced from a throng of Templars and gripped me in a hug. "Justin, you made it back! I was so worried about you. Well, and our deadbeat father, of course." She looked around "Where is he?"

Elyssa's eyes flashed wide. "Justin?"

The weight of the world seemed to collapse on my shoulders. I slumped. My chest constricted to a knot.

"David?" Mom's mouth dropped open a fraction. She looked around the control room. Templars streamed out of it and into the way station, but of course, Dad wasn't here.

My throat closed and the world blurred with tears.

"Please, no." Mom's voice sounded weak and scared. "Where is he?"

I hugged Mom tight and buried my head on her shoulder. "He's dead, Mom. He died killing the minders."

344

Her body shook with sobs as she clenched me tight. "No, not David. Please, no."

I wondered how much longer she'd want to hug me after hearing my part in his death. All because I wasn't fast enough. I felt a hand on my shoulder and looked at Elyssa. Tears filled her eyes. Pain and anguish tied my insides to knots. *I killed him.* "It's my fault."

Mom released me and backed away, shaking her head. "Don't blame yourself, Justin."

A wave of anger swept over me. "It's my fault! I tried to save him. I almost had him. I almost had Dad—" I choked on the word. "He let the minders grab him so I could get them inside the disruptor. I didn't pull him out in time before the disruptor went off and—" I could hardly finish the sentence. "It killed him."

Mom looked at me for a long moment. She took my hand in both of hers and squeezed. "It wasn't your fault, son. You did your best, and so did your father. The two of you saved us."

I wiped my face and took a deep breath, hoping to clear the anger and grief from my system for a moment. It didn't help much, but I was willing to take it. Mom's words soothed some of the pain, but not the regret. *If only I'd done things differently. If only.*

Mom gripped my shoulders. "Justin, you need to stop blaming yourself. It'll only lead you down a dark road. Believe me, I've blamed myself plenty for allowing Daelissa into this world. How do you think it feels knowing all this started because of my stupid curiosity?" She released me and looked away.

"You never would have met Dad if you hadn't activated the Grand Nexus," I said.

A smile flickered across her face. "True, though I don't think my love life was worth wholesale destruction and the enslavement of the entire human race."

Elyssa kissed my cheek. "I'm proud of you, Justin." Her eyes filled with emotion.

I hung my head. "I couldn't save him."

"Your father knew what he was doing. He sacrificed himself for the greater good." She pressed a hand to my chest. "Never, ever, lose sight of that."

345

Ivy tightened her hug around my waist. "You're a good person, Justin." Tears welled in her big blue eyes. "I kinda wish I'd had a chance to get to know him. He seemed like a cool dad."

"He was, Ivy. He really was." I ran a hand through her hair, choking back more tears. "I need to go back and get his body," I said. "I can't just leave him there."

Elyssa nodded. "I spoke to my father. His troops successfully secured the Exorcist church." Her lips tightened. "We still have access to the Gloom arch, but I don't know how safe it would be to go back to the fortress."

"I don't care." I slashed a hand through the air. "I'll take a carpet and fly to the roof, pick him up, and bring him back."

"I'll go with you," Elyssa said. "We can do it now while it's still night."

"Perhaps we could still retrieve the rune," Mom said. "If it fell into the quarry, it's possible we could reach it before Daelissa."

"Absolutely not," Elyssa said. "It's too dangerous."

"I want to go too," Ivy said. A yawn seemed to catch her by surprise, and her eyelids drooped.

Mom hugged Ivy. "No, daughter. You need to recuperate. You're not used to using so much power." She looked at me. "Be careful, son. Don't take any unnecessary risks."

I kissed her on the cheek. "I will, Mom." I took out my phone and called Shelton.

"Holy butt muffins," he said. "You're alive."

"Yeah." I tried not to sound terse, but it was hard. "I need you to open a portal with the omniarch. I'll send you a picture."

"Everything okay?" he asked, a note of concern in his voice. "Meghan got us patched up so we're ready to go if you need help."

"Just peachy." I didn't feel like talking. I just wanted to retrieve Dad's body and bring him home. I hung up and walked through the control room. I thought of looking for Vallaena. She needed to know about Dad, although his death might be a plus for her since she could assume full control over House Slade. I sent Shelton a picture, and a portal opened a moment later.

346

Elyssa and I stepped through the portal and into the omniarch room in the cellar of the mansion in Queen's Gate.

"What happened?" Shelton asked, a concerned look on his face. "You don't look so good."

"Too much to talk about right now," I said. "We need to go back to the Exorcist church and take care of some unfinished business."

"Alright, kid. Spit it out." Shelton's forehead pinched. "You look like somebody popped your balloon, knocked ice cream out of your hand, and stole your lollipop."

"Dad died, I need to go back to the Gloom to retrieve his body." My voice sounded flat. I felt emotionally exhausted.

A look of sympathy erased his brusque look. "Oh, man. I'm sorry. Anything I can—"

I held up a hand. "No, Shelton. We're good." I turned to the omniarch and, using a picture of the inside of the church, opened a portal to our destination. We stepped through and into the sanctuary. Borathen Templars were all over the place. I noticed the statues the Exorcists had used to ambush us earlier were smashed to bits or knocked off the upper ledges to reveal tunnels in the walls. Elyssa walked over to a Templar and requisitioned a flying carpet from the woman.

She rolled it up under one arm, but said nothing, apparently recognizing my maudlin mood. After speaking to a Templar guarding the Gloom arch, I opened a portal and we stepped inside the shadow world. The air was clear of fog since it was still night in Atlanta. Even though I doubted we had anything to worry about, I rode the carpet like a surfboard about ten feet above street level, using buildings as cover.

Elyssa held onto my waist but remained silent.

"I'm sorry," I said. "I'm acting like a child."

"No, you're not," she said. "I remember when I thought my dad had died after Maximus blew up his car. Even though my dad was more like my commander than a father, the pain was still awful. Almost unbearable." Elyssa squeezed me and kissed my neck. "I only

347

had a taste of what you're going through, babe. I understand if you don't want to talk."

I squeezed one of her hands. "I'm the luckiest guy in the world to have you."

We finally reached the outskirts of the quarry and stopped behind a worn building across the road so we could reconnoiter the area before moving in. Dust clouded a new hole in the ground where the arch chamber had once stood. A massive pile of rubble filled most of the quarry. Figures made tiny by the distance crawled over the remains like ants. I zoomed my vision, but could only barely make out Nazdal combing area. *They're looking for the rune.* I saw no sign of Daelissa or the Shadow Nexus.

"They're looking for the rune," I said. I looked over the front of the fortress and saw no sign of enemies. The tree line on the opposite side of the road looked as though it would provide ample cover for making our way to the roof where I'd placed my father's body. At the moment, I felt no fear of returning to the fortress. I felt no malice toward the Nazdal or Daelissa. It was just hard to feel anything. I'd probably passed the point of feeling and was comfortably numb.

Even so, I played it safe and guided the carpet low and behind buildings and trees until we were directly across from the part of the fortress where Dad should be. We flew low to the side of the fortress and angled up as we closed the gap. Gliding near the edge, we looked for the body. It didn't take long for me to realize it wasn't there. Someone had taken him.

I remembered Daelissa's desire for my father and wondered if someone had found the body and taken him to her. Anger pushed through the layer of numbness over my heart.

"Justin, there's a minder coming." Elyssa pointed to the direction of the road.

All minders looked pretty much the same to me, but even at this distance, I could detect a familiar vibe from this one. It reached me and put a ghostly appendage to my head.

348

Back already? Minder Justin sounded surprised. *You must really want a beer—or are you two here to help me seduce Elyssa's minder?*

I didn't feel like engaging my shadow self in witty banter. "They took Dad's body. Do you know where?"

I felt a hint of confusion from my shade. *I know exactly where his body is. Follow me.*

"Thanks." We flew away from the fortress, across the woods, and descended toward a side street pitted with potholes. I wondered if for some bizarre reason Daelissa had made her people dump bodies from the battle away from the fortress. I stifled a sob at the thought of Dad's body being dumped like garbage.

Chin up, dude. You did well.

"My father is dead," I growled. "I don't exactly feel like celebrating."

Dead? That's really strange, because isn't that him walking down the road?

I looked at the road and saw a familiar figure trudging down it. My heart climbed from the depths and dared to hope. I zipped the carpet down to street level and flew in front of the man. He looked up at me with a lopsided but devilish grin.

"Hi, son."

Dad was alive.

Chapter 42

"Dad!" I gripped him in a fierce hug and felt one of his arms tighten around me.

He grunted. "Easy, now. I feel like crap." His voice was a little slurred.

"Not that I'm complaining, but how are you still alive?"

He shrugged. "The disruptor whacked the ever-loving crap out of me, but since the Shadow Nexus was still open to Eden, I guess my healing abilities kicked in." He took a step forward, but his right leg dragged. "The portal obviously closed before I was done healing. I think I still have partial brain damage."

"Brain damage?"

He returned a lopsided smile, one eye twitching. "Either that, or I got drunk."

"But I saw your body. You were dead. It didn't look like you were breathing."

He shrugged. "It takes longer to heal in the Gloom."

"Justin, why don't we get him home, let his brain heal, and then you can question him?" Elyssa said, a huge smile on her face. "That twitch in his eye is super creepy."

We stepped onto the carpet and glided down the road. My spirits soared. *Mom's gonna freak!* How stupid had I been to think a man who'd survived so long could be killed by a little brain damage?

350

I'm glad you're feeling better, Minder Justin said. *You're such an angsty dude sometimes.*

As if you're not just like me, I sent back.

"Are Alysea and Ivy okay?" Dad asked.

I nodded. "Aside from thinking you're dead, they're fine."

He grimaced. "Well, at least they'll save money on the funeral costs."

I snorted.

Elyssa regarded us with pinched eyebrows. "You two certainly share the same demented sense of humor."

Dad elbowed me. "You hear that? We're demented."

"Cool," I said.

Cool, Minder Justin added.

Dad's smiled faded. "What happened after we killed the brain?"

I filled him in on the subsequent events. His eyes flashed surprise when I told him about the fight with Daelissa.

He looked in the direction of the fortress. "You're telling me the rune is buried in a mountain of rubble where the arch chamber was?"

"I think so." I bit my inner lip in thought. "I don't know if the Shadow Nexus was destroyed along with the room, or if it's buried under there too."

"Either way, this isn't a positive development."

Elyssa steered the carpet along the street. "Will the Gloom rune even work with the Grand Nexus?"

"It looked different," I said. "Its colors were reversed just like the arch. Maybe it's incompatible."

"That's a real big maybe." Dad pursed his lips, or tried to. One side of his mouth didn't quite work in conjunction with the other. "I don't think we can risk leaving such a powerful artifact for Daelissa to find."

Elyssa turned her head to look over her shoulder. "We can't exactly sneak in and steal it from under their noses. Even with their losses, Daelissa still has a sizeable force at her disposal."

351

"I think we can do it," Dad said. "Besides, they'd never expect it."

"True," I said. "Maybe we could get some camouflage armor—"

The carpet jerked to a halt. Elyssa turned, hands on hips and gave us a look that could melt steel. "In case you've forgotten, Daelissa is there. She's still extremely dangerous even with the Gloom dampening her abilities. Judging from the sheer power she demonstrated during our retreat, I have a feeling she'd have no problem squishing the two of you like bugs."

"Whether she does it now or later, what's the difference?" David said. "If that rune works—"

"*If* it works." Elyssa shook her head. "And look at you. You're half dead." She waggled her finger. "You two aren't doing anything until you rest in Eden."

Dad opened his mouth to speak. A severe look from Elyssa cut him off.

"You tell your bright plan to Alysea and see what she thinks of it." My girlfriend sniffed, turned her back to us, and set the carpet speeding toward the Exorcist church again.

Dad and I exchanged looks.

"She is definitely a keeper," he whispered.

"I heard that," Elyssa said without turning around.

I snorted.

"Alysea is a keeper," he said, almost to himself.

A pang of regret stabbed my stomach. "Isn't there some way we can satisfy Kassallandra without you marrying her?"

"Sure, I could cede power to her. I'd probably have to kill Vallaena first because she'd do everything she could to stop it." He tapped a finger on his chin. "That would, of course, ignite a civil war since there are many in House Slade who are more loyal to my sister than me, and the house would collapse. House Assad would, by default, become the most powerful Daemos house, and Kassallandra would likely ally herself with Daelissa, given the overwhelming odds."

352

I blinked a couple of times. "You've really thought this out, haven't you?"

"Over and over. Endlessly." He sighed. "I'm pretty damned good at finding loopholes and making the world bend to my rules. This is one of those conundrums I can't trick my way out of."

"We need to convince Kassallandra that joining Daelissa might pay off in the short term, but once the angel has power, it's doubtful she'll keep her promises." It seemed like common sense to me. Then again, maybe Daelissa had a heart of gold beneath that insane exterior.

"I've argued the same point with Kassallandra more times than I can count." He ran a hand down his face. "She wants what she wants and damned be the consequences."

"From a personal viewpoint, I think it's awful." Elyssa shuddered as if to underscore her point. "From a tactical perspective, we need every warm body we can get. If today was just a taste of what's to come, I'm scared to death about the real war. Imagine an army of Seraphim backed by vampires and Nazdal and whatever other horrors they haven't revealed to us yet."

"It'd be a slaughter," I said.

Wish I could help you there, Minder Justin chimed in. *Unfortunately, I have to go. I've been neglecting my duties tonight.*

Thanks for all your help, I sent back to him. *Tell the others thanks as well.*

I'm always willing and able to help you prevent world domination. Something like a laugh echoed in my head, and my minder glided away to tend to the dreams of the mortal realm.

We reached the church a few minutes later in a somber mood. I was so happy to have Dad back, but for how long, especially if Daelissa was able to use the rune from the Shadow Nexus? I hoped she couldn't, but in my experience, planning for the worst was usually the best course of action.

We stepped through the portal in the Gloom arch and back into the real world.

"Oh, man, this feels so much better," Dad said, rubbing the right side of his face. "It's not numb anymore." He gave me a serious

353

look. "Remind me to avoid extreme brain damage in the future. It's not a pleasant experience."

Elyssa called Shelton on her phone. He opened a portal using the omniarch at the mansion and we stepped through. Shelton's eyes sprang wide at the sight of my father.

"Holy—you're alive?" he said.

"It's something of a surprise even to me," Dad said with a grin restored to full working order.

"Is Meghan around?" I asked. I wanted her to check out Dad just in case.

I heard Shelton behind me. "Yeah, she's in the parlor with the others."

"What others?" I asked.

"Other women. They're, uh, figuring out how to console your Mom, and help plan David's funeral."

Dad's laugh echoed from somewhere behind. "This should be really good."

"Not funny at all," Elyssa called up behind me.

I felt a smile on my face and heard Shelton bark a laugh.

When we reached the parlor, the women looked up from what was apparently an intense and very somber planning session. Meghan, Bella, and Stacey were present. I didn't see Mom or Nightliss.

"Bloody hell, my lamb," Stacey said. She got up from the table along with Bella. "We are so sorry about your father."

I looked around. Shelton and Elyssa were there, but not Dad. I was about to call his name when he stepped from the shadows of the stairwell, an infernal smirk showing his teeth. He obviously wanted a grand entrance. *Showboat.*

The women gasped. Meghan didn't waste a second striding over and scanning his vitals with her wand. Cutsauce seemed overjoyed to see Dad, given the amount of yipping the tiny hellhound made as he danced around my father's feet.

Nightliss appeared at the second floor balustrade and peered over it. Her face was red and tearstained. When she saw Dad, her almond-shaped eyes went wide. She vanished from sight and reappeared, dragging Mom by the arm. Mom stared at Dad without

354

reacting, as if she couldn't believe her eyes. When the tears of what I hoped were from joy began to flow, she vanished in a puff of shadows and appeared in front of Dad.

He yelped and jumped back a foot. "Alysea, you know it startles the crap out of me when you blink like that."

She wrapped her arms around him and planted a kiss on his lips before he could say another word. I felt my face grow hot as the two of them made out like high school kids in the hallway. Elyssa took my hand and smiled at me through her own tears.

When my parents came up for air, their faces looked radiant.

"Where is our daughter?" Dad asked.

"She fell asleep the instant I put her to bed," Alysea said. "We should let her rest."

"I think it's time I spend some quality time with her," he said. "She's quite the little ass-kicker."

"Don't you dare tell her that," Mom said. "She already enjoys blowing things up far too much as it is."

He laughed.

Mom stopped his laugh with another kiss. "Besides, I'm the one who needs quality time right now."

"In that case, I have a story to tell you, my little angel." Dad took her by the hand and led her toward the stairs.

"You do, my handsome devil?" Mom replied with a note of seduction in her voice that ratcheted up the discomfort I felt by a gazillion degrees.

Dad looked over his shoulder. "We'll be back." He winked.

"I think I'm gonna be sick," I said.

Shelton slapped me on the back. "Don't think about it, man. Call of nature affects everyone."

"You're not helping," I growled.

"How bloody romantic," Stacey said. "Ever since you rescued your mother from Jeremiah Conroy, she's been pining away over that father of yours."

"All I can say is thank god," Meghan said, crossing her arms. "Regular sex with someone you love is very beneficial to good health. In my medical opinion, Alysea definitely needs some TLC."

Shelton laughed. "Way to make it clinical, doc."

"I've been keeping Harry very healthy," Bella said with a wink.

"That's for sure," he said. "I'm gonna have to magically enhance—"

"Not another word!" I said. I felt my palms break out in a sweat. "I'm beyond my TMI dose for the day." Holding onto Elyssa's hand, I pulled her behind me and into the kitchen.

Shelton called out behind us, "Hey, no more shenanigans on the kitchen table!"

Elyssa giggled.

I rolled my eyes and opened the fridge. "I'm starving."

"Make me a sammich, boy." She punched me on the shoulder.

"As you wish." I pulled out a haunch of ham and began slicing it while Elyssa grabbed a head of goat cheese and fresh bread from the Queen's Gate market. We made a couple of heaping sandwiches and sat down. It felt like the first normal thing I'd done in days. I took a bite of the sandwich and moaned. "This is so good."

"The ham is excellent," Elyssa said, wiping a dab of mustard from her lip.

I smiled and waved a hand at the sandwiches and us. "No, I mean this time right here and now. It's perfect. No fighting monsters, no running for our lives, just you and me and a couple of sandwiches."

Elyssa leaned over and kissed me on the cheek. "You're right. It is perfect."

"It's why we do what we do." I tried not to think about how many people had died today, or how many lives I had taken. "We fight so people can enjoy perfect moments like this."

"We still have Daelissa and the rune to worry about."

I nodded. "We can worry about that later. Right now, I just want to spend a little quality time with the woman I love."

I'd reunited my parents and Ivy had come home. It was hard to believe my entire family was beneath the same roof again.

We'd defeated Daelissa's Gloom army and hopefully shut down Serena and her experiments for the foreseeable future. But the

356

rune from the Shadow Nexus was still out there, and Daelissa still wanted to rule the world. Even so, I couldn't help but feel optimistic and hopeful.

After I enjoyed this quality time with Elyssa—not to mention this tasty sandwich—we'd mount up once again. We'd fight the good fight. And we'd kick Daelissa's ass once and for all.

####

Section A

MEET THE AUTHOR

John Corwin has been making stuff up all his life. As a child he would tell his sisters he was an alien clone of himself and would eat tree bark to prove it.

Years later, after college and successful stints as a plastic food wrap repairman and a toe model for GQ, John decided to put his overactive imagination to paper for the world to share and became an author.

Connect with John Corwin online:
Facebook: http://www.facebook.com/johnhcorwinauthor
Blog http://johncorwin.blogspot.com/
Twitter: http://twitter.com/#!/John_Corwin

Made in United States
Troutdale, OR
03/10/2024